...Headed for Love—
and Revenge!

Ellen gasped and whirled.

"You might have knocked!"

"I might," Harry agreed. "But it's not my custom to request permission to enter my own room."

"Is this a sample of the courtesy I can expect as your wife?"

Harry's eyes lightened and one corner of his mouth moved slightly upward. "Does this imply that you've accepted the situation?"

Pretending a calm she was far from feeling, Ellen surveyed the man before her.

"You look to be a proper man," she said with deliberation.

"Man enough for you, at all events." Harry's hand shot out to grip her wrist. She let him draw her close, so close she could feel the rapid thudding of his heart. Her own pulse beat even faster; he must feel it leaping beneath his sun-browned hand . . .

Books by Catherine Lyndell

Ariane
Border Fires
Tapestry of Pride

Published by POCKET BOOKS

Border Fires

Catherine Lyndell

POCKET BOOKS

New York   London   Toronto   Sydney   Tokyo

This book is a work of historical fiction. Names, characters, places and incidents relating to non-historical figures are either the product of the author's imagination or are used fictitiously. Any resemblance of such non-historical incidents, places or figures to actual events or locales or persons, living or dead, is entirely coincidental.

An *Original* Publication of POCKET BOOKS

POCKET BOOKS, a division of Simon & Schuster Inc.
1230 Avenue of the Americas, New York, NY 10020

Copyright © 1989 by Margaret Ball
Cover art copyright © 1989 Charles Gehm

ISBN: 0-671-64617-6

First Pocket Books printing May 1989

10 9 8 7 6 5 4 3 2 1

POCKET and colophon are trademarks of
Simon & Schuster Inc.

Printed in the U.S.A.

Border Fires

CHAPTER

❧ 1 ❧

The three-storied peel tower of the Irvines, with its vaulted chamber below and its narrow rooms behind thick stone walls above, was far too small to hold the gathering Carnaby Irvine had invited to celebrate his only daughter's nineteenth birthday. Every notable resident of Eskdale and Liddesdale, from the noble Crawfords to the raiding Armstrongs, had been bidden to this feast in Ellen's honor.

The stone-walled enclosure of the barmekin, surrounding the tower and providing a first line of defense in time of war or English raids, offered space enough; but Carnaby had decreed that this occasion should not be marred by the smell of farmyard beasts, that his guests should not be asked to find shelter in the humble outbuildings that normally sheltered cattle and horses against raiders. Instead, they were receiving their guests on the grassy hillside outside the barmekin wall, with hangings of rich velvet draped over the stunted trees to provide tents for the visitors. Ellen's aunt Verona called it a *fête à l'Italienne.*

"My birthday's not such a great occasion to be calling out the entire population of the west march," Ellen had protested when her father disclosed the extent of his plans for this party. "And as for eating outside like some wild foreigners, have you considered what we'll do if the English come over the border? We've not had a peaceful week since Lord Herries was named rebel against the king." The dissension between King James and his warden of the west marches had been like a signal to the English that it was open season on the Scots side of the border; what little law there was between the two countries had been lost in the scramble as Scots strove to dissociate themselves from the warden's rebellion and English streamed over the border to enjoy raiding without fear of being called to account at the next march day.

Carnaby Irvine's bushy gray eyebrows met over his nose as he scowled Ellen into silence. "Herries is down now, and no need to make trouble with loose talk. Lord Maxwell's been appointed the new warden, and he'll keep order along here."

"I hope the English know that." Ellen bit her tongue at the look of vexation on her father's face. When would she learn to curb her propensity for getting the last word? Carnaby Irvine was a pleasant-tempered man as long as his women-folk didn't argue with him—it was the poor man's cross that in Ellen herself and in her thrice-widowed aunt Verona he'd been saddled with two of the most back-talking women who ever lived. "I'm sorry, Da. You must know best, of course. 'Twill be a fine birthday party—much more than I deserve."

As always, her first word of submission was enough to bring the smile back to Carnaby's face. He reached out one rough hand to caress his daughter's smoothly braided hair, the exact color of pale-gold winter sunlight glinting off the burn at the bottom of the hill. "Nay, y'are a good lass, Ellen, and a rare comfort to me since your mother died. 'Tis true, I'd thought to hold such a feast for your betrothal, not your birthday, but since you're so set against Johnny Bell . . ." He heaved a sharp sigh. "It's time we saw some gaiety here. You've seen too much war and too little merriment, growing up here under the shadow of the English. Who knows, perhaps you'll meet a likely lad at the party. I'd like fine to see grandchildren at my knee before I'm too old to enjoy them." He sniffled unconvincingly and put one hand to the small of his back as though feeling the pains of rheumatism.

Ellen laughed and threw her arms about her father. She felt an upsurge of gratitude that he'd finally agreed to drop the matter of her marriage to Johnny "Fish-Mou'" Bell. Even had she yet seen the man she'd want to marry, it wouldn't have been Fish-Mou', a man old enough to be her father and afflicted with thick lips around a perpetually half-open mouth, which gave him his nickname as well as a misleading appearance of half-wittedness. She'd been surprised when her father suggested the match, just last month, and still more surprised when he insisted on it in the face of her unbelieving laughter. Carnaby and Fish-Mou' might think this a fine way to mend the old feud between the families, but Ellen had no intention of being the living sacrifice that brought together two stretches of barren hillside and two strong peel towers. It was a relief to have her father revert to his customary generalized grumbling about his lack of heirs. She could stand the discussion of marriage in general; in fact, Ellen told herself, she wasn't at all averse to it—providing the right lad appeared, one who could stir her blood half as much as her solitary dreams and her wild rides over the hills. It was just talk of marrying Fish-Mou' that set her teeth on edge.

"Never try to make me think you're tottering into the grave, Carnaby Irvine! Who lifted two dozen head of cattle from the other side of the border last full moon and led the men back so roundabout the pursuers thought sure they'd find their beasts in Hughie Nixon's barmekin?" She spoke of her father's feat with the simple pride of a girl who'd been brought up to know that taking livestock from an unguarded English farm was not stealing, merely good business and a small reparation for the similar losses they themselves suffered whenever they grew careless.

"Aye, well, could be the old man's not past it yet," Carnaby allowed with a self-satisfied smirk. "Mind, I'm not so sure Hughie will have forgiven me yet for getting him roused in the middle of the night by a parcel of English farmers on the Hot Trod." Pursuit of raiders across the border was legal so long as it happened immediately after the theft, when the trail was hot. If the defrauded parties waited, they had to go through the wardens of their respective sides for repayment—a matter that could take months or even years.

Now, on the day of the feast, Carnaby was in an even better mood than he'd been in when they sent out the bidding letters. Despite the chill wind that swept through the valley and curled the gray surface of the burn below the tower, he stumped around the hillside with a broad grin on his face, pointing upward to where a thin pale sunlight broke through the clouds and insisting that the weather was unseasonably warm for April—as indeed it was, Ellen had to admit. After all, it could have been raining. It could have been sleeting. The burn could have been frozen over.

"I'm damn't near frozen over," sniffed Ellen's aunt Verona from the depths of the dilapidated furs she had wrapped around her lank frame. "Wae's the day I ever told your da about Italian fetes—who'd ha' thought he would ha' tried to hold one at the tail end of winter?" A white starched ruff peeped out incongruously over the layers of dark fur, while at the other end the purple skirts of her farthingale and her neatly shod feet bore witness to the fact that Verona Irvine had not yet forsworn the delights of fashion.

"Hush, Aunt. Da's gone to a deal of trouble to make this a fine day for us—let's not spoil it by grumbling. Please?" Ellen softened her plea by an impulsive kiss on her aunt's withered cheek. Verona Irvine gave her niece a grudging smile and allowed her furs to drop a scant inch, revealing a little more of the glory of purple brocade underlying her ruff of finely pleated white linen.

"Aye, he's done the family proud this time," she allowed. "I just wish I knew what he meant by it. Carnaby Irvine's no' the man to go to trouble and expense without something to gain by it—and don't ruffle up your feathers at me, child, it's no insult I mean to your father! He's a sensible man, that is all, and to be making such a lavish display for a girl-child's birthday," Verona sniffed, "is *not* sensible, and well you know it!"

"Perhaps he means it as a peace offering," Ellen suggested doubtfully, "to make up for threatening to beat me and lock

4

me in the top story of the tower and keep me on bread and water for a month?"

"It's not as if he had the courage to *do* any of those things," her aunt pointed out.

"No," Ellen rejoined with an impish smile that made her slender, pointed face look more than ever like a kitten's three-cornered face, "and if he did, it would take more than a party to make peace between us, don't you think? Now stop worrying about Da. It's time to mingle, Aunt Verona. A whole party of Nixons just rode in and tied up their horses next to the Armstrong clan, and you know what happens when those two families get together. We'd best distract them before they start carving each other instead of the roast hogget."

With a swish of her dark green skirts, lifting the full petticoats that had been cut down from one of her mother's dresses, she skimmed across the hillside to welcome and distract the arriving guests. Verona Irvine watched her niece go with a smile for Ellen's pretty manners and an inward worried sigh for Carnaby's latest whim. What could it mean, this extravagant fancy of her brother's? Having insisted on an al fresco meal, as if they were celebrating Ellen's birthday in sunny Italy instead of gloomy Scotland, he'd spared no expense to make his whim seem like the most natural thing on earth.

Trestle tables had been set up outside the barmekin wall, on the grassy hill that sloped down to the burn below the tower. Costly silks and velvets, cloths laid away in chests since the death of Ellen's mother more than ten years earlier, had been spread on the tables and over the grass where the guests walked. A tree twisted from years of border winds glowed in pearl-strewn red velvet, creating a tent where the tender could shelter from that cutting April breeze; the hillside ran rivulets of oyster-colored satin among banks of sober broadcloth, and the roast meats and pastries were royally set out upon purple-dyed stuff fit for a king's wardrobe. It was like a wedding feast, not a simple celebration among neighbors. A wedding feast, and no groom in sight to claim the laughing fair-haired girl, the center of all this extravagance, who ran down the hill to

5

welcome her friends and neighbors . . . Where would the groom come from? Under the hill, perhaps, where the Fair Folk were said to dwell?

Verona Irvine shivered beneath her mound of furs and cursed herself for a superstitious old fool, seeing danger where no one else saw anything but a rare opportunity to gossip and drink and talk. She would help herself to some of the warmed ale being served up in a sheltered corner, and have a good chat with Effie Armstrong over the trials caused by Effie's seven wild Armstrong sons; that would serve to distract her mind from these causeless fears and to remind her of the blessings in her own childless state. Three times married and widowed, and never a bairn to show for it, while Effie had borne seven boys before she was thirty! No wonder Carnaby was eager to see Ellen married and breeding; he must fear lest she prove as barren as her aunt.

But the arriving guests were no more inclined to gaiety than was Verona herself. They had heeded Carnaby Irvine's bidding to the party out of neighborly friendship, or in respect to one of the richest border families—and he with only the one girl-child to leave it all to!—but the shadow of troubled times hung visibly above them, dampening the conversation and lowering the tones of the men who gathered in knots about the barrels of ale. There was worried talk of the Herries rebellion; Carnaby Irvine might insist that the matter was over and done with, but some feared that Lord Maxwell might join his friend and predecessor in open rebellion against the king.

"No warden on the marches?" Carnaby winked. "I've heard worse prognostications than that. Remember, friends, raiding parties can cross both ways in the dark of the moon."

"Aye, and happen they will—but I'd not care to ride out Fernshaws way these days," said Hugh Nixon, pausing with a mug of ale tilted at his lips. A heavy-set, black-browed man, he seemed to carry his own dark cloud of gloom about him, and his glum tones served to spread the dampening influence about the company. "Whether it's a bogle or mortal man remains to be seen, but *something* has been riding the border of late, and one of the old wives on my land swears this man who appears and disappears at will has black hair with a touch of red in the sunlight. Aye, and there's been lights seen in the old tower, and uncanny laughter heard—"

"Havers, man." Carnaby's hearty clap on the shoulder startled Hugh Nixon into hiccuping down the rest of his ale faster than he'd meant to drink it. "There's no ghosts at Fernshaws—I didna' leave enough stones standing to give them shelter! The Graemes are out of the borders for good—thieving, murdering English bastards that they were!"

His hard stare caught and held each man in turn, forcing a reluctant series of nods and mumbled agreements. Not a man there but knew why Carnaby Irvine had felt it necessary to burn out Fernshaws and extirpate the Graeme family eleven years ago; most of them had accompanied him on that terrible night of vengeance. And all of them had respected Carnaby's wish to keep the story behind that raid secret from his young daughter, who still believed that her mother had died in a riding accident. As Ellen came up now with a platter of fresh-baked cakes for her father's friends, their eyes shifted away from her and they sought for some way to turn the subject. But the fascination of Hugh Nixon's story held their minds as if in a spell trap.

"If it's not a ghost," mumbled Lang-Legs Armstrong, "it must be a Graeme—and that's worse."

"Havers!" repeated Carnaby, less happily. "There's none left—as you should know as well as I."

"The old wife who first saw him said this man looked to be in his late twenties," Hugh Nixon mumbled unhappily.

"And red lights in his black hair, like the flames of Hell lighting the darkness. Only one Graeme this generation had that hair," added an acquaintance.

"Red Harry Graeme," finished Lang-Legs, "would be twenty-eight by now, wouldn't he?"

"If he'd lived." Carnaby dismissed the subject with a wave of his hand. "But he died in the fire at Fernshaws."

"Did he?" Lang-Legs dipped his mug in the ale barrel. "How do you know how many bodies were buried in the rubble? Did anybody ever turn over the stones to find them all?"

"If he or any other man of the Graemes had lived,"

Carnaby said with careful patience, "you can be sure he'd have taken his revenge long before this. No, friends. Let Red Harry lie in his grave where he belongs, and try to lift those glum stares of yours! D'you want my girl to think you're not happy on her birthday?"

Despite his guests' nervousness, Carnaby was in an unshakably good mood. He circulated through the crowd, pressing ale on one and roast meat on another and telling a string of jokes that grew more and more bawdy as the day went on, laughing uproariously at his own jests when his guests failed to respond as he deemed appropriate. As the ale barrels emptied, the mood of the visitors grew more relaxed and some of them even joined Carnaby in a song. Ellen envied her father his inexplicable high spirits but felt there was one matter that she should draw to his attention.

"Da." She pulled at his sleeve to draw him away from the knot of men now rendering a lugubrious version of one of the border ballads. Their voices echoed down the hillside, with an eerie undertone added by the wail of the rising wind. "Father, did you invite the Bells? Not a one of them has shown up—not even Guthrie." The rest of the family might have stayed away out of pique at her refusal to wed Fish-Mou' Bell, but Guthrie was Ellen's special friend, the companion of her childhood. He'd already said that he didn't see the sense in pushing her to marry an ugly old man like his uncle, and Ellen couldn't believe that he'd have joined the rest of the Bells in snubbing her father's invitation.

To her surprise, Carnaby looked more guilty than worried. Could it be that he'd failed to send bidding letters to the Bells? That was no way to heal the divisions of the old feud. "Aye, well, that's all right, lass," he said, patting her hand and trying to detach her fingers from his sleeve. "You'll be seeing the Bell family soon enough, I warrant you."

"Oh, did they send word they'd be late?"

"Not exactly." Carnaby's pale, bright eyes darted from side to side, never meeting Ellen's gaze directly. "Come awa' out of the crowd for a moment, lass. There's something I wish to say to you."

Dutifully, Ellen followed her father down to the trodden

grass of the bridle path along the burn. The chill April breezes tugged at her skirts and bent down the tall grass on either side of the path, ruffling the icy waters of the burn as they passed. When they were out of earshot of the guests, he stopped and turned to face her, but he still wouldn't look into her eyes. "It's time we should be saying good-bye, Ellen my love."

"Good-bye?" Ellen felt a cold, unreasoning fear clutch at her heart. What was her father talking about? Could he be planning to leave on a raid in broad daylight? And what did that have to do with the Bells? "Da, where are you going?"

"Oh, I'm not going anywhere," Carnaby assured her. "You are. Now don't get upset, lass. I've thought it over carefully and this is the best thing for all of us. You'll thank me for it in a year's time, when you're bouncing your first babe on your knee."

"Thank you for *what?*" Ellen all but screamed into the rising wind that whistled about them, whipping her green skirts about her knees and making her father's curly gray locks dance over the top of his head.

"Everybody knows it's the bairns that matter to a woman, in marriage," Carnaby muttered. "The man's not so important, as long as he gives her children. Look at your auntie Verona, three times wed and three times widowed and never satisfied to this very day—that's because none of them could give her children, d'you see? Now Fish-Mou'—I mean, Johnny Bell's got six by his first wife, so there's no doubt he'll do the same by you, love, and you'll be happy. Trust me."

"Da." The chill wind was making her cold under the good thick layers of green velvet and white petticoats. "Da, what are you talking about? I'm not going to marry Fish-Mou' Bell. We agreed on that."

"No," said Carnaby with unexpected sharpness, "we agreed not to argue about it anymore. And now there'll be no chance for you to argue, my lass. Since you've refused to agree to my plans for your future like a sensible girl, we're going to do things the good old way."

"What d'you mean?"

"In the old days, border men didna' waste time in courting their brides, nor in haggling about the bride price.

9

They took their women when they were ready and paid up later. And that's the way Johnny's going to do it. Any minute now the Bells are going to come riding over that hill and carry you off, and if you scream and fight, I'll explain to our friends that you're just participating in the fun."

Ellen felt a cold sweat breaking out on the palms of her hands and under the tight sleeve seams of her underdress. "Is that what you mean to tell them? That he's not really abducting me—that it's a staged game? Da, are you mad to think I'd go along with such a thing? Or that our neighbors will let it happen? I'll call for help now!"

She made to dart past him, up to the brow of the hill where she could still see the guests drinking happily, but the wind tangled her full skirts about her legs and Carnaby Irvine's hand was tight about her arm.

"You'll no' disgrace me by calling out," Carnaby told her, "nor would it do you any good. Most of our good friends and neighbors are too drunk to stand by now, let alone to defend you; and who's to say they'd care to do so?"

Ellen looked up the hill and her heart sank as she acknowledged the truth of her father's words. He'd chosen the guests carefully; most of them were of his own generation, good solid farmers who'd nod their heads approvingly at a man who knew how to deal with his wayward daughter. The raiding Armstrongs probably still got their brides in this way, for what man would willingly give his girl to that clan? And the Crawfords, the leaders of what passed for society in the wilds of the west march, were drunk to a man—or to a woman, Ellen corrected, hearing Phemie Crawford's shrill giggle as she waved her glass and flirted with two of the Nixon boys at once.

There must be something she could do. If she could win to the safety of the peel tower, perhaps she could bar the doors herself. Carnaby wouldn't want to force her into marriage at the price of having his tower battered down, would he? But he was still gripping her arm, holding her between him and the icy burn, out of earshot of the guests and far away from the tower.

"Let me go, Da!" Ellen pushed unavailingly at his rock-hard strength. The blood was drumming in her ears, setting up a frightening rhythm of danger and haste and fright.

"All right. Go!" Carnaby released her so suddenly that she spun half around, only to see a troop of mail-clad riders bearing down on them. The drumming sound in her ears was that of horses pounding over the low pale grass; they were all but on her as she picked up her skirts to run. In their leather jacks and wide-brimmed steel helmets, with high gorgets covering their necks and chins, they could have been anybody: English raiders or Scots, come to drive off the Irvine cattle while the gentry of Liddesdale feasted. But the red and green sashes looped over their shoulders identified them as Bell men, and it wasn't cattle they were after. Ellen took two steps up the hill, hampered by her full skirts, and shrieked with pure rage as an arm clamped about her waist and swung her up to the saddlebow of the leading rider.

"You let me go, Fish-Mou' Bell! I'm not wedding you, I'm not! Help! Nixons, Armstrongs, Crawfords—"

The jolt of landing facedown across Fish-Mou's saddle knocked the breath out of her and ended her screams of protest with an undignified grunt.

"That's better," approved a voice muffled by the folds of red and green cloth. "Keep quiet, now, and we'll get on well enough."

Ellen drew breath for a scathing rejoinder, but before she could speak, the horse took off in a bone-jarring canter that shook her wits into jelly and her voice into a poor quaver. "It w-won't w-work, Fish-Mou'. They'll come for me."

"Will they?"

On the hillside in front of the Irvine tower, men were fumbling for their swords, tripping over the rivulets of oyster satin and dark broadcloth. Hugh Nixon, making for his horse, got entangled in the red hangings of the tent, and the Armstrongs were trying to drain their ale mugs and get their long pikes simultaneously.

"Sit down! Sit down, all of ye!" Carnaby Irvine's bellow drowned out the confused babble of the guests. "Ye're no' to follow them. It's all right. Now shut up and let me explain!" He reinforced this last order by clunking the nearest Armstrong boy on the head with a pewter mug. A deafening silence succeeded the questions and shouts for horses of a moment earlier. As Carnaby Irvine repeated his explanation, the guests began to chuckle and lay down their arms. So old Irvine had resorted to this desperate way of marrying off his lass? Aye, that one had been a handful, the way she'd been allowed to run wild since her mother died. Time she was wedded to a good strong man who'd knock some sense into her and give her a houseful of bairns to keep her close to home. A few men were sobered by thoughts of the Irvine lands and gold and gear that would go with Ellen, the wealth that had slipped through their fingers just now; but most agreed with Hugh Nixon's verdict.

"If Fish-Mou' was man enough to carry that one off, he's earned the right to her! I'd no' have credited him with such a bold stroke. He must have been right mad for the lassie."

Carnaby Irvine actually looked embarrassed for a moment. "He was that," he mumbled. "Right set on having her. And as she fancied no one in particular, I thought it best for her she should go to a man who wanted her so badly." He raised his head and repeated the last sentence as though he were trying to convince somebody. "Best thing for my girl. That's all I was thinking of. Time she was settled. Did it for her own good."

The men in the party mumbled agreement; the women looked doubtful but remembered that few of them had had much more say in their own marriages. First marriages, that was. On the border a woman might expect to outlive her husband; men were carried home from every raid, and many a woman there, like Verona Irvine, had been married two or three times while she was still young enough to bear children. Ellen might be widowed within a few years, and then she'd be free to make her own choice the next time around. Only one woman had the nerve to voice her dissent to Carnaby Irvine's face.

"Carnaby, you conniving, sneaking weasel, I'll have your guts out for this!" Verona Irvine dropped her furs and flew at her brother's face, hands clawing before her. "How could ye *do* this to the lass? Did ye no' understand she'd rather wed a barrel of stinking fish guts than Fish-Mou' Bell?"

Carnaby fell back before Verona's assault, trying rather ineffectually to restrain her without hurting her. "Verona, you ken fine the lass didna' have a mind to be wedded at all.

Don't you want to see her with children of her own before you die?"

"Not Fish-Mou' Bell's children," Verona contradicted flatly. "They'll likely have faces like great gaping carp in a pool." She swung around and appealed to the guests. "Is no' one of you man enough to ride after the lassie?"

There were sheepish mumbles from a few of the men, but no one stirred. Now that they'd had time to think it over, few of them were eager to risk a feud with the powerful and numerous Bell family. It had been noted that men who fell afoul of Fish-Mou' Bell didn't last long in the marches; several had been attainted of treason when Lord Herries fell, others had seen cattle disappear and barns fired in midnight raids that seemed to come out of nowhere, on nights when no one had sighted an English party crossing the border. Besides, it was a man's right to do what he liked with his own. If Carnaby Irvine had beaten Ellen into accepting Fish-Mou', no one there would have thought it his business to interfere; this mock raid was not so different. Also, it had been a damned entertaining end to a good party.

"None of ye?" Verona appealed again. "Dandie Armstrong, Ellen's aye been a good friend to you and yours—remember how she nursed your woman through the childbed fever? Hob Lang-Brand, are you afraid of mortal men like the Bells, you that watched three nights in a fairy ring to win a wager? Archie Douglass—"

Her appeal was cut off by a shout from one of the men standing near the brow of the hill. "Fish-Mou' Bell! What are ye doing back so soon?"

The trestle tables were overturned and the fine cloths trampled as everybody there tried to get to the top of the hill at once. Along the beaten path that led to the Bells' tower in the north limped a dejected party of men on foot, led by Johnny Fish-Mou' Bell himself.

"Where is the bastard?" he shouted at Carnaby Irvine. "I'll disembowel him over a slow fire! I'll have his guts to string my bow! Did he come this way? God, my blisters!" He sank onto the nearest bench with a theatrical groan, opening and closing his thick-lipped mouth like a carp out of water and massaging his feet.

"What bastard? And what did you do with my daughter?"

"He's taken her, then," Fish-Mou' nodded. "I thought that was his plan."

"Whose plan?"

"The smooth-talking, black-headed bastard who ambushed me on the road here with his gang of pirates. Foreigners, half of them. Spanish, I shouldn't be surprised. He had the gall to lead them in a song while they were tying up my men and stripping us of our armor and sashes. *And* the horses," Fish-Mou' mourned. "He took that sweet-gaited mare I lifted off the English side last time I crossed the border. I'd plans to breed a new line of racing stock out of her, and now—"

"To hell with your mare," Carnaby Irvine roared, lifting Fish-Mou' half off the bench by his shirt, "who's got my daughter?"

But the answer was obvious to him and to the men around him. It remained only for Lang-Legs Armstrong, as usual, to state the obvious while the women scattered out of the way and the men headed for their horses.

"Red Harry Graeme. And he's halfway to the border by now."

CHAPTER

2

In the first few minutes of the wild ride that had swept her up, Ellen struggled uselessly against the arms that held her prisoner before Fish-Mou's saddle. They splashed through the icy burn; droplets of water showered her feet and legs, dampened her petticoats so that they clung like bonds about her knees. The rider dropped his red and green sash across her face, blinding and half smothering her, so that she wasted her strength in trying to free her nose and mouth. With her arms pinned to her sides by Fish-Mou's firm grip, she couldn't pull the sash off. By twisting her head to one side she could just get enough air to breathe, not enough to scream for help. Wet strands of wool clung to her lips; she smelled the musty scent of woolen cloth that had been folded away wet too many times. Half consciously she registered the change in the mare's gait when they breasted the hill on the far side of the burn. The jarring canter changed to a smooth gallop that carried them in long, easy, swooping paces over the gentle slopes that stretched west and south from the Irvine lands, toward Solway Firth and the English border.

Solway? No. She must be mazed from the shock of being swept up like this. Johnny Bell's peel tower was close to Branxholme, north of the Irvine lands, deeper into Scotland and that much safer from English raids. There was no reason for them to be heading toward the border. Ellen shook her head vigorously, trying to get free of the damp sash that covered her face so that she could see where they were going.

"What's the matter?" A light, amused voice above her. "Oh—you can't breathe, can you? All right. If you promise not to scream, I'll take the scarf away. Not that it would do you much good," he pointed out. "No one is following us. But the mare's nervous, and it wouldn't really improve your position if she pitched us both off and maybe broke your leg, would it?"

"That's debatable," Ellen gasped as soon as the hampering folds of wool were peeled away from her face. "I'd sooner a broken leg than wed you, Fish—oh!"

Sheer astonishment robbed her of the first breath of clean air she'd taken since being scooped up to the saddle. This man was wearing Fish-Mou's old steel-plated jack and carrying his stinking sash, but he was lean where Fish-Mou' was bloated with good living, and the eyes that looked down at her between steel gorget and wide-brimmed salade were bright, hard blue like the June sky. Not brown. Momentary relief was succeeded by a cold sweat of fear that dampened the tight green bodice and made her dress cling to her in sticky patches. At least she had known what Fish-Mou' wanted of her, disgusting though it was. This man was a complete stranger—and now that she could see, her eyes verified what her other senses had told her. They were going toward the border.

"My name's not Fish," corrected the stranger. "It's Harry."

Ellen's thoughts flashed back to the conversation between her father and Hugh Nixon at the wedding. Could this be Red Harry Graeme? Her father had been so sure he was dead. The other men hadn't seemed quite so positive. If it was Red Harry, then he had taken her for vengeance—and she could only guess at what form his revenge might take. Her heart pounded so hard she thought he must hear it over the regular drumming beat of horses' hooves, and her palms were cold and clammy.

"Going to be quiet?" her captor approved. "That's a good girl. Now, look here. You can't be comfortable hanging over my saddle with your arms pinned under you, and you must see you'd be a fool to try to get away now, with all my men riding behind us and yours nowhere in sight. And I'm growing tired of trying to hold you down while I manage a strange mare. If you'll promise to sit quietly, I'll let you sit up before me and we'll finish this ride in slightly more civilized style—and without," he added, "your skirts tumbling up about your ears every time the wind shifts quarters. Fetching sight though it is, it's maybe not one you'd care to be showing to a rough lot like the men behind me."

It didn't require the veiled threat in the last sentences to make Ellen agree. She nodded and croaked, "I'll be quiet," in a voice she scarcely recognized as her own. Shaming fear had dried her throat and reduced her earlier stiff-starched resistance to a damp rag.

Red Harry hauled her upright without waiting for her cooperation, and Ellen found herself insecurely balancing before him, sitting sideways on the horse like a prim and proper lady going for a ride in an English park. Only this was the wild border country, not a tamed green park, and the horse was moving smoothly under her at a speed that made the hills with their gray-green coating of sparse winter grass brush past her eyes like clouds skimming before the wind. Ellen glanced down at the ground once, gasped and fought a wave of dizziness.

"Best put your arm 'round my waist," advised her captor, and she was only too eager to comply.

Fish-Mou's jack was inches too short for this lean young raider; in this unwilled embrace, Ellen could feel the smooth interplay of taut muscles and trained flesh, her arm clasped about a waist hardly thicker than a girl's. Her legs were pressed against his knee; she could feel each slight movement he made to control the horse, the subtle interplay of pressure and tension from knee to hand to shifting of weight with which he directed the mare along a narrowing glen. His hands were clasped loosely about the reins. Perhaps he wasn't paying attention to his riding; perhaps holding her

17

had distracted him. If she could snatch the reins from his hands, turn the mare's head about and set her at the hills behind them—

"I wouldn't even think about trying to get the reins," Harry observed before her free hand had stolen more than an inch toward the coveted prize. "Bear in mind that you're riding sidesaddle and I've got my legs clamped on either side of this fine English mare. Which of us is more likely to fall if it comes to any sort of a struggle?"

"I don't fall," Ellen retorted, stung by his assumption. "I've been riding since I was a bairn."

"Hmm. You're scarcely more than that now. And you didn't seem so secure a moment ago."

"You'd maybe be a wee bit dizzy yourself if you were snatched up out of a feast and carried off facedown on some total stranger's saddle!"

"And what are you complaining about? That I'm not Fish-Mou' Bell? Cheer up. I expect he's following us by now. Maybe you can distract me by your sweet conversation and slow us so that the Bells—and your loving father, of course—catch up with us before we reach the border. I'm sure you would find it so gratifying," said Harry in dulcet tones, "to be restored to Fish-Mou' Bell's loving arms. Looking forward to the wedding, are you?"

"What I'm looking forward to," Ellen snapped, "is the sight of what my father does to you when he catches us!"

"If," Red Harry corrected. "And it might be a question of who does what and to whom, mightn't it? I'm almost sorry that he didn't see through my little ruse and come after you at once. I, too, am looking forward to a meeting with Carnaby Irvine."

He spoke quietly, with no obvious menace; but Harry's calm frightened Ellen more than any threats. Eleven years ago the Irvines had all but wiped out the Graemes of Fernshaws, in a raid more savage than any ordinary border reiving. Now Red Harry Graeme was back and looking for payment from the last of the Irvines. Did he mean to take his revenge directly on her? Or, as his last words suggested, was she only the bait in a trap for her father? Ellen twisted to look over Harry's shoulder at the men riding behind them.

The sight was not reassuring. Half the troop had pushed back their helmets and loosened their gorgets as they rode; she saw swarthy, foreign-looking countenances hideously marked with scars. One man was positively black as the Devil! Colorful, if tattered, garments peeped out from under the edges of the armor they'd taken from Fish-Mou's men, and a variety of edged weapons of strange make hung from their saddles.

But there were not more than twenty of these fierce, strange-looking raiders. Her father, if he could sober up the guests at his party, would be able to put twice as many men into the chase after them—if he saw through Harry's trick in time to follow them.

"He'll come for me," Ellen insisted against her fears. "Now or later, doesna' matter."

"Oh, yes, it does. I've made some small improvements to the old tower at Fernshaws. Once we're over the border, we're as good as safe."

"We?" Ellen repeated sarcastically.

Red Harry shrugged. "Well, if you really prefer Fish-Mou' to me—"

He broke off in mid-sentence and reined in the mare. Behind him the other riders slowed at once. Harry's head went up and he seemed to be sniffing the wind, turning his face from side to side with a blind, questing look.

"Listen!" He held up his hand and the riders behind him stopped their horses. In the new silence the small sounds of the hills were all clear: the creaking of an old tree under the erratic wind that chased along the crest of the ridge, the rustling of the long pale winter grass at their feet, the splash of a tiny hill burn coming down to join the River Esk—and, far away, a distant drumming that seemed like an eerily delayed echo of their own horses.

"He's faster than I thought he would be," Harry murmured. "And more men too."

"All the gentlemen of the west march," Ellen affirmed. "Forty—perhaps eighty," she doubled her own estimate of the numbers without a blush. "You'll never get away from them! Best surrender at once."

"Oh . . . let's not be in such a hurry to part." Harry's

arms on either side imprisoned her, moving close as if to keep her from any thoughts of throwing herself off his horse. "We've barely met. I'm looking forward to a much longer acquaintance. Yohannon!"

A brown-skinned, slender little man who had discarded his salade in favor of a crimson kerchief tied around his head came forward. He and Harry conferred for a few moments in a strange language that sounded a little like the French Ellen's aunt had tried to teach her, more like the Italian that she'd heard only in songs. After a brief interchange the man called Yohannon laughed, and Ellen gasped to see the empty dark hole of his mouth where there should have been teeth. He raised his hand in salute and called out brisk orders to the rest of the troop. Harry wheeled his horse aside and waited while the other riders set off again down the glen leading to the border. When they were past, he walked the mare up the steep slope of the ridge to their right.

On the other side of the ridge a narrow trail led down through the thick-growing bushes of gorse and bracken that clustered on this sheltered side. The trail split into two parts, and Harry turned to the left, urging the mare into a trot. They rode on for some miles along this narrow path, parallel to the broad way used by the body of Harry's men but concealed from it by the low ridge of hills. Ellen strained her ears for the sounds of pursuit, trying to convince herself that Carnaby and the others were catching up with them. Was the distant thrumming of horses' hooves growing closer? Or fainter? Or was it entirely her imagination? It hardly seemed possible that she could hear such a faint, faraway sound over the hoofbeats of Harry's mare, the creaking of the saddle, and the whisk of the bracken being trampled underfoot. When she closed her eyes to listen better, all she was aware of was the sweet-pungent scent of the crushed bracken, the warm firmness of Harry's body against hers, the distant shrill song of a bird defiantly celebrating spring against all the evidence of a cold north wind.

The mare slowed and stopped; her head dropped and Ellen had to clutch at Harry to keep from sliding ignominiously forward. She opened her eyes and saw that they had paused where a tiny, icy-cold stream spurted out of the bracken on the hillside. The mare stood before the water, head down, breathing hard but not yet drinking.

"Wait, beauty."

"Impudence!" Ellen's eyes widened and Harry laughed.

"Oh, not you. You're well-enough looking in your way, but it was the mare I was addressing." He patted the horse's neck. "You can drink in a moment, but I think you need to catch your breath first. We have plenty of time now." He took off his helmet, his reddish-black hair startling Ellen as he regarded her attentively. "Time to get acquainted, don't you think? You must be tired too. Let me help you down." Instead of first dismounting himself and then lifting her down, he took her wrists and lowered her to the ground in one swift movement.

"D-Do you think this is a good place to halt?" Ellen tried to control the shaking in her voice. It had been bad enough to be riding in front of Red Harry Graeme, wondering what he would do to her when they reached Fernshaws. It was worse to be looking up at him from this isolated patch of turf, and not another person within miles, for all she knew.

"The mare needs to rest." Harry dismounted and looped the reins over the horse's neck.

"You're making for Solway Firth, aren't you? You'd be foolish to halt before you're at Fernshaws. My father and all our neighbors will be on you soon."

"Very kind of you to be so concerned for my welfare." His edged smile did nothing to ease her mind. "Does it relieve you to think that your father will doubtless follow the main body of my men? In his haste, I doubt he'll ever notice where we turned aside."

"You must be proud of yourself," said Ellen waspishly, "to have condemned so many of your followers to death just to make good your escape with one girl. I thought you were looking forward to a meeting with Carnaby Irvine!"

"Trying to shame me into chivalrous single combat with your father?" Harry laughed and shook his head. "It won't work. Even if he'd accept such a challenge, which I doubt, I prefer to meet with my enemies in my own time and place. As for my men, don't worry about them. They'll meet or evade your Scots rescuers as pleases them, or simply lead them over the hills till their horses founder. Yohannon knows a dozen tricks better than anything these simple-minded border reivers have seen. No, we'll bide here while the pursuit goes by, then ride south at our own pace."

"You mean to hold me for ransom at Fernshaws?" It was the poor best of all the alternatives that presented themselves to her.

"I mean to keep you there, certainly."

Ellen gazed longingly at the low ridge of hills that stood between them and the broad path southward. Harry was right. Even if Carnaby and the neighbors caught up with them in the next few minutes, they would sweep on after the tracks left by Yohannon and the others. In haste, still half drunk from the day of celebrating, they'd never notice the faint traces in the bracken where a single horse carrying two riders had turned off the main path.

The sound of horses galloping toward them was louder now, no longer a faint noise that she could have imagined. In a very few minutes they would have passed by. If she screamed, would they hear her from this side of the ridge before Harry got his hand over her mouth? It was all too slender a chance—but perhaps her best one. Unless she could divert him somehow, distract his attention for a few moments.

The mare had drunk her fill while they talked, and was now delicately mouthing the tender shoots of new ferns that grew up beside the burn. Harry stood with one hand resting on the saddle, looking up at the hills with a slight frown between his brows. His whole body was tense with waiting, ready to move at the first alarm. She would have to distract him somehow before she made her own move.

Ellen essayed an experimental moan and was pleased to see his head turn sharply toward her. Fluttering her lashes, she put one hand to her throat and swayed slightly. "The shock—my heart—I canna' breathe!" she murmured, letting her breath catch slightly on the last word as her knees gave way under her. She sank to the ground in folds of green and white, head falling limply forward onto her out-stretched arm.

"Women!" Harry sounded purely exasperated. But as she'd hoped, instead of hauling her bodily to her feet, he knelt by the burn and used his steel helmet to dip up the icy

water. Ellen watched through her lashes; when he was bending over the water, reaching down, she sprang up and placed one small foot squarely on his backside. A shove, a splash, an inarticulate roar from the burn, and she was ready to run for it. The mare threw up her head and whinnied with indignation at the cold water and the noise, and Ellen took one more precious second to slap her sharply on the rump. The horse cantered off one way, reins trailing behind her, and Ellen raised her petticoats to her knees and took off up the opposite slope as if the Devil himself were after her.

Bracken impeded her steps, gorse scratched at her legs, and the cold wind at the top of the hill seemed to draw the air out of her aching lungs. And worst of all, she could hear Harry behind her. Damn the man! Didn't he have enough sense to go after his horse first? Unmounted and in hostile territory, he'd have little chance of getting safely back to England—and much good his plight would do her, if she were caught with him. Breathing hard enough to burst the seams of her tight bodice, Ellen scrambled over the rocks at the brow of the hill and glanced about her for some help. The road was still concealed from sight by another gentle rise—close, it was, tantalizingly close, but there was no way she could reach it before Harry caught up with her. Nor could she be sure that her father's men would get there in time to save her.

A few steps away, to her left, was a half-ruined hut of gray hill stones piled haphazardly one on another, with the thatched roof fallen down on one side and nearly blocking the door. Ellen dived into the narrow opening between the roof and the stone wall and crouched in the shadow, hoping Harry would think she'd gone on down toward the road and pursue her that way. The ground was cold and hard against her aching limbs. She tried to stifle her sobbing breath, fighting the fire in her lungs.

The shadowy interior of the hut became even darker. Ellen looked up and saw Red Harry's figure blocking the narrow opening through which she'd come. This was the end, then. Oh, why had she driven his stolen horse away? He'd have no hope of survival now, and no reason to spare her life; and he'd be ready to kill her for the trick she'd played him. And she was exhausted, with no strength or will to fight any longer.

Would he never move from that doorway? She stared up at him, unable to move or speak. Once she'd seen a rabbit crouched on an open hillside, frozen into immobility while a hawk circled above. When the hawk stooped, Ellen had run forward, shouting and throwing stones, because she couldn't bear to watch the terrified rabbit just crouching there while its doom came down upon it. But nobody would appear to drive Harry Graeme away from her.

"Oh, don't look so like a frightened rabbit," said Harry irritably. "I'm not going to hurt you."

"You . . . aren't?" Ellen didn't really believe it.

"Of course not. I never intended to. Look, all I wanted to do was to stop you marrying Fish-Mou' Bell."

Ellen thought it over. She started when Harry moved into the hut and sat down beside her, clasping his knees before him and breathing hard. The cold burn water dripped down his arms and fell in rhythmic drops from his elbows; the straw under him was soaked where he sat down. "You run fast," he said in grudging tones, "for a girl. I'm out of breath. That's what too many years on a ship will do to you."

Ellen wasn't interested in comparing their athletic skills or in hearing about Red Harry's doubtless checkered past. "You wanted to stop the marriage? But why?"

"Does it matter?"

"I'm having a hard time in believing that a Graeme would risk his life to help an Irvine."

"Not to help you. To frustrate your father." Harry sighed and passed one hand over his sweaty forehead. Without the hard steel brim of the salade shading his face, he looked younger, less dangerous and less violent than the man who'd stolen Fish-Mou's horse and armor, snatched her out of a gathering of his deadly enemies, and carried her almost to the border. "Carnaby's obsession with seeing you married and with children is the gossip of the marches. And for some reason which I do not understand, he wants you to marry Johnny Bell." He laid his head on his knees. "I'm tired. It's been a long night and day."

"Feel free to take a nap," Ellen suggested politely, without any real hope that he'd take her up on it.

"And let you run back to your father? Do you really want to do that? He'll have you in Fish-Mou's bed before you can say aye, nay, or titty-tatty."

"He's gey set on wedding me to Fish-Mou'," Ellen agreed. "More than I realized." She shivered, thinking that had her father's plans gone as he wished, she might even now be suffering Fish-Mou's embraces. But at least then, she told herself, she'd know what she was in for; and she'd be among men of her own country, still close to her own home. Why was she beginning to think of her abduction as a lucky escape? Nobody with any sense would really prefer to be crouching in a tumbledown shepherd's hut with this strange young man. Why, she knew nothing of him—except that he was a Graeme. A man who might be expected to kill any of her family who came within his hands.

The straw around Harry was growing sodden with the water that dripped from his clothes. Ellen had no desire to sit in the puddle he was creating. She edged away from him; when he made no move to stop her, she cautiously inched over to the far wall of the hut. He was still between her and the door, but at least she was too far away for him to lay a hand on her easily. Perhaps he really was falling asleep; the black head on the sodden knees had not moved for several moments.

"Still afraid of me?"

Ellen started, tried to appear calm. "Can you give me one good reason why I shouldn't be?"

Harry shrugged and straightened his back, stretching his arms out in front of him. "I'm not Fish-Mou'."

"As a recommendation," Ellen said, "I've heard better."

"You could go farther and fare worse. Only consider—"

The clinking of harness interrupted Harry in mid-speech. A moment later Ellen heard a familiar deep-voiced roar from the direction of the road. "What are ye pausing for? The tracks are plain enough for any gowk to see."

It was Carnaby Irvine's voice.

Ellen and Harry stared at each other across the three feet of space that separated them. One good scream, and her father would be leading his men up the hill. Harry could not possibly reach her in time to stop her mouth. The men would be around the hut—far too many for one man alone to fight or escape, even did he still have Fish-Mou's swift new mare.

Without the mare he could hardly continue in his mad plan to abduct her. He'd be lucky to get across the border by himself, let alone dragging a screaming, reluctant girl. A shining plan began to form itself in Ellen's head. Maybe she could escape both her father's plans and Harry's. Making the mare bolt had already freed her from Harry Graeme, even if he hadn't realized it quite yet. Now she had only Carnaby to elude. Did she have the courage to risk it? Rescue was just outside the hut. She had only to call out.

And then what? Ellen remembered the flabby look of Fish-Mou's perpetually half-open mouth. His lips would be cold and soft, like something that had been underwater too long . . . She let out the breath she'd drawn in one long, shaking sigh. Below, the sounds of men and horses grew fainter.

Harry's chest rose and fell once as the jingle of harness and the clop of horses' hooves faded into the distance. Ellen realized that he, too, had been holding his breath while the Hot Trod paused below them. Now he spoke in a low, cautious voice. "Why didn't you—" He broke off again as the sound of someone tramping through the bracken came clearly through the walls of the hut.

"There's a shepherd's hut the other side of that rise. I'll just go up and check it out before we ride on."

It was Lang-Legs Armstrong. Of course the Armstrongs, border reivers and outlaws by profession, would know every hut, tree, and burn of the barren hills so close to their favorite crossing places. Ellen saw with a sinking feeling that Harry had put one hand to the short dagger slung from his belt. He couldn't fight Lang-Legs and the rest of the Armstrongs with that little knife. His other weapons had been lost with the horse. And he still was making no move toward her. Evidently he didn't intend to use her as a hostage to bargain his way to freedom. Did the man have no sense whatever?

A picture of the immediate future flashed before Ellen's eyes, so vivid that she could have sworn she'd already lived through it in the few seconds while Lang-Legs Armstrong came striding up the hill. Red Harry dead in the straw at her feet, his own blood covering him with a deeper, stronger red than the fiery lights in his own black curls. Herself hauled back to Branxholme, to be trussed up and handed over to Johnny Bell like a cheese in its hoops. A life of meek obedience and child-bearing to satisfy a husband she loathed and the father who'd given her to him.

Between one breath and the next she came to a decision without realizing it.

"Hide, you muckle gowk!" she whispered at Harry. Most of the straw in the hut was heaped up on the side where she knelt under the collapsing roof. Without waiting to see if he took her advice, she burrowed into the pile of straw and wriggled as close as she could to the stone wall. Here the roof was only a couple of feet above her head; there was just a chance that shadows and straw would conceal her from a cursory glance into the hut.

A moment later a lean, compactly muscular body dived into the straw and pushed her right up against the stone wall. The breath was driven out of her lungs with a most unladylike grunt. "Keep quiet, can't you?" Harry whispered in her ear. The steel plates of his jack cut into her sides and back; his legs imprisoned hers, holding her pinioned between the wall and him. His arms went about her, holding her as close as in a lover's embrace. They lay clasped together in tense silence while Lang-Legs' steps drew closer to the hut.

The steps paused. He must be looking inside now, Ellen thought, holding her breath. Her pulse was pounding and she was intensely aware of Harry's presence beside her, his arms holding her just under the curve of her breast, his cheek against hers. Tonight was to have been her wedding night; she would have been lying this close to Fish-Mou' Bell. Might still be. Would Lang-Legs never go away? How long could she hold perfectly still like this?

Harry shifted his grip ever so slightly, letting one hand open flat against her midriff. As Lang-Legs called out that there seemed to be nothing in the hut but a pile of sheep dung and straw, the long fingers moved slowly upward to cup her breast. She could feel each infinitesimal movement through the tightly fitted fabric of her bodice. Warmth flooded her body at the intimate touch, and the thrumming of her pulses deafened her to the sound of Lang-Legs Armstrong's steps. "Don't move," Harry whispered a warning. "He's still there. Watching." His hand moved slowly, tantalizingly, and Ellen felt shamed at her own involuntary response.

One slow, semi-drugged part of her mind worried at Harry's statement. How could he know that they were still being observed? If he could see Lang-Legs, he was too damned visible and they'd have been spied by now. As Ellen worked this out, she heard Lang-Legs' cheerful voice from the road below them, and the sound of the last horses in the pursuing party moving forward again. She kicked Harry away from her and shot upright in the straw.

"You lied!"

"Can you blame me for wanting to prolong the moment?" Harry grinned at her, unrepentant. "I didn't think you were exactly suffering." His black hair bristled away from his head like a most unsaintly halo, mixed with short ends of straw.

"Lang-Legs was right. You're nothing but a pile of sheep dung."

"He would have been referring to both of us. By the way, you have straw in your hair."

"So have you."

Ellen reached a hand upward and felt the truth of his statement. Her braids were bristling with it like a spiked crown.

Harry laughed at her expression. "You should see yourself!"

"I don't need to. I can see you, and that's funny enough. You look like Saint Harry of the Sheep Dung."

An irrepressible giggle spilled from her lips. While, on the road south, Irvines and Johnstones and Armstrongs and Nixons hurtled after the ghost of Red Harry Graeme, Ellen and Harry sat in straw mixed with sheep dung and laughed at each other like two triumphant children escaped from the grown-ups.

When the moment of mirth passed, Ellen stood up and tried to brush the straw from her gown. "I'd better be going. It's a long walk I have before me."

"And just where do you think you're going?"

She'd had time to reason it out, in those breathless minutes when they lay together under the shelter of the fallen roof. If Lang-Legs didn't see her, if she could escape being "rescued" by her father's men, she would find a place to stay out of Carnaby's knowledge until he gave up on this mad plan to force her into Fish-Mou's arms.

"Annan. My mother had a cousin there, a merchant. Salt fish or some such thing." Her nose wrinkled, remembering smells and sights from a childhood visit. "He'll take me in for her sake—I can help in the shop. It'll be a while before Carnaby thinks to look there." Let him wait and worry for a while, he'd be the more inclined to accept her final refusal of this distasteful marriage.

"No, sweetheart. You're going to Fernshaws with me. Remember?"

Ellen stared unbelieving at Harry. "You're mad! You'll have little enough chance to get through these hills on foot, with all the Scotsmen in the west marches after you. You can't possibly drag me along! Besides . . ."

"Besides?" Harry prompted gently as Ellen tried to put her thoughts in order.

"It wouldn't be fair. I saved your life just now. If I'd screamed, Lang-Legs and his brothers would have spitted you on their pikes like a fish in the burn. The only decent thing you can do is let me go."

"Now who," Harry asked of the shadowed air, "could have given you the impression that I had any interest at all in doing the decent thing?" He moved toward her and took her arm in a firm grip. "You couldn't possibly have mistaken me for a gentleman, could you, Ellen Irvine? A sad error on your part, if so. My pretensions to gentility burned down with Fernshaws. I'm nothing but a rude, crude pirate now, and not the least inclined to give up my prize on a point of honor. Now come along. We've a long ride before us yet."

CHAPTER
❦ 3 ❧

"We'll not be riding anywhere," Ellen pointed out as
Harry steered her out of the hut, his fingers closed about her
upper arm. "Your stolen mare will be halfway home by
now."

"She is that," Harry agreed with no change in his expression. As they emerged into the clean, cold air, he gave a
series of long, low whistles that could have been mistaken
for the cry of a bird. A moment later the mare came stepping
daintily up from a small grove beside the burn. "I may have
forgotten to mention," he said, "that it was me Fish-Mou'
stole her from in the first place. He left behind one of his
men who was too badly hurt to ride, and he was the one told
me about this plot Carnaby and Fish-Mou' had cooked up
together, to get you married off willy-nilly. All in all, it was a
very convenient raid—for me. I also learned—*who's that?*"
Following the mare was a frowsy-headed shepherd boy who
regarded them both with wide, interested eyes. He put one
hand up to the mare's mane and held on to it as she started
up the hill.

Ellen felt a shiver of fear go through her—not for herself,
but for the boy. She knew him, and it was clear from his

expression that he recognized her and was dying to know what Miss Ellen Irvine was doing out in the hills with this rough-looking stranger. Harry could not, dared not let him go free to warn anybody who might follow Carnaby Irvine about the side route they had taken.

"Run, Nellie's John!" she called urgently. There was no reason to suppose Harry's promise not to harm her would extend to a crofter boy who could betray him to her father's men. *"Run!"* she called again, even knowing it was hopeless. Harry could have overtaken the boy in three strides. And Nellie's John was still holding on to the mare's mane, stubby fingers twisting in the long reddish hair while his mouth slowly opened and closed. Ellen was surprised at the patience with which the mare bore this treatment.

"Who be he, Miss Ellen?"

"Oh, *hell,"* Harry muttered under his breath. He whistled again and the mare came forward to nuzzle against his breast, leading the boy with her. Harry stroked the mare's nose and went down on one knee to meet the boy at eye level. "What's your name, lad? Nellie's John?" His voice changed slightly, taking on the intonations of the Scots side of the border, losing his polished English accent. "Well, Jockie, I canna' just exactly be telling you my own name, for it's a terrible important secret just now. But if you'll promise to tell no one you saw me, I'll let you in on the story. You see, I'm a retired pirate."

Nellie's John's eyes widened. "Have ye killt anyone?"

"Only Spaniards," Harry lied without a blush.

"Och, that's nae killing. I meant real folk. Englishmen."

Harry's mouth twisted slightly. "No, but the Spaniards had a treasure ship loaded with gold and silver, and my friend Frankie and I took it away from them."

Nellie's John grinned. "Give over, now! Ye didna'!"

Harry reached inside his jack and brought out a thin, bright golden coin that glowed even in the dull-gray light of the clouded-over sky. He flipped the disk up and sent it in a spinning arc that ended in the palm of his hand. "I did that. And here's the Spanish coin to prove my tale. But there's more to it than that, Jock o' Nellie's, and this is where the secret part comes in. You see, it was this way . . ."

Ellen listened open-mouthed as Harry spun a lengthy and

quite fantastical tale involving pirate ships, maidens in distress, Spanish invaders, and a magic sword hidden in Caerlaverock Castle, which Harry must find if he was to defend Scotland's shores against the murdering papists. As he piled detail upon detail and introduced one complication after another, Ellen forgot to laugh at the sheer fantasy of it all and was quite carried away by the excitement of the tale.

So was Nellie's John—for the moment. Breathing hard through his open mouth, he clutched the shilling Harry gave him and could hardly be persuaded to leave them at the end of the story. Finally he trailed regretfully back to his sheep, turning every few steps to shout over his shoulder that he'd not betray them to a soul.

"Quick thinking," Ellen congratulated Harry as they rode away. She was still weak with relief and surprise that Harry had not, at the very least, tied Nellie's John up and put him in the hut to take his own chances on getting free before he died of exposure. But for some reason she did not want Harry to guess what she'd feared. Sitting very straight behind him, arms around his waist, she chattered on to keep her own mind off the doubtful future. "With beacons all over the countryside ready to be lit in case the Spanish send their fleet on us by way of Ireland, Nellie's John was primed to believe your tale of spies and magic swords. And the bit about having pirated Spanish treasure ships fascinated him from the first. Tell me, do you think up these stories on the spot, or do you lie awake all night planning them before you go on a raid?"

Harry didn't answer for a moment, but she could feel his shoulders quivering slightly. "You may be too quick to jump to conclusions, Ellen Irvine. How do you know I'm not a retired pirate and a secret agent for Queen Elizabeth?"

"Oh, don't be ridiculous," said Ellen briskly. "We may not have been formally introduced, but I know perfectly well who you are. Your name is Harry and you're taking me to Fernshaws and you look about thirty years old. How many clues do you think I need? You're Red Harry Graeme, and I'd like fine to know how you survived the raid eleven years ago. I assume you've kidnapped me on account of that feud, and I assume you're going to hold Carnaby up for a monstrous large ransom to pay for the rebuilding of Fernshaws, and now that I know I'm not in any danger personally, that's perfectly all right with me. The more money you ask for, the longer the negotiations will take and the better the chance that Fish-Mou' will get tired of waiting for an unwilling bride. So don't bother telling *me* any pack of lies about Spanish galleons and secret missions, thank you!" She stopped and took a deep breath, uneasily aware that she'd been talking too long and too fast.

"You believe I risked my neck over the border just to steal you from the bosom of your loving family?"

Ellen could feel her face turning hot at the sarcasm in his voice. "Not me personally, no. I'm just another counter in the game."

"Pawn in jeopardy." Harry's voice had an undertone of lazy laughter. "Insignificant pieces are sometimes . . . sacrificed. Aren't you afraid at all?"

"You've gone to some pains to convince me I stood in no danger from you," Ellen pointed out, "and there's evidence to support the matter. Back in the hut—when Lang-Legs came searching—you thought I would scream to draw the pursuit down on you, and you could have thrown your knife and killed me for your own safety, but you didn't. So I believe your promise."

"I promised not to hurt you," Harry drawled. "There are . . . other dangers a personable young woman can face."

Ellen decided the safest thing to do with that comment was to ignore it. She felt fairly sure by now—well, almost sure—that Harry Graeme had no intention of raping her. It would weaken his ransom demands, and he struck her as a young man with his eye very much on the main chance. But she felt even more certain that he would enjoy nothing more than drawing her into a teasing conversation full of double entendres, tripping her up and embarrassing her in a dozen ways at once.

"Besides," she said firmly, "you let Nellie's John go, and just how long do you think that fantastical tale you spun will hold up if he meets any of my father's men on the road? Don't try to frighten me! You're soft as butter, Harry Graeme, and the worst you're planning is to keep me at

Fernshaws till my father pays you for the rebuilding. I'm perfectly willing to wait for ransom, but I do hope you've made some repairs at Fernshaws. From what I hear of the way my father left it, it would be terrible drafty in this weather."

Harry's shout of laughter echoed off the ridges to right and left and startled an indignantly squawking bird out of its nest in the scrubby bushes beside them. "You've a rare gift for understatement, Ellen Irvine. Your father left no stone standing nor rooftree whole nor any Graeme living— that he knew of. If I were you, I'd be more feared of the ghosts of your victims than of a wee bit draft."

His family. Ellen blushed and bit her lip, angry with herself. She'd wanted to sound unconcerned, but not callous. "I'm sorry," she said in a small voice after they'd ridden in silence for a while. "I was forgetting they were your people. But . . . it was a long time ago, and I was a bairn at the time. It happened right after my mother died. That meant more to me, then, than hearing my father had been raiding across the border again."

"I'd forgotten about your mother," said Harry in the same punctilious tones of apology. "It seems we both have personal losses to forget. I'm told Carnaby mourned her too. But however sad he felt, it was a poor method of distracting himself he chose—rampaging across the border and trying to wipe out the Graemes. The feud was never that bitter before his raid."

He cut off Ellen's halting attempts at another apology with a brisk shake of his head. "No matter. As you said, you were a child at the time. I don't hold you personally responsible. And it's not as if I'd been that close to them. There were ten years between me and the next youngest brother, and none of them paid much mind to me, any more than they would to a runt-of-the-litter puppy. Nor did my dad. Seemingly he blamed me for my mother's death, for he never could bear the sight of me. I was left to run wild on the hills." Harry's lips thinned momentarily, as if remembering old pain and loneliness that still hurt within his breast. "That's why I—"

"Why you what?" Ellen prompted when he fell silent.

Harry turned his head to look at her. His lighthearted smile didn't reach his eyes, which now were cold and pale to match the faint April sky that occasionally shone through the clouds. "Oh, why I ran away to sea and became a pirate. The very night of the raid, in fact. That's how I survived—I wasn't there at the time. And since nobody knew I'd lived, it was some years before I got word of what had happened. I just assumed the family had forgotten me, as I had them. So you see," he said gently, "it was old news, and cold bones, by the time I heard of it. Not really a tragedy at all, in fact."

"But something you still mean to make the Irvines pay for."

"Aye," Harry said, tight-lipped. "Carnaby owes me—and I intend to collect the debt in the way that will hurt him most."

There didn't seem to be anything useful to say to that. Ellen bit her lip again, and they rode on in silence until, cresting the last low hill before the border, they looked down on the broad shallow sheet of water that was Solway Firth. Harry had ridden by wandering side tracks that brought them to the border just east of the ford at Bowness. For eight miles west of that point Solway Firth stretched toward the sea, so low at ebb tide that a man might wade it without danger of getting more than his breeches wet. But now the water was rippling with currents below the surface, and the sandy bars of the ford were half covered already.

Harry swore and raised one finger to test the wind. "The tide's coming up. And a southwest wind to speed it on its way. We wasted too much time back at the hut; I'd meant to be over and safe an hour ago. We'll have to ride back and ford the Esk."

As he turned the horse's head, Ellen gave an involuntary cry of warning. The ridge down which they had come glittered with steel points. Even as she watched, the quick-growing crop of steel raised stiff pikes above the level of the ridge, ripened into heads and shoulders of armed men, burst into a torrent of angry Scotsmen coming down the long slope at them.

"*Nellie's John.* He'll have set them on the right way again." Harry swore in a foreign tongue and set spurs to the

mare for the first time in the long ride, yanking at the reins
as he did so. "Hold tight, girl!" he shouted over his shoulder,
and then he had to give all his attention to the mare's
precipitous gallop down the long sandy edge of the Firth.

The wind of their passing whistled around Ellen's head
and whipped her long braids free to lash across her face.
"You're mad," she shouted at Harry's back. "We'll be
drowned; you'll never make it." The rising tide was roaring
up the channel now, foaming the smooth surface of the
Firth into a churning mass of white froth. Certain death,
and Harry riding into it, and herself like a fool clinging to
his waist instead of throwing herself off the mare while there
was still good solid sand under them. At worst she'd break a
few bones, which was better than drowning—but even as
Ellen told herself this, the sand streaking by under her
changed to foaming brown and white water, fetlock high
about the mare's churning legs, then up to her own knees.
She felt sick, closed her eyes, and tried to remember a prayer
with which to compose her soul. She could feel the force of
the rushing, incoming current like a live thing, tugging at her
wet skirts and making the mare's gait unsteady. The yards
and yards of soaking wet green and white cloth wrapped
about her legs, ready to drag her under if she lost her grip on
Harry. She clung to him with hands gone white and numb
with strain, felt the tension of his muscles beneath her arms
as he urged the frightened mare forward. What was the use
of hanging on? In a minute they'd be swept away anyway,
the last sounds in her ears the rushing current and the shouts
of the men who hung back on the bank behind them. The
water was deeper, the mare's ears laid back flat against her
head—in a moment she'd be swimming, and then the tidal
current would carry them all away—the sand washing out
from under them even now, deeper, deeper—

A jolt shivered through Ellen's whole body and she
blinked in surprise. The mare had found firm footing again,
and the water was infinitesimally lower. An inch, then
another inch, then they were moving forward again and the
wind was plastering Ellen's wet garments to her body and
the English bank was rising before them.

"Och, I never cared much for this side of the border

before, but today I could just be kneeling down to kiss the beautiful solid soil of it!" Ellen said fervently.

Harry laughed and flicked the reins; the exhausted mare moved on at a walking pace, head low and legs trembling, and every step carried them farther away from Carnaby Irvine and the Scottish shore.

CHAPTER

❧ 4 ❧

The cloudy day began to darken soon after they crossed
the Firth, the pearly gray of the clouds overhead turning to a
deep leaden blue. Soon the rain began, a gentle persistent
drizzle that would hardly have troubled Ellen if she'd been
out riding for pleasure. Now, though, she was tired, and
already soaked through to the skin by the fierce tide race in
Solway Firth; the cutting wind blew right through her damp
garments, and the rain falling persistently on her face made
her shiver. There was no warmth to be found in leaning on
Harry's shoulder, only the cold hardness of his steel-plated
jack with the drops of chill water rolling off the plates. She
gritted her teeth and set herself to endure the weary miles to
Fernshaws without complaining of what couldn't be helped.
But she could not control the convulsive shaking that
presently took control of her body. Her teeth chattered, and
her arms—locked around Harry's waist—trembled so
much that she was afraid she would lose her hold and slide
off the horse.

A jagged spear of light sliced across the darkening sky
before them, followed by a clap of thunder. Ellen started

convulsively and very nearly did fall off. Harry reined in
and grabbed behind him, blindly, to help her keep her
balance; he got a handful of wet petticoat and yanked her
back up just enough so that she could regain her seat.

"What's the matter? Not afraid of a small matter like
thunder and lightning, I hope?"

"N-Nothing's the matter," Ellen got out through chattering teeth. Harry twisted in the saddle and looked her over
through narrowed eyes. She could hardly meet his glance; it
was a gey foolish thing to be caring about at a time like this,
but she couldn't help thinking what a poor drowned creature she must look like, with her wet hair plastered to her
head, her clothes hanging about her like graveyard wrap-
pings, and what little color she possessed quite drained away
by the eerie storm light.

"We'll have to stop," Harry muttered under his breath.
He sounded aggravated; in Ellen's experience, men usually
were angry when they discovered women slowing them
down in some pet project.

"It's all right," she managed to say.

"No, it's not! You're wet. And cold. And I'm a fool to keep
you out in the rain and wind after dragging you through
Solway Firth by the hair. The trouble is, I'm not just exactly
sure how far I can trust the farmers hereabouts. This isn't
Fernshaws land, and half of these folk likely have kin on
your side of the border. I'd rather not risk it. Can you hang
on, do you think, if we pick up the pace a bit?"

"The mare will be tired," Ellen protested. "All this way
we've come, and her carrying double—"

"She's managed worse loads than that, in her time. And
it's not far now. Here, you'd better come in front of me so
that I can be sure you don't slip off."

Harry managed the transfer with a clumsy haste that was
a far cry from his usual deft economy of movement; Ellen
realized that he, too, must be tired. She ought not to let him
take the additional burden of supporting her weight, she
thought; but it was so comfortable to feel his arms about
her, warming her through and holding her safely on the
saddle. Best of all, he untied a bundle at the back of his
saddle and spread out a thick cloak of coarse wool with

which he covered her head against the rain. The cloak made a warm cave in which she could rest. "Safe now . . ." she murmured, and let her head fall back against his shoulder.

"On the English side of the border, in the power of the wicked English reiver who's kidnapped you on your wedding day? You've a strange notion of safety, Ellen Irvine."

Her lips curved slightly at this sally, but she was too tired to reply in kind. They rode on through the darkening land, Harry watching the path while Ellen half dozed in his arms and tried not to think about what would happen to her when they reached Fernshaws. Harry was being kind to her now, but the sight of his destroyed home might remind him that she was an Irvine, and daughter to the man who'd killed his family.

When she raised her head to look behind them, she could see the flickering lights of beacons on the hills rising on the Scottish side of the border, alerting the families who lived there—too late by several hours—that an English reiver had slipped in amongst them and out again. The beacons would have been burning on the broken hills of the English side, the night her father burned Fernshaws; and Harry's home the brightest flame of all. It didn't bear thinking of. Too many things couldn't be thought of. And the rain was coming down harder now. Ellen covered her head with the cloak and slipped back into her drowsy waking dream, conscious only of the steady gait of the mare under her and the strong arms sheltering her.

With the coarse woolen cloak pulled over her head, she could see little more than the path at their feet. Her first warning that they had reached their destination came when the mare halted atop a small rise. Before them, in the deepening twilight, the path led down to a valley where reddish flames lit the jagged outline of a broken wall, black against the deep purple shadows of the valley. Ellen sat up and pushed the damp cloak back from her face to see better.

Where the ground rose on the other side of the valley, there was a narrow peel tower surrounded by a broken wall. Half the stones of the wall had been pushed down to trundle across the valley floor to the bottom; all the way from the barmekin wall to the inevitable soggy creek the turf was speckled with whitish round shapes. Behind what remained of the wall she could see men moving before the fires. Light glanced off metal surfaces: pikes carelessly stacked in an angle of the wall, a salade being used upside down as a pot to boil water in, the steel plates of a jack being tossed aside just now by a lazy young sandy-haired giant. As the men strolled about or squatted before the fires, their faces were illumined momentarily as pale or dusky ovals, flashing into prominence for a moment and then disappearing into the velvety dusk outside the circles of light. The fitful light turned scraps of cloth into glowing jewels of color: Yohannon's crimson kerchief, the purple rags of a cloak that had trailed from under one man's borrowed armor, the flash of a stolen red and green scarf.

Harry's men were there, waiting for him, and Ellen knew a shaming instant of relief that they had not been annihilated by her father's forces. She felt disloyal for the thought —but more killing, just now, would only inflame the old feud further, and herself caught in the middle of it. She shivered at the thought, and Harry misunderstood.

"You'll be warm enough in a moment," he promised as they started down into the valley.

"But . . . this is not Fernshaws, surely?" Or was it? Could her father's raid have so destroyed the Graemes' manor that nothing had been left save enough stones to raise a single tower?

"It is not. The manor house," said Harry, "is some miles from here—what's left of it. Not a comfortable habitation at present, I fear. Until it can be rebuilt, I'm staying in this tower, which has the advantage of being defensible. At least it would be," he muttered, "if those lazy beggars of mine would trouble themselves to keep a watch out."

They were across the marshy area at the bottom of the valley now, the mare picking her way uphill around the stones that had been thrown down from the barmekin wall, and still they'd not been challenged. "Hollo, you sons of Spaniards!" Harry cupped his hands and shouted upward. "Who's supposed to be keeping watch tonight, and I'll hang him! What if I'd been Carnaby Irvine with forty blood-thirsty Scots?"

Before he'd finished his last sentence they were surrounded by a circle of pikes, the sharp points glittering inward like a thicket of thorns about them. The men seemed to have come from nowhere, five of them, rising out of the tumble of white stones that spilled over the slope like the ghosts of past raiders. In the lead was the black man Ellen had noticed earlier, his dark face and hands all but invisible against the shadows of evening; around him were four smaller men whose leather jerkins and dark breeches blended in with the same shadows. They had moved so silently and so quickly, they might have been Faerie warriors rising out of the hollow hill, or mist wraiths in the shape of men. But the long pikes, shining silver in the rising moon and red-gold where the firelight glanced off them, were palpable and real enough.

"We thought we'd not frighten your lady, Harry," explained the black man. "Seeing it was you alone, and not a pack of Scots raiders, we'd a mind to let you enter peaceably."

"Very generous of you." Harry pushed aside the pike that was leveled at his breast and swung off the mare with Ellen still in his arms. "Can you stand?" he asked, setting her on her feet without waiting for an answer. "Good. Go on into the tower, why don't you? My quarters are on the upper floor. There should be a fire." He turned back to the black man. "Where are the rest of the men, Eleazar?"

A flash of strong white teeth split the velvet mask of the face. "Well, now. There was a bit of a brangle with Carnaby Irvine and his friends, see? Mind you, we were getting the best of it when they pulled away. Got in a few good ones. And Johnny Bell won't be sitting a horse comfortably for some time—he got the seam of his breeches split by a pike, and you should have seen him flopping and wriggling like a fish on a stick!"

"They pulled away? Then what happened to Yohannon and the rest?"

"We'd have wiped them out entire," said Eleazar with some regret. "Yohannon and his crossbowmen were circling around to get them in the back—they were so ale-sloshed they never thought to guard their flanks, just rode down at us whooping and hollering—but before he could get into position, some fellow with legs eight feet long, conservatively, came galloping over the moors with his knees about his ears as if he was riding a donkey, shouting something in his thick Scots accent, and the pack of them sheered off and rode down toward the Firth. We thought you'd be long across by then, and you'd said not to go that way on any account, so we had to let them go. Pity, that."

"Where's Yohannon?"

Eleazar spread broad hands; Ellen was fascinated to see that the palms were pink, just like a real man's. Perhaps he wasn't kin to the Devil after all. "Seeing you'd left no specific orders about when to get back, a few of us took a small detour by way of some farms the other side of the border. It was thought that some Scottish beef might sit well for supper."

"Fools." Harry's lips were compressed into a thin line, and Ellen shrunk from the instant blaze of anger in his eyes, but Eleazar seemed unaffected. "Do they think we've come here to live like petty reivers? Have you all forgotten that there's more important game than that afoot? If we—"

Eleazar gestured toward Ellen, and Harry stopped abruptly. "Forgive me," he said to her with a slight bow. "I'm a poor host indeed to be letting you stand here in the wet. Let me show you to your quarters."

But Ellen had the distinct feeling, as he took her elbow and guided her toward the tower, that he had stopped rating Eleazar only because he didn't want her to hear what he was saying. And that he was taking her up to the top story of the tower for the same reason—to make sure she couldn't listen in on his discussions with his men. Through the haze of fatigue, apprehension, and cold that wrapped her around like a clammy sheet, she found a minute spark of curiosity rising within her. What might Harry and his men be planning that they didn't want her to hear about? Another raid? He'd called her a pawn; was taking her only the opening move in some diabolical campaign to crush Carnaby Irvine as he'd crushed out the Graemes?

Well, it was something to think about, at all events, and it kept her mind off other things; apprehension, for instance, about being alone with Red Harry Graeme at the top of his peel tower.

43

Ellen's full, wet skirts trailed on either side of her as she wearily mounted the spiral staircase. The heavy, water-logged cloth whispered against the well-worn stones and left a broad snail trail of shining dampness behind her. Her skirts would be picking up all the dust and filth from the stairs; no matter, she was too tired to lift them an inch. She should rightly have been too tired to worry about Red Harry's plans for her, but the closer they got to his private quarters, the colder she felt.

The low arched opening at the top of the stairs led to a room that glowed with color and warmth and light like—well, like a pirate's cabin. Ellen caught her breath in wonder at the careless luxury so lavishly spilled out around her. She'd thought her father's display at the party a fine show of wealth, but the contents of this small stone-walled chamber outdid anything Carnaby Irvine had ever shown her. The promised fire was burning merrily in the small fireplace in the outer wall, and tall wax candles fit for a prince's bedchamber stood in the iron sconces made to hold humble rush dips. A wooden tub before the fire promised the comfort of a bath in the near future, and a pallet on the floor offered a soft place to sleep.

These practical signs of comfort were overlaid by the luxurious furnishings that had taken Ellen's breath away. Lengths of cut velvet, deep and soft as the green moss whose color they borrowed, softened the crude wooden stools over which they were draped; the pallet of straw was swathed in glossy black stuff with the sooty texture of a black moth's wing; a blown-glass flagon held wine through which the candle flames sent ruby sparks. Beside the wooden tub was a shallow bowl which at first she took to be hammered brass; on moving closer, she thought that its soft luster could only be that of gold. It was filled with soft soap that smelled of musk and other richly exotic mixtures, unfamiliar to Ellen but far from the simple extracts of lavender and herbs with which she perfumed the soap they used at home.

More gold winked from an opened chest; chains set with jewels, hammered bracelets, all laid out on a puddle of night-blue silk threaded with pearls.

Behind her, Harry murmured with satisfaction. "We've no lady's maid to attend you here, but Eleazar knows how things should be done, having seen service in a Spanish grandee's house before I freed him."

"You really are a pirate," Ellen marveled. She wondered how many of the fine things around her had come from that same Spaniard's house.

"Didn't I say so?"

"Yes, but mixed up with so much other nonsense, how could I believe it?"

"How indeed?" Harry sounded quite satisfied with this answer.

"But—you've sailed to Spain, then?"

"And the New World. And more. But I'm not so poor a host as to let you freeze while boasting of my adventures. Eleazar!" Harry shouted back down the spiral stairs. "Where's the hot water? Do you want this poor girl to die of an ague before we've collected her ransom?"

Before the echoes of his shout had died away, Eleazar was at the door with two steaming cans of hot water in his hands and a smirk on his face. "Were you wanting me to let it grow cold while we waited for your return, then, Harry? Long enough you took to get here. We thought you and the lady must have been . . . admiring the scenery." His knowing grin made Ellen feel hot all over, even where her clammy garments clung to her skin.

"I called for water, not for backchat," said Harry shortly.

Eleazar raised both hands as if to protect his head and bent over to scurry out of the room, rolling his eyes and miming terror. In his dramatic exit he narrowly missed colliding with two more men carrying cans of hot water; they danced around each other in an unsteady waltz at the head of the stairs and then Eleazar plunged downward while the others added their water to the tub.

"All right," said Harry when the men had left, "let's get you out of those wet things and into the bath."

If his comment about her ransom had reassured Ellen, this order did nothing to allay her fears. "I'll do as I please and not as you command," she snapped, crossing her arms over her chilled breasts. If only he would leave and she could be assured of privacy, she thought longingly, there was nothing she'd like better than to strip off these soaked, clinging garments and take advantage of the luxuries he'd provided.

He moved behind her; Ellen jumped and whirled to avoid his outstretched hand.

"Sheathe your claws, kitten, I said I wouldn't hurt you. Don't you need some help to get out of that beautifully impractical gown?"

"No!"

"If you tear it to get yourself out," Harry warned, "you'll go bare until I can steal needle and thread for you to cobble up another garment. Or you'll have to wrap yourself in a length of silk, like a Roman lady. Very fetching, that would be. But not suited to our climate. Wouldn't it be more sensible to let me act as your 'tiring woman? It's not an altogether unfamiliar task to me; you needn't fear that I'll harm your gown with my clumsy hands."

"Clumsiness," said Ellen, "is the last thing I fear." She set her back against the wall and regarded him with stony eyes. "If you'll kindly leave, I can make shift to undress myself."

"Ah, so it's my skill rather than my clumsiness you fear . . ." Harry smiled at her blush. "What a pity. Very well, I'll not force you on such a small issue. Enjoy your privacy while I confer with my men."

He was gone on the last word, moving quick as a cat, and the door at the head of the stairs closed behind him on silent, freshly oiled hinges. Ellen slowly unclasped her arms and moved toward the steaming tub, noting as she did so that there was no latch on the inside of the door. Well, had she really expected him to give her the chance to lock herself away from him? That, she told herself, was more advantage than a man of Harry Graeme's acuity would ever give to a prisoner. And her own choices were very simple. She could freeze in wet clothes, or trust his word that he'd not interrupt her bath. The first choice would be a piece of prime stupidity; besides, if he came back to find her still cold and wet, she wasn't entirely sure that he wouldn't competently strip off her gown and dump her in the tub himself. And the water was cooling while she brooded . . .

Better hurry. His offer of privacy while he conferred with his men sounded as if he meant to be back soon.

The bath was wonderful. And by the time she'd finished, warm and pink and glowing with the effort of scrubbing off all that Solway mud, Harry still wasn't back. Ellen grimaced at her damp, muddy dress and shivered as she pulled it over her naked body. It would be so much easier to curl up in the softness of the pallet and its rich coverings! But now that she'd been revived by the hot bath, she felt it her duty to assess the chances of escape. If the door was unlatched, the stairway unguarded, the horses stabled close by, she might yet show Harry Graeme a clean pair of heels and make her way to the fishmonger cousin in Annan. Not that she really longed to be riding through the night, Ellen thought wearily. But oh, she did long to show Red Harry Graeme that he couldn't dispose of her person so high-handedly!

She was almost relieved, though, to see the two sentries at the foot of the spiral stair. No hope of escape that way, not tonight. She might as well go back upstairs, dry her clothes, and get some rest.

Just as she moved cautiously back, out of the sentries' sight, there was a clatter of horses and harness outside. Ellen froze where she stood against the staircase post, just out of sight of the sentries and the open archway into the first floor of the tower.

"Yohannon, you fool!" Harry's voice rose clear over the lowing of cattle. "What the hell did you think you were doing?"

The answer was inaudible. Ellen strained her ears to follow Harry's reply as he dropped his voice. "Oh, very well, you may have a point. The more this looks like an ordinary reiving trip, the better."

But what else was it? Ellen puzzled. Harry and Yohannon were talking more quietly now. As they came into the peel tower, she heard Yohannon say something in—could it be Spanish? Only the names he used meant anything to her. Something something Herries, mumble mumble Maxwell. It sounded as though Harry and his friends were interested in the Lord Warden's rebellion against King James. Well, no doubt a number of English thieves were interested; disorder on the Scots side of the border was like an invitation to come over and steal. Most of them didn't engage in detailed political discussions, though. They just took what cattle and movable gear they could find and got the hell out.

". . . Caerlaverock?" That was Yohannon again, asking a question.

"Aye, that's where it is, right enough," Harry replied.

A new voice asked, "Will I take the word south to Frankie? You'll give me a letter?"

"Nothing in writing. You'll take the message in your head. God knows it's empty enough, there should be room for my few words. Now here's what we'll need . . ."

They moved farther into the room, away from the stair-well, and Ellen could make out no more. And she was getting cold again from wearing her still-damp gown, and the sentries were still on duty. She crept up to the room at the top of the stairs, puzzling over what she had heard. Why was Harry concerned to make his trip into Scotland seem like an ordinary cattle raid? It must be obvious to everyone that he'd come to take his revenge on the Irvines by kidnapping her, and there was no reason she could see why he'd want to conceal it. The fact that Lord Herries had been replaced by another warden of doubtful loyalty might well be of interest if Harry were planning more raids. But what had Caerlaverock Castle to do with him, and what was "it" that Harry wanted to be sure was there?

"It's nothing to do with me, anyway," Ellen told herself. She stripped off her clammy wet gown and wrapped herself in a length of blue velvet cloth. She might as well be warm and comfortable while she waited. She dried her hair before the fire, combed it out with a tortoiseshell comb that she'd found under the jewels in the chest, and experimented with four different ways of braiding it. Then, belatedly, she shook out the crumpled wet mass of her discarded clothes and draped them over the chest, where they could steam dry in front of the fire.

Clutching the length of velvet about her, Ellen paced up and down the narrow room. Her fine, pale hair floated behind her, drawn away from the temples by two narrow braids and left free at the back. After rummaging through the chest, peering out the window slits, and testing the door, she had run out of things to do. The leather-bound books in the very bottom of the chest were in Latin. All she could see from the north-facing window was the darkness of night over the border hills, with no flares of beacons that might indicate that the Scots were over the border—that Carnaby was coming to take her back. And although the door was not locked, the only way out was by the narrow winding stair, and she felt sure the stair was still guarded at the bottom by two very alert sentries. Something told her Red Harry would not tolerate any slackness in his guards.

All of which left her nothing to do but think; and try as she might, she couldn't occupy herself for long with brooding over the political maneuvers hinted at downstairs. They didn't have much to do with her. More to the point, was the question of what Red Harry Graeme meant to do with her . . . He'd assured her again and again that he meant her no harm; he'd put himself at risk rather than hurt the innocent boy who'd stumbled across their path; he'd chivalrously left her alone in this upper room to bathe and dress again. And she'd chosen to be here, rather than letting her father's men kill Harry and send her back to Fish-Mou' Bell.

Ellen repeated these facts to herself over and over again, but she still could not smother her apprehensions. Had she been a fool to keep silence—to choose Harry's life over rescue for herself? In the shock of discovering just how far her father would go to marry her off to Fish-Mou' Bell, the gamble seemed worth taking. But that had been when she thought Harry would be forced to let her go. Now . . . now she was his prisoner in this tower on the wrong side of the border, and she thought that she just might have been very foolish indeed. The prisoner of an Englishman—a man with a deadly feud against her family, with as unsavory a set of followers as she'd seen outside of an Armstrong clan gathering—and, to top it all off, a genuine pirate! And herself with nothing to cover her, till her clothes dried, but a length of his stolen Spanish finery.

Ellen paused in her pacing to raise her chin and face the door through which Harry would enter. "Whatever he's in mind for me," she said aloud, "it canna' be worse than being forced to Fish-Mou' Bell's bed!"

She took two more turns up and down the room before

adding, "Besides, he's very likely no more intention than what I guessed: to get a big ransom out of the Irvines to pay for rebuilding Fernshaws."

It was the waiting made her so nervous, Ellen thought. How long had it been, anyway? Long enough for the water in the bath to grow cold. Two of the wax tapers were burnt down to the iron spikes that had held them, and the rest were very low. Puddles of wax crusted the floor under each candle; this room, for all its fine furnishings, was drafty, and the continual movement of air made the candles drip crazily so that they burned out sooner than necessary. All the same, some hours must have passed since Harry had left her alone up here.

"Besides," Ellen concluded wearily, "he's obviously not going to do me the courtesy of discussing it tonight."

Her legs were aching with exhaustion; she could no longer keep herself awake by walking up and down. She sank down onto the pallet and pillowed her head on her arm, not even troubling to extinguish the last candles. Within minutes she was breathing evenly, lost in a sleep too deep for dreams.

Harry found her so when, long past midnight, he finished his planning session and mounted the stairs to the upper room. The fire had burnt down to glowing coals, and the candles were all out; he stood a moment above the pallet, holding the branch of candles that had lighted his way upstairs. Their soft light made an enchanted circle about the two of them in the darkened room; it glowed off her white shoulders and the halo of fine, fair hair floating above the length of blue velvet in which she had wrapped herself after the bath. In sleep her face was soft, vulnerable, lacking the impish quality that had intrigued him when he first talked with her, after she'd begun to lose her fear of him.

Clothed and awake and defiant, she had seemed to be a sturdy girl of solid border stock, strong enough to ride for miles and ford the Solway in a rising tide and stand off a strange pirate in his own stronghold. Now, asleep and half exposed by the slippage of her velvet wrap, she seemed to him more fragile than he'd imagined, and more beautiful. There was something unearthly about her faerie beauty, the spun silver of her hair and the delicate molding of her long slender limbs. It might be an enchanted circle they stood in;

he might go downstairs in the morning to find he'd slept a hundred years and his men were all long dead and his plans as cold as last night's fires.

Harry shook his head, laughing at his own fancies. He must be tired indeed to let a pretty girl throw him into such mazed imaginings! But his hand trembled as he looked at her, and a drop of wax fell on her arm and started her out of her slumbers. Blue-gray eyes opened and looked at him, wide with confusion; then her face changed subtly as she remembered where she was. She sat up, clutching the velvet over her breasts, and stared at him with her little chin raised and her eyes mutely defying him.

"Don't come any closer!" she said in a shaky voice.

Harry shook his head again, meaning to tell her not to worry, and reached forward to set his candlestick down. She misinterpreted the movement and jumped up from the pallet, her hair in entrancing disorder, her eyes dark with fear. "If you dishonor me, my father won't pay any ransom."

"Highly unlikely." Harry couldn't resist the urge to tease her just a little. "A slightly used daughter could get him heirs just as well as a virgin one." He sat down on the pallet and wondered if she could be persuaded to help him ease off his boots. After two days in the saddle, sandwiched around a night of climbing around Caerlaverock Castle to spy out the information he needed for Frankie, he was beginning to doubt whether he ever would be able to get his boots off.

"I don't suppose you'd care to help?" He extended one foot and looked up at her with an appealing smile. "I've been wearing these things so long that my feet have all but lost acquaintance with my legs—and as for the state of my legs," he sighed, "that's hardly fit to discuss with a delicate young lady. A life at sea is poor preparation for two—that is, for a day of riding your border hills." No need to let the girl know exactly what he'd been doing in Scotland; if she thought herself the sole reason for his raid, the more likely everyone else would accept that story. And, in truth, she was a good enough reason for any man to risk himself over the border! Now that he saw her in this enchanting state of undress, he could hardly wonder at Fish-Mou' Bell's obsession with getting her for himself.

"Go away!" Her voice was shrill with fear, but she was making a valiant effort to control it; her hands were clenched on the blue velvet that bunched between her breasts.

"Oh, very well, I'll do it myself." Harry supposed he had been asking for it, teasing her like that when she was just startled out of sleep. He pulled his riding boots off, setting his teeth against the pain of new blisters making themselves apparent. His thighs were aching too. Had he really once ridden and climbed all over the border hills as a lad, making his forays into Scotland for the sheer impudence of outwitting the Armstrongs and the warden? Eleven years at sea were poor training for resuming that way of life. Not that there was any reason why he should resume it. "Once I've finished this task," he muttered, "I'll never go anywhere again but on the deck of a ship, the way men were meant to travel. Riding's a stark unnatural method of transport, and walking is worse."

"What task?"

How quickly she recovered from fright to curiosity. Harry made a note to watch his tongue around this girl; she was too quick-witted by half. Though there might be a way to profit from her quickness, make it his asset instead of Carnaby Irvine's . . . The thought pleased him, and he chuckled quietly. Yes, that would be the perfect way to be revenged on his old enemy, far better than extorting a ransom payment he didn't really need. But it needed thought, and tonight was no time to broach it to the girl.

"What task?" she repeated.

"Nothing that need concern you. Now blow out the candles like a good girl, will you? I'm going to sleep."

"Not here."

Harry took a blanket from the foot of the pallet and spread it out on the floor with ostentatious care. "Oh, not in your arms, if that's what troubles you. But I am most certainly staying in this room. In case you haven't noticed, the sleeping arrangements here are hardly as lavish as they would have been at Fernshaws, had your father not burned it down. I'm not going to share a truss of hay with my sweaty men and their sweaty horses just to spare your maidenly feelings. You're safe enough for the moment—I hardly ever rape virgins after midnight."

He rolled himself up in the blanket and was asleep almost before his head touched the floor, breathing deeply and evenly. Ellen stood where she had backed against the wall, hardly able to believe in this anticlimactic end to the evening. She watched in the candlelight for some betraying flicker of his closed eyes, some movement that would betray his instant sleep as a sham. After five long minutes Harry sighed deeply and rolled over onto his back, flinging one arm out across the pallet beside him. The utter limpness of his body betokened total respose.

It must be quite late, Ellen thought. Perhaps the sentries downstairs were asleep too. Perhaps, if she moved very quietly, she could get out into the barmekin, steal a horse, and make her escape through one of the unmended gaps in the wall.

First, though, she would have to get dressed. She edged quietly around the head of the pallet. Her clothes were still spread out before the dying fire. She'd not bother with all the laces and ties, just huddle them on somehow and stop to dress properly when she was safe away—

The hand that had been outstretched, limp and boneless, closed around her ankle with a sudden fierce grip. "If you were thinking of going anywhere tonight," said Harry's creamy-smooth voice from the floor, "you'd best change your plans. I forgot to mention that I sleep with one eye open, and the guards downstairs are relieved every four hours."

"With such fine precautions, I'm surprised Fish-Mou' Bell ever got close enough to steal your horse." Ellen jerked free and sat down on the pallet, glowering at Harry's half-closed eyes.

"He wouldn't have," Harry agreed, "if I hadn't wanted him to do so. The Hot Trod after him would have been a grand excuse to cross the border, d'you see, if his man hadn't told me the story that made you a better excuse yet. Fortunate . . ." His voice trailed off sleepily and he tucked his arm under his head as a pillow.

"Excuse?" Ellen prompted as he seemed on the verge of

53

going back to sleep. "I was only an excuse to cross the border? In God's name, then, what was your real reason, that was worth so much risk?" Not cattle; he'd been annoyed with Yohannon for that part of the raid.

At Ellen's intervention, Harry sucked in his breath sharply and his eyes opened, deep blue in the warm glow of the candles. "Forgive me for boring you with these details. What better reason could I have for crossing the border than to get revenge on Carnaby Irvine? And now, dear girl, will you kindly blow out the candles? I've a busy day ahead of me tomorrow." He closed his eyes again and began to snore ostentatiously.

Ellen managed to spatter hot wax over his face when she blew out the guttering candles. Even that didn't make the man admit to being awake. And a few minutes later, while she tossed and turned on the pallet, his fake snores gave way to deep, regular breathing again.

Ellen found it less easy to get back to sleep. She worried about what would happen to her. She brooded over the complexities of Harry's secret plans, half revealed by the words she'd overheard yet still unclear to her. And she was continually, maddeningly aware of the presence of the man beside her, inches from her pallet: long limbs taut with muscle, lighthearted and quick-witted, and in every way the opposite of Fish-Mou' Bell, who should have been sharing her bed that night.

Ellen turned over with an angry flounce, punched down the wad of straw that served her for a pillow, and told herself that it was entirely irrelevant what kind of man Red Harry Graeme was. Regardless of looks and manners and his passing kindness, she knew three things about him that made any thought of a closer relationship out of the question. He was an Englishman. And her family's sworn enemy. And her captor.

Obviously there could be nothing between them except the question of her ransom.

CHAPTER
❦ 5 ❧

I've decided what to do about you," Harry announced the next morning over a breakfast of bread and ale.

Ellen waited while he surveyed her over the rim of his ale mug, dark brows raised and deep blue eyes twinkling at her. This morning she felt very much at a disadvantage with this English pirate, very much aware of how completely she was in his power. The contrast between his appearance and her own only pointed up that discrepancy and made her feel even more awkward.

He was lounging on the corner of a broad oak table, one foot swinging free. The elegance of his dress belied the casual pose: he wore a close-fitting suit of black velvet, the sleeves slashed to let the fine white linen of his shirt puff through. By contrast Ellen felt dowdy and dirty in her once-fine clothes, now bedraggled from yesterday's long ride. Sponging and daubing had removed the worst of the mud stains, but she was dismally conscious that the skirt still smelled like a tired horse and that without her aunt's help she'd been unable to build her fine hair into the high coronet of intricately tucked braids she usually wore. Instead she'd been forced to leave most of her hair down, only drawing it away from her face with two narrow braids in the style she'd devised the previous night. She felt that she must look like a peasant, and a dirty peasant at that.

Harry, watching her face for some reaction to his announcement, was in no hurry to end the moment. She was even lovelier than he'd remembered from last night's candlelight glimpse, this border girl with her fine features lightly tanned by the same sun and wind that had bleached her hair to a rippling skein of silver-fair silk. Just now, waiting to hear his announcement, she was as still as a hunted thing; he could almost feel the tension that suffused from her limbs and drew her shoulders back under the green gown.

Today the gown draped softly around her, the full skirts flowing as gracefully as the draperies of an antique statue; she must have had to discard the petticoats which were stained worst, and their wetting in the Solway had taken the starch out of the gown. With her hair loose and her green gown so smoothly flowing, she might have been an elf maiden out of the hollow hills.

Instead she was the daughter of the man who'd wiped out his family, waiting in that tense silence to hear what he meant to do with her. And the longer they both waited, the harder Harry found it to explain what he had in mind. Damn the girl! He'd felt sure she would make one of her pert replies, give him an opening to slip the news in between a joke and a threat. "Yes," he repeated, diving into his ale mug for more courage, "I've decided on a fitting end to this feud."

"Let me guess," Ellen suggested. "You've decided to repay the debt of your life that you owe me by sending me back to my father, free and unharmed."

Harry sputtered into his mug and came up choking, his face wet to the eyebrows with the foaming ale that he'd spattered. "Girl, I don't owe you a damned thing! I could take any three Armstrongs with my bare hands against their pikes."

"Indeed? But there are seven of the brothers."

"You are the most provoking, difficult, irrational—" Harry upended his mug and swallowed the rest of the sentence, along with the rest of his ale, in a single heroic gulp. "Never mind that. No, I'm not such a fool as to give up my prize that easily."

"Then how much ransom are you demanding?"

Harry grinned at her. Now that she was back to asking questions, he felt in control of the situation once more. "How much do you think would be fair, Ellen Irvine?"

"My father is not a rich man," said Ellen thoughtfully. "You should bear in mind that he's had many losses in the past few years."

"My heart bleeds. He's about to have another."

"How much?"

"An interesting question. How much do you think it would take to compensate me for the loss of my entire family?"

"I don't suppose any sum of money would make up for that—to a man with proper feelings. So you might as well—"

"Send you back unharmed? How you do keep harping on that silly notion. Remember, Ellen Irvine, I'm only a pirate. I don't indulge in the luxury of proper feelings. All the same, you're quite right. We can't set off the deaths of my father and brothers against mere money, can we?"

Ellen felt sick with fear at the bright, unconvincing smile with which Harry ended this question—a smile that never reached his eyes, now darkly slate-blue, like thunderclouds over the west marches. For all he might claim there'd been no love lost between him and his family, it was still clear to her that any mention of her father's raid raised powerful feelings in him—as well it might.

"Besides," Harry went on after a moment's pause, "I don't need money. My years at sea left me with enough Spanish gold and other treasure to rebuild Fernshaws in princely style. And while it might give me some passing satisfaction to beggar Carnaby Irvine, I think there are sweeter and more appropriate revenges that I can take. Carnaby robbed me of all my relatives. I think it's only fair that he should give me a family to replace the one I've lost."

Ellen shook her head, bewildered. The two small braids that confined her hair at the temples swung forward and fell against her cheeks. "How?"

"You."

"Me!"

"I'm not sending you back," Harry told her. "Ransom or no, here you are and here you'll stay. Carnaby Irvine shall give me a bride in payment for father and brothers."

"No!"

"Oh, yes." Harry's foot swung back and forth, back and forth, in an irregular rhythm that reminded Ellen of a dance step. "I'm not asking you, girl—I'm telling you. Look about you. Have you forgotten that you are on the English side of the border, in the stronghold of a ruthless pirate? None of your kinsmen here to back up your refusal. Not too many kinsmen in any case," he went on in a meditative tone. "Carnaby's had bad luck with his own family, hasn't he? The Irvines are down to himself, one withered old lady, and a blooming virgin. No wonder he's so mad to see you married and bearing children to put some life back into the family tree. Yes—I think taking you from him, not for a week or two, but permanently—will be the best revenge I can possibly enjoy."

Ellen closed her eyes for a moment, unable to bear the sight of Harry's brightly mocking face. If there had been one word of tenderness for her in his—not a proposal, one couldn't call it that—in his announcement of his intentions, she might actually have been tempted to agree. He was a better man than Fish-Mou', and yesterday she'd thought him almost soft in his gentleness with her and with Nellie's John. But he'd made it humiliatingly clear that all he cared for was using her to obtain revenge on her father. How could he possibly expect her to agree to a marriage founded on hate? She'd be setting the stage for a long life of misery. And not the worst of the misery would be her own inner longing for some hint of love from the man who'd wedded her out of hatred.

"It is not possible," she announced. "I'll not consent."

"Then I'll marry you without."

"And where will you find a minister to do your bidding?" Ellen couldn't bring herself to look at him; her eyes were fixed on the swinging point of his shoe.

"I think I'll borrow one from the Debatable Land," Harry responded. "What's his name—Archie, Erchie, something like that? Any preacher willing to minister to the Armstrong clan should have no scruples about performing any ceremony that I require of him—especially with Yohannon's knife pricking his side."

Ellen knew that it wouldn't take the threat of a knife to make Wee Erchie Jamison perform the wedding ceremony. A few glasses of whiskey would make him happy enough, and muddled enough, to do anything Harry suggested. Fish-Mou' had probably been planning on using Wee Erchie to marry them—unless he'd meant to rape her first, assuming that then she'd be grateful enough for the form of marriage afterward. She shivered involuntarily at the thought and wrapped her arms around herself.

"Does the prospect arouse such distaste in you?" Harry's voice was cold. "I'd advise you to reconcile yourself, and quickly at that. You'll remain my prisoner until you become my wife."

Ellen tossed her head and forced herself to meet his eyes. "Well, the accommodations aren't that bad," she said, "and you've forgotten that my father will be over the border to rescue me soon enough. I don't mind remaining your prisoner until then." She dipped a curtsy and smiled at him; he should not know the effort it cost her. "Will I return to my cell now?"

Without waiting for his assent, she retreated toward the staircase. Harry's eyes had gone dark blue again, and he was scowling in a manner that boded no good for her if she stayed to take the brunt of his redhead's temper. But, with one foot on the threshold, she could not resist a parting shot. "Rather than making wedding plans, I'd advise you to rebuild your barmekin wall. My father's men will be through it like a knife through butter, and then where's your bride and your revenge?"

She whisked through the door and was past the first turn on the staircase before Harry's empty mug thudded into the wall just behind where she had been standing. Giggling, Ellen scurried up the remaining stairs until, at the top landing, lack of breath stopped her laughter and forced her back to contemplation of the situation.

He wasn't coming after her; soberly, she told herself to count that among her blessings. Which were few enough, these days. Her situation was untenable. After last night's

debacle it would take her father some time to assemble a
fighting force capable of coming across the border for her.
They would assume, correctly, that Red Harry Graeme
would be expecting them and that his tower would be well
defended, the approaches guarded by sentries.

They might also assume that Ellen herself would be safe
enough, that Harry was only keeping her for ransom and
that she would not be harmed as long as he thought he could
get money for her. So their best plan would be to wait until
the dark of the moon. And the moon had been at the quarter
last night. Three weeks! Would Harry's patience last so long?
She doubted it.

Ellen entered the top-floor chamber with dragging steps.
She left the door open; there was no way to bar it from
inside, and if somebody was going to come up the stairs, she
would rather have the door open so that she could hear their
approach.

In the clear morning light Harry's collection of stolen
finery and jewels should have seemed tawdry. Ellen had
been thinking to bolster her resolve by despising him and
his way of life. Unfortunately, the cool daylight that filtered
through layers of gray clouds only made the rich cloths glow
all the brighter against the pale stone flags of the floor.
Turquoise blue brocade, sky-blue velvet shimmering with
light, silk that blended the green and yellow hues of new
spring grass—there was nothing here that Ellen could
dismiss as cheap or second-rate. And if they were stolen, it
was only in the sense that he'd taken them from Spanish
ships. In a world where Scots and English raided cattle from
each other as moves in an international game, Ellen couldn't
see the sense in condemning Harry for taking treasure from
the Spanish, who were everybody's enemy. Sir Francis
Drake had been doing the same thing on a grand scale for
years, and everybody knew that the Queen of England,
though she promised the Spanish ambassador that she
would punish Drake, was secretly pleased with his exploits.
Especially these days, when the countryside was covered
with beacons waiting to be lit in the event of the expected
Spanish invasion, she could easier condemn Harry for
staying on shore now than for fighting the Spaniards in the
past.

"Well, there you have it," Ellen said aloud to the bolts of silk and velvet. She closed the wooden chest with a bang and plumped herself down on the carved lid, bunching her skirts behind her to shield her backside from the deep-relief carvings that made the lid an uncomfortable chair. Elbows on her knees, chin propped in her hands, she grumbled at the floor and tried to work up some proper indignation against Harry for something less personal than the scene downstairs. If he were a true patriot, she thought, he'd be joining Drake now, getting ships together to fight the Armada. Instead of which, he'd taken his ill-gotten gains and retired from the sea just when he was most needed, to pursue an old feud and rebuild an old burnt-out house.

But it was hard for her to condemn Harry on that score, when her own countrymen were just as guilty of ignoring the Spanish threat while they pursued their private interests. The Catholic lords, and those in rebellion against the king, might be as happy as not to see the Spanish attempt a landing in Scotland; there was a strong party that said England's enemy must always be Scotland's friend. And King James himself, though knowing the English fleet was desperately short of powder and shot, had refused to sell England any of the supplies stored in Caerlaverock and other border castles.

But that was different, Ellen argued against herself. It was a matter of national policy, or something—whereas Red Harry Graeme was just a sordid, selfish, unprincipled pirate with his eye on the main chance. He fought the Spanish when there was profit to be made out of it, but now that it was a matter of defending his country instead of robbing merchants and treasure galleons, he had retired to specialize in kidnapping girls.

Which didn't make her feel any better. It was all very well to enjoy a fine feeling of moral superiority over Harry Graeme, but it wasn't so pleasant to reflect that she was in the power of this selfish, unprincipled pirate. Ex-pirate. He wasn't a patient man, and for some reason he seemed extraordinarily annoyed that she hadn't fallen gladly into his arms the minute he announced his plan of marrying her for revenge.

"Really, how unreasonable can men be?" Ellen muttered.

Was she supposed to be madly flattered that he deigned to use her against her father? Anybody would think he was entitled to take it personally when she refused such a kind offer. Anybody would think he intended to be a real husband to her, not her jailer.

She caught her breath against a sudden, surprising feeling of hurt. Yesterday there'd been moments when she felt some mutual respect, something almost like friendship, growing between her and this strange young man who'd suddenly come out of nowhere to sweep her away from all she held familiar. His matter-of-fact announcement that he meant to marry her only to thwart her father's plans left her feeling battered and bruised by more than the long hard ride they'd shared. Being taken prisoner for revenge was bearable, especially as long as she could use her wits to keep him from getting too close and to bargain the ransom terms down. But being married for revenge? That carried her into unknown territory, a dark frightening land where independence and wit would do her no good whatsoever.

"Have you made up your mind to it yet?"

Ellen jumped up, hands pressed to her laced stomacher. There was an unpleasant feeling of emptiness inside her, as if she'd just stepped off a stair into a black hole, and her heart was thudding with the surprise of Harry's appearance. True, she'd been sitting with her back to the door, but he must have come up those stairs as softly and quietly as a great cat stalking its prey.

"What do you mean, sneaking up on a person and startling them like that?" she demanded.

Harry laughed softly. "Dear girl, I clattered up the stairs with no concealment. Why should I bother sneaking around in my own tower? I've been standing in the doorway a good five minutes, clearing my throat and shuffling my feet and trying to attract your attention, but you were so deep in thought I couldn't wake you from your trance. And a pretty picture you made," he added, moving to her side and lifting the long loose hair from her shoulders, "with the sunlight turning this stuff to a cross between silver wire and hackled flax; but I've never cared for a still picture when I could have the living, breathing reality."

"You can't." Ellen felt short of breath and unable to concentrate with Harry standing so close to her, his fingers brushing the back of her neck. She moved away and felt the pull of his hand; he'd closed his fingers about the fine, loose strands he had been fondling.

"No?" Still smiling, he tugged gently on her hair and drew her back to his side with steady, inexorable pressure until her face was against his shoulder. "Some might say I have it already." He halted between words, as if trying to catch his breath after running up the stairs. But he hadn't seemed out of breath when he came into the room.

His hand moved again, fingers weaving in among the fine soft strands at the back of her neck, and a gentle pull downward forced her to tilt her face up toward his. A flash of kingfisher blue illumined his changeable eyes; her cheek brushed the velvet softness of his black suit, and lips too warm and firm for the cruel mouth came down upon her own. Dizzy with new sensations, Ellen forgot entirely her resolve to treat Harry with cold, distant firmness. All her resolutions staggered under this unexpected attack; sweetness flooded her veins. His arm about her waist supported her, holding her so close that she could feel the fine-drawn muscular tension of Harry's body as if it were her own. Pressed against him from knees to breast, all but drowning in the flood tide of pleasure he released in her, she returned his kiss with no reserves, nothing held back.

"A short courtship, but a merry one. If you're so warm now, our wedding night should be delightful indeed." Harry's light, mocking voice broke the sensual spell his lips and hands had woven about her. Ellen felt cold as he released her and stepped back with a slight bow. Lost and frightened, she wondered what had almost happened between them.

You ken very well what almost happened. Her auntie Verona's tart voice sounded in her head, so real she almost turned to see if the old lady was in the room with them. *It's a warning, lass. Will you let the man master you so easily, like a peasant girl at haying time? A fine wedded life you'll have of it!*

"Is that what you call courtship? Forcing your embraces

on your prisoner?" Ellen's cheeks were hot; she put up her hands unthinkingly, changed the gesture into one of pushing her hair back.

"Not an entirely unwilling prisoner," Harry said. His smile made her cheeks burn. "Indeed, you surprised me. The notion of a Scots-English union takes on a whole new meaning in your arms, fair Ellen."

She wanted to hit that mocking smile off his face. Instead she shrugged and turned away from him, pretending to study the pattern on the roll of turquoise brocade that spilled like deep water across the stone floor and carved wooden chest. Beside the chest, on a three-legged stool, lay the comb and mirror that she'd found in Harry's chest of Spanish treasure, and something infinitely more precious to her—a tiny pair of bronzed sewing scissors, the handles worked in the likeness of a stork's head, with the small, sharp blades forming the beak. "I save my resistance for where it will do some good. Even Wee Erchie may think twice about saying the marriage lines over a bride who fights and screams and scratches on her way to the altar."

"He might," Harry agreed. "But you won't fight me. You'll come nicely as you're asked, and you'll assure this minister that the marriage is by your own choice entirely."

Ellen slid the scissors up into her sleeve. "Do you really think so?" If he tried to approach her again, he'd see whether it was so easy to tame an Irvine with a few casual kisses.

"I've told you before," Harry said. "Rape is not one of my pastimes. Nor do I want there to be any doubts about the legality of this marriage. You'll cooperate, or—"

"I know, I know." Ellen put one small hand to her mouth and made a show of yawning. "Or I'll be your prisoner here until my dying day—or until my father rescues me. Do you care to make a small bet on which will come first? 'Twould serve to while away the hours."

"No, I've changed my mind about that. Contumacious virgins bore me, and as I've told you, I've no need for ransom money. If you don't agree to marry me, I'll deliver you to Fish-Mou' Bell as originally planned. He may be a little annoyed with you when I explain that you went with me so willingly to escape his embraces, but I'm sure that in the long years of your married life you'll work things out somehow."

Ellen could feel the blood draining from her cheeks. Hadn't she just been telling herself that nothing Harry could do to her would be worse than being forced into marriage with Fish-Mou'? And now it seemed she was to be denied even that consolation.

"Of course," Harry added, watching her out of the corner of his eye, "you may not have that long a marriage to endure. I wonder at Carnaby Irvine's willingness to give you to such a man—I do indeed. How many wives has Fish-Mou' buried already? Four, is it? Or five?"

"Two," Ellen snapped, "and I'll not be the third."

"My, my," Harry mocked gently, "you're gey quick to say what you'll not do, Ellen Irvine. You'll not have me, you'll not wed Fish-Mou'—anybody would suppose you'd a wealth of choices for the immediate future. Perhaps, instead of saying what you won't do, you'd best devote some time to thinking what you will do. For you'll have either me, or Fish-Mou' Bell, before tomorrow morning—that I promise you."

He was gone as swiftly and silently as he'd come, leaving Ellen to stare at the door that swung shut behind him with a whisper of stirred air and dust. Would he carry out his threat? She didn't know. Nor did she know if she had the courage to find out. He was angry with her for refusing him, and she had no idea how far that anger would carry him. And her little scissors was no weapon at all against Harry's cold determination.

Downstairs, Harry found his lieutenants waiting to hear the outcome of the talk with Ellen.

"And what," he responded silkily to Yohannon's inquiries, "has it to do with you?"

"I'm in this venture of yours for . . . my own reasons." Yohannon's lips curled nastily around the black emptiness where his front teeth should have been. "If you're going to be distracted by a skirt, Red Harry, I might choose to take service with another captain."

"I'm not distracted. You know very well that taking the girl was a ruse—and a damned good one, for nobody will question why Red Harry Graeme risked his ass raiding into Scotland to strike at the Irvines. The old feud is damned convenient. Do you want to have the Scots asking what we were doing so close to Caerlaverock Castle? Ellen Irvine gave us a reason to take a party into Scotland, and raiding Carnaby Irvine a second time will give us an excuse for a second trip over the border when the time comes. There's nothing more to it than that."

"Something more," Eleazar corrected. "Seemingly you're set on marrying the girl."

"My private affairs."

"Not when they're tangled up with ours—and when there's bigger game in the offing."

"We need your brains, Harry," Yohannon said. "We need you to have your mind on the project, not on trying to talk this girl into marriage." He gave a disapproving snort. "What's she done to addle your wits? You don't have to marry her to—"

"Shut up!" Harry clutched at a handful of his springy dark hair. The red lights that glowed in his curls were like sparks in the darkness when he lost his temper. "If you want Red Harry Graeme to use his brains on your behalf, then you'd best stop trying to drive him mad with pointless squabbles. It may be months before Frankie sends the equipment we need. How do you want me to account for our presence here in that time? Feuding with the Irvines and rebuilding Fernshaws should fill in the time nicely. And I won't be wasting any more time on the girl. I've told her that if she doesn't consent by sunset, I'm going to wrap her up in a blanket and deliver her to Fish-Mou' Bell so the wedding can proceed as originally planned."

"You can't do that," Eleazar protested. "I've heard about Johnny Bell. Forbye he's old enough to be her father, the man's got a cruel streak. You give her to him, he'll take it out on her that she ran away from him once already."

"And it's wanton waste to risk your neck taking the girl and then to send her back without even collecting a ransom."

"You're both fools," said Harry. "Of course I'm not going to send her back." He touched his sword hilt, not in a threatening manner but as one remembering an old vow.

"Did you think the feud was nothing more than an excuse? It's thanks to Carnaby Irvine that I've no living kin. He shall have me to thank that the Irvine line ends with himself. Not only will he be losing Ellen to me, but I'll make damned sure she never gives him the grandchildren he's longing for. If I marry the girl, she'll not be free to marry anybody else. Even Fish-Mou' might be able to get her with child."

"Not after the wound he took in our little set-to."

"Can you be sure of that?"

Eleazar shrugged.

"It's irrelevant in any case. I've made my plans and I'm sticking by them. The girl will marry me, I'll spend the spring rebuilding Fernshaws, and when Frankie responds, we'll finish off the project as planned."

"If all you want is to chop down the Irvine family tree," Yohannon suggested, "no need to tie yourself down to the girl." He cleaned his nails with the point of a small dagger, frowning down at the blade with intense concentration. "Gives Carnaby Irvine a good reason to kill you too. Simpler to kill her and have done with it."

"It's to be a marrying, not a burying, and I don't recall inviting you two to debate the matter." Harry's hand dropped to his sword hilt again and he stared his two lieutenants down. After a moment Yohannon nodded and put away the dagger.

CHAPTER
❧ 6 ❧

What do you mean, there's no leeks?"

Ellen planted both fists on her hips and glared up at the lean six-footer called Jenkyn o' the Side whom she had dispatched to the ground floor of the tower in search of stores.

Jenkyn shrugged, shifted from foot to foot, twisted his blue cap in his hands, pursed his lips to spit into a corner of the room and then thought better of it. "No leeks. No carrots. Mistress, 'tis the tail end of winter, and us haven't been here but two weeks! What should we be laying in your fine luxury stores for?"

Ellen sighed. "I wouldn't call it luxury to provide yourselves with something more than ale and salted mutton to eat." The bowl of burnt meat scraps that had been brought to her at noon was so unappetizing that, between boredom and hunger, she'd cajoled her jailers into letting her downstairs to see if she couldn't cook something better for their evening meal. Red Harry Graeme was off on errands of his own; presumably, if he didn't get himself killed, he'd be back at sunset to receive her answer. That didn't bear

thinking of. So Ellen bustled about the corner of the
first-floor room that held the great fireplace and the iron
cooking pots, tried various ruses to get Harry's men to let
her out of the tower, thought about cooking and kept one
eye on the door at all times. If she could get outside on the
pretext of plucking herbs to season the broth, she might be
able to liberate a horse and be away before they noticed.

"There's no herbs on the ground, and precious little else."
The dour Yohannon vetoed that suggestion almost before it
was out of her mouth. "Anyway, this godforsaken land is too
cold to grow anything with any flavor to it. You'll stay inside,
mistress, where Harry told us to keep you."

"I suppose you come from a land that's flowing with milk
and honey!" Ellen snapped. "And I wish to goodness you'd
go back to it."

Yohannon's mouth stretched in that terrifying smile that
showed his mutilated gums. "Fruit and vegetables, anyway.
I'm as tired of salt mutton as you are, mistress. That's why
you've been allowed downstairs to cook. Don't abuse your
freedom."

"Marvelous freedom," Ellen muttered as Yohannon left
to pursue his own interests outside, instructing the two men
at the door to keep a sharp eye on her at all times. "I get to
go up and down stairs, and to be caged in two rooms instead
of one."

But, at that, it was better than being left to her own
unhappy circle of thoughts; so she swallowed her retorts and
tried another tack. If she could be allowed down into the
vaulted ground floor where stores were kept, she might find
something with which to flavor the stew. With a little luck
she might even find something that would make all Harry's
men sick as dogs. If she could feed them poisoned stew
before he got back, she might yet have a chance to escape the
decision that came closer with each hour.

That suggestion, too, was rejected—at least, the plea to be
allowed down into the storeroom herself; she didn't mention the rest of the plan. Instead, Yohannon had ordered
Jenkyn o' the Side to leave off his game of dice, right hand
against left, to act as Ellen's courier. So, in lieu of other
options, Ellen had resigned herself to the project of actually

cooking a decent meal for the evening. Now she was discovering that the paucity of stores made even that a most improbable plan.

"Salted mutton!" She threw up her hands. "Even my father's poorest servants would quit if he gave them nothing better, day in and day out."

"Oh, we've better fare than that, mistress," Jenkyn said cheerfully.

"You do?"

"Surely. Didn't Yohannon just bring home a goodly lot of Scots cattle? We'll have fresh beef the night."

"Roasted on sticks like the mutton, I suppose," Ellen said, "until it's nice and burnt on the outside and still half raw in the center."

From Jenkyn's confused look, it was evident that it had never occurred to him there was any other way to cook meat.

"Oh, never mind. If you're slaughtering, bring me a nice chunk of the loin and a good sharp knife to cut it up with. And oats—you do at least have a sack of oats among the stores, I suppose?" She could stew the beef in ale, and to go with it she would make flat crisp oatcakes on the iron griddle. Not a feast-day dinner, but at least it gave her something to do.

Ellen was concentrating on patting the oatcakes as thin as possible between her palms, trying to close her ears to the bellowing of the cow chosen for slaughter, when the thump of a sack behind her made her squeeze her hands together. The gritty paste of oatmeal and water squirted out in all directions. She looked in dismay at the splotches it had left on the front of her dress and turned to rate Jenkyn for his clumsiness.

Instead of Jenkyn's lanky, awkward form, she saw the big black man grinning down at her. What was his name—Eleazar? Ellen told herself not to be frightened. He couldn't help being black, it didn't necessarily mean that he was related to the Devil, and if he chose to decorate himself in a purple vest trimmed with gilt sequins, that was his own business. So what if it made him look like a pirate? He was a pirate. They were all pirates, and none of them had hurt her yet, and Harry had promised she shouldn't be harmed—

though he could hardly do worse to her than carry out his threat of delivering her to Fish-Mou' Bell.

"Onions, mistress."

The prosaic reality of the sack at Eleazar's feet, spilling forth round knobbly shapes that she tardily recognized, took Ellen's mind off her vague fears and longings. The sharp, pungent smell of long-stored onions beginning to sprout tickled her nose and aroused her senses.

"Onions! Wonderful!" She knelt and gathered up some of the treasure in her arms. "But Jenkyn said there wasn't anything in the storeroom."

"Jenkyn," said Eleazar in a gentle rumble of a voice, "does not appreciate good food. After all, he is an Englishman. I have observed that most of your compatriots think themselves well served if somebody burns their meat on the outside and gives them a tankard of sour ale to wash it down with."

The description so nearly matched what she'd been given at noon that Ellen giggled appreciatively. There was just one inaccuracy in Eleazar's statement.

"Not my countrymen, Eleazar," she corrected him. "I'm Scots."

"You will be English when you are wedded to Harry."

Ellen bit her lip and looked away. "Could you bring me a knife and a chopping block? I want to mince these onions fine to flavor the stew. Oh, and a bit of fat to fry them in—perhaps from the cow they're slaughtering?"

"We can do better than that." With a flourish Eleazar produced another, smaller bag from behind his back and began pulling out the parcels it contained. "Butter. A round of fresh cheese. Garlic. *And* my own supply of spices."

Ellen sniffed curiously at the small bags he offered her. Sweet and sharp, pungent and musky, the odors of distant voyages filled the air and made her head swim for a moment. "I don't know what all these are," she admitted, "but they should certainly make dinner more interesting."

"If you permit," said Eleazar calmly, "I will remain and teach you how to use them."

Under Eleazar's tuition, Ellen learned in that long afternoon that more strange and flavorful things could go into a simple stew than her father's cook would have used in a month of feast days. She chopped, fried, seasoned, and tasted; her forehead grew sticky with the heat of the fire, and wisps of hair clung to her flushed cheeks. Eleazar gave her no chance to slip anything untoward into the stew, even if she'd had it; he was always beside her, suggesting a better way to hold the great cleaver or recommending another generous pinch from one of his mysterious bags of herbs. Ellen knew she was being closely watched. But as they worked together, she lost her first instinctive fear of the tall black man, who had a gentle voice and large, competent hands. His slow, calming movements reassured her by degrees, and his tales of sailing with Red Harry Graeme fascinated her completely. Raiding Spanish galleons, trading with the sultan of the Spice Islands, navigating through the shoals and reefs of Indonesia—Ellen lived in another, enchanted world through that afternoon. Only between stories did she remember the threat of Red Harry's return at the end of the day.

"I don't see how he could have done so many things! He's not old enough to have lived such a life!" she exclaimed as Eleazar finished his story of how Harry had slipped into Panama by night, captured the governor, and held him for ransom aboard his ship.

Eleazar's deep, rich chuckle seemed to fill the stone-walled room. "Ah, well, mistress, Harry's been at sea since his seventeenth year. He was only a boy on that first voyage with Frankie—where he saved my life."

"Saved your life? How? Was it a sea fight?"

"No."

Eleazar frowned at the floor, seemingly lost in his own memories. Ellen took advantage of his abstraction to slip a paring knife up her sleeve.

"No, this was before I sailed with him, when I was a slave in Guatulco. That is a Spanish settlement in Guatemala," Eleazar amplified, and then, seeing that Ellen still looked blank, "In the Americas. I had been a house servant, until I grew too big and the lady looked on me with favor. Then I was sent to the mines . . ."

"What was that like?" Ellen prompted as Eleazar seemed to have lost the thread of his story again.

He sighed and shook his head. "You don't want to know, young mistress. It was not—men should not treat men in such a way." One hand absently caressed his right arm, and for the first time Ellen noticed a long ropy scar running the length of his arm, purplish against the smooth black skin. "I did not know then that I was a man. I was born a slave—I never knew my parents—but even so, I knew it was wrong, what the Spanish masters did to us. The priest told us to be humble and bow to the masters, but my heart was not humble. And then I found a friend."

"Yohannon?" She had already deduced as much. It was a strange partnership, the giant-sized black man and the wiry little man with the coppery skin and lank black hair, but this story went some way to explaining how the bonds between the two of them had been forged.

"Yes. He wasn't born into slavery, like me. He was captured on an expedition into the highlands. The Spanish soldiers raided his village and killed all those who they thought would not be strong enough to work for them. He saw them kill his two children, and they took his wife—"

Eleazar stopped, and Ellen was grateful to be spared the details. "Yohannon and the other men were bound and taken away to the mines," he said after a moment. "I think he wanted to die. He would not eat or drink. None of them would. The Indians don't make good slaves. The others did die, but Yohannon was feverish, and while he didn't have his sense, I got some broth down him. He was sick a long time, long enough to learn a little Spanish so we could talk, but he was still too weak when they dragged him out to work beside me in the mines. That was when the overseer beat him, and I—well, I had spent weeks sharing food with him, coaxing him to live. I couldn't stand the waste of it, that he should be killed the first day they took him out of the barracks. So I . . . stopped the overseer."

"And then what?"

"Oh, they beat me, of course, but they stopped before I was dead and took me before the court. I thought myself lucky they did not beat me to death on the spot, for that was the usual treatment for a slave who dared to resist an order. But when I heard the overseer talking in the court, then I thought I would have been luckier to have died in the mines.

He told the masters that I had been plotting a slave rebellion against them—that I wanted the slaves to rise and burn the town. So they decided that I should be burnt alive, as a lesson to the others. And Yohannon with me. They had drawn half his teeth, but he refused to 'confess' to their made-up conspiracy, or to say anything against me—so they said that he should burn too."

Ellen paled and her hands clenched white around the handle of the cleaver she held. "Beasts!"

"No," said Eleazar gently, "men. I've seen worse since."

"But you escaped."

"Harry and the other ship's officers were dining with my owner that evening. He invited them to stay another day and watch the burning—it was to be a public spectacle, and he thought they'd enjoy it. Harry thanked him and asked if he might return to the ship to invite his captain, also, to watch the show." Eleazar chuckled again. "And it was quite a show. He came back in the pinnace with twenty men, burnt the town and set all the slaves free. The Spanish fled into the jungle, and most of the slaves went to the Indian tribes or stole boats to go pirating on their own. But Yohannon and me, we chose to sail with Harry and his captain."

Eleazar's broad hands paused over the chopping block and he stared over Ellen's head with a faraway look, as if he were remembering horizons too distant to see clearly. "On the ship, when he got his strength back, Yohannon wanted to leap over the side. But Harry stopped him. I don't know how he did it, but Harry talked to him for three days and nights, in Spanish, English, whatever words he could find— and now Yohannon doesn't try to die anymore. But he still hates the Spaniards."

"So do I," said Ellen with feeling.

"No, don't hate them." Eleazar shook his head slowly. His smile was heartbreakingly sweet. "Hating eats on your insides. It eats at Yohannon. He won't let himself love anyone or anything—except Harry."

"And you."

"And maybe me, a little," Eleazar agreed. "But not enough to cure the hating that burns him up inside. No, it's not good to hate anybody. The Spanish are not different

74

from other men. Even here in England, I am told, men hunt one another down and burn houses and kill in the name of old feuds, even when they can no longer remember how they started."

He looked directly at Ellen as he said the last words, and she felt her cheeks turning red with more than the heat of the fire. Of course, Eleazar would know the story of how her father had finished off the Graeme-Irvine feud, or thought he had, by burning down Fernshaws with all its sleeping occupants. He would think she had little room to be feeling morally superior to the Spaniards w..° had enslaved Yohannon.

"Well, I don't like feuds," she said briskly, attacking a peeled onion with more energy than discretion. "All I want is for everybody to make peace, and then maybe—then—" The cleaver whacked down across the chopping block and bits of onion went scattering to the far corners of the room, filling the air with pungent fumes that helped to explain the tears at the corners of Ellen's eyes. "Then I could go home," she finished, suppressing the words that had first come unbidden into her mind.

Then maybe Harry would marry me for love, not for vengeance.

"Is that what you really want?" Eleazar asked gently. "To go back to Carnaby Irvine? The way I heard it, he would have forced you into marriage with this Johnny Bell. Still might, if you go home."

Ellen brushed her eyes with the back of her hand and set about reducing the onion to finely minced pulp.

"Harry Graeme is a good man." Eleazar delivered this opinion to the black stew pot over the fire, while he stirred the contents with a long wooden spoon.

"He d-doesn't love me." Ellen brought the cleaver down on the chopping block with a vicious hack. "Besides, he's going to send me to Fish-Mou' Bell, too, so where's the difference?"

"Not if you agree to marry him instead."

"And spend the rest of my life hoping for his revenge on the Irvines to turn into love for Ellen Irvine?" Ellen whirled and spat out the words before she realized how much of herself she was giving away. Blushing furiously, she bent over the chopping block and scraped its surface clean with the back side of the cleaver.

"If you think he's marrying you for vengeance," Eleazar told the stew pot, "you've not looked in your mirror lately, Ellen Irvine, or into his eyes. The boy needs some excuse, don't you see, to take the daughter of Carnaby Irvine to wife. Would you deny him that salve to his pride?"

"What about *my* pride?"

"Pride makes a cold bed companion."

Ellen sighed and laid the cleaver down, very carefully. "Oh, all right. Quit badgering me. You can all quit badgering me. I ken well enough I've no real choice, anyway." Had she ever thought she could choose Fish-Mou' Bell's embraces over any sort of marriage with Harry?

"You'll have him, then?"

"The stew's done. I'm going upstairs. And you can tell Harry there'll be no need to saddle fresh horses for a trip across the border tonight. I know when I'm beaten." At least Eleazar's stories had reassured her, a little, about the kind of man she was going to. As for his belief that Harry was really in love with her—that Ellen could not quite credit, but perhaps if she worked hard, she could make herself believe that he cared for her a little bit, or enough to salve her own pride at entering into this loveless marriage.

She knelt and rinsed her hands in the corner bucket. As she stood, Eleazar's pink-palmed hand closed about her left wrist, gentle but too strong to resist. "In that case," he said, "you'll not be needing the paring knife you slipped up your sleeve earlier, will you?"

Cheeks burning, Ellen retired to the upstairs chamber with just over three hours left to repair her dignity and her bedraggled green gown.

He was Red Harry Graeme, who had raided a Spanish settlement in Guatemala before he was twenty, who had slipped into Panama alone to tweak the nose of the Spanish governor, who had cheated Chinese merchants and flattered sultans and sailed into Cadiz to singe the king of Spain's beard. And now, at twenty-eight years and some days, he was trembling like a maiden outside the door to his own chamber in the ancient peel tower that was all Carnaby Irvine had left of the Graeme inheritance.

For the third time Harry raised his hand to knock at the door; for the third time his hand fell back of its own accord. What a time to be stricken with doubts! The minister was downstairs, half drunk already and ready to mumble whatever words Harry required of him. His men were waiting for him to come back down with his bride. Ellen had had a full day alone in his chambers to think over his threat of delivering her to Fish-Mou' Bell. The choice between them shouldn't be that difficult—and in any case, he did not really have to give her a choice. She was the daughter of his worst enemy, the man who'd all but wiped out the Graeme family, and she was in his power. Instead of refusing him, the little snip should have thanked God fasting that he meant to marry her!

So why was he hovering outside his own door like an anxious suitor? Because if Ellen was still fool enough to refuse this marriage, he would be left with only two choices. He could drag her downstairs kicking and screaming, hold his hand over her mouth long enough for Wee Erchie to solemnize a marriage of doubtful legality, and then lock her back in the upstairs room. Or he could carry out his threat to give her to Fish-Mou' Bell.

Neither course of action was acceptable. The one would leave him tied to a bride who hated him, the other would lose him Ellen forever. Irritable, resentful, tired from his long ride to get Wee Erchie, Harry wavered on the edge of admitting an unacceptable truth to himself. He didn't want to force Ellen, and he would not give her up. He wanted her to come to him of her own will; he wanted her, God help him, to want him! As though there could ever be such a thing as desire between a Graeme and an Irvine! If the ghosts of his family didn't haunt him for such an unmanly thought, Ellen Irvine herself would laugh in his face at the mere suggestion.

So what would he do if she still refused to have him?

He didn't know, but nothing could be worse than lingering outside the door like this. Impatient with his own fears, Harry pushed the door open and marched in to meet his fate.

Watching from the tower window, Ellen had seen the horsemen returning from their expedition to the Debatable Land, Red Harry's unmistakable figure in the lead, then a knot of his men surrounding a rotund little man who swayed and sang in the saddle. Wee Erchie Jamison, that was, and the man was drunk as a lord already. Harry'd have no trouble in getting him to agree to any ceremony he wanted performed.

Ellen had been oddly relieved to think that her consent was going to be irrelevant. Somehow, she felt, if she gave in to Red Harry at all, he would sense that in her folly she'd already begun to—well, to like him better than any of the nice boys and worthy gentlemen she'd met on her own side of the border. As if there could ever be anything but cold courtesy, and not much of that, between a Graeme and an Irvine! How could any good come of this marriage? Every time he looked at her, he must remember the burning of Fernshaws.

And yet—he wasn't a cruel man. Eleazar clearly worshiped him. He must be a good leader; his men were willing to follow him anywhere, even on a crack-brained expedition over the border to masquerade as a troop of Bell men and kidnap the child of his worst enemy. He'd been kind and considerate, as far as the circumstances allowed, on that long hard ride to the English side of the border.

Her father hated the Graemes, always had, as long as she could remember. He must have had reason.

Harry had let Nellie's John go unharmed, though by doing so he put his own life in jeopardy.

He hadn't troubled to ask her to marry him, he'd simply informed her of his plans; and he'd made it humiliatingly clear that his only interest in her was as an instrument of revenge.

He rescued slaves and let shepherd boys go and dragged a strange Indian captive back from the brink of despair by the sheer force of his will.

Eleazar thought he loved her; but it had been nearly an hour since he returned with Wee Erchie Jamison in tow, and where was he? Drinking downstairs with his men, no doubt, without caring that prisoned in the top room of the tower was a girl whose entire future hung on the events of this one night.

She thought bleakly that it was not a very good augury for their married life. But wouldn't even being ignored by Harry be an improvement on Fish-Mou' Bell's attentions?

"Oh, *damn* the man!" Ellen burst out, wheeling to stare out the window at a barmekin now empty and shadowed with the approach of dusk. "Why can't he be one thing or the other? I don't know whether to love him or hate him!"

"You haven't to do either," remarked a suave voice behind her. "Only to marry him."

Ellen gasped and whirled. Her long green skirts, no longer held out by the stiff layers of petticoats, swished across the floor behind her and slowed her quick motions.

"You might have knocked!"

He had crept up on her without warning, cold and quiet as the north wind that was presently sweeping gray clouds down over the hills and ruffling the steel-gray waters of Solway Firth. His eyes were dusky blue-gray in the chilly light of early evening; he had exchanged his riding clothes for a suit of mouse-gray velvet, the doublet sprinkled with brilliants. Only the dark reddish glow of his dark hair lent warmth to his appearance in the darkening room.

"I might," Harry agreed. "But it's not my custom to request permission to enter my own room."

"Is this a sample of the courtesy I can expect as your wife?"

Harry's eyes lightened and one corner of his mouth moved slightly upward. "Does this imply that you've accepted the situation?"

Ellen's heart thudded annoyingly whenever he looked at her with that tantalizing half smile. Against her will she was remembering the impudent caress he'd taken when they were hiding under a pile of hay in the shepherd's hut, thrust closer together in the narrow space than man and wife would lie in a decent-sized bed. Her breast felt sensitive and tender, aching for something—surely not for a renewal of that caress! She clasped her hands before her and stepped back, remembering this time to move slowly so that she wouldn't risk tripping over her own skirt. She forced herself to meet his laughing look with her own level stare. Slowly, pretending a calm she was far from feeling, she looked up and down the length of his body until his smile began to fade.

"You look to be a proper man," she said with deliberation. "Not very tall, perhaps, but straight in your limbs and healthy and strong. If I must be had by somebody, I suppose you'd be better than Fish-Mou' Bell."

"What do you mean, not very tall! You're a fine one to talk, Ellen Irvine, and you standing no higher than my chin if I measured you against me."

Ellen shrugged, pretending indifference. "Aye, well, in Scotland men get to their full growth. But I've heard the English were stunted wee souls, and no doubt you're man enough by these Southron standards."

"Man enough for you, at all events." Harry's hand shot out to grip her wrist. Unresisting, she let him draw her close enough to measure the truth of his assertion that she stood no higher than his chin. Her cheek brushed the soft gray velvet of his doublet, and she could feel the rapid thudding of his heart under the fine new suit. Her own pulse beat even faster; he must feel it leaping under his hand, where his sun-browned fingers lay across her wrist. They stood close enough now, but they'd lie even closer tonight, without the barriers of her green gown and his velvet doublet—if she acceded to Harry's mad plan. But then, what choice had she? The word she'd spoken was true enough; better Red Harry Graeme than Fish-Mou' Bell, if she were to be forced to take one or the other.

The deep throbbing of her pulse, the way her breath wavered when she thought of the wedding night ahead, the fact that given half a chance she could love this reckless fellow as she'd never hoped to love any of the douce-quiet gentlemen who courted her at home—none of these things counted, Ellen told herself. She was being forced into this marriage, and for her own salvation she must pretend to take it as Harry did—as a matter almost of business, as one step more in the interminable feud that had plagued both their families since long before any living man could remember.

Lips brushed across her floating hair, ending with an

unexpectedly warm and tender kiss on her forehead where the fine braids left her face bare. Harry's arm went around her and Ellen tilted her face upward without thinking, eyes half closed, waiting for the inevitable conclusion.

Instead of kissing her lips then, Harry released her and laughed, shakily, on a long exhalation of breath. "Well, Ellen Irvine? You see I'm tall enough to kiss the top of your head. Do you admit you've no need for a long Scots beanpole of a fellow?"

He was laughing at her and her response. Laughing at her naiveté in expecting this strange contract to be sealed with a proper kiss. Probably he didn't even mean to lie with her tonight; he'd shown little enough sign of being interested in her that way. She was purely an instrument of his revenge, nothing more.

Shame burnt in Ellen's cheeks and sent bright warm flushes all along her neck and breasts. She stepped back and raised her eyes to meet Harry's. "I felt no need of any man at all, Red Harry Graeme. And naturally I'd rather wed one of my own countrymen, if marry I must."

"That option," warned Harry, "is still open . . . assuming Fish-Mou' will still have you, after you've spent a day and a night in the chambers of a lecherous pirate. Do you want to ride over the border and find out?" What devil was in him, teasing the girl this way? He'd be finely served if she said yes. Then he'd have to admit he'd no intention of giving her to Johnny Bell, and she might soon deduce that any other threats he made were pure bluff where she was concerned— that he melted like butter in the sun under one look from her clear eyes, and would have given her anything she asked for. A fine thing, for a man to be the weak-willed slave of his worst enemy's daughter!

"But since you seem so insistent on this marriage," Ellen said hastily before Harry could expand on his threat, "I suppose I can put up with an Englishman. After all, it's not like a real marriage."

"And just what do you mean by that?"

His eyes were the smoky dark blue of storm clouds rolling in from the west. Ellen knew a moment of pure, unreasoning fear at the suppressed anger in his face.

"Well—I—It's not as if you cared anything about me

personally, or I about you," she stammered, stepping back to get away from that accusing look. "I m-mean, you don't hate me in particular. I'm just a representative of my family. And I feel the same way about you. How could there be any more to it than that? We hardly know one another!"

"So you don't think a ride over the border and a wetting in Solway Firth constitutes a proper introduction, Ellen Irvine? How formal you Scots ladies are!" Harry swept off his feathered bonnet and made her a mocking bow, bending so low that the white plumes in his bonnet brushed the floor as he stretched out his hand.

"May I have the honor of your hand, fair lady?"

"Oh, stop clowning and let's get this over with." Ellen picked up her trailing skirts and stalked to the door.

On the way down the spiral stairs she heard Harry murmur behind her, "Such eagerness in a young bride! I'm touched, faith I am."

It was not possible to go down the stairs any faster without risking a broken neck; not in these long skirts. *"Must* you tread so close behind me?" Ellen snapped without turning her head.

"Don't you want to be close to your loving husband?" He mocked an injured tone.

"I'm very glad that this is only a formality." Thank goodness he was behind her, so he couldn't see how the color rose into her face every time she thought of what it would be like, to lie next to Harry Graeme in the darkness and privacy of that small upper chamber.

All Harry's men were drawn up in rows in the lower chamber where Ellen had been cooking just that afternoon, their leather jacks freshly cleaned and steel accoutrements burnished. Even cleaned up and standing still, they were an impressive and untoward sight—faces of every hue from Eleazar's glossy black to Jenkyn o' the Side's milk-pale skin with its spattering of freckles; garments wildly decorated according to the wearer's fancy, with gilt sequins along the edge or with bright silk scarves knotted at the elbows; arms as homely as a borderer's pike and as exotic as the enameled and inlaid gun in Yohannon's belt.

Ellen checked involuntarily at the sight, and Harry took advantage of her pause to come up beside her and put his arm around her waist. "Don't be frightened now, Ellen Irvine," he murmured. "A girl who'd run off with a pirate rather than marry Fish-Mou' Bell should have the courage to face the pirate's men. And there's not a one among them but will be your slave, when they know you as I do."

Ellen saw Yohannon in the front ranks, thin lips closed over his empty mouth, dark obsidian eyes sparkling at her with a resentment all too clear to read, and took leave to doubt this statement. Besides—"You hardly know me at all," she pointed out.

"Perhaps that's what I meant."

"You—ohh!" Ellen sucked in her breath as she grasped his meaning, and Harry grinned unrepentantly.

"Slow on the uptake, aren't you? Never mind. I intend to know you better. *Much* better. Come on, now. Wee Erchie's just at his prime—two more drinks and he'll be too far gone to mumble the words for us."

Ellen glanced at Wee Erchie, bobbing back and forth on his heels like a round little doll, and wondered if there were any way she could delay Harry until the minister had had those two last drinks. But Harry was already urging her up to face the minister, and one of the men was opening the book for Wee Erchie and helpfully pointing out the place where he should begin reading.

Ellen looked behind her for some way out and saw only Yohannon's thin-lipped, mirthless smile. Know and love her? At least one of Harry's men would be perfectly happy to see her set over the border for Fish-Mou' Bell; of that she felt sure, without exchanging a word with Yohannon. And if she disrupted the ceremony now, Harry might just be angry enough to let Yohannon take her away. She'd had experience already of how short his temper was and how badly he took being rejected.

She knelt in response to Harry's downward pressure on her arm, bowed her head and folded her hands. Beside her Harry's sword scraped on the stones as he, too, knelt. She could just see his knees and the brilliant-trimmed edge of his gray velvet doublet.

Her hands were cold, and the fingers were white where she clasped them so tightly together to keep from trembling. Her whole body was cold under the green gown. What was there to be afraid of? This marriage was only a formality; Harry had made it clear enough that he had no interest in her person; if this was what it took to keep him happy until her father could rescue her, it was little enough to agree to. The bonds could always be annulled once she was back in Scotland—she doubted that Harry, having been out of the country for so many years, knew that the parliaments of both countries had agreed to make illegal any marriage between English and Scots.

There was really nothing to fear.

Just before it came time for them to make their responses, Ellen glanced up at Harry's face; she didn't know why. He was looking boldly and openly at her instead of bowing his head as he ought and his eyes burned with a blue fire that destroyed all her careful chain of reasoning. A formality? A meaningless, illegal form of words? There was nothing so cold and passionless in that glance. Nothing cold at all about Red Harry Graeme, except his determination to have what he wanted. All the rest of him was a leaping flame, bright as the dancing lights in his hair, quick as his movements, dangerous as his edged tongue. A flame that could consume her, if she let it.

If she consented to it.

And if she did not?

"Aye," said Ellen Irvine in a clear small voice that trembled hardly at all, when Wee Erchie turned to her for her response.

CHAPTER

❧ 7 ❧

There was no chance afterward to think over what she'd consented to and possibly to rue it. As soon as Wee Erchie Jamison shut his book, Harry's men surged around them, clapping him on the back, wishing her well, filling a great chased-silver tumbler for her from the barrel of wine they'd broached in the barmekin.

"Come awa' oot and see the bonny fire, mistress," urged a man whose name she didn't know, but whose tongue proclaimed him Scots by origin.

"And there's a fine beef stew to eat by the firelight," teased Eleazar, "the work of two great international cooks!"

The bonfire must have been laid hours before, the wood soaked with melted tallow, to produce the instant blaze that shot toward the sky as soon as Harry tossed a lighted torch into the midst of the pile. The center of the barmekin blazed red and orange and hot against the cool gray hills and the darkening sky, brighter than the last faint glow of the setting sun. Harry kept his arm firm about her waist, and Ellen was thankful for the heat of the fire, which could explain the warmth of her face. What was he thinking, this strange quicksilver young pirate whom she'd wedded? Did he mean to lead her upstairs presently, to share the pallet in that small upper chamber, or were they to sleep in chaste separation, as they had last night? She didn't know what he meant to do—nor what she wanted. Her body wanted to nestle into the comfortable space between his side and the crook of his arm. But she was used to being ruled by her cool, clear head—and now her head was dizzy with too many drafts of the strong sweet wine, and all of her was warmed with an inward heat that rivaled the heart of the bonfire. She wished he would let her go. No, she didn't, or why did she make no move to escape his light embrace?

"It's all ver—very confusing."

When he smiled down at her, the flames from the bonfire danced in his eyes and made her want to smile back. "What is confusing you?"

"I—The—" Thankfully, Ellen found a safe ground of conversation. "Is the wine from a Spanish ship?"

"No."

The monosyllable ended that line of conversation.

"Hey, Red Harry," called the merry little Scotsman who'd invited Ellen out to enjoy the lighting of the bonfire, "whar's the bride's gift?"

Harry clapped one hand to his forehead and cursed himself in plain English for a cloth-headed bumpkin. "Here am I in all my finery, and forgetting entirely that I'd a gift for you in my pocket. I'm sorry there was not time to have a suitable dress made," he said, "but I'd hoped that this might make you forgive me for making you kneel before the minister in your torn green gown. And after all, it went completely out of my head when I saw you."

Reaching inside his doublet, he drew out a chain of heavy, flat silver links that draped over his hand like a living silver serpent, turning and shooting off silver sparks in the firelight. The serpent's eyes were green . . .

"Not Spanish gold?" Ellen teased. She felt a little shy at this unexpected gift; it was something any real bride might be delighted to receive from her loving husband. But if she responded so, Harry would laugh at her again for taking this mock marriage seriously.

"The emeralds," Harry said, unsmiling, "are from a ship

86

of the Spanish plate fleet that I once had the good fortune to intercept. But the silver comes from Fernshaws. There was once a small silver mine on our land; it never produced enough to repay the money my father put into it, but he did get out enough good silver to have a set of chains worked for my mother. She died when I was born, of course, and the chains were put away. After the fire, a neighbor found the lump of melted silver and saved it—in case any Graemes ever came back, she said, we should have one thing left that had belonged to the family. I took it to a jeweler in Carlisle and had him work it into a new set of links."

"Why?"

Harry glanced down at her, unsmiling. "Oh, I thought it might come in handy someday."

In one careless motion he tossed the silver chains over her head. The heavy flat links were cold against her neck. A single chain in the back, in the front the necklace was elaborated into a series of chains that hung down over her breast in ever-deepening arcs, each link winking with a green emerald eye.

"But Harry—you mean this is your one heirloom from Fernshaws?" Ellen protested. "You can't mean to have me wear it!"

She started to lift the necklace from her bosom, but Harry's hand came down over hers and stopped her. His fingers lay warm against the hollow of her throat; he must be able to feel the tumultuous pulse that his touch had stirred to life.

"And why not?"

Ellen turned her head and regarded him with a level, serious gaze. "You know why not. I am the daughter of Carnaby Irvine, the man who burned your home and killed your father and brothers. You only married me because you thought it would hurt my father. Every time you look at me you must remember the burning of Fernshaws. You cannot want me to wear this!"

"Perhaps," said Harry silkily, "I want you to wear it for just that reason. So that I won't forget."

Ellen would have torn off the necklace and thrown it at him, but his hand still weighed hers down, and it would have been undignified to struggle before his men.

"Enjoy the memories while you can," she said. "When I leave here, I'll leave the necklace with you for your real bride—if you can find one."

"You'll not leave here," Harry contradicted, "and you're as real as any bride I might take. Did you think it was a joke, the words Wee Erchie read over us? Drunk or sober, he's a minister and the marriage stands."

"If you hadn't gotten him drunk, he might have broken the news to you that no such marriage can possibly stand. It's against the law!"

"What the devil are you talking about?"

Ellen hadn't meant to go so far, but now she couldn't retreat. "You've been out of the country too long, Red Harry Graeme. It's against the law for English and Scots to wed without their sovereigns' consent. No court either side of the border will uphold this mock marriage. It'll be annulled as soon as my father rescues me from your hold."

"That," said Harry between his teeth, "he'll never do. And if I have to get the queen's consent to marry you, I'll have it. And for now—why don't you come upstairs with me, *wife,* and we'll put a swift end to all this talk of an annulment. This marriage will hold—you might as well make up your mind to it."

"You can't want that. Not really. Think!"

"I have thought of little else since I took you from the burn below your father's hall," Harry told her, "and what I think is—I don't want any wife but you, Ellen Irvine. I'll have no other. So you might as well wear the Fernshaws silver, in token that we're bound for life. Now come. We've dallied below long enough."

Ellen caught her lower lip between her teeth and looked around the barmekin. Harry's men were all about; there was no room to run, no place to run to, no chance to escape his touch. And, weak-willed fool that she was, she hardly wanted to do so. The Fernshaws silver lay cold and heavy upon her neck; when she glanced down, the emeralds set in each link winked their green eyes at her. He was serious about this marriage. He wanted her—and perhaps not only for revenge upon her father. Eleazar thought he loved her but could not admit it to himself. Perhaps, in time, she could make a real marriage out of this thing begun in haste and revenge.

There was no other man she would rather make a life with. After a day in Red Harry's company, she couldn't imagine any other man who could even come close to stirring her blood as he had. Surely it was worth the effort!

And if she failed?

Ellen shivered at the thought of the loveless years that lay ahead.

"Cold? Come on upstairs. I'll warm you."

"So will the fire."

"Ah. But I'll enjoy the task more." His lips were close to her neck, sending new voluptuous shivers through her body; his hands guided her toward the peel tower, and she resisted no longer. In a daze of wine and anticipation she slowly climbed the winding stair inside. If her mind was half drugged, her senses were achingly, thrillingly alive. She heard the quiet swish of her long skirts on the stones, the chinking of the silver chains about her neck, the soft undercurrent of Harry's breathing and the click of his heels on the steps behind her. She felt the weight of the linked silver chains like a living thing caressing her neck and bosom; the brush of air along her cheek as she mounted the drafty stairway was like a promise of the touches to come. Harry had lit a torch at the bonfire just before they came inside; it flared in his hand behind her, sending her shadow long and black and wavering up the stairs.

The door at the top of the stairs swung open easily at the touch of her fingertips, moving quietly as a breath of wind on its oiled hinges. She felt her way into the dark room; Harry, following her, set the torch to the fresh candles fixed on their holders all around the walls. Golden flowers of light blossomed wherever he passed, until they were standing in a ring of lighted candles, surrounded by the carelessly heaped-up spoils of his pirate years.

Harry upended the torch and laid it in a corner. He came toward her with empty hands, palms up, but stopped before he reached her. He looked younger, now, than his twenty-eight years; young, and serious, and almost vulnerable. The restraint that held him back was as palpable a thing as if he'd been in chains. Ellen could read the blaze of desire for her that lit his eyes, made his palms tremble. It frightened her, to be wanted so much, and by a man who still hadn't made up his mind whether to love or to hate her.

As he reached for her hand, she flinched; then, willing herself not to reveal her fear, she stood quite still, her chin upraised. Whatever was to happen now, she reminded herself, Harry Graeme was not a cruel man, and she'd chosen this ending of her own will rather than give herself to Fish-Mou' Bell.

"Afraid?"

"No," Ellen lied. But her eyes would not quite meet his.

He laughed softly. "Of course you are. Don't be. Didn't I tell you that I don't make a hobby of raping virgins?"

As he made no further move toward her, Ellen felt her confidence—and her curiosity—growing. Did he really mean to leave her untouched? Had he just been bluffing, downstairs, with his talk of wanting to keep her forever, to make this a real marriage? A moment ago she'd been afraid of the unknown, now she felt almost disappointed.

"What you actually said was that you very seldom rape virgins after midnight."

"True. Well, that gives us several hours, doesn't it? Don't be afraid of me, Ellen Irvine. I may be only a rude pirate, but I've better sense than to throw you down on the straw like a farm boy with his first love. Contrary to what you may have heard," Harry said with a wry smile that did not quite reach his eyes, "not all my women have been forced to my bed at the point of a sword. Some of them even rather enjoyed the experience."

"Which ones?"

Harry looked surprised.

"I'd just like to know what percentage of them enjoyed it," Ellen explained politely, "so that I can estimate my own chances."

Harry laughed again. "Now, you'll call me a conceited fool if I say they all did, and you'll get all nervous again if I say there were some who didn't. Why don't we sit down and talk it over? It's been a long day, and I'm not used to all this riding; truth to tell, I've been looking forward to this nice soft bed." He grimaced and rubbed his thigh as if easing the strain on a pulled muscle.

"Nice soft bed," Ellen repeated, looking at the straw pallet with its luxurious covering.

"You slept all right last night, didn't you?"

Ellen blushed, remembering the long hours of lying awake and listening to Harry's breathing, the sense of his presence beside her in the dark quiet room.

"Neither did I. And perhaps for the same reason." Harry took her hand and drew her down to the pallet with him, and Ellen did not resist. She folded her legs under her and sat quietly, her free hand lying open in her lap, her head bent so that her loosened hair fell forward and partially obscured her face. Her heart was pounding so hard that she thought the flat silver links of the Fernshaws necklace must be quivering, all her awareness concentrated in the hand that lay in Harry's grasp. His finger traced idle lines in her palm; it was hardly a lover's gesture, but even that light touch made her feel dizzy with impatience and imagination.

He was sitting tailor fashion, legs crossed, looking quite relaxed and comfortable, as though all he'd ever had in mind was an hour's quiet conversation with her. And yet his fingertips kept up those teasing light caresses, now venturing as far as the white inner surface of her wrist, tracing the blue veins just below the surface of her clear skin; and Ellen couldn't breathe or think properly as long as he kept doing that.

"Now, Ellen Irvine, what would you like to talk about?"

"You were the one wanted to sit down and talk," Ellen pointed out. "I rather think you were going to tell me the story of your conquests."

Harry's brows shot up and the reflected lights from the candle flames danced in his eyes. "Now, who's so tactless as to tell one lovely lady the story of . . . other lovely ladies? Besides, it's not relevant."

"Not?"

"Not," Harry said firmly. "This is different."

"Oh, you mean you didn't have the threat of a Fish-Mou' Bell to get your other ladies into bed with you."

"I mean that I never married the others."

"I'm honored. Or do you just mean that you didn't have any way to blackmail your Spanish ladies into cooperating? How did you make your conquests," Ellen asked in tones of polite inquiry, "if you didn't have threats to hold over their heads and if you really are above forcing them at the point of a sword?"

"Like this."

His fingers glided up her arm, brushing over the softness beneath her tight sleeves, lingering in the crook of her elbow. Somehow, with his other hand, he was gently lifting the fine strands of her hair and letting them fall again, a continual waterfall rippling across the back of her neck and tantalizing her with the nearness of his touch.

"And like this," Harry added, letting his hand slide on up to her shoulder, his fingers across the soft bare curve between shoulder and neck, slipping under the links of silver. "You've warmed the necklace with your body," he murmured. "You're warm behind those cold eyes, Ellen Irvine, and too lovely to lie alone night after night. Haven't you ever been troubled by the waste of your beauty, nights when the moon is high and you've just sent another poor suitor about his business? Doesn't your blood call to you at midsummer, don't you want to dance in the night and know the full joy of life?"

"It's April, not midsummer, and too cold to be dancing after dark." The words seemed to come from someplace far away, from some girl whom Ellen barely knew. She was melting like wax in the fire under Harry's gentle, unending caresses, but some part of her warned her to hold back.

"Ah, my sensible border lass." There was a ripple of light laughter underlying the words, and another ripple that was her bodice parting all along the back lacings where his hand had been busy and she'd thought he was only playing with her hair. Now his fingertips stroked down her spine, and she half closed her eyes in anticipation of the moment when his hand would slide under the cloth in front to cup her breast. Her nipples were taut and aching, and not from the cold; but she longed for his palm to warm them.

"Do we need this?" He eased the dress down over her shoulders, unhooked the skirt, and Ellen lay back passively, letting him do what he would, until she was naked but for the Fernshaws necklace spilling in a waterfall of silver chains over her shoulders and breasts. Eyes half closed, she trembled in anticipation of what was to come, expecting every moment to feel the weight of Harry's body on hers. Instead she felt only his fingertips trailing across her skin, tracing patterns of desire over her body. Every sense was painfully alive; she heard the rapid catch of his breathing, felt the tumultuous beat of her own pulses, sensed the candles burning as a red light through her closed eyelids. His hands roamed where no man had ever touched her, and she gave herself up to the pleasure he awakened, the pleasure and the gathering longing for something more that possessed her.

"Candlelight," said Harry thoughtfully, "is not your best light, Ellen Irvine."

Her eyes flew open and she half sat up, but his hand rested on her shoulder and pressed her back down onto the soft coverlet. Beneath the thin fine fabric, straw prickled against her naked back.

"And just what is wrong with me by candlelight?" she demanded.

Instead of answering, Harry rose and circled the room, blowing out the candles one by one. She watched his lips pursing to extinguish each flickering light with a gentle puff of air, until the last flame died and the room was transformed into a black and silver pattern of moonlight and shadows.

"Am I so ugly that you can only bear to have me in the dark?"

He knelt beside the pallet but did not touch her. "No. I meant what I said. Fire and candlelight aren't right for you, and gold looks coarse beside your hair. Silver is for you, Ellen, and moonlight, and the first pale light of day."

Ellen felt a strange stirring within her at his words, as though they were a charm to spirit her away into a strange land. "No one ever talked to me like that before," she murmured. "Are you a poet, Red Harry?"

"You could make me into one." His eyes were dark and serious, his face half shadowed; the moonlight killed halftones and subtleties, turned his curling hair into a dark cap. She longed for him to touch her again, but he only sat beside the pallet with hands open upon his knees, drinking in the sight of her in the silvery light as though all he needed was to look at her.

"I don't think I have any power over you at all."

"No?"

If he wanted her so much, why didn't he come to her now, instead of sitting and looking and spinning pretty phrases?

"I don't think anyone does. You go your own way in all things, don't you, Harry? I've heard stories." Ellen raised herself on her elbow, drawing a fold of her discarded skirt over her body. "They say as a boy you were wild as a hawk, roaming both sides of the border and playing tricks on Scots and English alike. You've not changed much, have you?"

Harry shook his head. "Oh, yes. I've learned patience since then. I used to take whatever I wanted. Now I wait until what I want comes to me of its own accord."

"As you waited for me?" Ellen couldn't help riposting. "Forgive me, but I seem to recall a small matter of a kidnapping and a ride through Solway Firth. It will maybe have slipped your mind, being so long ago as yesterday?"

"As I'm waiting now."

Hands open, eyes fixed on her face, he compelled her attention with the naked intensity of his gaze. Ellen could not look at him and doubt that he desired her; and the thought sent answering fires leaping in her own blood. This was the man she wanted, never mind how or why he'd compelled her into this strange marriage. Red Harry Graeme, the wild rover who'd come back from the dead and swept her over the border, who had never taken no for an answer, who had the patience to spend half his wedding night kissing and caressing her into such a state that she didn't think she could live if he didn't finish what he had begun.

Ellen's lips curved in a slight, delicious half smile and she put out one white hand to cover Harry's open palm. "Then I am thinking we have both waited long enough."

Harry leaned over her at last, but still without touching her. "Kiss me," he commanded in a voice husky with suppressed desire.

Ellen raised herself to comply, clasped her arms round his neck and pressed her lips against his. A wild leaping fire sprang to life between them with that first touch; eyes closed, she gave herself up entirely to the primitive sensations of Harry's body, warm and heavy against her own, his mouth covering hers and demanding all the surrender she had been unable to put into words. There was a frustrating moment while he fumbled with his own clothing; then there was nothing but the two of them, together under the pale silver light, making a wreck of the silk-covered straw pallet that was Ellen's marriage bed. Joyous and unashamed, she forgot all caution, finally allowing herself to respond to the desires he'd awakened with his slow patient seduction. She could not have said whose hands were where, who took the lead and who followed down the sweet paths they discovered together; nothing mattered except their mutual discovery of each other. They had entered into a magical world where there were neither Scots nor English, feuding Irvines nor vengeful Graemes, borderers nor privateers. What Harry wanted from her, Ellen gave gladly, twining her limbs around him and making equal demands of her own. There was a moment of fear when he entered her for the first time, but she thought it a shame to hold back or to wince at the pain he caused her. She'd known that must happen; the girls and young women she knew at home gossiped freely enough about such things, and after all, it was not so bad as they would have made her believe.

"Did I hurt you?" Harry whispered tenderly.

Ellen shook her head and held him closer.

"It won't hurt again."

"I know."

But what she hadn't known was how the pleasure could mount after that in long, slow, sweet waves, each one seemingly about to crash over her head and carry her away into a new world. Harry was holding her close now, controlling her movements and his own with a certainty and a mastery that she gladly ceded to him. Nothing had prepared her for the dizzying joy she experienced, the unbearable ache of longing that built up within her in response to him. With each breath she thought, *It's too much, I can't go on!* And yet she didn't want to stop, didn't want him to stop; there was a secret just beyond her vision, a wave that would lift and carry her away, if only they could go on and on.

There was light everywhere and a surging, lifting feeling that didn't cease; her body was shaking, but she was somewhere else, floating above the man and the woman who were locked together on the pallet. With a dazed feeling of incomprehension, she heard herself cry out, felt Harry trembling and heard him groan as he broke free of her clasping arms. Warm sticky fluid gushed over her thighs and stained the silk beneath her legs. Harry faced away from her, and Ellen came back into her senses feeling confused and somehow sad.

"What did you do that for?" she demanded, sitting up. "That's not how it's supposed to happen."

Harry looked over his shoulder at her, brows drawn together and lips compressed. "What do you know about it? I thought you were a virgin!"

"I should think you would know that!"

Harry's expression softened. "I'm sorry. I didn't mean to impugn your virtue. Just that you can hardly consider yourself an expert in the details of the marriage act."

Ellen felt a flush traveling from the tips of her naked breasts to the crown of her head. Her skin was hot under the cool silver links of the Fernshaws necklace. "My dear sir," she said crisply, trying to hide her embarrassment under a trenchant manner, "the Irvines have been breeding horses and cattle for generations, and you don't keep a stallion at stud or send a cow to the bull very often without understanding a few basic facts of anatomy." She'd heard stories, too, from a giggling, loose serving girl whose lover in the stables had claimed he could always pull out in time to keep from getting a girl with bairn. As far as Ellen knew, he'd been right. "And one thing I do know is that there'll be no more Graemes to follow you if you insist on that style of lovemaking."

"They'd be half Irvine," Harry said.

"What?" For a moment Ellen thought she must have misheard him.

"Our putative children . . . who will not, as you so astutely pointed out, exist."

Ellen's flush was succeeded by a chill that started at the center of her. "You hate my family that much? You can't

96

bear to have children who would share my heritage as well as your own? A' God's name, why did you marry me?"

"I should think the answer to that would be obvious." Harry ran his open palm down over Ellen's shoulder and laid his hand flat against her spine. She flinched away from the touch.

"To own me? To hate me at your leisure?"

"No!"

Eyes snapping with anger, Harry grasped Ellen by the shoulders and forced her to face him. "Have I seemed to hate you?"

"You can't bear to have children by me. I wouldn't call that love." She'd promised herself that she would not mention, would not even hint at, her hope that love might somehow grow out of this loveless act of revenge. But that was before Harry's casually brutal explanation had shattered that hope. What difference did it make now? Eyes stinging with unshed tears, she pushed him away from her. "I could have cared for you, Harry Graeme. We could have made this an end to the old feud. But all you want is a new beginning—a new way to hurt people. Starting with me."

"No, Ellen, never you," Harry protested, and the pain she heard in his voice made her look up at him. "But I'll not give Carnaby Irvine the heirs he wants. He longs to see you with children, strong healthy sons to succeed him. Every one on both sides of the border knows how much he wants that—so much, for God's sake, that he would see you forced into marriage with a man twice your age just because Fish-Mou' Bell has proven his ability to get sons on two wives before you."

Ellen's last faint hope died away before Harry's calm reasoning. Where she'd thought to find love and hope, life and peace within their marriage, he saw only a clever move on the chessboard of his game of revenge. "Did you plan all this," she asked in a voice made toneless by all she was holding back, "when you came into Scotland to carry me away?"

"No. It was only—" Harry stopped for a moment. He looked almost confused. "That is, I hadn't thought so far ahead. It seemed like a good way to let Carnaby Irvine know that there was a Graeme on this side of the border again. To thwart his cherished plan of marrying you to Fish-Mou' and get his only daughter in my power—I knew that would drive him wild." His eyes softened and he lifted one strand of her hair, gleaming as silver as the Fernshaws necklace in the white light that poured in through the unshuttered windows of the tower.

"You were . . . not what I expected," he went on, and there was a slight catch in his voice. "I couldn't hurt you, Ellen, and I couldn't take a ransom for you and send you back to let Carnaby go on with his plans to wed you to Fish-Mou'. Marrying you seemed like the ideal solution. I get to keep you with me, you're spared Fish-Mou', and— well, is it so bad then, marriage with Red Harry Graeme? Is it?"

His voice challenged her to deny the pleasure they'd found together. Ellen could not do that. But neither could she conceal her disappointment. "I had dreams that this might be the end of the feud," she repeated, staring up at Harry's face. There was no hint of softness there to give her any renewed hope. He looked cool and calculating, a man used to planning his strategy and carrying it through without flinching from the cost. The waste of their two lives would mean nothing to him beside the satisfaction of working harm on his ancient enemy. Still, Ellen could not refrain from one last try. "You said my father wanted grandsons, Harry. That's true. But you—don't you want children to come after you? By tying yourself to me, by taking this cold revenge, you're also denying yourself a son."

She thought she saw a flicker of doubt on Harry's face; or perhaps it was only the shadow of a cloud crossing the moon. Still, it gave her courage to go on. "Our children would be Graemes, Harry. Wouldn't that be revenge enough on Carnaby—to see his longed-for heirs bearing your name, to know that his wealth would pass to the Graemes? Revenge for you, and reparation for his burning of Fernshaws. Oh, Harry!" She rose to her feet, forgetting her nakedness, and took his hands in her own. "Let us make this a real marriage, an end to the feud."

"The feud will end," said Harry. They were the words Ellen had prayed to hear—but his voice was cold and the hands gripping hers had no gentleness in them. "It will come to the surest possible ending. There'll be no one left to carry it on—on either side. I'll get no sons on you, Ellen Irvine. The Graemes and the Irvines end here, in this room. After us there'll be peace in this section of the west marches."

"I suppose," Ellen said through a throat constricted with the desire to cry, "being dead is peaceful enough."

Harry crooked one eyebrow at her. "Aye, but I've no intention of carrying the argument to its logical extreme. We can have a lively time of it yet, Ellen Irvine. There are all sorts of interesting things we can do that won't result in progeny. Let me show you?"

"I'm not interested," said Ellen. "You might as well go to sleep." Withdrawing her hands from Harry's, she wrapped a sheet around herself and retreated to the window. She stood there, cold in the moonlight, staring out over the wild undulating hills that stretched between her and Scotland, until Harry's deep, even breathing told her that he had taken her advice. Only then did she cautiously lift one corner of the coverlets and slip into the warmth of the pallet, taking great care not to brush against his body.

CHAPTER

❧ 8 ❧

Shouts and the blaze of torches woke Ellen from a confused dream in which she was standing naked on the fells, begging Red Harry Graeme to return her dress.

The reality was just the reverse. Harry, half dressed in riding breeches and linen shirt, had tossed the covers over her and was holding out her limp green gown. A crude pine-knot torch lit the corner of the room from which stairs led to the beacon at the very top of the tower; men in leather and steel were tramping through the room, carrying out the chests and other furniture.

Bemused, not sure whether or not she was still dreaming, Ellen sat up with the coverlet held to her breast and took the dress Harry thrust upon her. "What's the matter?"

"Raid," said Harry tersely. "Carnaby, no doubt. We've just enough advance notice to pack up and get out of here." He swung the door shut on the last man with his load of gold and brocade in a cedar chest. "Hurry up and dress. I can give you five minutes' privacy, no more; then they'll need to be stacking the peat in here."

Ellen shook her head to clear away the cobwebs of dreams from her brain, ran her fingers through the crackling fine mass of her hair and began obediently to fasten her bodice. As she dressed there was an urgent pounding on the door. Eleazar called through the oak panels, "Captain! They're past the Stone Riggs. If you don't fire the tower now, we'll not have time to get the peats burning."

This time Ellen was sufficiently awake to understand what Eleazar meant. One of the commonest methods of defending a peel tower was to fill the inside with smoldering peat so that the attackers could not get in to blow it up. The defenders simply withdrew into the hills or took shelter with another, stronger family until the raid was over. When they returned, they might have to repair the woodwork of the tower, but the stone structure would be intact.

The burning peats were frequently used by weak families or those who had not the stomach for fighting. But why would Harry, with his crew of retired pirates and border reivers, choose to run away like this? Ellen's eyes met his with the unspoken question between them.

"It's your father," Harry said. "With a fresh force, not twenty-four hours after his defeat on the Esk. Sooner than I'd have expected him." He gave a short laugh. "The old man's no weakling, whatever else I might have against him. To mount a second trod into England immediately! At his age one would have thought the first trod would have had him in bed for a week. He must want you back very badly." He pulled on his riding boots and took Ellen's hand. "Come on, we'd best leave this room for the men to do their work."

They could barely sidle down the narrow staircase past the line of men carrying peats to the upper room. Once the top of the tower was full, one of them would plunge a burning torch into the mass of turf squares. While the peats smoldered, they would retreat down the stairs, filling the stairwell and the lower floors as they went, until the narrow tower was one mass of burning peat from beacon-terrace to cellar. Although Carnaby Irvine, with his large retinue and his well-defended tower, had never been forced to evacuate his home in this fashion, Ellen had heard the method described often enough by weaker neighbors who would shelter with the Irvines during an English raid. As a rule the men chuckled at their quick wit in saving the towers from destruction, while their good wives sighed over the blackened timbers and smoke-damaged furnishings that would greet their return home.

The barmekin enclosure was a mass of bawling, frightened cattle and horses rearing as they were saddled, their eyes rolling back to show the whites and their coats gleaming with sweat in the torchlight. Through the confusion Ellen could discern the lineaments of order: one party of men worked with spades and levers to bury Harry's chests under the stones of the old wall, another group drove the cattle outside in a milling, lowing mass.

"Can you ride? Of course you can, you're a border lass. Up, now!" Harry boosted Ellen into the saddle of his own English mare and took a rough-coated border gelding for himself.

"Why are you running away?"

The noise of frightened cattle and the shouts of the men directing the working parties drowned out her question. Harry cupped one ear and leaned toward her.

"Why are you running?" she shouted again.

Harry shrugged and pointed at the broken gaps in the barmekin wall, then at her and at himself. His lips moved, but she could not hear what he was saying. She shook her head and pointed to her ears; he leaned closer, but just at that moment a shout of triumph came from the tower behind them. Ellen turned in the saddle and saw a cloud of white smoke billowing forth from the top of the tower, stark against the night blackness of the sky. Moments later the windows of the lower rooms sent forth gushes of smoke. As she watched, Eleazar stumbled backward out of the tower, a length of cloth tied over his mouth and nose, his fine purple vest covered with crumbs of peat and blackened with ashes. He dropped his torch on the ground and stamped on it while pulling the cloth free so that he could breathe the cool night air.

"Done!" Harry's cry of triumph sounded high and clear over the noises within the barmekin enclosure. "Now we ride!" He waved one arm in a half circle, pointing to the hills in the east, and they swept out of the barmekin in a cheering, grinning crowd with Ellen trapped among them.

The darkness outside came down upon her eyelids like a mask of black velvet after the torchlit confusion inside the walls. How could Harry and his men see where they were going? Already there were angry shouts ahead of them—and the ring of steel! Ellen pulled at the reins of the English mare, but the press of men behind her forced her on. The clouds overhead parted and the cold glimmer of moonlight shone from raised swords, glanced off steel plates and helms. Her heart leapt, whether with excitement or fear she could not tell. Carnaby Irvine had tricked Harry this time; his men had been lying in wait just outside the barmekin wall while Harry thought them to be nearly five miles away yet, just at the group of standing stones called the Stone Riggs. She should call to her father and make herself known.

"A trap!" Harry's call came too late to save the men in the lead. "Back! Back!" But could they defend the smoldering tower? It was an impossible task. And now the attacking men had already cut down the riders in the lead. A pike was thrust toward Ellen. She shrieked and twisted down in the saddle to avoid it, and Harry thrust himself between her and the attackers.

"Don't strike, you fool!" he cried. "Will you kill your own?"

A sword crashed down on his bare head and he slumped terribly in the saddle. Ellen reached to hold him up, imagining him trampled beneath the hooves of the horses that milled about them; but the sturdy little border gelding he rode tossed its head and plunged sideways, carrying him out of her reach, and somebody had the reins of her mare out of her hands and was forcing her out of the melee.

"Get out of it, you fools!" called a voice behind her. She recognized Yohannon's accent. "The master's hurt."

Hooves thudded into the night; Ellen's mare threw up her head and tried to follow, but Carnaby Irvine had the reins in his own hand. The chestnut gelding he rode stood almost two hands higher than the mare; from that vantage point, behind his steel breastplate and old-fashioned salade, he glared down at his daughter. Torchlight behind him shone into Ellen's eyes and turned her father into a dark, accusing silhouette.

"A fine lot of trouble you've given us!"

"I?"

Carnaby snorted. "Don't try to play the innocent with

me, miss. Nellie's John told us you seemed right friendly
with the Englishman, else he'd have been worried to see you
going off with him toward the border. You wanted him to
carry you off, didn't you? You stupid, light-skirted little—"

"Well, I damned sure didn't want Fish-Mou' Bell to do
it!" Ellen rose in her stirrups and shouted her defiance up
into Carnaby's face. "And yes—even an Englishman is
better than Fish-Mou', to my way of thinking. While you're
throwing around your black names, what name would you
put to a man who'd arrange to have his own daughter
kidnapped by an old rake who's killed two wives already?"

"Johnny Bell's a good, solid citizen, and better than you
deserve," Carnaby shouted back. His face was in shadow,
but Ellen could imagine how the purple veins were knotting
and standing out on his forehead.

"Then it's as well I can't wed him!"

"You can't? How did you—"

"I'm married already. To that Englishman you just did
your best to kill."

Carnaby's figure seemed to grow another couple of inches,
looming over Ellen. "You're *what?* You canna'! It's march
treason—the English warden will have him hanged for
this!"

"That's his problem, not yours."

"Stop answering back, you idiot! Do you know, do you
have any faint, flickering, beglamoured notion what you've
done? Red Harry Graeme, of all men! You'd as well have
wed the Devil himself!"

"I'd as soon wed the Devil as Fish-Mou' Bell."

"And stop calling Johnny Bell by that byname! It's not
respectful." Carnaby yanked at the reins and the mare
whinnied in protest, stretching out her neck and sidling on
the uneven ground to keep from having her mouth torn by
the bit. "Anyway, the marriage willna' stand, not once we're
back in Scotland. You'll come back with me now and we'll
do what we can to straighten out the trouble you've caused
your family. This once I'll forgive you, Ellen, but you'd best
be a douce obedient girl in future and do as your daddy bids
you—understand?"

Fury rendered Ellen incapable of speech for a moment.
She gripped the pommel before her and breathed slowly and

deeply until she was no longer shaking with rage. "Yes, Da. I understand."

"That's more like it. Come along now, we've a long ride before us, and no telling when that Graeme will come back with his damned pirates." Carnaby tossed the mare's reins to Ellen and turned his own horse's head toward the border, waving to his men to go on. He and Ellen rode at the tail end of the cavalcade, following the host of tired, sweaty men in armor who had come at Carnaby Irvine's bidding to rescue his only daughter out of England.

As they left the smoldering tower behind, moonlight broke through the clouds again and showed Ellen the broken hills around the tower. This desolate country, with its irregular low ridges and its secret valleys, was not unlike the land she knew so well on the other side of the border. A band of armed men or a herd of stolen cattle could vanish into such a countryside without a trace. One person could disappear even more easily.

"I understand you better now," Ellen said in low tones that only Carnaby could hear. She reined in the mare so that they dropped a little behind Carnaby's men. "You're telling me that if I behave myself, keep my eyes down and my skirts around my ankles, maybe in time I may be forgiven for my indiscretions."

"Ah, lass, no need to draw such a long face! All will be well enough, if you'll just have the sense to do as I say." Carnaby was jovial now, having gained his way.

"I may be forgiven," Ellen went on as if he hadn't spoken, "for the heinous crime of having been kidnapped by an Englishman."

"No' just an Englishman," Carnaby corrected her. "A Graeme."

"Instead of having doucely waited to be carried off by Fish-Mou' Bell."

"A decent body of a Scotsman, and the man your father chose for you!"

"Exactly."

Carnaby glanced sharply at his daughter. The moonlight was not bright enough to reveal her expression, but she didn't sound like the quiet chastened girl he'd expected to get back, pathetically grateful for having been rescued from

Red Harry Graeme's clutches and ready to do anything her father required of her.

"What exactly are you getting at, girl?"

"I'm tired of being dragged from one side of the border to the other," Ellen told him. "You and Red Harry are one as bad as the other." What was it Harry had called her? A pawn in jeopardy. "You both just want to use me as a pawn in your stupid games."

"Damnit, girl, I rescued you! Now shut up and ride."

"I will." On that low-voiced promise, Ellen kicked the mare in the side and laid the reins across the right side of her neck.

The mare wheeled in one stride and set off to the left, galloping over the smooth pale grass that covered the border hills, while Ellen lay flat along her neck and urged her onward. Behind her she heard Carnaby's shout of dismay, then the clatter of armed men suddenly changing direction to come after her. Let them chase her! The wind of her passage whistled free and cool through her unbound hair, and Red Harry Graeme's English mare moved smoothly under her. The mare was fresh, the horses her father's men rode were tired from the long journey across the border; Ellen was a featherweight, the men pursuing her were strong and heavy and weighed down with armor. And if Ellen didn't know the country on this side of the border, the mare evidently did.

They were over the first ridge; the mare turned down a narrow winding path between large rocks, and Ellen gave her her head. Behind them the sounds of pursuit grew fainter, but she dared not slow down yet. They passed a clump of trees, a ruined tower, splashed through a small icy-cold stream. More hills ahead—but the mare turned toward a shadowy rock-strewn place, and a pass opened as if by magic. Ellen heard hoofbeats behind her and gripped the mare with her knees. "Come on, my beauty," she whispered urgently. "Come on, show those men your pretty heels!"

While the moon shone overhead, Ellen could tell that they were traveling west, in the general direction of the sea— toward Annan, where her mother's cousin the salt-fish merchant might or might not take her in. If she could evade

Carnaby and his men, if she could head north and across Solway Firth before they went too far west, if the mare didn't put her foot in a rabbit hole or throw off this strange rider with the flapping skirts . . .

"If, if, if!" Ellen mocked herself. "Can you do more than count the possibilities for failure?" At least her sudden dash away from the troop, when Carnaby least expected it, gave her the chance for freedom. If she could but win safe to Annan, both her father and Red Harry might rot in hell before ever she returned to be the pawn in their ceaseless games. And for now there was a good horse under her, the clouds coming back over the moon in good time to hide her, and all the wild, free border hills stretching before her. Ellen put her head back and laughed soundlessly at the cloudy sky. She was free of her father's machinations, free of Red Harry; and if one rebellious corner of her heart ached for the memory of a dark head pressed to her bosom and a night of love in the moonlight, she would forget it in time.

Time passed and the moon set behind clouds, and they'd reached no landmark that Ellen could recognize. If they had been heading west all this time, she should have seen the English stronghold of Rokele rising before her, with the waters of the Firth glistening beyond its stone towers. But in the darkness she'd been forced to let the mare go where she would, and the constant twists and turnings forced on her by the broken country had quickly destroyed her sense of direction. Well, if she had to wander until dawn, a night in the open was no such great hardship; and with the coming of light, surely she would get her bearings and meet some honest country folk who could direct her toward the border and Annan town.

Of course, honest country folk weren't the only sort to be met with in the wild border country; nor were all reivers disciplined bands of men like those supported by Harry Graeme. There were masterless men and rogues abroad, and dens of thieves that lived by preying on undefended homesteads. Men who would kill for a good horse like the one she rode; men who would think her an additional prize and who might not wait to hear who her father was and what he'd pay to ransom her. Ellen consid-

ered the possibilities soberly and came to the conclusion
that she'd be better off to take shelter in some fold of the
hills until daylight rather than riding on aimlessly wherever
the mare's whim took her.

Besides, she was desperately tired and likely to fall asleep
in the saddle.

Ellen dismounted and looped the mare's reins loosely
over one arm. She could hardly see an arm's length ahead of
her, but the mare's gait had warned her that they were
traversing an uneven path between rocks. Perhaps she could
shelter in the lee of a large boulder until daylight; at least
she'd be out of the wind there. Kilting up her skirts to the
knee, Ellen stepped cautiously forward. She stretched out
her free hand, fighting the irrational sense that she was
about to walk into some obstacle in the darkness, and
moved quietly through the night in search of shelter.

Her groping fingertips brushed something warm and
smooth. Ellen gasped and leaped back, reaching for the
pommel of the mare's saddle. She was seized by the wrist
and yanked away from the horse before she could even
attempt to mount. Her back was pressed against a man's
leather-clad chest; something cold and sharp lay under her
chin.

"It's the Scots girl!"

The speaker sounded disgusted. Ellen recognized Yohannon's accent. She stood very still, conscious of the knife
at her throat, remembering the hostile look she'd seen more
than once in Yohannon's black eyes. He hated everyone and
everything but Harry, so Eleazar had said. And he hated her
in particular, for being a danger and a distraction to Harry.

"You'd best take me to Harry at once." Her bluff worked.
The knife dropped away from her throat, Yohannon's hard
fingers released her wrist, and Ellen found that she could
breathe again.

"I suppose so," Yohannon said slowly. "He's been asking
for you."

Then he was alive!

And why should it matter to her?

She did not know—but she did care. Well, it was only
sensible, Ellen told herself. Under the circumstances. If

Harry had died trying to keep her out of Carnaby's hands, his men might not have felt very fond of her.

Taking her by the arm, Yohannon pushed her ahead of him down a rough path. Ellen stumbled over the rocks, trying to feel her way with her feet, straining her eyes for some glimmer of light to show the location of Harry's hiding place. The mare followed them like a well-trained, beloved pet, sure of her welcome. She must have been making for this place ever since Ellen gave her her head. Of course, Harry and his men would have been here before; they must have lain in the hills while they were scouting out the border territory and secretly rebuilding the old peel tower. The mare would have known the way between here and the peel tower as well as she knew the way to her stable.

So much for her bid for freedom! The night's ride had served no better than to throw her back into Red Harry Graeme's power. Ellen could have laughed at the bitter irony of it.

"At least we can draw in the guards now," Yohannon commented as they rounded a tall boulder beyond which the faint glow of a fire could just be seen. "He's had half the men out watching for you ever since he came around. One would think that blow on the head had disordered his senses."

"Is he badly hurt?"

"Does it matter to you?" Yohannon sighed and answered his own question. "I suppose it must. You did come to him, after all. Just as he swore you would, if you could get away from Carnaby. He claimed you loved him and wouldn't be parted from him."

"Oh, he did, did he?" Ellen ground her teeth together. "He felt that sure of me?" What a simpering fool he must think her! When she saw Red Harry, she'd have a few words to pass with him on the subject. Did he prize his skills in the bedchamber so highly that he thought she'd run away from home to enjoy more of his attentions? Even knowing that he was only using her as an instrument of revenge?

Yohannon missed the bitter sarcasm in her tone. "He did. I thought he was delirious."

"He must have been. This is the last place on earth—"

"Not quite so remote . . . as all that, sweetheart." Harry's voice interrupted her; Ellen recognized the clear, carrying timbre and the English accent. He had risen from a seat beside the fire to greet them, a black shadow against the background of flame. His body swayed perilously as he spoke, and he put out one hand and leaned on Ellen for support.

"You are hurt! Yohannon said—I thought—"

"Nothing the sight of you won't cure." But the staggering weight of him against her told a different story. Even as Ellen put out her other hand to support him, Red Harry Graeme sighed deeply and slumped against her. "The rocks—" He gestured toward a tall ring of sheltering rocks, where Ellen saw that some rough beds had already been made of hacked-down bushes and heaped-up grass. She helped Harry to lie down there and worriedly touched the bandage that came down almost to his closed eyes.

His eyelids flickered at her touch, and when he saw Ellen bending over him, he made an effort to raise himself. "Ellen? I thought I was dreaming. You did come, then! I was afraid you would not be able to get away."

Ellen swallowed hard. She could not tell a wounded man, one possibly dying, what she'd set out to say: that Harry Graeme's camp was the last place on earth she had been looking for.

"Oh, you didn't think I'd go meekly back with Carnaby, to be forgiven and thrown back into Johnny Bell's arms, did you?"

A ghost of a laugh escaped Harry's lips. "No, not my Ellen. But you might not have been able to find the way here."

"Your mare knew the way." That was true enough; the fact that Ellen looked on it as an atrocious piece of bad luck could be saved until Harry was strong enough for her to quarrel with properly. If he ever got that strong. Now he was slumping back against the pile of grass that made his bed, exhaustion and pain showing in every line of his white, strained face. Ellen frowned at the bandage covering half his head. There was little blood showing, not nearly enough to account for this extreme weakness. She began to unwrap the bandage so that she might examine his head wound, but Harry's eyes flickered open again and he put up one hand to restrain her, gripping her fingers with surprising strength.

"Not a pleasant sight for a lady."

"I've seen wounded men before. Do you think you're the first fool ever to take a cut on the head because he was in too much of a hurry to put on his helmet?" Ellen spoke sharply to cover her growing anxiety. Scalp wounds generally bled profusely. The fact that Harry was hardly bleeding at all would have reassured her if it hadn't been coupled with his weakness and pain. There must be something else wrong, and she meant to find out what.

"Let Eleazar tend to it. He's done such work on my ship. I trust him."

And not me. But Ellen could hardly quarrel with that judgment. Harry might have wed her, might have the egotism to think she'd come back to him when she had the chance of freedom, but he would never forget that she was an Irvine. She withdrew at his command and sat on a stone by the fire, resting her head in her hands, while Harry and Eleazar held a whispered colloquy in the darkness.

She was so very tired! She strained to hear what they were saying, but the few words that came to her ears were in a foreign tongue—Spanish, she thought. Nothing she could understand, anyway. And in the midst of listening for a familiar word or two, she nodded off in a daze of exhaustion, then snapped herself awake as her head fell forward. She thought she heard Eleazar laughing; then he was squatting on the ground before her, his large black hands enfolding hers, a look of sympathy on his face that could have but one meaning.

"He's dying, isn't he?" Stupid tears were running down her cheeks. It must be because she was so tired. She sensed Yohannon's sardonic, mocking glance from across the fire, and wiped her wet cheeks. There was no reason, Ellen told herself, to feel so sick at heart just because another border freebooter had got himself fatally wounded in the aftermath of a raid. Especially when the death of this particular reiver would release her from a loveless marriage with an enemy. But she was greatly relieved when Eleazar shook his head.

"With care, and rest, and good nursing, he'll live. It was a bad blow your father's man gave him, though."

"He should have been wearing his helmet," Ellen snapped. "For that matter, he shouldn't have stolen me in the first place, then my father would have had no reason to come over the border after him."

Eleazar shook his head again, more slowly. For the first time Ellen noticed glistening silver hairs mingling with the tight black curls that covered the big man's head. The silver gleamed in the firelight, rivaling the small gold rings set in his ears. "Do you think so, mistress? That's not how I understood these border feuds. Harry told me they go on and on, until one side finally kills off all of the others. He thought that once Carnaby Irvine knew there was a Graeme at Fernshaws again, there'd be no peace for him in any case."

"It does not appear to me," said Ellen tartly, "that Red Harry is very interested in keeping the peace. You didn't amass those chests of gold and jewels with your hands folded in prayer."

"Is that how Carnaby Irvine increases his herds?" Harry called from his improvised bed. "By prayer?"

Ellen stalked over to the rocks where Harry lay and glared down at him. "I'm not defending my father. I told him, and I'll tell you the same—you're either one as bad as the other, and I want no more of you and your feud!"

"Bravo!" Harry clapped his hands together weakly. "And how do you propose to live in peace between us? Do you think men will stop fighting on the border and feuds will be replaced by brotherly love because Ellen Irvine decrees that she is tired of all this nonsense?"

Eleazar knelt beside Harry, frowning, and placed dark fingers over his wrist. "You are getting too excited, Master Harry. If you do not want this feud to end with the extinction of the Graemes, you will lie quietly and let the young mistress tend you."

"Oh, but he does want that," said Ellen. "Didn't he tell you? After himself, there are to be no more Graemes, no more Irvines. Our marriage bed is to be the deathbed of both families."

"You are tired also," said Eleazar with gentle persistence. "Why don't you lie down, mistress, and I will bring some more blankets to cover you both?"

"I'll find my own bed."

"No—stay with me."

Harry's plea was almost a whisper; his brief moment of animation was past, his face pale and drained of strength in the flickering light of the fire. "Please?"

Ellen shook her head, but she knelt beside him. "Why? So we can quarrel some more?"

"Because . . . I need you. You came back to me, Ellen. Don't leave me again tonight."

She hadn't come back to him, not in any sense that mattered, but how could she insist on that point to a wounded and possibly dying man?

"I'll sit here until you go to sleep."

Eleazar brought a blanket to put around her shoulders, and Ellen sat holding Harry's hand in her own while the night sky slowly lightened with the approach of dawn. The fire died down to a few reddish coals, and when she looked over her shoulder, she saw only sleeping forms rolled in blankets. Her own fatigue made her eyes feel as if they were full of sand; confusing half dreams danced before her when she closed her eyes, and her head was so heavy she could barely hold it up. If only she dared lie down! But every time she tried to leave Harry's side, his fingers tightened and he murmured in protest.

Even when Harry finally fell into a fitful slumber, his hand gripped hers so tightly that she dared not free herself for fear of waking him. It was bitterly cold in these quiet hours before dawn, the hours when Ellen had learned that a man's soul most easily leaves his body. Despite the blankets covering him, Harry was shaking with cold on his bed of grass and branches; and she was cold too.

"This is ridiculous," she said under her breath. Harry did not stir, nor did the men sleeping all around the glen. She lifted one corner of his blankets and nestled in beside him, drawing her own blanket over them both for more warmth.

She wrapped her arms around him and felt the convulsive shivering stop.

"It's only until dawn," she told herself. "Then I'll . . ." She was too tired to think what she would do when daylight came, and sleep overcame her in the middle of the thought.

CHAPTER
❧ 9 ❧

"Come on! Get moving! Get your blood circulating!"

Ellen rolled over in the warm nest of blankets and gave a drowsy murmur of complaint. It seemed she'd only just gotten to sleep. Her head and all her limbs felt too heavy to move. And some sadist was striding through the camp, shouting and kicking blanket-wrapped men and generally raising the devil. He ought to shut up, whoever he was, he would wake—

Harry.

There was no one beside her.

Ellen sat up, rubbing her eyes, and glared at the blackhaired man who was now using the flat of his sword to encourage a few laggard risers. When he noticed her movement, he whacked Jenkyn o' the Side once more for good luck and came to her, squatting on his heels.

"Ah, you're awake at last! Good."

"I could hardly sleep through the row you've been making." Ellen squinted at Harry through sleep-swollen eyelids. She noticed that his head was not bandaged this morning. "You seem to have made a rapid recovery from the verge of death."

"Oh . . . that." At least he had the grace to look momentarily embarrassed. "Well. I wasn't really hurt. Just stunned."

"Trust an Englishman's hard head to break a Scots sword, instead of the other way around!"

"I dodged—not fast enough. The side of the blade knocked me on the head. It stung like blazes, too, and I've got a knot on my head the size of a rock! Don't you have any sympathy for your poor battered husband?"

"I used it all up last night," said Ellen, "on my poor, practically dying husband, so weak he could barely whisper a plea that I'd clasp his hand during his last moments. What was the point of all that, anyway?"

Harry shrugged. "I heard you and Yohannon talking as he brought you into camp. He may have thought you came to visit us of your own will, but from your tone of voice, I wasn't entirely sure of it. You sounded as though you thought me a conceited bastard who needed to be taken down a peg or two."

"You've never had that experience before?"

"Some have tried," said Harry with sublime confidence, "none have succeeded. But I didn't want you to give me a tongue-lashing just because Yohannon spoke out of turn. I thought I'd better play on your womanly sympathies until you calmed down. That," he added, "was when I thought you had some. What happened to those gentle arms I remember going around me in the dark of the night? The soft bosom I laid my head on? The loving, tender, concerned glances?"

"I reserve my womanly sympathies for men who need them."

"And a damned hard knock on the head doesn't qualify me for the position?"

"Not in the slightest."

Harry gave a mock sigh. "You're a hard woman, Ellen Irvine. Perhaps I can find some way to soften your heart toward me while we're camped here. As soon as I've got these lazy rascals up and about, we'll have some fighting practice. Would you care to let me wear your token in the melee, like a knight of old?"

"I would not," said Ellen. "How long are you going to skulk in the hills?"

"As long as I think it advisable."

"Aren't you afraid that I'll sneak out of camp and tell somebody where you are hiding?"

"No," said Harry simply, and turned away to organize his men for the morning exercises.

During the rest of the morning, under Harry's merciless direction, his men practiced riding at a target with pikes, mounting and dismounting at speed, and forming into a military line that could dissolve on command into a screaming savage horde encircling the designated enemy. Ellen watched for a while and was unwillingly impressed by how hard they worked.

When she grew bored with the war games, she explored the perimeter of the camp and discovered just why Harry hadn't been concerned about the possibility of her leaving without notice. On two sides the rocks formed a natural barrier; on one, the hills fell away steeply to a cold burn bordered by the path along which Yohannon had marched her the previous night. Two quiet men in steel helms were stationed on that path now, one watching each way.

After a midday meal of cold meat and bread, the men resumed their war games and Ellen went back to exploring the camp. She hadn't yet examined the fourth side of the campsite for its escape possibilities.

Here, looking to the south, the hills fell away from this high point in long, deceptively smooth, rolling curves. Nothing but short pale grass grew here; there were no trees, no gullies in the smooth earth, no place where anything bigger than an insect could shelter.

Ellen stood a long time watching the shadows of the clouds sliding over the grass. She stood so still that a family of rabbits emerged from their burrows and began skipping about on the hill not ten yards from her feet. While she watched, a darker, fast-moving shadow appeared out of nowhere. The rabbits froze, exposed on the hillside, and a kestrel stooped with deadly speed to seize one of the family. Ellen ran forward, shouting, to drive the kestrel away. It skimmed out of its dive and soared again; the rabbits disappeared into their holes; and two men whom she had not seen until that instant appeared at her side, courteously offering to escort her back to camp.

"I can find my own way, thank you." Ellen walked slowly back to the camp, thinking that not even a rabbit could leave or approach Harry's hideaway unobserved. She spent the rest of the afternoon turning over and discarding plans for escape, without any strong desire to put them into action. But it was something to think about—something that didn't make her throat close up with unshed tears, as nearly every other thought did. She and Harry had been so close during a few sweet moments, so far away the rest of the time. If only she could trust and believe in that sweetness, build it into something resembling a real marriage!

Thinking like that hurt too much. Ellen sat cross-legged, her chin in her hands, and stared with resolute concentration and an empty mind at the lengthening evening shadows that crept across the smooth hills below the campsite. Harry's sentries were invisible again, but she could feel them watching her all the time.

"I'm glad to see you weren't trusting in my deep love for you to keep me here," she challenged him over the food that Eleazar produced when the fighting practice was over.

Harry grinned and bit into a heavily spiced chunk of roasted rabbit. "Why? Don't you want me to trust you, fair Ellen?"

"I'd be sad to see any man deceiving himself with false hopes," Ellen said primly. "Last night, from what Yohannon said, I had the impression you thought I'd be throwing myself at you from the great love I'd acquired in the course of our one night together."

"I never deceived myself that you loved me," said Harry. "But I flatter myself that you still prefer me to Fish-Mou' Bell. And was I wrong? After all, you're here, not with Carnaby."

"Don't flatter yourself overmuch. I left Carnaby, yes, but not to come to you. It was your mare led me here in the darkness. I was hoping to reach Annan."

"Annan?" For a moment Harry went blank, then his blue eyes twinkled with secret amusement. "Oh, yes. The worthy merchant of salt fish. You really prefer his company to mine?"

"At least he's neither a Graeme nor an Irvine." Ellen regarded the inevitable roast meat before her with resignation. Too bad Eleazar couldn't have gotten away with the big caldron as well as with his mysterious packets of spices! "I'm tired of feuds and fighting. I wish you Graemes had never started this one."

"Started it! How do you figure that?"

"Didn't your grandfather Harry kill my three great-uncles at the ford of the Esk? And on a day of march truce, too, when both sides were bound to keep the peace!"

"Accident. He was always a bad shot."

"Three accidents?"

"Surely. He only meant to shoot them in the legs so they couldn't get away before his men got there to take them prisoner."

"Aha! So you admit it! The whole thing started when old Harry Graeme tried to capture a bunch of Irvines for ransom."

"It did not! I mean, he had good reason! He wanted to trade them for my great-aunt Gilda, whom *your* great-uncle Lowrie had carried off!"

Ellen dismissed this paltry argument with a wave of her hand. "No such thing. Gilda Graeme ran away with Lowrie of her own free will. The poor lassie was nearly six feet tall. Where could she find a man to match her among all these wee Englishmen?" She gave Harry a sweet smile intended to point up his own lack of inches.

"Well, what about the time your auntie Verona threw all the Irvine crockery out the window and broke my father's arm?"

"She was defending our tower."

"The hell she was. She was just trying to keep the Graemes busy while your father sneaked over the border and lifted our best herds. And she didn't need to throw the chamber pots."

"They're as good as any other crockery."

"Not after everybody in the tower had been *using* them for three days!"

Ellen choked, sputtered, and put both hands over her mouth. "I never heard that part of the story. And Auntie Verona is so proper! Clouting your dad with a jurden! I'd not have credited her with such a good move!"

"You Scots have no sense of shame. There's conventions and decency to be observed even in war."

"You English have no common sense. If you were fools enough to spend three days pestering an old lady while my father lifted your herds, you deserved to lose them."

"She wasn't so old then," said Harry, a reminiscent gleam in his eye. "In fact, to hear my father talk, there was a time when he'd happily have taken Verona in exchange for the cattle. Of course, that was before the chamber-pot incident. I'm afraid he never felt the same about her after that."

"You'd think he would have learned not to mess with Irvines!"

"If he didn't," said Harry, suddenly serious, "your father drove the point home, didn't he?"

Ellen put down the anonymous roast meat she had been holding in one hand. Suddenly she did not feel the least bit hungry.

"Look here, Ellen Irvine." Harry rolled over on the grass, took the skewered meat from her hand and began playing with her fingers. "Has it occurred to you that there's something damned strange about the burning of Fernshaws?"

"Must you always come back to that?"

Ellen snatched her hand from Harry's and jumped up. It was her own fault, she knew, for letting him get her into a discussion of how the feud started. Some of the things that had happened in earlier generations were funny, now that the years had taken the sting from the incidents. But all their laughing together could only drive home how unforgivable her father's final action against the Graemes had been. Eyes burning with unshed tears, she ran across the sparse pale grass to lean against a rock on the other side of the campsite. Here she could pretend that it was the smoke from Eleazar's cooking fires that made her eyes water, and not the reminder that there could never be true peace and amity between her and Harry—between a Graeme and an Irvine.

She understood perfectly why Carnaby had been so upset

to hear that she was with Red Harry Graeme, why he'd pushed himself to the verge of exhaustion by mounting two major pursuits in as many days to get her back. After his vicious and unprovoked attack on Fernshaws, he must have been in terror that Red Harry would take an equally vicious revenge on her—that he'd send her back over the border hacked into little pieces, or something.

"Oh, Da," whispered Ellen into the smoky breeze that blew past her. "You don't understand. He's taking the worst revenge of all—one that will last my life long. He's making me love him." Wasn't it a man like Harry Graeme she'd been waiting for, while she put off her father's suggestions of a good marriage with this man or that? Brave. Daring. Dangerous. A man who could make her think of nothing but bed, just by the way he glanced sidewise at her from across the room. And a man she could laugh with, whose quick verbal wit was more than a match for her own.

And a man who could never forgive her for being Carnaby Irvine's daughter.

"I didn't mean to upset you, Ellen."

He had come across the grass so softly that she had no idea he was standing just behind her, trapping her between his body and the boulder she leaned on. His hands dropped lightly on her shoulders.

"You don't have to hold me," she said, staring out over the smoldering remains of the fire. "I won't try to run away from you again. I can't run far enough to make any difference, anyway." It was too late for that. Whether she stayed with Harry or escaped, his image was already imprinted on her heart.

"If you find the camp's boundaries too confining, perhaps we can ride out together from time to time. Once it's safe to return to the tower, I'd like to take you over to see Fernshaws."

"So you can rub in the lesson of what my father did? It's not necessary. I understand perfectly. There was no excuse for such a savage attack. That was why you wanted to rehash the whole history of the feud, wasn't it—so I could understand the guilt we Irvines bear toward you?"

"Ellen Irvine!" Harry's fingers bit into her shoulders and he swung her round to face him. "I meant no such thing."

"Oh, I suppose you just like thinking about how my father burned your family in their house? The memory gives you such pleasure that you can't help reverting to it? Or did you think to please me by bringing it up?"

"Women!" Harry followed the exclamation with a string of Spanish words, then looked at Ellen with suspicion. "Er—you don't know Spanish, do you?"

"Fortunately I do not."

"Good. Now. *Will* you try not to be so damned emotional for a moment?"

Ellen could have laughed and cried at once. Here was the man who'd snatched her from her father's tower and made her love him in three tempestuous days, the one man in all the world who could never possibly love her, holding her by the shoulders and staring her down with those brilliant blue eyes. His mouth was inches from hers, his hands warm and strong on her body, forcing her to remember the sweet madness that had possessed her the night before last. And he wanted her not to get emotional about the small matter of this feud that stood between them!

"I meant exactly what I said back there," Harry told her. "There's something very strange about Carnaby's attack on Fernshaws. What was the feud before that? A few cattle lifted back and forth on both sides, some hotheaded young men getting into a fight on a day of truce, a pretty girl dumping a chamber pot on my dad's head. Not much more than an excuse to cross the border and have some fun with the opposite parties. Then suddenly, out of nowhere, Carnaby Irvine decided to wipe the Graemes off the face of the earth. Why? He must have known that if one of us survived, anywhere, he'd never know a peaceful night again. What made him do such a thing?"

"I don't know." Ellen twisted against Harry's hands. "I don't know!"

"He must have said something about his reasons!"

"Harry, I was eight years old! My mother had just died! I had other things to think about!"

"And in all the years since? He's never given you a clue?"

"Unlike you, he does not care to harp on the memory."

"I'm not surprised." Harry's fingers relaxed slightly, and

Ellen winced as he shifted his hands and she felt the soreness where he'd been holding her. "I've hurt you . . . I'm sorry. But doesn't it seem a mystery to you?"

"It seems a terrible crime to me," Ellen told him, "one that nobody can make up to you. And I'm sorry, Harry, truly I am. But . . ."

She shook her head. What had she been going to say? Don't hold it against me? I was a child at the time? She was still an Irvine. By the harsh border code, she was as guilty for acts of the feud as any other of her family, whether she had personally participated or not. It was a code that could keep the cycle of killing and retaliation going on for generations, children slain for the sins of the fathers, descendants taking revenge for crimes committed before any one living could remember. For the first time she began to appreciate Harry's harsh ending of the feud.

"Perhaps you're right," she whispered. "After us, there'll be no Graemes, no Irvines—and no more killing. How else can we end it?" Certainly not by Harry's agreeing to forget her father's unprovoked attack on Fernshaws. That was too much to ask of any man.

"How, indeed," Harry agreed. "But don't think I hold it against you, Ellen Irvine. You and I—we can end the old feud. We don't have to live at one another's throats just because our ancestors had no better sense." One hand opened slowly, gently glided along the curve between neck and shoulder.

Ellen half closed her eyes. If only she could know nothing, feel nothing but the magic of Harry's touch! Last night she'd come to her bridal bed half ignorant. She'd known, at least in theory, what happened between a man and a woman. What she hadn't guessed at was the way this simple action could make your bones melt inside you with longing, the way it could last in memory so that the light brush of Harry's fingertips was enough to conjure up images of desire that left her dizzy and breathless.

If only they were an ordinary wedded couple, she thought, she could come into his arms now and they could share that pleasure again, with nothing to care about but the long sweet hours of the night before them. She wouldn't have to keep a guard on herself lest she confess the love for him that made this marriage so uniquely painful for her. She wouldn't have to wonder, every time she looked into his eyes, whether the blue fire there meant desire for her or anger at the wrong her family had done to his.

How sweet and simple it would be, if they had nothing to worry about but the two of them!

"I don't know if we can live together at all," she murmured. But at the same time she leaned her cheek against Harry's open palm, resting in the warmth and tenderness of that caress even while her mind shrieked warnings. It was too dangerous to trust this man, infinitely dangerous to show him how she could care for him.

"Of course we can." Harry's other hand slipped behind her, drawing her close against his chest. A slight pressure from the hand on her cheek urged Ellen to look up at him. She did so, and saw no anger, no remembered hatred, in the grave loving look he bent on her. The shadows of evening softened his face and hid the lines marked by years of fighting and seafaring. The sounds of the camp were muted by the soft breeze that whispered over the grass. For a long enchanted moment they might have been any young man and his sweetheart, stolen out to meet in the privacy of the hills.

"We can. We will. We'll put an end to the feud, Ellen Irvine. If you can forgive me for the rude way this marriage started? God's my witness, if I'd known what you were, I would have come properly courting to your front door, hat in hand, and you should have had time to know and love me before we wed."

Ellen had to giggle at the sublime self-confidence in his voice. "You sound very sure that would have been the result."

"Is it conceivable you could know Red Harry Graeme and not love him?"

No. But she wasn't ready to confess that yet.

"I've never much cared for pincushions," Ellen said meditatively.

"For . . . ?"

"Which is what you would have resembled," she pointed

out, "had you approached Irvine lands in other than disguise, and without full armor on, and giving my father time to take aim at you. When could a Graeme ever simply call on an Irvine?"

"When indeed!" Harry shook his head, laughing soundlessly. "Very well. You concede that I was forced to employ a small ruse of war to get you at all. But now that you're mine, Ellen Irvine, can we not put an end to the war?"

He bent his head to kiss her, and the shock of delight she felt as his lips met hers was enough to send all caution and all warnings out of her head. Her arms went around him and they were locked together. A single current of pleasure ran through their two bodies, as swift and irresistible as the hidden strength in a burn fed by melted snows.

It was over. Ellen knew that now, in her bones and blood. The feud was over, the talk of revenge was buried. The delight they took in one another was the promise of a new day. The miracle was here; they could be together like any man and any woman, alone under the stars with their love.

Harry snatched blankets from the pile of grass that had served as a bed last night and found them a place under the shelter of the far side of the rocks, out of sight of his sleeping men and yet protected by the cliffs that rose above them. Here there was a narrow space of soft grassy earth between the boulders and the cliff, hardly wide enough for one person to lie down. Harry knelt and spread a blanket.

"It'll be close quarters tonight, Ellen Irvine." He looked up at her from his knees, a question in his blue eyes. Did she mind the rough sleeping quarters, the lack of privacy?

She was suddenly shy, unable to tell him what was in her heart: that the blanket they shared would be a finer bed than any other she could imagine. Instead she stooped to kiss him on the forehead, where the crisply curling dark hair swept back to reveal a brow as smooth as a maiden's. He trembled under the pressure of her lips, and when she sank to her knees to look him in the face, it seemed to her that his cheeks were flushed; but it was growing dark, and she could not really tell.

Then there was no more need of words, as with hands made clumsy by the strength of desire they rediscovered each other under the cover of darkness. Harry drew the other blanket over them both, and they lay clasped together in a warm, soft nest that smelled of sweet, half-dried grass. An errant blade of grass tickled Ellen's nose and she sneezed, then giggled.

"Is that any kind of response to your loving husband?" Harry demanded under his breath.

"I was just remembering," Ellen whispered back.

"Yes. The shepherd's hut, and you and me under the straw for fear of Lang-Legs Armstrong." Harry's arms tightened about her, and Ellen marveled at the unique joy of having a husband who could pluck the thoughts from her mind, no need for long explanations. "You didn't give me away then, Ellen Irvine. Is it possible you'd already discovered some small fondness for me?"

"Even an Englishman," said Ellen sweetly, "is some small improvement over Fish-Mou' Bell."

"*Small* improvement! Get those skirts out of the way, girl, and I'll teach you how lucky you are to have wedded an Englishman. Last night," Harry promised her, "was just the beginning. Tonight I trust we won't be so rudely interrupted —and you won't be so contumacious?"

Ellen smiled agreement and caressed his cheek in the darkness, feeling the slight roughness with her fingertips. Red Harry Graeme, who was so meticulous about his person, had not found leisure to shave since they fled the peel tower. The slight falling off from perfection reassured her; how could she live up to a husband who never forgot the smallest detail?

"I've nothing now to quarrel with you about," she murmured. Last night she'd been hurt by the abrupt conclusion to their lovemaking, by the discovery that all the sweetness she'd discovered in Harry's arms meant nothing to him beside the chance to hurt her father by denying him heirs. But tonight hadn't he said that the feud was over—that the two of them should begin a new life together? And what better way to bury the ancient wrongs than with love?

Ellen felt as if her heart would burst with joy and gratitude. How lucky she was to have found Harry. Not only was he everything she'd ever dreamed of in a man, he was more than she'd possibly hoped for. No borderer of her acquaintance would have had the courage, the generosity, and the magnanimity to bury so deep a wrong as her father had done Harry Graeme, all for the sake of love. The law of the border was as harsh and uncompromising as that of the Old Testament: an eye for an eye, cattle reived for sheep lifted, a killing for a killing, until no man could ride abroad without casting his glance about for old enemies. Only a man like Harry would be brave enough to set that unwritten law of revenge aside, with no fear that he'd be thought a weakling and a coward for doing so.

He must love her very much, to be willing to take Carnaby Irvine's daughter to wife and to forswear his revenge.

"Oh, Harry," Ellen whispered at the shadowy figure that shared her blankets, "I do love you so very much."

"And I you." His arms went about her again, and the two shadows melted into one.

Overhead the north wind chased away the clouds; the moon set behind a high broken ridge, and the stars wheeled about the heavens in a spiraling dance of blue-white fire. The covering blanket fell away from the two lovers, but neither of them felt the cold of the night. Ellen was warmed, inside and out, by the thrills of delight that Harry's caresses sent through her; nothing mattered now but being as close to him as she could, in every possible way. She clasped his lean, tanned body to her, feeling the lines of old scars with her fingertips, knowing the leaping surge of bone and muscle and blood under the skin as intimately as she knew her own white body. As the ecstasy within her mounted to an almost unbearable pitch, her head fell back against the grass and her eyes opened, wide and blank, to the fiery cascade of a meteor shower spurting across the cool black sky.

Her whole body sang with the stars; she cried out, grasped Harry's shoulders, felt herself freed to go floating upward into the crystal sphere. In the same moment Harry shuddered and withdrew from her, rolling away to spill his seed uselessly upon the rocks beside them.

Nothing had changed after all. That cold, hard knowledge was waiting for Ellen as the fires of passion died down within her. For all Harry's talk of love and ending the feud, the need for revenge was still so strong within him that he could overrule his body's most basic urges for its sake. Tears sprang, unbidden, to her eyes; she tried to blink them away, not to let Harry know how terribly disappointed she was.

"What's this?" His finger traced the line of moisture on her cheek where it glittered under the starlight. "Sweet Ellen, did I hurt you again? Ah, I'm a fool, I forgot it was only your second time and you'd that long ride in between. Why didn't you tell your brute of a husband to let you alone?"

She couldn't let him feel guilty for a hurt that existed only in his imagination. "Not that. You didn't hurt me." *Not my body.*

"Then what's the matter?"

He sounded as if he really cared. Well, no man would want to be saddled with a wife who burst into tears after sex. "I thought—when you said the feud was over—" She couldn't go on; her throat was closing up.

"Ah. You thought I was ready to beget a batch of mixed Graemes and Irvines, to carry on the feud in their own breasts? To make a son who would only learn, when he was old enough, that his Irvine grandfather killed his Graeme grandfather and uncles? No, my love. I don't forget my vows so easily."

She'd thought that he loved her enough to bury the horrors of that night when Fernshaws turned into the biggest beacon ever to blaze over the west march. But after all, nothing had changed. She was still just his tool for revenge.

Or was she? He'd said he loved her. Perhaps he meant it, but not in the way she'd hoped for. Perhaps, in time, she could make Harry forget revenge for her sake.

In any case, there was no point in repeating last night's quarrel. They would only come to the same unhappy ending. And by now Ellen knew that she could never willingly leave Harry. Better this half a marriage than a real marriage with any other man.

"Of course you don't forget your vows," she conceded. "It was foolish of me." She wouldn't argue with him again—

not in words. If he loved her at all, then it was worth waiting to see what time would do—time, and perhaps a little feminine encouragement. One thing was certain. He wanted her. And men didn't always think quite coldly and logically when they were gripped by desire. Who knew? Perhaps one of these days Harry would forget himself. And once she was with child by him—once he held his son in his arms—then he'd have no choice but to forget the feud. What man could reject his own son?

"That's a sensible lass," Harry approved. Ellen clamped her teeth together to keep from telling him that he sounded just like her father—all smiles as soon as she capitulated. "After all, children aren't the only thing in marriage. And there are lots of interesting things we can do that won't result in children to thicken your body and complicate my life."

"There are?" Ellen asked doubtfully. Harry's confident tone suggested that his years abroad had taught him something more than she'd picked up from living in close proximity to a horse-breeding concern. But then, nobody had ever suggested that a stallion at stud could or should do anything that wasn't likely to result in foals. That would contravene the point of the whole business!

"There certainly are. Lie back, Ellen Irvine. It's time you had another lesson."

Harry kissed away the traces of tears on her cheeks, but when Ellen would have raised her lips to his, he pressed her back down against the blanket. He tantalized her with light fluttering kisses that traveled down her throat and across each of her breasts in turn, raising the nipples to taut peaks with the pressure of his tongue. Ellen gasped in surprise at the coiling of desire within her again, rising expectation replacing the sleepy contentment she'd felt a moment ago. And still Harry's lips traveled downward, across the smooth curve of her stomach, lingering over the silvery triangle at the juncture of her thighs. Surprise yielded to a bewildering intensity of sensation; this was like nothing she'd ever imagined as part of the act of love, but the demands of her own body coupled with those of Harry's insistent kisses were drawing her out of the realm of thought.

The stars seemed to dance overhead, and the wind sang in her ears.

"Well?"

He was lying beside her again, one arm over her midriff, the other pillowing her head. Ellen felt almost too limply relaxed to answer.

"Do all married folk do . . . things like that?"

"And more," Harry assured her. "What do you think?"

Ellen thought it was wonderful. If Harry could teach her to do such dizzying, sense-destroying things to him, it shouldn't be long at all before she made him completely forget his vow not to have a child with her.

"I think I'd like to have you teach me more."

Harry's self-satisfied, totally masculine chuckle told Ellen that he took her words at face value, as tribute to his skill in satisfying her. Well, that was a part of it; and if he wanted to think that was all, it was perfectly all right with her. In time, Ellen thought with her own brand of satisfaction, she would make this marriage just what she wanted it to be. He loved her and wanted to make her happy; that was as good a first step as she could hope to achieve in just over twenty-four hours. Who knew what the next twenty-four would bring?

Ellen fell asleep with a smile curving her lips, her head resting on Harry's shoulder. He traced the soft line of her mouth with one finger and shook his head in bemusement. What an enchanting witch of a girl, and how close he'd come to forgetting everything else in her embrace! Perhaps it was a good thing she was an Irvine. If she'd been just any girl of the west march, a girl he could love without reservation, he might have been tempted to forget the projects that had brought him back to the border, to settle down at Fernshaws and live as a quiet country gentleman.

But she was Ellen Irvine, and she had a good streak of Carnaby Irvine's stubbornness in her to remind him of where she came from, and it was probably a good thing there was that to keep them a little bit separated, to keep him from making her his whole world and life.

Harry shook his head again, shaking away the faint tinge of regret that accompanied the thought. Very carefully, so as not to awaken her, he slipped out of their nest of blankets and dressed himself again. It would be as well to make the rounds of the camp before he slept, to see that all the sentries he'd posted were alert. And the walk in the cold night air would help him to collect himself against this dangerous attack of sentimentality.

CHAPTER

❧ 10 ❧

It was over a week before they could return to the peel tower. Carnaby Irvine and the main body of his men might have returned to Scotland on the night of the raid, but the smoldering peats with which Harry's men had filled the tower had to be allowed to burn themselves out before anybody could enter there again.

They passed that time pleasantly enough, in the manner of the first day: some of the men practiced mock battles under Harry's watchful eye, while others hunted to bring meat for the pot or went to a farmer's cottage to buy bread and oatmeal. Harry teased Ellen, Yohannon watched her with suspicious dark eyes, and Eleazar produced mysterious packets of spices out of the recesses of his gorgeous garments to flavor the food they brought in. And at night, Ellen and Harry retreated to their little nest of blankets between the boulders at the edge of camp.

They were blessed with a long spell of clear sunny weather, and Ellen found living outdoors no hardship. She bathed in the burn after Harry posted guards who were under strict orders to keep their backs turned. She helped

132

Eleazar with the cooking, and developed quite a taste for an exotic way of roasting meat slowly in smoke, called *barbacoa*. And after she happened to mention that her dress was getting positively filthy, Harry himself made an expedition to the farmhouse and returned with the best dress belonging to the oldest daughter—a plain kirtle and bodice of home-dyed brown wool, with a yellowish linen petticoat underneath. Ellen washed her own dress, rejoicing, didn't complain about showing her ankles in the peasant dress, and wondered aloud what the oldest daughter was wearing after Harry took her clothes.

All in all, it wasn't a bad life. She was almost regretful when Harry's scouts announced that the peats were burnt out and they could return to the tower. On that last day, while they were packing their saddlebags for the return, she wandered around the perimeters of the camp as she had done on the first day. In only a week the place had been filled with sweet memories for her. Harry had worked himself and his men mercilessly, to what end she preferred not to imagine; but he'd also found time to be with her, light-hearted lovers' time which she feared would not come their way again.

The little stream where she washed her body and her clothes had also been the site of a mad tussle in which she'd tumbled Harry head over heels into the shallow water, only to be rolled over the pebbles herself—and that scuffle had ended in the predictable manner, too, with the two of them damp and giggling like children and seeking a quiet corner out of the way of his men. The nest of blankets between the rocks where they'd lain together every night held sensual memories that now, in the broad light of day, made her face burn. She'd grown bolder and more inventive as the week went on, sometimes following Harry's lead, sometimes surprising him by taking the lead herself. So far she'd not managed to make him forget his scruples in the matter of begetting children, but once or twice she'd come close enough to give her hope of eventual success.

She paused in her wanderings at the brow of the hill, the opening in the circle of rocks from which the long grassy slopes swept south in smooth undulations. Here, where she'd scared the hawk away from a rabbit, she and Harry had lain in the grass one long sun-speckled afternoon and put names to the clouds that passed above them. Chewing on a stem of grass, he'd talked idly of the wonders he'd seen in his life at sea, of pearls the size of a hen's egg in the turban of a sultan the size of a child, of fish that skimmed above the surface of the water like birds and birds that waddled on frozen water like sheep. And from there he'd drifted into stories of his own adventures and those of his friend Frankie, the older mariner whom Harry seemed to respect above all men.

"I'd like to meet this Frankie," Ellen had said idly when Harry paused.

"Would you? Perhaps some day, when all this is over, I'll take you to court and introduce you to him."

"Court! You've highly-placed friends, Harry Graeme. Are you sure you don't mean a court of inquiry into acts of piracy?"

Harry laughed and lazily agreed that one might find Frankie in just such circumstances.

Behind her teasing, Ellen wondered: when all *what* was over? The feud with her father? Harry had said often enough that the feud could only end when both families died out. Did this mean he now foresaw an earlier peace? She dared not ask, but that evening she'd redoubled her efforts to make him forget, and had come as near success as she'd ever been.

What would happen now? For a week they'd been cut off from the world, able to play at being only themselves, with no dark family history of blood and violence to separate them. When they went back, the world would break in on them again. There'd be messages and threats and probably more raids from her father, trouble with the wardens on both sides about this unauthorized cross-border marriage. In addition, the English warden would expect Harry to supply men for the coast watch against the threatened Spanish invasion, while the Scots warden would demand that the English husband of an Irvine give bond not to raid into the border lands he guarded.

There would be no forgetting who they were, no way to

ignore the network of obligations and family ties and national loyalties that pulled them different ways. Ellen sighed again, wishing they could stay here on the hill forever.

"Sighing again? Do not worry. Tonight you will sleep under a roof again."

Ellen jumped, her heart thudding erratically. Yohannon had come up behind her so quietly that she'd had no sense of his presence until he spoke. All Harry's men moved that way, like great hunting cats. It was hard on the nerves.

Now he stood inches from her, his red head kerchief glowing under the cloudy sky, black eyes sparkling with that mixture of open amusement and hidden malice that she had grown used to. At first Yohannon had disconcerted her, with his precise English coming from that unreadable foreign brown face, with the dark gap of his mouth where there ought to have been teeth, with the undercurrent of resentment that she always felt in his presence. Since Eleazar had told her his story, she had worked on feeling sorry for Yohannon—enslaved, losing his family, tortured by the Spanish. Some days it worked better than others. Today she felt no sympathy for him at all, but neither was she inclined to back off as she usually did in the face of his hostility.

"You misread my feelings," she replied crisply. "I've no great desire to return to Red Harry's tower. I would rather stay in this place."

To her surprise, Yohannon nodded slowly and his mouth opened in the dark crescent that was his attempt at a smile. "Yes. You stand the hard life well. Most women would have been wailing and screeching for their maids and their looking glass." His thin lips closed again and he folded his arms, looking her up and down with those button-hard eyes.

Ellen had the sense that he had not finished what he'd come to say. The week with Harry, the effort to wear away at his planned revenge without ever mentioning it aloud, had taught her the beginnings of patience. Now, instead of snapping at Yohannon to say what he wanted and be done with teasing her, she folded her own hands and waited with at least the outward appearance of tranquility.

"When Harry took you," Yohannon said at last, "I

135

thought it was a mistake. Women can make a man weak. A man will become a slave to protect those he loves, yet nothing can ever make them completely safe."

The suppressed pain in his voice tore at Ellen's heart. Without thinking, she put out one hand to touch his arm. "I know, Yohannon. Eleazar told me what happened—"

"We are not talking about me." Yohannon shook off her touch as if it burned him. "I have no woman. Red Harry Graeme has a woman, and maybe he was not wrong to take you. He ran away from the Scots raiders because he did not want to endanger you in a fight. But I have been watching you this week, and I think he should not have run away. I think you would have chosen to stay and fight. Yes?"

Ellen nodded. It would have been better to have faced Carnaby then, to have gotten it over with. Now they would only have to deal with him again when they came back; and if Harry really had avoided a siege for her sake, that worry for her might cripple him again when the odds were worse.

"I don't like to run away," she said at last.

Yohannon's mouth opened again in that crooked, dark hint of a smile. "Neither do I. So perhaps I was wrong about you. If Red Harry had to take a woman, maybe he chose the right one."

He turned on his heel, as if afraid she would take this grudging concession for an offer of friendship, and marched back across the camp to busy himself with packing and repacking his saddlebags. He kept his back turned to Ellen while he prepared to ride away from the hill camp. But when Harry brought the English mare for her to ride, Yohannon very deliberately bent and offered his linked hands for a step to help her mount. And he rode just behind her and Harry on the way back to the border.

They crested the last hill, to find the peel tower emptied of its half-burnt peats but little improved by the week of smoking and slow fires. The men Harry had sent to reconnoiter had pulled the peats out of the tower with long hooks, stacked them around the tower in blackened heaps, and had cut wood to prop up the sagging timbers where the supports of the upper floor were partially burned through. This much done, they'd considered the tower repaired and had prompt-

ly moved into the lower floor to sleep away the re̶
hours until Harry's arrival.

"Good work," Harry congratulated them. Ellen caught
her lower lip between her teeth, uncertain whether to laugh
or cry. Indignation won out over the other feelings as Harry
went on to give instructions, clearly considering the task of
cleaning out the tower satisfactorily completed. He hadn't
even asked what she thought of it!

If she meant to make a place for herself by Harry's side, as
his wife, here was as good a place as any to start—though it
was a far cry from the secret sweetness of their shared bed,
where she kept trying and failing to make him forget
himself. But she couldn't afford to overlook any opening.
Besides, the tower really was filthy.

She interrupted Harry in the midst of giving orders to the
men about their turns of sentry duty and war games.

"You call this good work? I thought you said the tower
was habitable again. Only pigs would inhabit such a sty as
this! Would you go to sea in a ship with a soot-blackened
deck and timbers half burnt through?"

Harry pulled off his cap and ran his fingers through the
tight coils of his dark hair. "Well, no. But that's different.
This is only temporary, you know. I'm going to rebuild
Fernshaws."

"Different? Not to me it isn't. I'm not living in squalor for
the months it could take you to build a new house."

"After sleeping on grass and bathing in the burn for a
week, I should think you'd be happy to get back to four walls
and a bed."

"The grass," said Ellen, "was at least clean."

Harry sighed. "Women! What do you want now? Do you
want me to wave a magic wand and turn this place into an
English manor house?"

"Just give me four men to carry water and scrub," Ellen
said, "and I'll do all the wand waving that's necessary. And
get out of my way!"

For once in his life Red Harry found himself retreating,
having lost the battle before he quite knew that one had
been engaged. "You'll not get my fighting men to wield scrub
brushes," he warned as he backed down the stairs.

Ellen grinned. "Four. With good strong backs."

Harry sent up four men with buckets, crossed himself a few times, and announced that he was going hunting while Ellen turned the place inside out. "And she'd better be done by the time I get back!" he muttered, but he didn't have the courage to say so to her face.

Of the four men Harry sent up, one was Jenkyn o' the Side, whose boils Ellen had lanced and dressed on the second day of their stay in camp; one was an elderly sailor whom Ellen had listened to for hours in camp while he lamented Harry's freakish decision to leave the sea; and the other two were frankly afraid of Yohannon, who had chosen to lounge in a corner of the stairwell until he satisfied himself that Ellen had everything she needed. In short order they formed a willing, if not enthusiastic, scrubbing party.

By nightfall the walls of the old tower were whiter than they'd ever been; the burnt woodwork had been replaced; and new-cut grass filled the barmekin enclosure, drying to make beds for all Harry's men as well as for himself and Ellen. One of Eleazar's mysterious stews was bubbling in the great iron cookpot, and only the slightest hint of a burnt-peat smell lingered about the crisp oatcakes Ellen was taking off the griddle as Harry entered. She straightened, flushed from the fire, and held out the plate of hot oatcakes.

"There's water heating outside," she said, looking at his mud-spattered boots and breeches and the soggy ruin of his cloak. "You might want to wash before dinner."

The fire behind her turned the loose strands of her fair hair into a gilt halo about her face, outlined the curves of her slim figure in the farmer's daughter's gown and kirtle, and left reddish lights dancing on the polished flagstones at her feet. After the cold, wet, muddy afternoon of fruitless hunting, Harry felt as if he had entered into a paradise guarded by a sweet Scots houri.

"I can think of things I'd rather do." He took the plate of oatcakes from her hands and, momentarily distracted by the appetizing smell, bit into one while trying to clasp Ellen around the waist with his free arm. She retreated, and he found himself holding only a muddy, crumbling oatcake.

"Wash before *that* too," she informed him.

"Am I no longer master in my own house?"

Ellen set down the platter of oatcakes and moved toward the door. "Let's discuss that upstairs."

In the refurbished upper chamber she faced him somewhat nervously, clasping and unclasping her hands. She'd been thinking out what she wanted to say all afternoon—but it was a very different matter to make this speech to an imaginary Harry who nodded and agreed obligingly to all her important points. Now she was facing the man himself, muddy and tired but vibrantly alive, with suppressed energy evident from the flash of the red lights in his hair to the impatient tapping of his dirty riding boot. He wanted her, and he wasn't accustomed to being put off, and she had better get what she had to say over with before his quick temper exploded over this temporary refusal.

And all her tactful circumlocutions had completely fluttered out of her brain.

"You're master in this house," she said at once, before he could explode. "But if I'm to be your wife, then I have to have my sphere of authority too. Under you," she added, and then cursed her unlucky tongue as Harry's wicked grin gave a double meaning to the last two words.

"Sweet Ellen, that's precisely what I had in mind!"

Ellen felt her whole body shaking with the buried anger she had been denying all week. "I'm sure it is. And it seems to be all you can carry in that thick English head of yours. Is that what you want? A woman who couches with you in squalor without making the least effort to remedy it, a woman you keep for your pleasure while making damned sure you don't get children on her? Do you call that a marriage?"

Harry's brows were drawn together and his eyes had turned the dark smoky blue of a summer thunderstorm. "I do, and the Church does. We were wed by a minister, Ellen, and all my men heard your consent."

Ellen snapped her fingers in the air. "I don't give *that* for words out of a book—especially words read by Wee Erchie Jamison when he was too drunk to know what he was saying. If this is a marriage, you'll treat me with the respect due to your wife. If all you want is a leman to lie down with you in your muddy boots, you can satisfy your needs in the stews of Carlisle."

Unexpectedly, Harry grinned. "I usually take my boots off first, sweet Ellen. And you've not objected to lying down with me, have you?" His hands flashed out and caught her around the waist before she could step back; slowly, inexorably, he drew her to him, until her head was pressed against his shoulder and she could feel the tension of his body under the mud-splashed riding leathers. She was still too angry to relax against him, but an involuntary shiver of pleasure went through her as his arms held her close.

"There, that's better." One hand stroked her hair rhythmically, very gently, as though she were a wild kitten that he was trying to soothe. "Now, if you'll calm down for a moment, Ellen Irvine, perhaps you can tell me what we're quarreling about?"

The slow, sensuous movements of his hand were drugging her. The fire crackled in the fireplace behind them; leaping pale flames, consuming the small dry twigs at the edges of the blaze, while in the center the great log burned with a steady heat that warmed her back through the coarse homespun gown. Ellen drew a deep, shaky breath and tried to recapture her carefully reasoned arguments. "I didn't want to quarrel. You made me lose my temper."

She looked up at Harry's face and was relieved to see that the stormy look had left his eyes. But it was a mistake, looking at him; his mouth was so close, and she couldn't forget, now, the feel of those firm, sensuous lips on hers. She closed her eyes and tried to think. "Harry, you said you regretted forcing me into this marriage. If you want to make it a real marriage now, then I must have my proper place. I don't want to keep thinking of this tower as my prison. I want to think of it as my home."

"Fernshaws will be your home. When I've rebuilt it."

"And until then?"

Harry was silent for once, and Ellen pressed her advantage. "All that's outside is your business, Harry, the ordering of the men and their war practice and the keeping of the beasts. But inside is a woman's domain. I can't think of myself as your wife if I don't have authority to keep your home in good order."

"Ellen, sweet, you shall have all the scrubbing brushes

your heart desires," Harry promised carelessly. "Now, if that's all, will you come to bed?"

"It's not all."

"I thought you understood my feelings about children."

"Oh, I do. Completely," Ellen hastened to reassure him. "I won't argue with you again on that score." She would simply act like his proper wife—mistress of Fernshaws, when the time came—until he was so used to her that he could forget for one minute that she was an Irvine. And when that minute came, she knew what she'd do with it!

"What, then?"

"You agree that I'm in charge within doors?"

"I just *said* so!"

"Then," said Ellen demurely, "won't you please take off your muddy boots before we go to bed?"

As she'd hoped, Harry laughed, and she had the sense of one very small victory won. Once he granted her the outward place of a wife, it was only a matter of time before she made him forget that his reasons for taking her had had very little to do with love. Today a clean tower and a decent plain dinner on the table, thought Ellen as Harry wrestled with his riding boots; next year, mistress of Fernshaws; and before very many years are out . . .

She reveled in visions of children playing at her feet, of her father riding over the border to see his grandchildren, of the two families reconciled and she and Harry growing old happily together amidst a crowd of their descendants. That was what life should be: a man and a woman making a home, a family, and a future together. That was the proper way to heal this feud that had so drastically pruned both family trees.

Then Harry got the second boot off with a thump, and instead of standing, reached up one lazy arm to draw her down onto the floor in front of the fire. And all Ellen's roseate visions dissolved in the solid reality of his arms about her, his hunger for her body, and the leaping delight in her blood which answered his caresses.

Over the next few weeks Ellen's life in the peel tower settled down into an approximation of the wedded life she'd expected to have one day. Granted, it was strange to be living with no other women about, but she didn't entirely mind that; there was no one to cast disapproving glances if she chose to spend the day riding with Harry instead of sitting at her needlework like a lady, and no Aunt Verona to insist that she keep her unruly hair braided up and her back as straight as a board.

Ellen sighed a little, and Harry stretched out his hand to her. They were seated together on a deep wooden bench that Ellen had discovered in the storeroom and had commandeered for their chamber, padding the seat with cushions to make it more comfortable. She suspected that the bench had begun life as a church pew, but it didn't do to be overscrupulous about where you found your furniture in the west march country. Chances were that particular church was one that had been burnt in some border fighting, anyway, and folk couldn't be blamed for salvaging what was left and putting it to good use.

"What's the matter?"

She missed Aunt Verona. But what was the point of bringing that up? Harry would never allow her to visit her home, for fear that Carnaby would keep her there; and Aunt Verona could hardly be expected to traipse across the border, at her age, to risk her neck among a parcel of English for the sake of a visit to her niece.

"I can't see to braid my hair properly," Ellen lied, holding up the small round Spanish mirror she'd been using since she found it in one of Harry's treasure chests.

"Then don't braid it. I like it better loose, anyway. You look like an elf maiden." Harry took the mirror out of her grasp and tickled her nose with one of the floating strands of fair hair. Ellen sneezed, giggled, and reached unavailingly for the mirror; Harry demanded a kiss as ransom; and somehow she forgot all about braiding her hair.

But two days later, when she awoke to find that Harry had taken half his men on one of those "practice" rides that kept them all in shape, there was a large square mirror in a carved wooden frame propped against the wall beside the straw-filled mattress they used for a bed.

Another day she came home from a ride with Harry to

find that in her absence a high wooden bed with a feather mattress had replaced the pallet.

And nearly every day Harry surprised her with some gift or other for her comfort. He extravagantly traded Spanish gold and West Indian jewels for whatever luxuries Carlisle could supply, from a stack of books newly arrived at the stationers' to a chandelier that could hold a dozen wax candles over the table where she liked to sit and read.

"You'll have this tower furnished better than many a fine southern manor house," Ellen protested.

"And you'll have the manor house too," Harry promised, "as soon as the roof is well on. Tomorrow I'll take you to see how the work is progressing."

Ellen fell silent. She knew that Harry's frequent trips to Carlisle were not just to buy her gifts, that he had also hired carpenters and a master mason and glaziers and lead setters to restore Fernshaws to its former glory. But up to now he had not suggested that she come with him to see the work. Their rides had all taken them the other way from Fernshaws, and Ellen supposed it was because Harry could not bear to have her around him when he was repairing the devastation her father had wrought.

On the morrow, when they rode toward Fernshaws, Ellen braced herself for the sight of the fire-blackened shell of a house, its rooftree burnt through and the roof fallen in, weeds growing through the window frames and thistles sprouting in the hall. She was prepared, too, for the hurtful jibes that Harry could not resist whenever the subject of the feud came up. She promised herself that whatever he said, she would not be trapped into answering him sharply. If this strange marriage had any chance of succeeding, surely one requirement was that she accept her family's guilt toward the Graemes and not try to defend her father's indefensible savagery. But oh how she dreaded being forced to see what he had done!

What she actually saw, when they topped the last rise, was a scene of ordered activity quite unlike anything in her memory. All traces of fire had been removed; the remaining stones and timbers were scrubbed almost white; the grass and weeds that must have overgrown the place in eleven years had been scythed down; and the park was full of wagonloads of new building stone from the quarries south of Rokele. Workmen moved purposefully through the shell of the old house, here erecting new walls, there cutting timbers for a high arched roof over the hall.

"Well? What do you think?"

Ellen was speechless.

"You do like it, don't you?"

It dawned on her that Harry was waiting for her approval.

"I didn't want to show you before, because I was afraid you'd think it would take forever to rebuild the house."

As Ellen still didn't answer, the words came spilling out of Harry in an anxious rush. "Now we're far enough along that you can see it taking shape. But maybe I should have consulted you earlier? You said the house was your domain. Maybe you wanted it done differently? It's not too late to change things. I've pretty well followed the old plan, except I cut the end off the great hall to give us a private parlor and sitting room. And there will be more windows—all the upper story should be full of light—you'll like that, won't you?"

Ellen swallowed the lump in her throat. She'd expected recriminations and jibes; instead he was trying to please her. He hadn't even mentioned the burning. If he could show her Fernshaws without even hinting at what Carnaby had done, just to spare her feelings, then surely one day soon he would be willing to drop the feud entirely. They had come so far in so short a time; she had found such generosity in him; couldn't she even repay him, now, with the words he wanted to hear?

"Och, Harry, it's beautiful," she said honestly. "It will be a bonny, bonny house. You're repairing it so well, one could scarcely tell there'd been a—oh, I don't deserve that you should be so kind to me!" The silly tears were coming, she couldn't stop them; she'd been steeled for his anger, and this new kindness was breaking her heart.

Harry brought his horse beside hers, put one arm around her shoulders, and pressed a clean linen kerchief into her hand. "Now blow your nose and look happy, or my master mason will think you don't like his stonework. And if you hurt his feelings, he's liable to put down tools for a week while he sulks it out, and you'll be that much later moving into your bonny new house!"

Ellen obediently dried her tears, smiled at the workmen and made approving comments. She even managed not to suggest to Harry that a house the size of Fernshaws, with all those bedrooms in the upper story, would be wasted on a childless couple. After all, he was coming along nicely; she was willing to bet they wouldn't be childless long! Indeed, with any luck she could take advantage of Harry's high spirits this very night, shake his resolution a little.

On the way home Ellen was silent, revolving plans to take Harry by surprise and seduce him past his obstinate stand against children. One problem might be that he usually initiated their lovemaking, so he always had a chance to plan how it would go. And then he teased her, and distracted her, and drove her half crazy with new positions and strange caresses, until she was beside herself with wanting him—and he stayed well in control the whole time!

That would have to change. And today was as good a time as any to alter the pattern. When they got back to the tower she would plead fatigue from the ride, slip upstairs and put off her daytime clothes for the nightgown of gossamer-thin green silk she'd been sewing in her spare time. Then she'd send a message to Harry that she needed his help in the upper chamber—and in mid-afternoon, with the sun streaming through the thin silk gown, perhaps she'd be able to take the lead for once and make him forget everything but loving her.

When Harry helped her dismount within the barmekin wall, he was grinning as if he'd read her mind. "I think I'll come upstairs with you."

"Now?"

"Why not? I want a wash. Or do you prefer a husband who smells like his horse?"

Oh, well. She wouldn't be able to surprise him, but if he meant to take a bath—well, that could be surprising, too, in its own way.

Yohannon stopped Harry as they entered the tower. "I've a message for you from—"

"Can't it wait?"

"From *him.*"

"Oh, well. Love, I'll be up in a minute."

Ellen hardly paid attention to the exchange; her mind was on other matters. She ran lightly up the stairs, thinking about sprinkling some of the scent Harry had got her into the bath water, slipping out of her own clothes while he was scrubbing and—

There was a strange young woman standing in the middle of the chamber: a buxom girl with fat, dark braids hanging down to her tightly-laced waist. Ellen stopped in the doorway, cheeks aflame. Had Harry been dallying with one of the local girls? And what possessed the chit to think she could install herself here?

Fortunately, she was somewhat out of breath from the run upstairs. Before she could betray her thoughts, the girl gave a self-possessed little bob of a curtsy and moved forward to greet her.

"Good afternoon, mistress. I'm Ruthann. Harry brought me to be your maid."

Ellen heard a delighted chuckle behind her, from Harry. "Well, you said you couldn't think what more I could possibly bring you for a present. And I had a feeling you might be lonely for another woman. So . . ." he bowed and extended one arm toward Ruthann, "your new present!"

"Harry, she's a person, not a gilt mirror or a sack of nutmegs!" Ellen turned back to Ruthann. "Did he constrain you? You needn't stay if—"

"I only abduct my brides," Harry interrupted. "I pay my servants."

"I'm Ruthann Turner," the girl repeated with perfect composure, "and that's my best dress you're wearing."

Ellen glanced down in dismay at the homespun kirtle and gown, now irreparably stained from weeks of use as a riding skirt.

"My father was the one furnished you with bread and cheeses when you were hiding in the hills," Ruthann explained. "And I've not been forced here. He"—she jerked her head toward Harry—"hired me from my father, and perfectly happy he was to see one of our family serve the Graemes again. And I'm a good hand with a needle, my lady, to make the dresses you need, and I can comb and braid hair, and I'd like fine to stay here, if so be as you'll take me with you to Fernshaws when the building's done. Always had a fancy to serve in a fine house, I have, but there's been no proper gentry around here since . . ."

For the first time she seemed to lose some of her self-assurance. Her voice trailed off and she glanced uncertainly at Harry, then back at Ellen. It was only too clear that Ruthann knew the whole story of the feud and Harry's marriage.

"Well, there. I always did talk too much for my own good, and my mam said it would get me in trouble someday!" Ruthann gave a small vexed laugh and stooped to gather up the bundle at her feet. "You'll not be wanting me now."

"No, stay." Ellen's innate kindliness responded to the girl's discomposure. "I *have* been lonely, and it was kind of Harry to think of bringing you here, and I'll be glad of the company. Only—"

She faltered in her turn. Where was Ruthann to sleep? And what could she do with her right now, when she so desperately wanted to be alone with Harry?

"That's good," said her husband, oblivious to the under-currents of doubt and love. "She can share your bed for the next few days, Ellen. I have to go away for a little while, and I didn't want to leave you lonely. I must go today, in fact, though I wasn't expecting it would be this soon. So Ruthann's coming is in good time. You two girls can keep each other company, and I'll be back—oh, within the week."

"Away," Ellen repeated blankly. It would be the first time since their marriage that Harry had absented himself for more than a day. "Carlisle? About the building?"

"It shouldn't take more than a week," Harry answered obliquely. "But I'll have to leave as soon as I've bathed and changed. I'm taking six men with me—the rest will stay here, and Yohannon will guard the tower while I'm gone."

He clearly had no intention of telling her where he was going, or why; and she had too much pride to question him in front of Ruthann.

CHAPTER
❧ 11 ❦

It was more than a week, and the men Harry had left behind were maddeningly close-mouthed about where he was and what he was doing. Ellen was handicapped by the pride that forbade her to question them directly; she felt she must act as if she knew as much as she cared to know of Harry's business. Eleazar was perhaps the one person to whom she'd have been willing to admit her ignorance and her curiosity, and he had gone with Harry.

"Well, naturally he'd want to take Eleazar," Jenkyn o' the Side said in an unguarded moment. "Either him or Yohannon—the three of them having been with Frankie longer than anybody else and knowing how he likes things done. And Yohannon had to stay here to guard the tower."

"Frankie," Ellen repeated. Harry's pirate friend. She didn't want to think where that piece of information led her, but her tongue outran the guard she'd placed on it. "He's going back to sea—to be a pirate again."

"Privateer."

"What's the difference?"

"We don't raid English shipping."

"I can't tell you how much better that makes me feel,"

said Ellen bleakly. She wandered away to contemplate a married life spent pacing the halls of Fernshaws, waiting for her husband to come home with bales of goodies liberated from the hold of a Scots merchantman. Would he expect her to rejoice when he preyed on ships belonging to her countrymen?

Or would he go farther afield? Perhaps he was trying to talk his friend Frankie into another voyage to the Caribbean. Perhaps he would sail directly from wherever he'd gone to. It could be years before she ever saw him again, years of a barren married life. He might die of fever or in a fight.

Ruthann's cheerful, ceaseless stream of talk had flowed around Ellen's ears for days, somewhat distracting her from her concern over Harry and subtly erasing the barriers between them, until Ellen found it quite easy to share these new worries with her maid.

Somewhat to her discomfiture, Ruthann burst out laughing.

"Sorry, my lady," she apologized, clapping one hand over her mouth. "But you sound as mazed as me, trying to think all contrary ways at once. Now, you can't worry about all these things, surely?"

"Why not?" Ellen snapped.

"Well, stands to reason—if he's raiding Scots ships, then he won't go to the Caribbean. I mean, either he'll be robbing your countrymen and coming home to you at night, or he'll be a long ways off but won't be fighting anyone you know personally."

"Vastly comforting!"

"Same with your other worries," Ruthann went on, undaunted by Ellen's peevish tone. "If he gets killed on the Spanish Main, you mourn his death but you're free to marry again. If he sails away and doesn't get killed, you can feel happy that he's alive even if he's never home. But you can't possibly have both problems at once, so why don't you pick which one you'd like better?"

"I must be the only woman in England fortunate enough to have a philosopher for a maid! Why don't you apply some of that philosophy to finishing the new gown you were cutting out for me?"

"It's done." Ruthann gave a final twist to Ellen's hair,

inserted a silver pin to hold the coils in place, and held up the carved mirror for her to admire the result. "So's your hair, and you do look a treat if I say so myself. Want to try on the new dress now? P'rhaps your man will come home tonight to admire it. And if he don't, I'll see what *I* can find out from the lads downstairs. Some of them must know more than they're letting on. That Yohannon, he's a tough nut to crack, but a few of the others like me."

"I don't need you to spy for me." Ellen saw Ruthann's hurt face reflected in the looking glass and realized how unreasonable and peevish she was being. "Oh, I'm sorry, Ruthann. I know you meant to cheer me up, and all I'm doing is quarreling with you."

"Oh, well, if you don't have your husband to quarrel with, you might as well keep in practice with me. I don't mind," said Ruthann cheerfully, whisking away the mirror and returning with a dress of Spanish brocade cut in the English style, with skirts wide enough to accommodate the new farthingales, should Harry bring such fashionable toys home as a peace offering.

Harry did not return that night, and the next day Ellen felt a sharpening of interest in spite of herself when Ruthann came dancing up the stairs with a beaming face. "What did you find out?" she demanded.

Ruthann shook her head, momentarily sobered by the intensity of Ellen's question. "Not much. Except that he's gone south, which I should think he'd hardly do if he wanted to go back to pirating, would you? There's the sea less than a day's ride to the west. Why would he go down into England?"

Ellen shrugged. "He's meeting this Frankie. Could be anywhere. Maybe Frankie has a ship somewhere to the south."

"Aye, but he rode *inland,*" Ruthann urged.

It wasn't enough to cheer Ellen, particularly in the face of Harry's prolonged absence.

"Never mind, then," said Ruthann, "I've got other news will take your mind off. The Gypsies have come back!"

"Gypsies?" Ellen was aware that she seemed to be stupidly repeating other people's words a great deal lately. But the people around her kept saying things that had no possible connection with anything she'd been expecting. "What have Gypsies to do with Harry?"

"Not a thing," Ruthann beamed, "but there's more to life than one wayward man, isn't there? They usually come through here in the fall, but this year they're early. They set up their tents outside the village, just for the night, 'cause there's not enough folk in these parts to make it worth their while to stay—they'll be going Carlisle way tomorrow. There's a dancing bear, and a man can make things vanish with a flick of his hands, and an old wife telling fortunes, which they've not done before and I can hardly wait to hear what she says, can you? When shall we go to hear her? Or do you want her to come here? They sent a boy to say she *specially* wants to read the hands of the two lovely young ladies in the Graeme tower—that's you and me, my lady!" Ruthann giggled with delight and swung her long, dark braids back and forth, admiring the effect of the new ribbon bows Ellen had given her.

"Mmm. I suppose we'd better go there," Ellen decided. "I don't think Harry would care for a visit from the man who makes things vanish with a flick of his hands. There's too much gold and silver plate around here that just might vanish." And it should be safe enough to go as far as the village, she thought, if Yohannon would give them an escort. Her father hadn't mounted another raid since his last attempt had ended in failure. Ellen suspected he was putting pressure on the wardens of the marches to get his daughter back—but that was something for Harry to worry about, and Harry wasn't here, and she was bored! "A dancing bear, did you say?"

The Gypsies made a yearly journey north as far as Edinburgh, passing unharmed through Scottish and English border lands alike. Ellen was familiar with the sight of their ragged tents with one side open to the wind and weather, the naked brown children who seemed impervious to cold, and the old women huddled over their cooking pots. Many a time she and Guthrie Bell had run to the Gypsy camp, strictly against the orders of their elders, to watch with wide-eyed awe at the strange dark men who had a byname for doing magic and stealing children. They never saw anything more magical than a tinker healing a broken pot with quick sharp strokes of his hammer, or anything stolen that couldn't be cooked in the same pot when the work was done; but something of the aura of magic and romance and forbidden escapades lingered about Ellen's memories.

This visit had something of the flavor of the forbidden too; Yohannon had grumbled and dallied until it was almost too late for Ellen to set out for the camp that day, and then he'd insisted on escorting her personally. An armed guard of six men, all old shipmates of Harry's and none of them native to the border country, accompanied Yohannon and the two girls.

"They'll think it's an army coming to arrest them," Ellen complained. "Do you want to frighten them away before we see the fun?"

"Frightening is little to what would happen to them, did any harm come to you," Yohannon told her. "I want to be sure they understand that."

Ellen sighed, and resolved when Harry got back to speak to him about Yohannon's evident desire to keep her safely inside the upper chamber of the peel tower forever, like a heathen woman in the Grand Turk's harem. She'd lived all her life with the threat of raids from English reivers or Scots outlaws; did Harry think she couldn't take care of herself, that she hadn't wit enough to scent danger on the wind and stay out of its way?

But the danger that awaited her in the Gypsy camp was of another sort, subtler than the pounding attack of armed men on horseback swooping down to carry her away. Even Yohannon did not sense it.

The camp was somnolent in the late afternoon sunlight, men and women slowly waking up from a long drowsy day of huddling in their rags away from the cutting east wind, undernourished horses placidly cropping the thin pale grass and enjoying their brief rest. Even the dancing bear—a thin, shabby creature with the fur on his neck and shoulders worn away by an ill-fitting harness—could hardly be roused to make a few dispirited circles before Ellen. The girl who held his lead banged a tin circlet of bells listlessly against her knee, glanced up at Yohannon with dull dark eyes and swished her skirt from side to side in a limp imitation of a dance.

"We should have come at night," Ruthann complained. "They dance and sing all night long sometimes. In the daytime there's nothing to see."

Yohannon would never have allowed them to make the excursion at night. Ruthann knew that as well as Ellen.

"Never mind," said Ellen. "When Harry comes back he'll take us to see the dancing at night." Unless he, too, wanted to keep her safely locked away? Ridiculous! He'd not expect a girl raised on the border to live like a timid city lady—and if he did, he'd soon learn his mistake. Besides, anybody could see that this poor, undernourished band of Gypsies posed no possible threat to anybody. Ellen glanced once more around the semicircle of dust-colored, patched tents. All but one had their flaps raised so that the inhabitants could bask in the brief afternoon sunlight. Unfortunately, that same light also showed with merciless clarity that the Gypsies' colorful clothes were threadbare, the gold and silver trim nothing but tinsel beaten fine, the jewels in the bear's collar bits of colored glass.

The camp looked better seen through a child's wondering eyes, Ellen thought, remembering how she and Guthrie had stared and marveled at these strange, exotic folk. Or at night, by torchlight, when the magic of fire and darkness could lend the Gypsies the glamour they lost by day. Now the sight of their shabbiness and poverty depressed her unreasonably. She felt in the purse hanging from her belt for some coins to give the girl with the bear. Two half-naked children ran to cling to her skirts, cupping their hands and mutely begging for more.

"Yohannon, send down a cow for them to kill and cook when we get back."

"Why? You've already overpaid the girl for that miserable performance."

"Och, well, if we don't give them the cow, they'll only steal it, and at least this way we get to pick which one they have." That had always been her father's excuse for feeding the Gypsies when they passed over the Irvine lands. His blustering and shouting about "the damned thieving Gypsies who'll steal your eyes out of your head if you don't give them something first" had covered his embarrassment at dispensing charity. Now Ellen felt the same determination to know that these children had at least one good meal while they were near her lands.

Harry's lands.

The correction came unbidden to her mind. She frowned into the low afternoon sun. Harry did care for her; she no longer doubted that. He had begun, under her constant, discreet pressure, to give her the place of a wife. But until he forgot to take precautions against having children, how could she forget that he'd married her only as an act of revenge?

Soon, Ellen promised herself. Soon he would forget the feud. She would make him do so. Perhaps when he came back he would be so glad to see her that he wouldn't think about revenge. She wouldn't give him time to think! He'd said he would be gone about a week, and it had been nine days already; perhaps he would be back tonight. Perhaps he was back now, and she was wasting time with a bunch of Gypsy tinkers when she should be home preparing a welcome for her husband that would burn all thoughts of revenge and restraint straight out of his mind.

"Let's go back now, Ruthann. There's nothing to see here." Cheeks flushed with the heat of her visions, Ellen turned to leave the Gypsy camp, only to be stopped by yet another child tugging at her sleeve. This one was a half-grown boy with bright eyes almost concealed under the long curls of dark hair that fell over his forehead, and he did not have his hands cupped for a penny.

"Please, lady, my mistress says will be bad luck if you do not visit her."

"Your mistress?"

The boy pointed at the one tent that stood apart from its neighbors, the closed flaps giving it a secretive, almost sinister air.

"The fortune-teller," Ruthann breathed. She gave Ellen a pleading look. "Be a pity to come so far without hearing what she has to say, my lady. They do say Gypsies can look at your hand and see the past and the future all spread out there, plain as lines on a map for them as has the sight to see it!"

"They say Gypsies steal children and do magic too," Ellen observed, wryly remembering the tall tales she and Guthrie Bell had told one another to build their fears of the mysterious Gypsy camp.

Ruthann nodded vigorously. "They do! But we're safe with Yohannon and these great fine men he's brought along." She dimpled and gave the six men of their guard a generous smile, then turned her pleading glance back on Ellen.

"All right. You go first, Ruthann, and if there's time, I'll go in."

Ellen felt a strange reluctance to enter the darkened tent where this fortune-teller sat waiting for them. She thought it must be some memory of her escapades with Guthrie. They'd been quite convinced that if they were separated for a moment, if one of them wandered behind a tent, the Gypsies would snatch that unwary child up in a moment and vanish like smoke.

"As if anybody would have taken either of us for pay, hell-born brats that we were!" Ellen laughed at her own shadowy fears. She still remembered the clutch of Guthrie's sweaty palm in hers, and half hoped that Ruthann would dally in the tent until darkness approached and she could use Yohannon's nervousness as an excuse for hastening home.

Her hopes were in vain. Ruthann emerged in only a few minutes, pink-cheeked and smiling.

"You must have had a good fortune."

Ruthann grinned and set her thick braids bouncing with emphatic nods. "But I'm not to say what, or the luck will be gone . . . It's your turn now, my lady."

Ellen hesitated, but the boy who'd guided them to the tent grasped her hand and pulled her forward. "Please, yes, very bad luck to pass my mistress by, good luck to see her . . ." She would have had to fight the boy's tight, insistent grip to get free, and if Yohannon saw her struggling, he might set his armed men on the boy. He was tense as an overwound spring already. And so was Ellen, though she didn't know why.

The inside of the tent was double draped with some dark, heavy stuff that shut out all but the faintest glimmer of light. Tiny circles of glass and steel hung in strings along the draperies, moving with every breath of air, catching those faint gleams of light and reflecting them like a thousand dancing eyes.

In the dead center of the tent, seated cross-legged on a rug, was a bent figure swathed in black veils which completely covered its head. One hand moved, slowly beckoning to her, and Ellen felt a tremor of superstitious awe that annoyed her immensely. It was all tricks, tricks to get her in here and to build up her fears so that she would be too nervous to doubt the fortune-teller's vision. Doubtless the Gypsies had picked up all the village gossip about Red Harry Graeme and his young wife from over the border, and now this old woman thought to win a purse of gold from her by promising that everything would work out all right in the end.

"You are the one who was sent for. Come down, pretty lady, come down where I can see you."

The sibilant whisper set the circles of glass and polished steel dancing, like stars trembling in the night sky. Ellen knelt before the bent old crone in her black veils, half wondering in spite of herself if some startling truth were about to burst upon her.

For a long moment the old Gypsy studied Ellen's face, her own features hidden by the artful drapery of black veils. Kneeling, Ellen realized that the old woman would be taller than she was if the Gypsy stood up and straightened her back. She was large-framed, too, for a Gypsy.

There was nothing in that to intimidate her, not with Yohannon and his men just outside the tent and ready to respond to her slightest call. She had nothing whatever to be afraid of.

But the prolonged, silent scrutiny was making her very uncomfortable. "All right, I'm here. What did you want to tell me? I haven't got long." The words came out blunter, more ungracious than Ellen had meant them. She was almost relieved when the fortune-teller made no direct response.

"He has not harmed you yet, the man from over the water. I see no marks of suffering on your face."

"Everybody in the village knows that my husband is Red Harry Graeme and that he's been at sea for eleven years. You'll have to do better than that if you want to impress me with your occult knowledge. And I'm not paying good silver to be told that my own husband hasn't hurt me. Why would he?"

"Why indeed? Your mother might have asked the same thing, pretty lady. There is danger in the house of Graeme." One pale hand shot out from under the draperies of black and captured Ellen's wrist. The grip was too strong for her to break away easily. But what had she to fear? At any moment she could call for Yohannon, save that she'd feel like an idiot to cry out before she was hurt.

"Will you come away, Ellen Irvine? Come away with the Gypsies now, before the fire burns you too. I can see danger for all who shelter in the house of Graeme—danger, death, and fire . . ."

The whispered, crooning words were like a spell weaving around her. Ellen stared down at the strong fingers encircling her wrist and willed herself not to show any feeling. A prickling sense of unease stirred the small hairs on the back of her neck. She wanted to look behind her, but that was ridiculous; nobody could have come in without setting all the dangling mirror disks to jingling on their cords. She scowled at the Gypsy woman's long, strong fingers, gleaming white in the shadowy tent.

White?

All the Gypsies Ellen had ever seen were brown-skinned.

And she'd never seen an old woman with such a strong, smooth hand. A hand with blunt fingers, ridged nails, a dusting of yellow hairs from knuckle to wrist, and a tiny white crescent-shaped scar between the thumb and forefinger . . .

"You can stop crooning at me now, Guthrie Bell," said Ellen, "and tell me what mad folly possessed you to come alone into the heart of Red Harry Graeme's lands."

"Fire and death, come away—Hell! How did you recognize me?"

"Your hand. I mind when you got that scar, trying to carve our initials into your dad's prize apricot tree that he grew against a wall—and a fine whipping you got for it too!"

Guthrie straightened his bent back and pushed the black veils away from his head. Yellow curls gleamed in the shadowy tent; he gave Ellen the crooked grin that had accompanied his worst bits of mischief when they were children. "Aye, but it would have been worth it, if I'd finished."

"It would?"

"You promised to give me a kiss if I carved our initials into the tree. Remember?"

Ellen flushed. She had managed to forget that she had inspired that particular piece of mischief. "Well, I never thought you'd be fool enough to do it! And just what do you think I'm going to give you for this crazy prank, Guthrie Bell?"

"You're going to come back with me," Guthrie said with an assurance that shook Ellen's self-confidence.

"No, I'm not. And you must be mad to cross over to the English side all alone, there must be a dozen men between here and the Solway who know that yellow head of yours and would like fine to hold it for ransom."

"Ah, but they're not looking for a poor old Gypsy woman," Guthrie pointed out. Ellen relaxed slightly. Twice now she'd asserted that he was here alone, and he'd not contradicted her. Her fears of a camp full of armed Scots lying concealed under the Gypsy tents receded. Alone, Guthrie could not force her to anything; not with Yohannon and his men waiting just outside the tent.

"And just what was the point of all that eldritch crooning?" Not that she needed to ask. Guthrie's sense of mischief was running hand in hand with his notion that she stood in need of his rescue. He would have thought it great fun to scare her with his impersonation of a fortune-teller before he revealed himself and offered to carry her away.

"The Gypsies were a great help to me." Which wasn't exactly an answer. "When they came through Johnny's lands, I asked them to come down here early and promised they shouldn't lose by it. Tonight they'll move on south, so if Harry thinks you've gone with them, he'll be hunting the wrong direction."

"He'll think no such thing, for I'm not going anywhere at all."

"Ellen, you must!" Guthrie reached for her hand again, but this time Ellen was anticipating the move and drew back quickly.

"Guthrie. I assume you had some half-baked chivalrous notion of rescuing a damsel in distress. Please don't think like that. I'm wedded to Red Harry Graeme now."

"By force—with a drunkard to say the lines! Oh, I've heard the tale; d'you think Wee Erchie could keep his mouth shut on such a fine story? You can deny the marriage, Ellen. Say you were constrained, no Scottish court will hold you to it."

"I've no intention of denying it, even if I could."

Guthrie blanched on the last words; in the half light his freckles showed clearly against his milky skin. "Ellen! You're not—I never thought—are you with child?" He recovered quickly. "It doesn't matter. Come with me. We'll say the baby's mine."

Ellen didn't know whether to laugh or cry at his facile assumption. She thought that she should be grateful to know that one part, at least, of the story of her marriage was not yet common currency.

"No. There's no child." *Nor likely to be.* No, she mustn't think that way; she must recapture the gay confidence in Harry's love that she had felt—was it only a few minutes ago? What was happening to her? Guthrie's white, strained face, the risk he had run to save her, the musty darkness of the Gypsy tent, and the tinkling mirrors were all working powerfully on her mind, making her startle at shadows and see danger where there was only a dear friend trying to help her.

Guthrie saw the shadow of doubt cross her face. "And you're not happy. Ellen, you must come away with me!"

"One doesn't look for perfect happiness in marriage. Adults know how to make compromises, how to wait—"

159

Ellen caught her breath at the thought of how, if she judged Harry wrong, that waiting might stretch out into long, barren, lonely years.

"I would make you perfectly happy," Guthrie promised. "Ellen, if you're staying with him for fear of being forced into marriage with Johnny, you needn't. Johnny can't marry anyone now. Your fine pirate of an Englishman saw to that! The wound he took in the fighting has—well, it's made him less of a man."

Ellen drew in her breath sharply. "He must hate Harry very much. Is he seeking revenge?"

"What do you think?"

"Is that the danger you spoke of? That Fish-Mou' Bell will come raiding over the border?"

"That, and . . . other things. Ellen, come with me now. You can't truly want to stay with this man! You know nothing of him—where he's been, what blood has soiled his hands, what foul crimes he may have committed in his life of piracy—"

Ellen stood. "Guthrie, I've stayed this long for the kindness we had to one another as children, but I'll not stay to hear slurs on my wedded husband. I know Red Harry Graeme as you could never know him, and there's no crime or foulness in the man. As for blood, what man on this troubled border is so free of killing that he dare turn up his nose at Harry for his sea battles? At least he has only killed Spaniards, not his own neighbors."

Guthrie sat crouched at her feet, still wrapped in the Gypsy skirt and cloak. He should have looked ridiculous in the disguise; she should have been able to laugh at the boy's fancy that had sent him on this mad, chivalrous quest over the border. But his stillness made her nervous.

"You'd better go now, Guthrie. I won't tell anybody you have been here, and I wish you luck in getting back safely over the border. Thank you for warning *us* about Fish-Mou'." She emphasized the pronoun, to remind him that she and Harry now stood as a unit. "But you needn't fear for us. I assure you that Red Harry is well able to defend what's his."

As she turned to go, Guthrie scrambled to his feet. The

flowered Gypsy skirt flopped about his brawny legs, revealing the boots and spurs beneath. "No, Ellen. You're wrong."

"You think Harry can't defend his tower? Guthrie, he ran away before because he didn't want to fight his father-in-law. He'll have no such compunctions about cutting down Fish-Mou'. If you've any fondness for your cousin Johnny, you'll warn him to stay at home and nurse his wounds in privacy."

"No. Not that. What you said—about Harry only killing Spaniards—I wish it were so! Carnaby is out of his mind with worry for you. You must come home with me, now. You don't know what Harry has done."

"Stop right there, Guthrie! I told you before, I'll not stay to listen to slurs against my husband." Ellen put one hand to the tent flap. Already, in her imagination, she was outside in the clear pure air of early evening, breathing the wind from the hills instead of the musty aroma of this tent full of lies and secrets.

"Not slurs," Guthrie flung at her, "but facts! Will you stay with the man who killed your mother?"

CHAPTER

❦ 12 ❧

I'm sorry!" Guthrie blurted out into the silence that followed his accusation. "Carnaby said you weren't to be told, that I must get you away from here some other way. That's why I tried the Gypsy warning. I thought maybe you would have sensed that something was wrong with Harry— that you'd be ready to go without having to be told why."

Ellen's hand fell away from the tent flap, and the sliver of cool blue sky that she'd glimpsed for a moment disappeared behind the stifling dark folds of dirty cloth. "I think you had better explain yourself, Guthrie." What he said made no sense—no sense at all. Her mother had died so long ago! Ellen could just remember a laughing presence scented with rosewater and lavender, a soft cheek pressed to her own at night. She'd been only a bairn then. How could Harry Graeme have had anything to do with that long-ago loss? Still, she felt cold with foreknowing; dates and stories were coming together in her head. Her mother's death, the burning of Fernshaws: both had happened eleven years ago. With relief Ellen remembered the one fact that put the lie to whatever tale Guthrie had made up.

"No one killed my mother. She went out riding alone and

was thrown from her horse; they found her body in the hills."

"That's what you were told. You were too young to know the truth."

"It is the truth!" Ellen protested. "I can remember when she left."

Was it that last time she remembered, or another? Carnaby away on a raid or a political visit, and her restless young mother calling a man to saddle her horse; the disapproving frowns of the groom who brought the horse, her mother's gay laugh and assurance that no harm could come to her in the hills she had ridden since her childhood. A swift stoop to plant a kiss on Ellen's cheek, a promise that next time they would ride together, and then she disappeared.

It was a scene that Ellen must have observed many times. But today it was as painfully clear and sharp in her memory as though it belonged to one particular day. "It had been raining, and the sky was all clear and washed to a pale blue. There was an east wind. The grass was wet. Somebody warned her not to gallop on the slippery grass."

Old feelings of mourning, betrayal, and anger swept over Ellen. At eight years old she had been able to understand Carnaby when he told her that her mother was never coming back; not old enough to understand that she hadn't been left behind on purpose. "She can't be dead! She said she would take me with her next time!" the child Ellen had screamed, trying to deny what had happened.

"Thank God she didn't." Carnaby's rough hand fondled her silky blond hair. "You're all I have left now, Ellen."

Thank God she didn't. But if her mother had really died of exposure after a fall from her horse, would Carnaby have said those words? Wouldn't he have wished Ellen had been there, to ride home and get help and tell the searchers where to find her mother?

"Ellen, Ellen, I'm sorry." Guthrie's arms were about her; he brushed away the tears on her cheeks with the scraps of black veiling that still hung over his shoulders. She clutched him, grateful for that strength and warmth. "I did not want to tell you. But now you must know. She went out riding alone, Ellen, that much is true, and that's what you remember. The rest was a lie your father made up to spare you the truth. She didn't die of a fall and exposure. She was waylaid in those hills, raped and strangled. They thought Carnaby would go mad when they brought the body to him. That's why he burned Fernshaws, Ellen."

"Because he went mad."

"Because Red Harry Graeme killed your mother!"

"How do you know? Were you there?"

"They found his ring lying by the body." Guthrie fumbled under the folds of the Gypsy skirt and brought out a heavy gold-seal ring. "Carnaby gave me this in case I had to tell you—in case there was no other way to convince you. Look!" His broad palm thrust under her nose, forcing her to see the ring. "You should know the Graeme arms by now."

She did, too well to mistake them. The Graeme device, the eagle within a circle, stared at her, arrogant in polished gold and quite unmistakable. All right; there was this much truth to the monstrous lie. A Graeme had been involved. That made sense of her father's terrible act of revenge, the burning of Fernshaws. But to say it was Red Harry, her Harry, the man she loved—that was just nonsense. She knew him far too well to think any such thing of him.

"A Graeme, maybe, but not Harry. His father—brothers —one of them might have done it. He was only a boy then!"

"He was seventeen, and a man grown, and in the habit of slipping over the border on his own errands. His father had threatened to throw him out of the house for the wild tricks he got up to."

Ellen tried to speak calmly through the anger that possessed her. It was not fair to be so furious with Guthrie. He did not know Harry as she did, could not know how wickedly unfair his accusations were. But he must not be allowed to go on believing such a thing. "Harry's told me of his escapades. A lone raid or two over the border, fooling the Scots into thinking he had an army when it was just two other boys clapping pieces of tin together to make a noise. Some nights of hard drinking with men twice his age, who should have borne the blame for misleading him. And, yes"—she looked Guthrie steadily in the eye—"some exploits with the local lasses. He's told me those stories too.

And it's a long way from such boyish pranks to rape and murder, Guthrie!"

"Do you think he tells you everything?"

"I know he does!"

"Ah. Then you know where he is right now?"

"Of course I do," Ellen lied.

"And you don't mind?"

"Guthrie, are you trying to trap me into telling you where Harry is?"

Guthrie smiled, but his eyes remained calm and cold. "You fence well, Ellen, but I'm better armed. Your maid already let slip that Harry left nine days ago with no word of where he meant to go. He has secrets from you, Ellen. And this is one of those secrets!" He thrust the gold ring at her and she turned her head away, blind, sickened by the monstrous accusation.

"Why do you think he married you—a Scotswoman, the daughter of his enemy? For love? For obsession. He was in love with your mother; when he couldn't have her love, he forced her, and killed her to keep his crime secret. You're the image of Eleanor—even your name is almost the same. He wants to possess her through you. He's mad, he's a murderer; you're not safe with him, Ellen! You must come away with me now, this very night, before he returns from his mysterious errand!"

Guthrie's hands gripped her arms; he held her so close that she could feel the heat of his face. The strings of mirrors swayed and tinkled around them.

"Let me go," said Ellen mechanically, "you're hurting me."

"Am I? I'm sorry." Guthrie looked at her pale, set face and repeated his apology. "If you were fond of him—Ellen, I am sorry for everything. I wish you hadn't had to know this. But I had to make you understand. You can't stay with him."

"If this is true," said Ellen, "no, I cannot stay."

"*If?*" Guthrie's voice rose in an outraged yelp of disbelief. "How much more do you need? Shall I drag your aunt Verona over the border to tell you how Harry Graeme used to send love poems to your mother?"

"He may have had a boyish crush on her. If she was as lovely as I remember her, I wouldn't be surprised. But Harry would never kill where he loved."

"Not if he lost his temper?"

Ellen remembered Harry's anger when she refused to marry him. He had the quick temper to go with the red lights in his hair. And from the tales she'd heard of his life at sea, she knew he had the capacity for violence.

"No." She clung to the bare hard fact of her denial even as her faith slipped away. "You are mistaken. He wouldn't do such a thing."

"You're not sure of that!" Guthrie had caught the wavering in her voice. "Ellen, you can't go back to live with that man, always wondering if he killed your mother and when he might destroy you in the same murderous frenzy."

"No," Ellen agreed. "I can't do that."

She lifted the tent flap again; Guthrie's hand closed over her wrist and spun her bodily back into the darkness of the tent, with all the clattering mirrors jingling around them. "Where do you think you're going?"

"Home."

"I'll take you. That's what I'm here for."

"Home," Ellen amplified, "to Harry Graeme's tower."

"Are you daft? You just agreed that you couldn't go back there."

"No. I agreed that I couldn't go on living with Harry and wondering if he killed my mother."

"So you must come back with me!"

Ellen regarded Guthrie with a slight smile. The longer he argued, the stronger she felt her returning faith in Harry Graeme. Why was she allowing herself to be troubled over some stories eleven years old and a ring that could have belonged to any of his family? These were shreds of gossip. She knew the man himself, and she would not permit herself to doubt him. "Why, no. I am going back," she said gently, "to ask Harry himself. Who else could give me the assurance I want?"

"You can't do that! I won't let you!"

"I have seven men within call," Ellen pointed out, "who will become very suspicious if they don't see me leave this tent soon. You would have had a hard enough time spiriting me across the border with my cooperation, Guthrie. You haven't a chance without it."

She meant to leave him then, a faintly pitiable figure in his tawdry half disguise; to leave him and the foul lies he'd brought in the dark tent where they belonged, while she escaped to the free, clear air and the light. But Guthrie managed a last word of sorts.

"The Gypsies don't move on for three days. I'll be here until then. When you come to your senses, I'll be here to take you away."

The narrow windows of the peel tower were golden slits of light blazing against the blue dusk; inside the barmekin wall there was a tumbled confusion of tired men and sweaty horses. And in the middle was Red Harry Graeme, his black hair shining with the Devil's own red flames by torchlight, loudly demanding to know who'd been fools enough to let his lady go off across the moors with only six men to guard her.

"Six men and Yohannon," Ellen heard somebody point out as her little party drew rein just outside the barmekin wall.

"Oh, well, in that case she'll have come to no harm."

Yohannon glowed with dark pride and lifted Ellen down from her horse. Three of the guards behind him jostled to give Ruthann the same attention.

"Ellen!"

He cleaved like a blade through the mass of men to greet her, mud-splashed and weary in his riding leathers, blue eyes sparkling in the golden light of the torches set around the half circle of wall. She looked in his face, alight with joy, and told herself that she could never, not for one moment, believe Guthrie's accusations. She held out her hands to Harry, and he took her into his arms with a crushing embrace.

But her father had believed him guilty; had believed it strongly enough to come down on Fernshaws by night with one crushing blow that should have destroyed the house of Graeme forever.

Despite herself, Ellen stiffened in Harry's embrace. The hands that clasped her so firmly were strong enough to kill; she'd seen for herself the blaze of his temper. She couldn't keep out of her mind the image of those hands going around a woman's throat.

"Is something wrong?"

He was too sensitive to the slightest nuances of her movement, the feelings she could successfully conceal from everyone else.

"Nothing," Ellen lied. "It's just—" She wrinkled her nose as the distinct aroma of sweating horses gave her an excuse for the momentary withdrawal. "My dear Harry, you smell exactly like your horse."

He gave a shout of laughter and released her. "I should never have given over the running of the keep to you. I'll wager you have worn out all my poor men with having them bring buckets of water to scrub everything down to the mortar between the stones. Well, if the burn's not gone dry, I'll wash upstairs and present myself to you in a more fitting state."

He bounded up the spiral staircase, his overflowing vitality not even slightly diminished by the long hard ride, and Ellen watched him go with a frown creasing the space between her brows. If only she had not gone to see the Gypsies! This afternoon she would have joined Harry upstairs, to see if she couldn't make this bath as interesting as the one she'd been planning just before he left. Of course Guthrie's stories were nonsense—but there was that shadow between them, subtly chilling her and making it quite impossible for her to greet Harry with the love she wanted to show him.

She'd told Guthrie she would ask him, but now she feared she had not the courage. How could you say to your husband, "By the way, did you happen to kill my mother eleven years ago?"

Of course she would not ask him. There was no need.

The signet ring lay cold and heavy between her breasts, like a cursed treasure.

I have to know the truth.

In her heart she did know it, knew Harry incapable of any

such thing. But she had to dispel that faint shadow of doubt before it poisoned both of them.

Maybe she could do so without actually questioning him.

He was damp, toweled, and dressed in one of his fine Spanish suits, when she came into the upstairs chamber. A fire blazed in the wall fireplace, turning the puddles of water on the floor into pools of red and filling the recesses of the room with dark, trembling shadows; the candles were unlit.

"You're grown nesh indeed, to be having a fire in the chamber, and it nearly June!" Ellen teased. She picked up a discarded towel and knelt to mop up some of the water he'd spilled on the floor. The red reflections of the flames in the pools of water troubled her, making her think of fire and blood.

"Ah, but the water," Harry pointed out, "is cold enough to make up for it. Would you care to try it out?"

"No, thank you. It's not I who was riding for days and days."

"Oh, we didn't go that far."

She noticed that Harry didn't say where they had gone, though, and that troubled her. All right—so he didn't tell her everything. Why should he? He was a man, he was used to managing his own business, and she was as yet only half a wife to him.

Ellen seated herself before the tall mirror in its carved frame, one of Harry's first gifts to her, and began unplaiting her hair. In the shadowed room, with the fire behind her, a strange pale face looked back at her from the glass; a face with large bruised-looking eyes and a floating cloud of silvery hair, like a ghostly apparition. Ellen hardly recognized herself. She felt as though she were looking back into her own past.

"I wonder if I look very much like my mother," she said, idly twisting one lock of hair that fell over her shoulder. "I'm told I do, but of course I can hardly remember her."

"She was the most beautiful lady in the west marches."

"Then I can hardly claim to resemble her."

"But you do." Harry came to stand behind her, his hands warm on her shoulders where the loosened strings of her bodice allowed it to slip down a few inches. She watched his face in the glass and could see no shadow but that of memory. "You might be a copy of her, though you are silver and moonlight where she was gold and sun."

A lesser copy—a shadow. Doubt clutched painfully at Ellen's heart.

"You talk as though you were in love with her!" She tried to turn the trembling of her voice into a laugh.

"I was—as much as a boy can love. Which is to say," Harry amplified with a wry smile, "I was full of my own importance and my own exploits, and I think I wanted to be in love with a beautiful but unattainable lady. It seemed a much more dignified reason for unhappiness than being the unregarded runt of the litter in my father's house. And when I saw your mother at a march-day meeting . . ." He shook his head slowly, smiling at his own folly. "She was very beautiful, and married, and Scots to boot, and in love with her husband. Quite safely unattainable. Of course I convinced myself I was in love with her! I used to sneak over the border to get a sight of her, and come home with a few scrawny beasts as excuse for my journey. Which did not make me any more beloved of my father, who very sensibly pointed out that if I wanted to get us embroiled with all our Scots neighbors at once, I might as well lift enough cattle to make it worth the fight."

Ellen didn't want to talk about cattle raiding. She wondered if Harry was deliberately drifting away from the subject of her mother. "And what did she think of your devotion?"

"She never knew." Harry's hands gripped her shoulders a little harder, not enough to hurt. "I was a fool, Ellen, but not enough of a fool to go making love to a wedded woman twelve years older than me. Besides, she thought the sun rose and set in Carnaby Irvine; that was clear enough to all who ever met them. Oh, I used to tell myself romances about how she was tied to an old man and would welcome a young gallant riding into her life—but I must have known, even then, that I was lying to myself."

"So you never even spoke to her?"

Harry turned away, releasing her. "Never."

His voice was different. Ellen could have sworn, if he'd never lied to her before, that he was lying now.

Or was it just Guthrie's suspicion that infected her mind? She had all the assurance she could possibly ask from Harry, without asking him straight out. Ellen told herself firmly that she would comb out her unbound hair, go to bed, and never entertain the slightest suspicion of Harry. So he had confessed to a boy's fancy for her mother—what did that prove? If she was as beautiful as everybody said, half the men in the west march must have sighed over her in their time.

The silver-backed comb was lying on top of a low chest beside the mirror. Ellen bent to reach for it, and the forgotten signet ring fell out of her loosened bodice and rolled across the floor.

"You've dropped something." Harry stooped and picked up the ring. "No—Well, I'll be damned! My old signet ring. The only thing of the Graemes my father ever gave me, and he grudged that, but my mother had said I was to have it. I haven't seen this since I left home—thought I must have left it when I ran away. But then it would have been melted in the fire, wouldn't it? Well, I used to come here for solitude at times; I suppose it must have fallen into a cranny of the walls and lain here undiscovered all these years. What happened, did you find it when you were cleaning the place?"

"It—It turned up unexpectedly." Ellen was surprised to find herself speaking so steadily. "Someone thought it might be yours."

CHAPTER

❧ 13 ❧

A single bright bar of moonlight sliced across the chamber, pouring silver light into the massive bed, its curtains drawn back to the posts at each corner. Red Harry Graeme, the fiery lights in his hair damped to pure inky black by the silver light, sighed deeply in his sleep and rolled halfway onto his back, so that his face was in shadow again. Ellen froze where she stood in the dark half of the room, and only dared to move again when the even rise and fall of his chest assured her that he had not wakened.

He slept as sweetly as a tired child, as though there were nothing on his conscience to send him shouting into nightmare. It was Ellen who couldn't sleep. She had lain long awake in the bed, rigid beside Harry's sleeping form, turning and twisting the facts she had learned and trying to keep them from fitting the monstrous shape they had assumed.

Finally, unable to put aside the truth any longer, she had slipped quietly from the bed to dress herself by moonlight. Harry had admitted his desire for her mother, had confirmed Guthrie's story that he used to slip across the border regularly, had recognized as his own the signet ring that was found beside her body. And he'd lied when he claimed he

172

had never spoken to her; Ellen felt sure of that. Never before had Red Harry Graeme avoided her eyes.

The facts were there, cold and hard and undeniable. Twist them how she would, she could not avoid the conclusion Guthrie had forced upon her. Harry Graeme had brutally murdered her mother and fled the country just in time to avoid Carnaby Irvine's revenge. Ellen could see, now, just how it would have happened. He'd come across her, riding alone in the hills as she had the habit of doing; had seized the moment to confess his love, and had been laughed at for his pains. She'd seen for herself the blaze of his quick temper; she could imagine—

No. She couldn't imagine him using violence on a woman. Or was it just that she didn't want to? Because that was how it must have happened, in a fit of blind anger when he didn't really know what he was doing. And when he came to his senses, he would have fled without ever noticing the ring that he left beside the dead body.

And everything she'd thought she saw in the man, his kindness and strength and living warmth, had been no more than a foolish girl's self-delusion. Because he pleased her senses, because she didn't want the marriage Carnaby would have forced her into, she had wanted to believe that Red Harry Graeme was really a good man.

She had even deluded herself that he cared for her.

What a blind fool she must have been! Neither the love she'd imagined in his eyes nor the story of revenge he'd told her had the least thing to do with why he had kidnapped her as soon as he returned to his home. He must have known that he could not live here in peace, that Carnaby Irvine would be bound to kill him whenever he returned to the west marches—unless he protected himself somehow. She was that protection. He hadn't demanded ransom for her because she was infinitely more valuable to him here, alive, in his power. As long as he had Carnaby Irvine's daughter, he was safe from Carnaby's vengeance. No doubt that was why her father hadn't raided south again, after the failure of his first attempts to rescue her. Harry had probably let him know that his beloved daughter was alive and well and likely to remain so—as long as Carnaby left him in peace.

How convenient to make the hostage love her captor!

Ellen wondered bitterly whether Harry got much pleasure from her resemblance to her mother. Did he feel that by possessing her and making her love him, he'd finally wiped out the pain of her mother's rejection? Or was he so shallow that he never thought about his past crime at all? There'd been no trace of guilty memory to be read in his eyes this night; he'd spoken of her mother as though he hardly, now, remembered the desire he'd once felt.

At least, Ellen thought, she could understand now why he didn't hold the burning of Fernshaws against her. It was his own fault that the house of Graeme had gone up in the fire of Carnaby Irvine's revenge; it was his own guilt that he wanted to erase when he built a fine new house over the fire-blackened ruins of the old one. And it was his own line he wanted to end; that was why he would beget no children on her.

Yes, he must feel some guilt. But not enough! Not enough for all he'd done to her and hers! Ellen clenched her fists and tried to feel hatred for the man sleeping in the four-poster bed. When she shut her eyes she could call up those bloody images of rape and murder and fire, and could despise the man who'd done all this—as he deserved to be despised. But when she looked at Harry's face, the lines of tension and worry smoothed out by sleep, the dark hair tumbling over his forehead and the arm flung out where she'd been lying beside him—then she could remember only a thousand tender kindnesses, all the words of love and caresses that had passed between them.

All the *lies.*

The sky was streaked with red and amber to the east by the time Ellen reached the Gypsy camp. The hem of her skirt was sodden with dew, and her shoes were rubbing blisters on both heels. In the cool gray-blue morning light the camp looked as it had when she was a child: silent, shrouded, mysterious.

"Why didn't you ride?" Guthrie wanted to know.

"I told the men on guard duty that I wanted to gather some herbs before they lost their virtue in the sunlight. It would have looked funny if I'd taken a horse." And she had wanted to leave the peel tower with nothing of Harry's, not even one shaggy little pony that had probably been stolen from somewhere else to begin with. "What's the matter? Didn't your great rescue plans include arranging for two horses?"

Guthrie went white, and Ellen regretted her jibe. It seemed she was correct. He had only the horse he'd ridden, and it was tired and not up to carrying the two of them back, not if they were pursued.

He'd risked his neck to warn her and help her; it would be unkind to make fun of him, unkind to betray the fidgets that possessed her as she waited for him to deal with the Gypsies about a second horse. But the dickering seemed to take forever, and the sky grew lighter with each passing moment, and Ellen kept thinking she heard someone coming. If Harry believed the guards when they said she had only gone out to gather herbs, they might get half a day's head start, enough to win over the Solway before he even began the pursuit. If he didn't believe them, he might be down on the Gypsy camp at any moment. Ellen walked to the edge of the camp and gazed back the way she had come, tensely alert for any movement along the line of smooth barren hills.

"I'm sorry it took so long," Guthrie apologized when they were at last mounted and riding for the north. "They wanted more gold than I could well spare for the second horse—well, more than I had." He flushed to the eyebrows under Ellen's cool, considering gaze, and she decided not to ask just why he had come on a rescue mission without either horses or arms or gold. Surely her father would have supplied him, if he'd had the sense to ask!

Guthrie reached out to touch her hand. "Ellen—you can't consider yourself bound by this marriage. Now that you're free of him, I—well, I just wanted you to know that I mean to take care of you."

The sun was up now, sending long black shadows over the hills. Harry would be up too; and if he sent men after them, men better armed and better mounted than Guthrie, there'd be scant chance of escape. Guthrie would be dead on the turf at her feet, and she would be dragged back to the tower.

"We're not free yet." Ellen urged her horse into a canter,

glad enough that she needn't respond to Guthrie's clumsy courting just yet. He was a dear boy and an old friend, but how could he think she'd take him seriously after a man like Harry Graeme?

A murderer.

She made the correction in her mind, but she couldn't change her heart. He was mad, he was a murderer, there was a crushing weight of evidence to prove it; he was the man she ought to hate above all others; and with every stride the horse under her took toward the border, her heart ached the more.

"There's no need to tire the horses. I told the Gypsies to say, if any came inquiring after you, that you'd gone into the hills to the south after those herbs you're supposed to be gathering." Guthrie was just barely keeping up with her, sitting at ease, as though he thought they were out for a morning's pleasure jaunt.

And he thought a weak story like that would fool Red Harry Graeme once Harry decided to look for her? If he doubted her story at all, he'd be out after them with Yohannon, who could read the hoofprints of a dozen ponies in the hardest ground and tell you what weight each had carried. *"Ride,"* Ellen said between clenched teeth. She reached over and slashed at Guthrie's mount with the doubled ends of her reins, then gave her own horse the same dose.

The pounding, desperate gallop that followed had at least the merit of keeping her thoughts off what she was leaving behind. She crossed streams and hedges and galloped down narrow pebbled hillside paths without care for her own bones, much less for Guthrie's, and only stopped when the horse was panting under her and its flanks were lathered with sweat.

"Are you trying to get us both killed?" Guthrie shouted angrily when he came up beside her. His face was flushed red with the effort of urging his horse on to keep up with her, and he was sweating as badly as the horse.

"No, trying to avoid that. Do you *want* Red Harry to catch up with us?"

Guthrie's face changed subtly and his eyes slid away from

hers. One hand dropped to his waist where he wore a short knife, his only weapon.

"You do!" Ellen shook her head in disbelief, slid off the lathered horse and looped the reins under her arm. "You'd be pleased if he caught up with us."

"I'd like a chance to fight him," Guthrie admitted, "for what he's done to you. Will you be angry with me for that, Ellen?"

"No, but I'll fear you're a worse fool than I thought." Ellen tugged the recalcitrant mare downward, off the beaten path and toward a clump of trees at the bottom of the hill. "You can't take Harry Graeme, Guthrie. He'd kill you in the first two minutes."

"Oh, I wager I'd have a better chance than that in a fair fight. I've been riding with Johnny a few times, you know, Ellen—I was with him in that fight with the Musgraves. I can handle myself all right."

Guthrie's self-satisfied chuckle grated on Ellen's nerves. "And what makes you think there'd be anything resembling a fair fight? Harry would be more likely to have a few of his men jump you from behind and tie you up like a Christmas parcel, for delivery to Fish-Mou' with his compliments. He's not one to waste effort on a stripling."

Guthrie's ears turned bright red, but at least he stopped posturing about his desire to meet Harry Graeme in fair fight. He even helped Ellen shove the horses behind the trees, where they could rest with some chance of escaping observation from the path.

"Though I don't know why you're bothering," he grumbled, "seeing you seem to think Red Harry can see through hills and trees to track us down if he wants to."

Ellen pointed out that other travelers might conceivably use the path they had been on. "Harry almost got caught when he was crossing the Solway with me, because one of Da's men talked to a shepherd and found out we'd gone that way."

"So the great Graeme makes mistakes!" Guthrie smirked. "To hear you talk, one would have thought him invincible."

"At least I learned from him not to make the same mistake twice."

While the horses were resting, Ellen splashed cold burn water over her face and tied her hair back, then announced herself ready to go on.

"I don't want to tire you," Guthrie demurred. He moved behind her and put one arm around her shoulders. "Ellen, I know this must be painful for you. It must have been a nightmare, being in that monster's power!"

Ellen thought of shared words of love in firelight and moonlight, kisses warm on her lips and a profusion of thoughtful gifts for her comfort and pleasure.

Lies, all lies.

"It's over now. We needn't talk about it." Ellen freed herself from Guthrie's arm and busied herself with adjusting the girth on her horse.

"I only wanted to make you feel better."

"I'll feel better," said Ellen, "when we're safely out of England and in my father's good peel tower."

Her eyes burned, but it would be no comfort at all to cry on Guthrie Bell's shoulder. She didn't think anything at all could soothe the ache deep in her chest; certainly nothing could atone for the black shame she carried in her heart, the shame of still loving the man who'd killed her own mother. "Let's ride on."

"Of course you're not married, girl!"

Carnaby Irvine's booming reassurance must have carried to the very top of the great square tower. Ellen shook her head, smiling wearily at her father's persistence. Last night she'd all but fallen off her horse before the walls of the Irvine tower; he'd given her one night to sleep and wash and be clucked over by Aunt Verona, and already he was hard at work arranging another marriage for her.

"I don't care what words Wee Erchie read over you. You're Scots and he's English, and neither of you had your warden's permission to wed, let alone your sovereign's. Besides, you were forced. Besides, for him to marry you is march treason by English law. Besides—"

Carnaby temporarily ran out of *besides,* and Ellen shook her head again. "If I'm not married, then what am I? Red Harry's whore?"

"You're my daughter and heir to my lands and goods,"

Carnaby shouted, "and I'll not hear words like that in my daughter's mouth again! You've had an unfortunate experience. It's all over now. You can consider yourself free to wed where I tell you to."

"'Free'? It's an odd word to follow with your orders."

"If you'd followed my orders to begin with, you'd not have gotten yourself kidnapped!"

"Oh, so now that's my fault too?" Ellen jumped up from the bench where she had slumped and faced her father, arms akimbo and fair hair crackling like lightning around her face.

"Go to it, lassie!" Verona Irvine cheered from the doorway. "Show the old tyrant your mettle. 'Twas a dirty trick he played on you, and serves him right if it rebounded in his face."

"You keep your long neb out of it, Verona!" Carnaby bawled. "This is between me and my daughter and the good man who's willing to take her in her slightly used condition, never minding the fact she cooperated to the hilt with that dirty murdering pirate who snatched her out of my dooryard." He stopped, gasping and clutching at the air in his indignation.

"And how was she supposed to know what Harry Graeme was, and you keeping the truth from her all these years?"

"Aunt Verona's right!" Ellen put in before Carnaby could draw breath to shout them both down again. "And another thing, Da. I'm not wedding Fish-Mou' Bell, and there's an end to it. You can make up your mind to that. I'd sooner go back to Red Harry Graeme, murderer or no!"

A thousand times sooner. Oh, Harry, my love . . .

But he wasn't her love, wasn't the hero she'd dreamed him to be. Why had she even mentioned Harry's name? Just the thought of him was like knives going through her chest. She'd been a fool, and Carnaby was right. The only way to bury her folly was in dutifully obeying his commands. Marry, give him grandsons, keep your house and forget your life. Ellen sat back down on the bench again and leaned her aching head on her hands.

"You don't have to marry Johnny Bell. Even he, mad as he is for you, knows better than to think I'd give you to a man who can't get children on you. But he still wants you in the family. You're to wed Guthrie." Carnaby Irvine rubbed his hands and beamed at Ellen, certain that this masterstroke of policy would meet with her approval.

"I don't want to wed Guthrie."

"Damnit! Can't a man get a little cooperation from his womenfolk? Listen, Ellen. Johnny Bell is a very powerful man on the border. More than that—he's got the king's ear in Edinburgh! It's a good clan to ally ourselves with."

"What your dad means," put in Verona, "is that if you marry into the Bell family, they might help save his neck if the king ever finds out how friendly he's been with Maxwell and Herries."

The casual mention of the two rebel wardens widened Ellen's eyes.

"Not to the point of treachery," Carnaby put in quickly. "When they started talking about how the Spanish fleet could put men ashore off Caerlaverock, I left their counsels. I'm no papist, to prefer Spanish rule to that of our own King James."

"Nor no loyal Scotsman, either, to have dipped in as deep with the Catholic lords as you've done."

"You keep out of it, Verona!" Carnaby's graying hair bristled as he turned to face his sister. "By God, you always were a righteous nag, and three husbands did little enough to beat it out of you. Lord Herries wanted more freedom for us on the border to manage our own affairs our own way. I went along with him on that. But since he went to open rebellion, and Maxwell following him—"

"He means," said Verona to Ellen in an instructive tone, "now that the king's taken all but one of the castles Maxwell held, and has him under siege in Lochmaben, rebellion doesn't look like a paying proposition. So your dad would like fine for everybody to forget that he's been holding hands with Maxwell and Herries under the table. Which they might well do, save for one little detail he omitted to mention to me last month when he was trying to shove you into Johnny Bell's arms. It seems Johnny Bell has some letters that passed between Carnaby and Lord Herries, letters that might be of uncommon interest to the king. He's offered them to your dad as part payment for you. And if you want my advice, girl, wedding a nice upstanding young man like Guthrie Bell is an easy way to buy your dad's honor out of the gutter he's been dragging it through."

"You've got a damned nasty way of putting things, Verona," Carnaby said sulkily.

"All right. I'll do it," Ellen said without giving herself time to think.

"But a persuasive way." Verona smirked. She sat down beside Ellen on the bench and took her niece's cold hands in her own. "Ellen, dear, you've made the right choice."

Ellen nodded, trying to smile over the dreary emptiness that filled her. She felt very sensible and dull. What else was she to do? Spend the rest of her life breaking her heart because Red Harry Graeme wasn't the man she'd dreamed him to be? And what better way to show him how little he'd touched her heart than to marry the man who brought her out of England and away from him?

But she didn't feel the relief she'd expected after she made the decision. Yes, it was unquestionably the right thing to do, to put Red Harry and his lying love behind her. Yes, Guthrie Bell was a fine upstanding young man, as Verona said, and there was nothing to object to in him as a husband—and it was black unfair of her to keep thinking how much cleverer and more amusing and more competent Harry Graeme was. Yes, she was lucky that Guthrie was willing to overlook the fact that he was getting a slightly used bride, and very, very lucky that the mutilation Johnny Bell had suffered in the wedding-day fight had made him unable to take her for himself.

Ellen agreed somewhat listlessly to all these cheering propositions whenever Aunt Verona tried to rally her spirits in the few days before the wedding could be arranged. She let Guthrie kiss her on the cheek whenever he rode over with yet another bride gift, and told herself that they'd be as happy as any other wedded couple. And whenever he left, she would go up on the roof of the tower where the beacon stood ready to light in the event of raids or invasion.

"You spend a lot of time up in the wind here," commented Verona once when she had panted her way up the last stairs with samples of cloth for the wedding dress.

"Da won't let me go outside the tower. And I need fresh air."

"Yes. You must keep up your health." Verona tactfully pretended not to notice that Ellen spent most of her time on the roof looking south, toward England and Fernshaws. Why nag the girl? In time she'd forget the man and learn to settle for what she could have, like every other woman.

CHAPTER
❧ 14 ❧

The walls of Johnny Bell's fortified house, with the two stone towers rising at either end to guard the central block, were sparsely guarded on the day of the wedding. With rare generosity, Johnny had allowed most of his men the day off to cram themselves into the galleries lining the great hall and watch the wedding ceremony; those who remained on guard duty had a barrel of ale and the promise of relief in time to join the festivities, as recompense for missing the ceremony itself.

Clarty Lewis, at nineteen the proud possessor of a red-bristled mustache that almost covered the pimples around his mouth, was the one man of the guard who wasn't consoled by the ale and promises.

"You're a fool, man," hiccuped Brown Jock, contentedly swilling down his fourth or fifth cup of ale from the generous barrel. In his middle years, Jock had long since come to the conclusion that a full paunch, a sunny day, and a warm girl in his arms were the only victories that counted. Let the young men get holes poked in their skins just to steal somebody else's cattle, or depress themselves longing for somebody else's bride. Jock was happy enough to draw a nice quiet spell of guard duty and doubly happy to enjoy the ale that had mysteriously appeared out of nowhere with Johnny Bell's compliments.

"Would you rather stand in the gallery, hungry and dry, to watch some skinny girl being wedded? Here's more ale than the entire staff could drink, and no one to count our cups—and after, won't you be free to join the servants' dance?"

"I don't drink," said Clarty Lewis stiffly, "and I'd have liked fine to see the bride in all her finery and jewels. They say she's the fairest girl on the marches."

"You talk like a girl yourself. Jewels! Finery! At the servants' dance there'll be some girls you can put your arms 'round, who won't squeal too much if you find a nice dark corner with them. That's better than gawking at some fine lady who's so wrapped up in corsets and whalebone that you wouldn't feel anything if you did get to squeeze her."

Clarty Lewis sighed and stared out over the featureless grassy hills to the south, trying to ignore his vulgar and half-drunken partner. He succeeded so well in blocking out the sight and sound of Brown Jock that he also managed not to notice what was going on in front of him. The rider who had appeared on the crest of the nearest hill was hammering on the doors before Lewis snapped out of his self-induced daze and ran down to let him in.

"News for Johnny Bell," the rider panted when he tumbled off his horse. "Urgent—I must see him at once!"

He had been riding without saddle or stirrups, his skin dark and his head covered by a gaudy purple scarf. A Gypsy, Lewis thought, and wrinkled his nose with distaste. Funny, this one didn't smell as bad as Gypsies were reputed to. But everybody knew they were dirty thieves. "And what makes you think a Gypsy thief would be let into the house? You'll just have to wait until the wedding is over. Maybe then Bell can give you a minute."

"He'll want to hear my news before then," said the Gypsy. "I've ridden over the border to warn him. Red Harry Graeme is coming this way with eighty men, to steal back the bride. Johnny Bell had best put off the wedding an hour or so. First he should double the guard and fire the beacons."

"Too late," said Lewis with sour satisfaction at spoiling someone else's pleasure. "It's already started."

"Then let me in, quick, to warn him!"

"Hey!" Brown Jock's shout startled Lewis out of the concentration he needed to decide whether the Gypsy should really be allowed inside. Rolling down the stairs, thumbs tucked in the armholes of his worn leather jacket, Brown Jock spread his legs and grinned at the Gypsy. "I know you. You were with the party that delivered our ale—and a nice surprise that was, coming from a man as tight as Fish-Mou' Bell. What's this nonsense about having just ridden over the border?"

The Gypsy shook his head. "Must be my cousin you're thinking of. He went bad—took an honest job as a wagoner's assistant. For *pay*. From a *gorgio*." He spat out the two words as if clearing his mouth of something dirty.

"Oh, well, honest mistake," said Brown Jock. "All you dirty thieving tinkers look alike, anyway. But I'd like to know what makes a Gypsy so public-spirited as to wear out his horse in the service of somebody else's feud."

"I thought Johnny Bell might pay for the information," said the Gypsy simply.

"Wouldn't it have been simpler to let Red Harry Graeme pay you to keep quiet? Save yourself a ride, that way."

"That pirate? Pay?" The Gypsy's dark brows arched and he stared at Brown Jock in ironic astonishment. "Have you ever seen the man?"

"Of course not."

"That's clear enough. Far from paying, he turned our camp upside down looking for this girl. Stuck pikes and swords through the bedding, terrorized the old ladies—oh, he was in a right rage! Seemed to think we had something to do with her getting away."

"Didn't you?"

The Gypsy shrugged. "At least Guthrie Bell paid us for services rendered. Red Harry's a bloody pirate. Call us thieves? One of his men spitted poor old Adelina on his pike and wouldn't even pay for her!"

Clarty Lewis' lips felt dry. What kind of brute were they about to face? "Did he—was the old lady killed?"

"No lady," the Gypsy scowled. "Adelina was my best pig,

the one that followed the camp since she was a weanling, eating our scraps and growing almost fat enough to slaughter. Now Red Harry's men are feasting on pork cracklings while I wear myself out to warn Johnny Bell in time, and he'll not be grateful if you two keep me out here until Harry Graeme takes the house!"

Brown Jock pulled up his leather jacket and scratched his stomach where the fleas had been nibbling on him. "Aye, and he'll not be pleased to be interrupted in the middle of his nephew's wedding by a dirty Gypsy tinker thief either!"

Lewis resented the way Brown Jock was taking command, without even a pretense of consulting him. "Just a minute, Jockie. This man's news is urgent. I think he'd best come inside. We'll not interrupt the wedding, but I'll escort him to where he can talk to Johnny immediately after. You can keep watch out here." He pushed the Gypsy ahead of him and tried not to feel Brown Jock's accusing stare between his shoulder blades. After a moment the imagined pressure lessened and he concluded, correctly, that Jock had shrugged and returned to the ale barrel.

"What's this about a nephew?" the Gypsy asked. "I thought Fish-Mou'—er, Johnny—was marrying the girl himself."

Lewis snorted. "Not after the wound he got fighting with Red Harry's reivers. He's giving her to Guthrie. Lucky girl, to be getting a well-set-up young man instead of that old fart."

"Lucky Guthrie," suggested the Gypsy. "She's very beautiful."

"Aye, but soiled goods. And she must be a bold piece, to stand up in front of all these folk, and all of them knowing she's been a pirate's wanton for a month."

A low growling sound came from the Gypsy's mouth and his brown hands clenched convulsively.

"Here, now, what's the matter with you?" Lewis demanded, alarmed. "Not going to have a fit, are you?" Fish-Mou' would likely forgive him for introducing this man among the wedding guests, for the sake of his news. But if the Gypsy fell down in a fit, what was the point of bringing him inside?

186

"Sorry, lad. It's the thought of that bloody pirate and the damage he did to our camp."

Lewis nodded understandingly. "Well, you'll get your revenge. There's nothing the Irvines and the Bells would like better than another chance at Harry Graeme."

"It's mutual," the Gypsy muttered just before Lewis opened the massive carved doors leading into the great hall and put a finger over his lips to warn the Gypsy to silence. Inside, men and women in silks and velvets were packed like herring drawn up into a net, filling the high-ceilinged room with the warm effluvia of so many bodies perfumed with so many different kinds of scent, and all pushing to see over one another's shoulders.

Ellen had moved through the days between her agreement and the actual wedding like someone walking through deep water. If only she didn't breathe, it would be all right. Once she was married to Guthrie Bell, all this would be a dream behind her from which it was safe to waken. Then she could come back up to the surface of life, breathe and laugh and eat. For now, it was too dangerous to allow herself to feel anything. Any incautious movement, a word, a gesture, the sight of the sun on the flowers, could bring back the stabbing pain of her memories.

"You must eat *something*," Aunt Verona would fuss over her.

Dutifully, Ellen would pretend to pick at the morsels on the tray before her. When she had a moment unobserved, she slipped some of them to Verona's little lapdog, who had learned to crouch by Ellen's skirts in wait for the goodies that came slithering down to him.

"It's time to fit the wedding gown."

Ellen would stand as calm and still as a statue while Verona and the maids and seamstresses lifted her hair out of the way, pinched and patted and fussed, pinned and stitched while arguing whether the creamy white satin gown should be ornamented with pearls or just with knots of silver thread.

"We'll have both," Verona would decree one minute, and the next she would be screeching that the idiot seamstresses

187

were making her niece look like a fashion poppet on a stand, with all those jewels crusting over the smooth lines of the dress.

"Oh, it doesn't matter," Ellen said when Verona demanded her opinion. "Have them make the dress any way you like, Aunt. It's not worth all this fuss."

"Oh, yes it is," Verona snapped back. "In the first place, you're my dearly beloved niece and I'm going to turn you out in style for your wedding, whether you like it or not. In the second place, you owe it to Guthrie Bell to make a fine show. Don't you realize half the gawkers and whisperers there will be wondering why he's willing to take a girl straight from Red Harry Graeme's tower? I want them to see how beautiful you are, so they'll not have to wonder any longer. And in the third place, if you weren't dressed in the best this house has to offer, folk might think your father and I were ashamed of what Red Harry did to you. This isna' just a wedding, girl—it's a show of family solidarity."

"Family, family, family! I'm sick of that word, it's all I ever hear around here. If Da hadn't been so wild to force me into marriage to give him heirs, none of this would have happened in the first place. And if it weren't for these damned feuds—"

But feuds weren't what had made Harry Graeme into a murderer, and none of Ellen's wishing could obliterate what had happened on a lonely bridle path when she was only a child. Her momentary anger dissolved into sobs that shook her slim body from shoulders to toes. Verona nodded to the seamstresses and they hurriedly scooped up their materials and departed while she steered Ellen to a bench in the corner, where she could crouch and cry as long as she needed.

"It's all right, love. It's going to be all right now," Verona crooned, wishing she knew what words could cure Ellen's wounds. "You're going to marry a fine young man and forget all that happened. Nobody blames you."

"Well, they should!" Ellen hiccuped between sobs. "Oh, Aunt Verona, I'm so black burning ashamed—"

"You couldn't help it that he forced you."

"Not that." Some desperate impulse to have the truth out

for once, to see if it drove away this woman who'd been a mother to her for the last eleven years, pushed Ellen on. "He didn't force me. I went to him willingly."

Verona caught her breath at this revelation, and cradled Ellen's head on her shoulder until she had control of her face. "Well, no shame in that either," she said, too brightly, "for you weren't to know what the man was, and I'm sure he can put on as fair a courting face as any of the Graemes. They were always a gey handsome lot of men and turned too many women's heads in their time."

"It's not that either." Dry-eyed now, Ellen pushed her aunt's hands away and sat up very straight. "The shame is that even now—knowing what I know—I still love him."

In the last day before the wedding, Verona had ceased pestering Ellen with details about the wedding dress and the attendants' trains and the display of the bride gifts that Guthrie had brought over. Ellen lapsed back into her dreamy solitude, refusing to let herself remember any of the happy days with Harry. Days based on lies, she told herself, and few enough of them to boot. And in time she would forget—that's what they all said.

Did one ever forget love? Ellen tried to imagine herself middle-aged and calm, the happy mother of a half-dozen children by Guthrie Bell. But the picture wavered and blurred in her mind; the oldest dream boy looked up at her with Harry's eyes, and she bit her lip hard to stop the painful feelings that threatened to overwhelm her. Better not to think at all.

That self-induced calm carried her through the bustle of the last day, when bride clothes and bride gifts and attendants and Ellen all had to be packed up and moved to Johnny Bell's home.

"Why there?" Ellen asked listlessly, without really caring about the answer.

"It's Guthrie's home now too," Carnaby told her. "His father's farm is hardly big enough to support three sons, and Johnny has kindly offered Guthrie a place with his men. Now that Guthrie will be setting up his own household, it seemed the best time to make the move."

"Oh . . . You mean I'll be living in Fish—er, in Johnny Bell's house?" When Ellen thought at all about the time after the wedding, she had assumed she and Guthrie would share a room somewhere in his father's fortified farmhouse —cramped quarters, perhaps, but enlivened with the cheerful laughter of his mother and two young brothers.

"You'll have a suite of rooms to yourselves. Johnny is being most generous, especially since he has sons of his own to provide for. But they're all married and living away from home now, so he's got the space to spare."

"And why must I be married from there?" Ellen asked idly, again not caring about the answer. It would be far for their friends and neighbors to ride, and the sudden change wouldn't give them much time to make plans. But she lacked the energy to bother about such trifles.

Carnaby's brief hesitation made her look up. "Safer," he barked at last. "There's a rumor of English coming over the border."

"Harry!" Ellen's heart leapt with joyous expectation. He was coming for her, after all. He wouldn't let her go to Guthrie Bell. He truly loved her. He—

He had killed her mother.

And she was evil herself, that she could still feel anything for the man who'd done that. Ellen subsided into her old leaden silence while Carnaby directed the move to Johnny Bell's house and Verona packed her possessions.

Standing stiff and straight in a dress whose jeweled seams felt like the wires of a cage, she stared at the minister's black robe and waited for it all to be over. This wasn't Wee Erchie, but a tall dignified man specially imported from Edinburgh for the occasion. Was that generosity on Johnny Bell's part, or simply a desire to make sure that the minister hadn't heard any rumors of Ellen's previous marriage? Carnaby and Johnny and Guthrie had had no trouble convincing themselves that a marriage to an Englishman, being performed by force and illegal anyway, didn't really count. Not on the border, where the law between march days was whatever the border lords wanted it to be. But an ordained minister might take a more straitlaced view of things.

The witnesses to this marriage were not a band of pirates and reivers dressed in a rainbow of gaudy rags, but gentlemen and ladies of the border in their fine silks and velvets. Which was to say, Ellen thought, a slightly higher class of pirates and reivers. Behind her was old Andrew Kenneally, who'd made his fortune by intercepting English merchant ships between Carlisle and Ireland; flanking him stood her father and Johnny Bell, two reivers whose superiority over the Graemes consisted solely in the fact that they'd crushed the Graeme family in their last great raid.

Ellen's unruly mind insisted on going on to catalogue the differences between this and her last wedding—as if that were anything to remember! After today, she vowed, she would put that unhappy episode out of her mind for good. But today she could hardly help remembering, comparing, trying to comfort herself with the visible luxury surrounding her. Instead of a cold stone-walled tower, she stood in a hall rich with carved wooden paneling and overheated by three unnecessary fires in the series of fireplaces that made such a great show down the west side of the room. Instead of pirates waiting to drink to the bride in stolen Spanish wine, she had the assembled nobility of the west march waiting to do the same thing.

And the greatest difference of all was in the man standing beside her. Guthrie was tender, kind, honest. If he hadn't thought to bring extra horses and gold when he came to rescue her, it was because he'd been so eager to reach her. If he'd seemed a bit peevish on the ride home, it was because his view of the world called for the man to do the protecting and leading, not for a woman to push on ahead and think out the safest routes.

Ellen swallowed hard over the lump that formed in her throat. She, too, would have been happy to have a man to protect and lead her. But Guthrie needed somebody to guide him, and he always would. He was a natural follower. It wasn't his fault that he hadn't been trained in the rough school of necessity that had made Harry a leader of men.

Harry.

It was definitely too hot in this crowded hall with its three fireplaces all being put to use. Ellen thought she might faint if she had to stand here much longer while the imported minister from Edinburgh delivered his speech on the rights and duties of married life. Couldn't he get it over with, say the words that would make her and Guthrie man and wife and put Red Harry Graeme out of her life for good?

Even the invited guests grew weary; Ellen could hear the rustle of silk gowns behind her as ladies changed position, a wave of whispers traveling the length of the hall. Harry would never have stood for a minister lecturing him at such length. He'd have interrupted the man without ceremony and told him to get on with it; the image of him doing so was so vivid that Ellen almost thought she could hear his voice.

"Stop!"

But that wasn't what he would have said!

A lady shrieked behind her, and there were the sounds of people shoving each other to get out of the way. Ellen whirled, trailing the heavy jewel-encrusted skirts of her wedding gown behind her, and saw a dark-faced, shabby Gypsy advancing through the elegantly dressed crowd.

A Gypsy with Red Harry Graeme's blue eyes.

As she watched, he repeated, "Stop! This wedding is against the laws of God and man. The lady has a husband living."

"By what right do you make such a claim, young man? Were you a witness to this previous marriage?" The minister clapped his book shut and peered over the tops of his reading glasses at Harry. Behind Harry a pimply-faced boy with a spreading red mustache pushed through the crowd to grab his arm and drag him backward. Harry pushed the youth out of the way with one hand while with the other he pulled off his purple head scarf. Everybody else, from Fish-Mou' Bell to the bridegroom himself, was too shocked to move.

"Better than a witness," Harry replied with a cheerful, impudent grin. "I'm the man himself. And I'll not stand by to see my lady given to another, tricked into bigamy by the lies of those who told her I was dead."

Carnaby stepped forward; Harry's hand went to his waist and came away with a short blade that glittered free and cold in the center of that overheated, overluxurious room.

"Don't be in such a hurry, Carnaby Irvine," he warned, swinging the blade around him in a circle that cleared the space about him of spectators. "I've a natural aversion to killing my father-in-law, but it's a feeling that could be overcome if you make it necessary. As for the rest of you," he addressed the wedding guests, who had fallen back before the menace of his blade, "you'd be well-advised to take this minor interruption calmly. The house is surrounded by my men. Some of them brought a barrel of ale to your guards, Fish-Mou', and I fear that most of the men are half-seas-over by this time, while my men have taken their place."

He grinned and reached for Ellen with one hand. "Come, my loving wife. You're wanted at home—the other side of the border."

For a moment it seemed he might almost get away with it. Then Guthrie Bell yelled, "Husband living, has she? Not for long, you murderer!" and launched himself upon Harry with fists upraised, careless of the dagger.

Ellen shrieked, and time seemed to stand still for a split second. Harry flipped the dagger around in his hand with a juggler's dexterity, brought the weighted hilt up to meet Guthrie's chin, and without pausing, swung his hand backward to place a long rip down the doublet of the young guard who'd brought him in. Guthrie crumpled, his eyes rolling up in his head, and the pimply-faced young guard bellowed over the shouts of alarm, "He's leein'! There was no' but twa men brought the ale, and he's one o' them! Come on, you—we can tak' him!"

Grinning like the madman he'd been proved to be, Harry Graeme leapt onto an oaken stand and rained the books from Fish-Mou's one library shelf onto the guests with one hand, simultaneously kicking out at those who got too close and feinting with his dagger to keep a healthy fear in the rest.

He'd seen this moment coming for hours now—ever since, arriving from one direction at Carnaby Irvine's tower while his men were supposed to be coming another way, he discovered that the wedding had been moved at the last minute. He would barely have time, himself, to get to Johnny Bell's in time to stop the marriage; he could only hope that his men would arrive at the rendezvous, get the message he left, and shortly follow and back him up. With the guards fuddled by ale, he might just have had a fighting chance—if he could wait until his men arrived.

But there was always the chance that things would turn out the other way, that the wedding would be done before help came. A sensible man would have waited quietly and snatched Ellen back in his own time, even if that waiting meant allowing her to spend a night with Guthrie Bell. Harry discovered, when he saw his runaway bride standing up beside that big stupid Scots boy, that he was not nearly as sensible as he liked to think. Never mind that she'd fooled him, pretended love, then ran away at the first opportunity. She was his woman, and it was physically impossible for him to stand there and watch her marrying another man.

Besides, his men might just have arrived while he was inside. Except, given the uproar and the lack of reinforcements, it seemed that they had not. Oh, well, at least he'd knocked out the bridegroom; that should delay the wedding for a few hours, and—always supposing Fish-Mou' Bell didn't hang him out of hand—that should be all he needed. Harry kicked the head of a young sprout of the Gordon family and slashed with his dagger at a leather-jerkined, paunchy guard who'd joined the fray on the other side.

What he needed was something to throw, to keep them from pressing him so close. Ah! The shelf above his head still held a hefty leather-bound volume with iron clasps. A bible? Never mind, it made a fine dent in Sim Armstrong's head.

The conclusion of this fight might not be in doubt, but Harry took a savage delight in doing as much damage as he could before the inevitable end. Besides, one never knew; even now Yohannon might be storming the gates. He might yet ride out of Johnny Bell's house with his lovely, false, deceitful Ellen in his possession again.

The books were all gone now; with his free hand he wrenched at the iron candle holder set in the wall to his left. The mortar was too firm. He had to put all his weight on the thing for a moment, and in that moment somebody grabbed his boots and somebody else knocked his hand with a log of wood, numbing the fingers so that the dagger fell useless to the floor. And he never saw the third man, the one who hit him on the head while he was struggling to free himself from the fellow holding his legs. He tumbled into stars and darkness, his last conscious thought one of triumph that he'd managed to thoroughly delay the wedding. While he lived, no one else would touch Ellen Irvine.

CHAPTER
❧ 15 ❧

The chamber to which Ellen had been shown after the fight was far larger and more luxurious than she would have expected Fish-Mou' Bell's charity to provide for a mere nephew like Guthrie. Despite the spacious floor and high ceilings, though, the overall effect of the room was to make her feel confined and watched. On two sides the walls were hung with dark red velvet hangings covered with lavish embroidery in black and purple, in a twisting design meant to suggest vines. To Ellen's aching head and tired eyes the crawling curves of purple and black resembled snakes twining up the hangings; she could almost hear them hissing at her.

The other two walls were covered with dark paneling, hand-carved around the borders with strange curving shapes. Flowers became the misshapen heads of monsters, horses sprouted lions' heads, demons rode goats, and no-where in the exuberance of line and curve was there a harmonious smooth place where the eye could rest. In the shadowy chamber, lit only by the candle a servant had given her, Ellen almost fancied she could see the carved figures slowly moving; one little demonic head in particular, set halfway up the wall where it was level with her eyes, seemed to wink at her.

Impatient with her own foolish fancies, Ellen pushed back the heavy, dusty velvet hangings covering the windows and immediately wished she hadn't. The faint summer twilight was swallowed up, defeated and annihilated, by the layers of cut velvet, embroidered stump work, and ornamented brocade in which the room was so overdressed. Ellen herself felt as weak as the fading light, still trapped as she was in the stiffly-boned wedding dress with its jewel-weighted skirts.

There was a single massive chair beside the bed, an old-fashioned box chair with high carved arms and a carved wooden seat that also served as the lid of the box underneath. That chair, Ellen thought, was just like the rest of Fish-Mou's house: luxury, ostentatious wealth, but no real comfort. Try to sit on it, and you'd likely find your backside stamped with the carved eagle design of the seat when you got up. But there was no other place to sit, except for the high bed shrouded in its embroidered hangings.

The bed she was to have shared with Guthrie. There seemed to be a curse on her wedding nights, Ellen thought. First she was kidnapped practically out of Johnny Bell's arms—not that she objected to that—and now Guthrie Bell was lying downstairs with a knot on his head that might keep him unconscious all night. Even if he roused, he'd be in no state to say his vows or enjoy his bride; and anyway, there was no one left to marry them. The Edinburgh minister had left soon after the fight was over, calling them all a parcel of border heathens who'd try to marry a woman to two men at once and enjoy the free-for-all that resulted.

"Why, man, what's the point of having a good fight if ye dinna' enjoy it?" Carnaby Irvine had boomed jovially. His annoyance at seeing the wedding disrupted was cured by the thought of Red Harry Graeme out of his life for good. "We're all friends here, and the villain that stopped the wedding is to be hanged in the morning—so, married or no, my girl will be free to wed again after that! Why don't you stay and have a dram with us the night, and—"

The minister was already in the saddle, declaring that he had rather ride through the night than stay any longer with such undisciplined heathens.

"Don't take it so hard, lass," Carnaby Irvine had advised Ellen, seeing her as white as her dress and with her hands clasped together before her. "We'll have Wee Erchie here tomorrow, as soon as Guthrie's fit to stand up beside you again. First we'll hang Red Harry, then marry you all right and proper—a double celebration, eh?" And he rubbed his hands together, beaming jovially.

Carnaby and Verona and the other wedding guests had departed soon afterward, some promising to return in the morning, some apologizing that they dare not leave their own homes unguarded two days running. In the lawless state of the borders since Herries and Maxwell had rebelled, few gentlemen cared to spend the night away from their homes. Still, Ellen was surprised that Fish-Mou' did not urge at least some of his guests to stay the night, if only to spare them the long double ride.

Surprised and . . . what? Nervous? Ridiculous. This house was where she and Guthrie were to begin their married life. She ought to be happy to be here, settled at last—or almost so; with the scandal of the past month safely behind her—or almost so. Ellen clasped her hands tightly beneath her breast, pressing inward, as if that could ease the pain she felt. She ought to feel glad that Red Harry Graeme, madman and murderer, was to die in the morning.

Perhaps, after all, it was as well that Guthrie had been knocked out. A bride in tears wouldn't augur well for the rest of their life together, would it? By morning, Ellen promised herself, she'd be calm and composed and in control of her unruly emotions. Only, she would not watch Harry die. They could not ask that of her.

Her gown was too stiff and too hot. And here she was, without even a woman to help her undress! Were there no servants in this vast, dark house? Before she'd come to the chamber, somebody had brought up trays of cold meats and cakes and wine; now, though, there was no servant to be seen. Ellen didn't even know, in the confusion, what had happened to the girls she had brought with her for her personal attendants. Surely they hadn't gone back with Carnaby; that would make no sense at all.

Ellen shook her head and freed her hair of the jeweled pins that held it crimped and stiff to her head, wishing she could free herself as easily of the shadows of grief and foreboding that surrounded her here. It was an inauspicious start to a marriage, for a bride to see her first husband hanged; liar and madman and killer though he was, surely no one could blame her for feeling some oppression of the spirits. And that was all it was. She would not lift a finger, she told herself fiercely, to save the man, even if it were in her power.

As, of course, it was not. What could she do? Seek out Fish-Mou' Bell and beg him for mercy? Suggest that it might be better to obey at least a form of law, keeping Harry locked up for delivery to the English warden on the next march day?

Even if Fish-Mou' acceded to such a plea, Carnaby Irvine wouldn't. Her father was mad to see her married, and more, he needed this marriage to keep his own head well attached to his shoulders; how could she so quickly have forgotten the threat Fish-Mou' held over him? He wouldn't let a man live who might, at his trial, call the legality of Ellen's marriage to Guthrie into question. He wouldn't let a man live who had kidnapped and, by his way of thinking, dishonored his daughter. And most of all, he would hardly trust an English justice to take revenge on the man who'd murdered his wife. He hadn't waited for the law before, but had taken his own vengeance on the house of Graeme in fire and blood. He would hardly be more patient now, when the man who'd done the deed was actually in his power.

And she shouldn't even want him to be. If she were a good woman, she'd rejoice in the thought of Harry Graeme's lithe young body dangling at the end of a rope, the fiery lights gone out of the black hair, the dancing of his blue eyes ended forever.

At the very least, she wouldn't cry over the notion. Ellen stared out the window and willed herself to feel nothing but the emptiness of the darkening summer sky. Her chest ached and her head kept whirling with futile, hopeless plans to save Harry; the last light went from the sky while she stared with unseeing eyes.

"What's this! In tears, and on your wedding night? Dear, dear, this will never do."

Fish-Mou' Bell's jovial voice shocked Ellen. She turned

and found him standing so close that she would have had to push past him to get away from the window. The heavy door had opened silently on its well-oiled hinges; the thick Turkey carpet that covered the floor had muffled his footsteps, and the enveloping draperies that filled the room had absorbed any lesser noise.

He looked uncommonly cheerful for a man who'd just recovered from a crippling wound, then to see the girl he'd wanted wedded instead to his nephew. Ellen could hardly reconcile the sprucely dressed gentleman in his suit of sober gray with the disheveled figure she'd last seen standing on a bench downstairs, shouting encouragement at his men while they overwhelmed Harry Graeme. Then, the excitement of the fight had made Fish-Mou's thinning hair bristle up like a hedgehog's back and his face drip sweat. Now the strands of hair that fell across his shining pink scalp were carefully combed into place once again. His thick lips, slightly rolled out in the perpetual pout that gave him his byname, glistened in the fading light, and his eyes were brightly calculating behind the bulbous protrusion of his nose.

"Are you feeling lonely, with your dear bridegroom having been so uncivil as to get himself knocked out by that young ruffian? Very thoughtless of Guthrie to sustain an injury upon his wedding night. I shall have to do what I can to make up to you for his absence."

Fish-Mou' slipped one arm around Ellen's slim waist. "It's not much of a wedding celebration you had, but we can catch up now, eh? I've ordered wine and food sent up here. Ah, good, I see it's arrived already. We can be private now."

Ellen tried to move out of his encircling arm, but the heavy stiff skirts of her wedding gown trapped her in the cramped space where the window bowed outward. "That's all right. I've no objection to dining downstairs. In fact," she added rather desperately, as Fish-Mou' showed no sign of releasing her, "I had rather do so."

"No, no. You've had a terrible shock. You need rest and seclusion. Don't worry about a thing, my dear girl. I've given strict orders that no one is to bother us here."

So that explained why she hadn't seen her maidservants. Ellen felt relieved as Fish-Mou' moved away and seated himself in the box chair, beside the bed. But the way he kept staring at her made her uneasy.

"Now, why don't you make yourself comfortable? That gown—it's quite lovely, of course, but don't you find the weight of the silver embroidery too much? You'd best take it off."

Ellen's laugh sounded shrill and unhappy, even to her. "Well, I can hardly do that while you're here, can I? If you'll send one of the maids to me, I'm sure she will help me."

"I'm sure she would," Fish-Mou' agreed. "But I think you'll find that I can do everything for you she would, and more besides. Take it off."

Ellen didn't know what to say. Had he gone mad?

"Hurry up," Fish-Mou' ordered with a tinge of impatience in his voice. "I've waited a long time for this."

"I think you forget that it's Guthrie I married, not you!"

"Oh, no. I could hardly forget that—or the reason why." Fish-Mou's hand moved toward his groin, and Ellen closed her eyes briefly. "Your father's mania about getting male heirs to his lands forces me to share you with Guthrie. He'll have his chance to get sons on you. But I can still find pleasure with you in many ways, even if I can't do that one thing your father cares about. You'll find life with the two of us quite . . . interesting."

Ellen felt the blood draining from her face as she stared at Fish-Mou's thick-lipped, confident smile. In the twilight his balding head and his large white teeth glimmered with a ghostly pallor. *Don't faint,* she commanded herself. The dizzy weakness that had been troubling her for several days had returned, making her head spin until she wanted to collapse on the bed. *That's the last place you want to collapse just now. Especially with this crazy man in your chamber.*

The tart words sounded in her head just as if Aunt Verona were standing beside her, lending her strength with her own brand of acid commentary. Ellen surreptitiously pinched the inside of her arm through the tight inner sleeve of her wedding dress. The sharp little pain helped to keep her alert.

"I will never believe that Guthrie agreed to such a monstrous bargain," she said, surprised at how calm she sounded, even to herself. "You will leave now, Johnny Bell, and never suggest such a thing to me again. And Guthrie and I will be leaving this house as soon as he is recovered."

Fish-Mou' shook his head, still smiling, and Ellen's faint hope that she might be able to bluff her way out of the situation vanished. "If you want to see Guthrie recovered, you'd best please me tonight. Of course he did not agree to my plan, but where he is now, his agreement makes no odds."

"In God's name, where is he?"

"Oh, he's well enough—for the moment. I've had him placed in the cellars below the kitchen. Red Harry in one cell, Guthrie in the next. A pretty symmetry, don't you think—both your husbands in one place? Don't worry about Guthrie. If you cooperate, he'll wake in the morning with nothing worse than a headache."

"And if I don't?"

Fish-Mou' shrugged. Ellen backed away as he rose from his chair. "I see no need to afright your ears with the gruesome details. I will have to leave him in condition to get sons on you, but he may not be nearly such a pretty lad by the time I release him to do that duty. Now please be reasonable, Ellen, and don't force me to do anything unpleasant. I've got it all worked out perfectly. Guthrie will come to you once a week until you're pregnant. In between those visits, and after you're with child, you will do everything you can think of to pleasure me. You can begin now, by taking off that gown. Now, here's what I want you to do tonight . . ."

Ellen covered her ears as Fish-Mou's voice droned on, calmly detailing gestures and acts she'd never imagined, much less heard spoken of in decent company. He was serious. And they were alone in this deserted wing of the house—the servants ordered to stay away, the guests sent to their homes, and Guthrie locked in the cellars. His attack on her had been as meticulously planned as one of the raids that left the Bell family so rich and powerful in the marches.

And he was, for all his detailed planning, quite mad. Ellen had no doubt of that as she listened despite herself to his catalogue of perverse desires. His voice droned through the hands she had clapped over her ears; it vibrated through her head like a stonemason's chisel cutting through rock, inscribing disgusting images on her brain. She thought briefly of appealing to her father to get her out of this house, then dismissed the thought. Even if she could get a message to him—and she had no doubt that she'd be closely enough watched to make such a thing difficult—she could not even try to reach him before morning. And after such a night as Fish-Mou' had planned, Ellen thought, she herself might be a poor draggled madwoman. At best, she'd be too sick and ashamed ever to look decent folk in the eyes again. What would be left for her, then, but to live on as Fish-Mou's prisoner?

"But enough talking. It's time for the play to start."

Fish-Mou' lumbered toward her; Ellen darted to the far side of the bed, but he moved with surprising agility for such a heavy man, catching her wrist and dragging her back to him with a twist that sent tears of pain to her eyes.

"First the dress can go," he panted, struggling with the stiff cloth, "then you can start earning the price of Guthrie's pretty face. Or shall I drag him up and cut his nose off in front of you? Would that make you more cooperative? Ah, you—"

She drove an elbow into his stomach, hard enough to hurt, and as she dived for freedom, he cursed her and yanked at the back of the white satin dress. The fabric parted with a rending sound; pearls bounced into the carpet, and Fish-Mou's hands slid inside the dress to grasp her naked skin. Ellen felt sick and deathly weak at that touch; her head spun as she was drawn back toward the great curtained bed. There was no escape; he was all around her, greedy hands feeling her body and wet lips slobbering at her neck. Her stomach heaved with nausea and her legs folded under her as Fish-Mou pushed her onto the bed.

"That's better," he said with satisfaction. "Now we'll have some light to see you by."

He left her lying, sick and dizzy, on the bed while he dealt with the matter of light. The one candle Ellen had brought with her was burnt down to a feeble flame in a pool of wax. Fish-Mou' shielded it carefully with his hand while he lit the tapers around the walls of the room. The old-fashioned pricket stands, consisting of an iron spike mounted in the center of a large round dish to catch the melted tallow and wax, were fixed to the walls wherever there was a break in the hangings.

In the growing light Ellen could see the room all too clearly—the embroidered hangings, the heavy Turkey carpet, the velvet draperies. She felt smothered in softness. Oh, for a knife, a pair of scissors, anything with which she could surprise Fish-Mou' for a moment! She fought the nausea and the whirling in her head to sit up, cautiously gathering her feet under her. Somehow she would have to get to the door; if she could just escape from this room, perhaps she would be able to outrun him and get to a part of the house where there were sane people. Now, while he was fussing with the candles on the far side of the window, with the bed between them—no, he'd turned his head to look at her again.

The flame leapt from candle to candle, flaring up with a hot drip of wax that spluttered onto his hand.

Now.

Her fingers were on the iron handle of the door when his weight dragged her back again into a soft, damp embrace. "No, Eleanor," he whispered into the coiled braids of her hair.

The unexpected sound of her mother's name on Fish-Mou's lips made Ellen falter for a moment, and Fish-Mou' clasped her more firmly while he continued his soft, mad whisper. "You won't fight me this time, will you, Eleanor? I don't want to have to hurt you again."

He threw her bodily onto the bed, so hard that her head cracked against one of the carved wooden posts, the weight of his body upon her before she recovered. His hot fingers were ripping at the dress, fumbling under layers of cloth to get at her naked skin, and one arm was crooked about her neck so that she could barely breathe. And all the while the eerie, gentle whispering went on.

"You're so beautiful, Eleanor. I always wanted you. Now you won't laugh at me. We're going to be happy now, Eleanor. You're going to do everything I say, and I'll have you by me always to play with, and we're going to be happy."

Ellen lay rigid with fear and disgust under Fish-Mou's body. He was mad, quite mad. He thought she was her mother. Had he wanted Eleanor Irvine too? Was she some kind of substitute for her dead mother? Dear God, what would he do if she managed to break through his mad illusions?

"Are you happy, too, Eleanor?"

Numbly, Ellen nodded her head.

"Good. Now you shall dance for me."

Ellen could hardly believe her reprieve, but Fish-Mou' lifted himself off her, and she could breathe again.

"Go on," he urged, "stand up. Dance for me, Eleanor!"

His eyes were blank and glittering in the candlelight. Ellen had the horrible feeling that there was nobody there behind the eyes. And that frightened her more than had Fish-Mou's vicious, sane, controlled threats against her and Guthrie. She slid off the bed and stood on shaky legs. The shredded ruins of her dress fell about her waist. She tried to hold it up, but Fish-Mou's abrupt gesture startled her into letting go.

"That's better. You can take the skirts off in a minute. Dance!" He was breathing heavily through his moist, half-open mouth.

Ellen raised her arms above her head and turned slowly to the left, then to the right.

"Bounce up and down."

Two obedient bounces carried her toward the wall. Her fingers fluttered in the air and brushed against the base of the lighted candle that had been luring her since she stood up. She didn't dare to look, just grabbed blindly at the candle. She felt iron bite into her fingers, knew a moment's sick despair—she had grabbed the pricket stand, not the candle itself—then exulted as the whole thing came loose from the paneled wall, wax bowl, spike, and candle together. She threw herself at the bed, the candle extended before her, and dashed the flaming end straight at Fish-Mou's eyes.

He screamed, a high, thin scream that seemed to go on forever, and flung up his hands too late to protect himself. The soft wax and tallow mixture of the candle crumbled in his face and the iron spike slid into his eye before Ellen realized what was happening.

"Oh, God." Her fingers opened to let go of the horrible weapon she had accidentally seized, but it didn't fall. It remained where it was, sticking out of Fish-Mou' Bell's face, the iron bowl vibrating slightly and covering most of his blood-streaked face. He had fallen backward against the bolster, slumped over sideways, and after that first high scream, he'd made no noise at all. The only sound in the room was a steady quiet dripping as his blood fell into a growing puddle in the brocaded coverlet.

"I've killed him," Ellen whispered, staring with horror at the still, slumped form before her.

CHAPTER
❧ 16 ❧

With one desperate sweep of her arm Ellen pulled the heavy curtains shut all along the side of the bed. But two sides still remained open to the room; if she moved at all, she would see Fish-Mou's body with the iron candle stand sticking out of his eye. Eyes closed, Ellen felt her way around the bed, drawing the curtains shut as she went. Only when the bed was totally enclosed in its shroud of embroidered curtains did she give way to the trembling in her knees. She sagged down onto the carpet, the white skirts of her dress billowing about her, and covered her face with her hands. Her whole body was shaking now, and she felt deathly cold.

A wave of nausea swept over her, surprising her with the intensity of the force that gripped her body. She wanted to spew up everything she'd eaten in the last twenty-four hours. But the jurden was under the bed, and Ellen couldn't even imagine crawling under there to retrieve it.

"Don't," she commanded herself. Her forehead dampened with a chilly sweat, but she didn't vomit; and after some moments the weakness passed and she could sit up again.

That small victory over her body gave her the hope that somehow she would get past this moment. Oh, it was over already; time hadn't frozen in the moment when she felt the iron spike going into Fish-Mou's eye. Life went on, Ellen told herself, and she had to go on with it. And she had no intention of spending the night locked in this eerie chamber with a corpse. Only, would Fish-Mou's men just let her walk out of the house? Not very likely. And what if they discovered the body before she got away?

Ellen drew up her knees and wrapped her arms around her legs while she tried to think. The white shreds of her dress dangled about her, moving slightly in a draft from some unseen source. Her bare shoulders showed the marks of Fish-Mou's hands. She felt soiled all over.

The simple, honest course would be to go downstairs, just as she was; to tell the folk there that Fish-Mou' had attacked her and she had accidentally killed him in struggling to protect herself.

Ellen felt sick with shame at the thought of exposing herself before all those people—Bells, too, or men who looked to the Bells for their hire; and she was an Irvine. No. She had to get clean away from here, that was the first thing. When she was safe on Irvine land again, then they could take up the matter of why she had killed Fish-Mou' Bell.

Her father would doubtless be back in the morning, to see—Ellen's thoughts skittered away from the memory. Dear God, she'd actually forgotten the fate that awaited Harry Graeme! She couldn't help that, but she would not stay to see him die. Nor would she spend the night in this chamber, listening to the drip of the blood that still fell from Fish-Mou's body, waiting to be discovered in the morning. She had to get away from this accursed house, now, this very night.

When Ellen tried to get up, her knees crumpled under her. She hung on to one of the posts of the bed until the wave of sick dizziness passed. "Get *hold* of yourself!" she whispered with fierce, desperate anger, clenching her free hand until the nails bit into her palm.

She was tired and frightened, sick and hungry, but no consideration would have persuaded her to eat from the plates set out in this chamber for a dead man's feast. Very well. She would just have to go on without. All it required was resolution . . . and remembering not to think about the thing on the bed.

With grim determination Ellen concentrated on the practical problems of making her escape without alerting any of the Bell retainers below.

Clothes were the first thing. She wouldn't get very far wearing only the shredded remains of her wedding dress. Fortunately, the chest containing her clothes had been brought up to this chamber. Ellen searched through the contents and selected a plain, serviceable dress of dark green stuff, with narrow skirts that could be worn without the cramping fashionable apparatus of farthingales and stays. Over that she threw a dark cloak with a hood large enough to cover her head and most of her face.

Now what? She looked respectable enough, but she would need a horse out of the stables if she were to get home. A new-wedded bride demanding a horse at this hour of night would be questioned, surely; and if she masqueraded as one of her own gentlewomen, they might not give her the horse without some authority.

They would do it on Fish-Mou' Bell's orders, though. Perhaps one of his rings would be a sufficient sign of authority—the carved signet with his arms on it, which he used to seal letters, would be the perfect thing. Ellen tried to remember if he had been wearing it. She felt sick at the very memory of his hands on her. But she could have sworn those fat, hot fingers had been bare—thank God! She didn't think she had the resolution to strip the signet ring from a dead man's hand.

Where would he keep such a thing? If this sumptuously decorated room was Fish-Mou's private chamber, the signet should be somewhere in here; Fish-Mou' wasn't the man to let his valuables go far from him. There were no chests, though, save the one in which her own clothes had been brought. A secret hiding place behind the paneling? The candles would be burned down before she'd pulled and pried at a tenth of the knobs and faces and symbols carved into the panels. Ellen glanced about the room and saw the old-fashioned box chair. Perhaps that was the answer. The seat was constructed to serve as a storage place, and she could think of no other reason for Fish-Mou's keeping such an ugly old piece of furniture in this luxuriously appointed room.

When she pulled up on the seat and found it locked, Ellen was sure she was on the right track. A second candle stand, with the iron spike freed of its candle, made a perfect lever with which to attack the box part of the chair. The old, dry wood split into two pieces as soon as she put any pressure on it. Below was a length of cut velvet on which reposed the ring she'd been looking for—Fish-Mou' Bell's signet, with the Bell arms cut deep into the flat top of the ring.

When she reached to get it, Ellen realized that the cut velvet was actually wrapped around some other things. Could any of them be of use to her? She lifted out the velvet and shook it out over the carpet. A miscellaneous assortment of treasures spilled out onto the floor: a dirk, an inkwell, and a gold picture frame. As they tumbled forth, Ellen thought she saw a momentary flash of red fire.

The gold frame was bright in the candlelight, decorated with a smooth tracery of engraved lines that Ellen could not read without picking it up. The silver handle of the dirk was quite black with tarnish. But on the flat silver side of the inkwell the tarnish had somehow spared the engraved lines, so that they stood out as a bright silvery tracing against dullness. And the picture Ellen saw was the eagle within a circle, the Graeme device that she'd last seen on Red Harry Graeme's signet ring.

Hands shaking, she caught up the unsheathed dirk and examined it carefully in the candlelight. Yes, the same emblem was worked into the chased silver handle here, and the blinking dots of red she'd seen before were chips of ruby stone that formed the eagle's eyes. And the delicate lines on the gold frame spelled out the Graeme motto, *Ne Oublie*.

Ellen's hands fell open, and the three treasures lay untouched on her white skirts where she knelt beside the ravaged box chair. She stared unseeing into the flame of a candle on the wall before her, thinking furiously. Here were Graeme family possessions, not so valuable in themselves, but treasured heirlooms from the look of them. There must have been many raids back and forth across the border in which such things could have been stolen.

Stolen goods in themselves didn't bother Ellen; from all the stories she'd heard in her growing up, the English had taken as much from the Scots as the other way around. The mystery was in why Fish-Mou' had kept the things by him all these years, hidden away like this. That was unusual. A reiver might display the English silver in his house, as testimony to his success; or he might sell it to a jeweler for the equivalent in good coined money; or he might, if it had sentimental value, sell it back to the original owners for twice its monetary value. But he didn't stuff it in a bag and lock it in the bottom of a chair!

"He called me Eleanor," Ellen murmured. "My mother's name." Why did she think of that now? She felt as though something tremendously important were almost within her grasp, something she had to figure out because her life depended on it. Something she was afraid to think about.

Why hadn't the Graemes bought these things back from Johnny Bell?

After the raid of 1577 there had been no Graemes to buy them back.

Had her father stolen the things, on that terrible night when he burned Fernshaws? Ellen shook her head slowly. He had been on a mission of vengeance, not of reiving. The thought of Carnaby Irvine pausing in his vengeance to pop a few pieces of Graeme silver into his pockets would have been comic, if the whole story hadn't been too sad for laughter.

The things must have been stolen just before that climactic raid, then. But why, with the Graemes of Fernshaws gone, had Fish-Mou' not sold them?

Could it have been dangerous, for some reason, for him to admit possession of these things?

The truth came to Ellen all at once, like a jumble of lines that resemble a child's scribbling until you hold it the right way up and see that it is a picture.

Harry said he had thought his signet ring lost. Might it not have been taken in the same raid where Fish-Mou' acquired these other three pieces? And if so, then Johnny Bell, not Harry, had subsequently lost the ring.

Beside Eleanor Irvine's slain body.

Johnny Bell, who had just now called Ellen by the name of

her dead mother, who had displayed an obsession with winning her that passed the bounds of reason.

Ellen knew, as certainly as though she had heard his confession, that she had just killed the man who was responsible for her mother's death.

The story that seemed so improbable, pinned on Harry Graeme, made perfect sense to Ellen when she pictured Fish-Mou' Bell in the leading role. He was patient and subtle enough to watch Eleanor Irvine's movements until he knew just when and where he could find her alone; he was mad enough to force her, sane enough to kill her before she could tell her husband what he had done.

He had left Harry's ring beside Eleanor's body, whether by chance or calculation hardly mattered; but once it was seized upon as evidence that a Graeme had done the killing, Fish-Mou' dared not admit to possessing the other pieces of gold and silver he had stolen from Fernshaws. They had lain hidden all these years, keeping his secret well.

She stared at the closed curtains around the bed, with loathing for the object inside. "I'm *glad* I killed you," she whispered.

Clarty Lewis had been set to watch the cells overnight as punishment for his stupidity in letting Red Harry Graeme into the house. "And no ale to be sent down either!" Fish-Mou' had ordered before going upstairs to see to the young bride, who he claimed was hysterical. Seemed strange to Lewis, the whole affair. The girl hadn't seemed hysterical when she went upstairs; only white and still, with big bruised-looking eyes in her slender face. And the order to keep Guthrie Bell in the cells below, next to that dangerous brute Red Harry Graeme, seemed stranger still. Fish-Mou' said it was for his own protection, that Guthrie would be weak and dazed when he came around, and in no state to defend himself were Red Harry's men to mount an attack. All the same, you'd think the man would want his nephew upstairs where he could be looked after.

So Lewis wasn't too surprised to see the bride herself coming down the cellar stairs, a candle in one hand and a pitcher in the other.

"Feeling better, are you, my lady?" She would have come

to see to her husband, of course. But it would be pleasant if she could be persuaded to stay and talk with him for a few minutes first. Lewis hadn't had many chances to be around such a lovely girl. And after what she must have been through in Harry Graeme's hands, she might not object to a bit of a cuddle with a nice young Scotsman for a change—especially since her husband was unlikely to do much for her on this wedding night.

"I am, thank you. And I thought it was time someone saw to Guthrie. Has he come 'round yet?"

"He has that. At least—not sensible, but he's been groaning every now and then."

"Oh, poor Guthrie." The girl's eyes seemed to grow larger and darker. "Pray open the door to the cells. I must go to him at once."

"Er, I'm not sure I should. Fi—Johnny told me to keep them both locked up safely. In case of an attack, y'see."

"Idiot!" Ellen's chin jutted out ominously. "Johnny told *me* to come and see to Guthrie. Here's his ring, if you don't believe me." She thrust the signet ring under his nose. "Now let me in to my husband *at once*. You needn't come with me—just give me the keys."

As Lewis swung open the heavy door under the stairs, he was tempted to ask the snippy little piece which husband she meant—the one she'd tried to wed this afternoon, or the one who'd interrupted the wedding? But she didn't seem to be in the mood for a little joke. Pity, that. He squatted on his heels before the open door and resumed his game of dice, left hand against right.

The space beyond the door was divided into a narrow hallway and two small chambers, both closed off with heavy doors. Ellen held up her candle and was dismayed to find no gratings in the doors, no way she could tell which chamber held which man. She could call to the young guard to show her, but then he'd hang about and watch her, and she'd have no chance to let Harry out.

A whimpering groan sounded from the right-hand chamber, and Ellen made up her mind. Harry might be in pain—she had no idea what condition he was in after the fight—but he wouldn't whine. More likely he would enlarge her Spanish vocabulary with a few choice phrases. She turned the key in the lock of the left-hand door and slipped in, praying in one confused breath for all manner of mercies: that the guard wouldn't look in, that Harry would be conscious, that no one would think to disturb Fish-Mou' upstairs for some hours yet.

As she pushed the door shut behind her, a hand gripped her wrist and pushed her arm up behind her back. The candle fell into the straw on the floor and a boot stamped out its flame. Harry's lean, wiry body pressed her against the closed door. "If you came alone, you made a mistake," he hissed into her ear. "You're going to help me get free."

"That's what I *came* for, you great gowk," Ellen whispered back.

"Oh, of course. Why didn't I guess that?" Harry's arm slipped around her waist, holding her tight in a most unlovely embrace. "After all, you've already shown your tender concern for my welfare by running away from me for no reason, repudiating our marriage, and giving yourself to that pretty boy Guthrie."

"That was before I knew you didn't do it."

"What did you come down here for? To tell me you were sorry I had to be hanged in the morning, but surely I'd appreciate the vast inconvenience a living husband made to your plans? Well, my dear wife, I must apologize in turn for upsetting your plans, but I have no intention of being hanged. I'm going back to England—and you're coming with me."

"Damn you, Harry, will you let me explain?"

"Not now. You can spin all the fancy stories you've a mind to once we're safe the other side of the border, and maybe I'll even listen. At the moment, though, I don't want to hear your fantasies. The only thing I want to know is how many guards are on the other side of that door. No, never mind. Why should you tell me the truth? Tell me something else instead." He was holding her close as any lover, and his breath was warm on the back of her neck. "How did you tear yourself away from the marriage bed so early? Is your new young husband not so amusing as your rude pirate was? Can't he—"

"Guthrie's in the cell next to us!"

That surprised Harry into releasing her. Ellen spun

around and pressed her back against the door, holding out her hands to him. "Please understand, Harry. Fish-Mou' got me alone upstairs—he—I—"

Memory of the bleeding corpse slumped on the bed stopped her voice for a moment. Harry nodded. "I understand. He cheated you? The wedding to Guthrie was just a device to get you into his house?"

"Yes. And—"

"And so you thought that the nasty man, Red Harry Graeme, might not be so bad after all. You contrived to slip away from him, and you thought I'd save you. Well, you were right. I can't do without you, false though you are. And I must thank Fish-Mou' for ensuring your cooperation. It will be easier to get away with you helping than if I had to knock you out and sling you over my shoulder. Now, about the guards outside?"

"One only. But Harry—"

"Hush!" His hand was over her mouth a second before she understood the significance of the muffled cries outside. There was a fight going on somewhere; steel clashed against steel; a man shouted, and his voice gurgled to a stop in mid cry. Huddled against the cell door, with Harry's body over hers and his hand covering her mouth, Ellen listened tensely for a clue to what was going on. There were steps coming into the cellar now; many men on the stairs, tramping without attempt at concealment.

Had they found Fish-Mou's body? Ellen tried to push Harry's hand from her mouth, to whisper a warning, but he was too strong for her. The door swung open and she closed her eyes.

"I thought you'd be here."

It was Yohannon's voice, creamy smooth and very pleased. Ellen opened her eyes and saw the narrow hall outside the cell full of faces she recognized.

"I may have been a thought impetuous," Harry admitted. He released Ellen and shoved her forward into Yohannon's arms. He caught and held her like a parcel. "But as you see, the lady kindly offered me a way out. It seems she's thought better of her bargain. You brought fresh horses?"

Yohannon's dark face opened on a darker smile. "What need? The Bell stables supply us. But we'd best be moving.

There was a slight disagreement about the manner of our reception here, and we had to invite the folk in the house to step outside."

"He's meaning," put in Jenkyn over Yohannon's shoulder, "we fired the house to keep the Bells busy, and it's spreadin'. Could get hot, even down here."

"Harry!" Ellen found her voice at last. "You'll not leave Guthrie locked up in here?"

Harry laughed. "Why, no. We'll take him with us. I think I might have a use for the boy."

Guthrie, still only half conscious, was dragged outside and slung over a horse in front of Yohannon. A group of dazed, sullen Bell relatives and guards watched the looting of the stables in silence, their hands and feet bound. Behind the stables flames crackled out the windows of Johnny Bell's fine new house with its carved paneling, and mortar cracked between the stones of the flaming towers.

Harry paused after looking over the men Yohannon's party had captured. "I don't see Fish-Mou' here."

He glanced toward the inferno of the upper story, now sending out orange-black billows of smoke and flames together.

"He's dead." Ellen proffered no explanation, and Harry asked for none.

"And we're riding." Harry scooped her up to sit behind him, arms around his waist. Ellen leaned forward and rested her forehead on his leather-clad shoulder. Harry still thought her false to him; she could feel the tension in his body, resisting the embrace. And she wasn't fool enough to embark on explanations in the midst of a body of sweaty horsemen riding full tilt for the border. But when they were home again, she thought, then Harry would listen. She would make him listen. And then everything would be all right again.

CHAPTER
❧ 17 ❧

A rainbow shower of light danced over the black and white tiled floor of the long gallery at Fernshaws, sunlight splintered into many colors by the beveled edges of the new windows. Ellen laughed with pleasure, picked up her skirts and danced to where the rainbows met her face. She held up her cupped palms as if she could catch the light like a fountain of water; the bars of red, blue, and green danced over her fingers and disappeared again as the sun went behind a cloud. Suddenly the gallery seemed dull and cheerless, with its cool tile floor and its empty long wall where the portraits of Harry's ancestors should have hung.

"You seem to have recovered remarkably well from yesterday's exertions."

Harry's voice was as cold as the tiles underneath her feet. And he had come so quietly through the double doors at the far end of the gallery that she'd not even been aware of his approach until he spoke. How long had he been watching her?

His eyes were the dusky blue of the sky before a storm; his mouth was set in a firm, unsmiling line. The dark velvet of his doublet matched the blackness of his hair, and in the shadow of the clouds there was no warm light to bring out the dancing red undertones that had given him his nickname.

As he stood with feet slightly spread apart, hands on his hips, Ellen felt that she was facing an accuser rather than a husband.

"Would you think better of me if I locked myself in my chamber for three days, crying and fainting and complaining?" In fact she'd had nightmares last night, starting from her sleep in the newly furnished bedchamber with memories of Fish-Mou's face turning into a bloody mask. And Harry had not been beside her.

A smile tugged at the corners of Harry's lips. "There's no need to go to extremes. But you don't have to pretend to me that you're delighted to be here. You made your preferences quite clear when you ran away with that boy. All I wish to make clear to you is that you are indeed my wife and that I've no intention of allowing you to contract a bigamous marriage in Scotland or anywhere else."

"Harry, it was a mistake. I thought—"

"You thought you'd be happier with a boy of your own age? In your own country? Tell me, was that before or after he told you that he meant to share your favors with Fish-Mou' Bell?"

"It wasn't—"

"Now that Fish-Mou's dead, you may be thinking of taking another chance with Guthrie. You can forget that."

Ellen's hand clenched over the folds of her skirt. "You've not killed him!" Not now, not when they were so close to ending the feud once and for all. Only let her explain what she'd discovered in Fish-Mou' Bell's chamber, and Harry would have to forgive Carnaby Irvine for his attack on Fernshaws; her father would have to stop trying to kill Harry; Harry would understand why she'd left him. Oh, it was all about to unravel under her fingers, and if Harry had Guthrie Bell killed, then it would start again and there'd be no end to the fighting in her lifetime. She felt sick at the thought. "Please, Harry. Tell me you haven't killed Guthrie."

"At the moment," said Harry with a trace of regret, "I see no need for that."

Ellen's knees sagged with relief. She longed for a bench to rest on, but Fernshaws was just barely finished and hardly furnished at all. This long gallery on the second floor was completely empty, decorated only by the pattern of tiles on the floor and the beveled glass in the new windows.

"Then you'll let the Bells ransom him?"

"No. I've better use for him here." Two steps brought Harry to Ellen's side, his hand gripping her arm, his blue eyes burning into her face. "You're very concerned about young Guthrie. Are you so fond of him?"

"As an old friend!"

"A good enough friend for you to marry?"

"Harry, I thought . . ." It was so hard to say.

I thought you had killed my mother. She couldn't just blurt it out like that without explaining the seemingly irrefutable evidence Guthrie had brought her, without showing Harry how his own words had fed the belief. "It's hard to explain."

"I wonder you even try! Never mind. You lied enough to me before. Do you know, I was fool enough to think you loved me as I loved you? I suppose it was all an act to gain my trust, so that you could run away."

As I loved you. A warm glow began somewhere deep inside Ellen, protecting her from the hurtful cold sting of his words. He did love her; he admitted as much; and when he calmed down, she had only to explain to him why she'd thought she had to leave. Only, when would that happen? Last night he'd left her alone, and truth to tell, she had been too tired to want anything but her bed. And this morning, which had begun with rainbows and delight, had degenerated into a pointless quarrel. If only he would stop shooting those angry words at her and give her a chance to explain!

"Well?" Harry shook her arm slightly.

His knuckles brushed the curve of her breast, and a sharp, sweet longing sang through Ellen's body. *Oh, my dear, my dear, why aren't you embracing me instead of holding me like a prisoner? Why won't you let me make you understand how it all came about?*

"You used to have a tongue quick enough in your own defense. Aren't you going to tell me that I forced you in the first instance, that you had every right to run away from the man who kidnapped you? Aren't you going to tell me that I was a fool to believe your words of love could be anything but a pretense?"

"Would it make you feel better if I did?"

"It would be honest, at least. But who am I to look for honesty in an Irvine?"

"If you despise me so, I wonder you want me to stay with you." He was going to be sorry for all these harsh words when he understood her reasons. She needed to find some way of stopping him. But she was getting too annoyed to try. There was a limit to how long a person could be expected to put up with being reviled and abused and insulted.

"God's truth, and so do I! Call me a fool again for that if you like, Ellen, but understand this: you are my wife and will remain so. You will not run away again. You will be my sweet, loving, dutiful wife, in public and in private. Especially in private."

Oh, yes, yes, especially in private! What more had she ever wanted? Ellen's momentary annoyance evaporated and she smiled blissfully at the thought of all the private times to come. "All right, Harry. Whatever you say."

"D'you think I'll trust such an easy capitulation? You won't take me in a second time with your smiles and promises, Ellen. I've a way to ensure that you will at least act as if you love me."

If he'd only stop ranting at her, she'd have no trouble convincing him of the truth of her feelings! Just as he stood beside her, blue eyes dark with anger and suspicion, fingers holding her arm so tightly, vibrant with life, he was worth a round dozen of any other men she'd known. When would he finish with the quarreling and get to the kissing? That would be when she could explain everything without getting her head snapped off. If she had the breath left in her to do so! Harry's brand of lovemaking didn't leave a woman with much leisure to spare for idle conversation, as Ellen remembered; and it had been too long since they'd loved each other. Much too long. If he wanted to take her right there on the tiled floor of the gallery, she'd not refuse him.

"Remember Guthrie Bell?"

Ellen sighed. Deliberate patience with an angry man

could last just so long. "Yes, Harry. I'm not likely to have forgotten Guthrie Bell so quickly, and I care about his fate as I would for any—*any,"* she emphasized, "of my friends and neighbors who were taken prisoner by the English. But I don't necessarily want him in the bed with us!"

"Maybe the thought of him will help your acting. Understand this, Ellen: your pretty Guthrie, whom you were so quick to join with in bigamy, is still in my power. As long as you act the loving wife in every way, he's safe. The day you even think about leaving me again, I'll hang him from this balcony!"

Well, Guthrie was safe enough in that case. Ellen had no intention of leaving Harry for, oh, another sixty or seventy years at the least. But if it made him feel more secure to blackmail her into doing what she wanted to do anyway, that was perfectly all right with her. Anything that would get him relaxed enough to listen to her story without exploding like a squib in the fire!

"Very well, Harry." She smiled up at him. "When do I start being your loving, dutiful wife?"

"Now."

The building of Fernshaws had just been completed in the week that Ellen ran away, and Harry had, understandably, other matters to think about than furnishing his fine new house. The bedchamber where Ellen had spent the night, where Harry led her now, contained only a tall bed whose posts looked oddly naked without curtains. The windows were bare, too, and as the clouds rolled away, sharp morning sunshine spilled into the room. From the bed Ellen could see a vista of gently rolling hills and groups of trees, all green with the beginning of summer.

"You can start by taking off your clothes. Slowly."

When Fish-Mou' had issued the same order, in his dark chamber closed in with carved wood and heavy curtains and heavy, clinging scents, the thought of his slavering enjoyment had made her sick. Shadows and curtains couldn't mask the obscenity of his desire. Now, in this almost empty room, she had neither curtains nor darkness to cover her, and it didn't matter. She was proud to give all herself to

Harry, and it seemed right that the sun and the wind should be their witnesses. After this day, when everything was made clear, nothing more should be hidden between them, no more old secrets and family tragedies lying in the darkness to trip them up. And this was how it should begin.

Slowly, gracefully, proudly, Ellen stripped off her garments until she was standing quite naked between Harry and the window. She watched his face all the while. He was standing by the door, untouched by the flood of sunlight that poured over her, a step removed from all that dazzling. He made no move toward her; his hands were locked behind his back, and maybe he thought his still face masked his feelings. But Ellen could read the blaze of desire that lightened his blue eyes, and she understood the unnatural stillness and tension of his body. He wanted her so much it was hurting him, but he was determined to play out this game he'd started. He wanted to be in control, she thought. To be the impassive, unfeeling man, taking her for his pleasure without really needing her, ordering her to serve him.

Unfeeling? She turned toward the window to hide the smile on her face. The man was aching for the touch of her, as she was for him. He was only holding back because he thought she didn't love him, because he feared to trust her again. Soon she would be able to soothe that hurt. But for now—if he was unhappy, it was his own fault for being too impatient and angry to listen to her explanations. And if he wanted to play at keeping his distance—well, it would be interesting to see how long he could make that last.

"What shall I do now?" she inquired, pirouetting before him. Harry's eyes were fixed on the movement of her white breasts; he gulped, and she thought it possible he could not speak.

"Should I undo my hair?" she prompted.

"Yes—Yes, do that." His husky voice was hardly more than a whisper.

Ellen raised her arms gracefully and took her time about unfastening the long plaits wound about her head. She combed out the fair hair with her fingers and spread it slowly out over her breasts, caressing herself with long, slow, downward strokes. The light gilded her hair and made her skin glow, and Harry's arms trembled as though he had clenched his hands together behind his back. How she wished he could touch her!

"And now?"

He swallowed and opened his mouth, but no sound came. She laughed to herself and reached out her hands to him, slim and naked and unashamed, feeling the glorious flood of warmth and light that streamed through the windows onto her bare skin. Harry took a halting step forward, then another, and then he stood in the circle of light with her.

"What are your orders now—husband?" she inquired meekly, resting her hands on his shoulders.

Harry drew in his breath at the light touch, and his arms went about her, imprisoning her in a hard circle of flesh beneath the black velvet of his doublet. He swung her off her feet and carried her to the bed without speaking.

"Just let me look at you." But he couldn't keep his own orders; his hands were already roving over her body, his impatience and tension communicating themselves to her as a palpable thing. His fingers brushed lightly across the erect tip of her breast, and Ellen felt herself trembling deep within. He stroked her cheek, and she turned her head to press her lips upon his open palm.

"Love me, Harry," she whispered into his hand. "Please love me."

Sunlight spilled over the bare uncurtained bed, playing over the two bodies locked together there. With her head thrown back, Ellen could see the clouds scudding across the sky, high wisps of white against the pure rain-washed blue that filled her vision. Harry was holding her close at last, quick and demanding, and she felt as pliant under his hands as a willow branch bending into a pool. And this time there was no holding back, no careful calculation on his part; his need for her drove past all the barriers he'd set up between them. In the midst of her own pleasure Ellen felt him trembling with release, his hands biting into her shoulders as his body arched and he drove deeply into her. Above her the clouds danced across the blue squares of the window, the sun dazzled her eyes, and the world was all blue and gold and glorious.

"Why are you lighting the candles? It's still day."

"It is most wonderfully summer and sunlight," Harry agreed, "and I want more light yet. I want gold and fire and sun all together. I want to see you in every light at once, and we'll finish by moonlight." He pushed the casement open; a summer breeze, a warm breath of flower-scented air, rushed in and extinguished the candles he'd just lit. Ellen giggled.

"All right, you can just walk 'round the room and light them again!" Harry ordered. He returned to the bed and lounged there, hands behind his head, watching Ellen's graceful walk with appreciative eyes. She had to lift her arms high to light the tapers, and her fair hair spilled down over her shoulders like a faerie cloak of sunlight and moon. "And when you've finished with that little task, I've thought of a few other things I want you to do."

They'd both dropped the pretense that she was obeying him out of fear for Guthrie. Ellen came back to the bed and knelt beside Harry, drawing her long hair over his naked body until he shivered and reached for her.

"Woman, can't you wait till I order you?" he murmured into her neck while his hands roamed down her body. She moved softly above him, implicitly offering all that he discovered of white skin and gentle curves, joying in the manner of his possession of her. "What's the use of obedience if it comes before I give you my commands?"

Ellen laughed and nipped his shoulder gently. "How much obedience have you the strength to command, husband?"

"As much as you can give."

"Och, is it a contest, then?" Ellen straddled him, laughing, and her lips formed a soft, surprised bow of delight as he drew her down onto him and demonstrated that he was still in the contest.

"Are you calm enough for an adult conversation now?"

Harry was sprawled, limp and relaxed, diagonally across the bed. "Calm, yes. For the rest—wasn't our conversation these past three hours sufficiently adult for you?" He passed one lazy hand over her body, and Ellen curled in closer to his side for a moment. The sun was too high now to come in at the windows, and the warm, scented summer air that wafted in through the open casement was cooled by the thick, fortified outer walls of Fernshaws.

"Harry, we need to *talk*," she protested as his lazy caress changed to something more specific. "And you can't—"

"How do you know what I can or can't? D'you need another demonstration, then?" His free hand arced over to capture her, pinning her between his arms while he held her down by the weight of his body.

Ellen prudently retreated from the implied challenge to Harry's virility. "Well, then, I can't. I'm exhausted!" She slipped one long leg off the bed and began fishing around on the bedroom floor with her toes for the garments she'd discarded earlier.

"And just who gave you permission to get dressed?" Harry stretched lazily and pulled her skirts awry before she'd properly got them on. "Maybe I'll keep you naked in my room indefinitely. It's one way to keep you from running away."

"That," said Ellen, twitching her skirts out of his grasp, "is what we have to talk about. But first you have to promise not to lose your temper—"

"I? Lose my temper?"

"Or shout, or yell, or shake me, or threaten to hang anybody."

Harry made his blue eyes very round. "Lord save us, girl, you misunderstand me entirely. I'm the meekest, mildest country gentleman—"

"Pirate," Ellen interrupted.

"I had letters of marque from the queen!"

"What does that make you? A private merchant specializing in robbery on the high seas? Trading English steel for Spanish gold? With your crew of nice quiet clerks and— damn you, Harry. We're quarreling already, and I haven't even gotten to the hard part."

"Oh, if you want to see a hard part—"

"No!" Ellen was off the bed in a flurry of skirts. She

retreated as far as the open casement window, where the summer breezes blew her long hair about her face and pulled strands of it out the window.

"If you're thinking of letting down your hair for the prince to climb up and rescue you," said Harry, "I might remind you that young Prince Guthrie is under lock and key in a very secure place, and is likely to stay that way for the foreseeable future."

Ellen sighed. She could just envision a future in which Harry alternated between suspicion, jibes about her untrustworthiness, and unbridled lust. Actually, the lust part wasn't bad at all, but they did have to do something about the other things. Otherwise she just might be driven to murder him from sheer irritation.

"Harry. Please. Five minutes. No more cracks about how you can't trust me. All right?"

"I suppose I can restrain myself for five minutes," Harry agreed, lying back with both hands locked behind his head.

"Did I ever tell you how my mother died? And when? It was the day before you ran away to sea, Harry. The day before my father burned Fernshaws. You see, he thought you did it."

That caught Harry's attention. He lay still and tense while Ellen spilled out the old unhappy story of love and death and fire.

"And did he raise you to hate me?"

"No! I never knew any of this until after you brought me here. Do you think I'd have come with you, believing that you raped and killed my mother?"

"But you believed it later."

Harry's words were evenly spaced, dropping onto the warm summer air like cold stones. Ellen wished she had not extracted that promise to keep his temper. Better his rage than this freezing control!

"Guthrie told me—he showed me your ring, Harry! The ring that was found beside my mother's body. And later, you owned it was yours. And more, you admitted that you'd loved my mother. What was I to think?"

"You might have *thought*," Harry growled. "If I'd killed Eleanor Irvine, would I have been fool enough to admit later that I'd ever wanted her? If I left my ring beside her body, would I own it later?"

"N-Not if you knew that was where you lost it."

"All right. So after living with me and sharing my bed, you judged me rapist and murderer on evidence that wouldn't have convinced a flea. I suppose I should be grateful you didn't feel it your duty to kill me in my sleep before you fled with Guthrie."

"Carnaby said I should have." Ellen twisted her hands together. "But I couldn't have done anything to hurt you, Harry. I just—do you understand why I had to leave?"

"Do you think that didn't hurt me?"

"Harry, please try to understand! I left you, yes, I couldn't stay after that. But I—I fought it, but I still loved you, Harry."

"You seem to have fought it most successfully! How long did it take you to accept Guthrie's proposal? Did he ask you to marry him on the way back across the border? Or did he sample the goods first and then make up his mind to purchase? I'm sure you two had a merry ride of it, and I must apologize for interrupting your efforts to forget me."

Ellen bowed her head and let the angry words wash over her. Of course Harry was hurt and angry. She'd known he was. But she'd hoped he would feel better, knowing she had what seemed at the time to be unassailable reasons for leaving him.

There was no point in trying to explain how she'd come to accept Guthrie—the complicated deals her father was making with Fish-Mou' Bell in an effort to save his own neck, her own dead feeling that nothing mattered and her life was over anyway. Whenever she mentioned Guthrie, Harry got too angry to hear her out. All she could do was finish the story as quickly as possible.

Quietly, when Harry was through with his sarcastic speech, she went on to describe the scene in Fish-Mou' Bell's private chamber after the fight. She tried to keep her voice calm and unemotional, but she couldn't look at Harry while she was talking; even the memory of that experience made her feel soiled and ashamed. She stared out over the sun-dappled hills, her hands clenched around the iron casement frame so tightly that her fingers were white and numb, and told him what had happened in as few words as possible. Even so, when she came to the part where she struck at Fish-Mou' with the candlestick and felt the iron spike go sliding into his eye, her voice faltered and she couldn't go on for a moment.

A warm body pressed close behind her and two arms went around her waist, cradling her back against Harry's chest. "Poor frightened girl. And there was I locked up down below, and no use to you. That—" He said a few words that Ellen took to be Spanish, and of a sort that she'd better not understand.

"Well, it's over now," she said. "And it was worth it, for when I was searching for his signet ring to help me get away, I found a whole cache of things he'd stolen from Fernshaws." With Harry's arms around her to keep her safe, she found it was quite easy to speak of those terrifying moments in Fish-Mou's chamber; she felt as if she were describing events that had happened a long time ago to somebody else. "And he called me Eleanor several times—did I mention that, Harry? He must have done it, and left your ring by the body to make folk blame it on you."

"And that's why Carnaby burned Fernshaws," Harry mused, "having the bad luck to miss me by only a few hours. I think I owe Fish-Mou' Bell something. Too bad he's dead already."

He released Ellen, very gently, as if she were fine porcelain that might break in his grasp, and moved back into the chamber to don his clothes. "No wonder you had bad dreams last night. Would you like Ruthann to be your bedfellow tonight?"

"Ruthann!" Ellen gasped. "But Harry, I thought you— now that you understand—Harry, I love you! I've always loved you! I thought you'd be happy to know I didn't run away to wed Guthrie."

"Oh, I am. I'm stark delighted." But his tone was as dull as an ill-cast bell, and he kept his head bent while he fastened his clothes again.

"And to know that I've proved your innocence of . . . that other matter?"

At that, Harry's head came up. "Ah, well, you've married a sad cross-grained fellow, Ellen Irvine. You see," he said gently, a self-mocking smile on his lips, "somehow I can't help wishing you had been able to believe in me before you found this grand proof."

CHAPTER
❧ 18 ❧

Ellen wasted nearly a week prowling around Fernshaws, exploring pantries still smelling of nothing more than freshly planed wood and sawdust, checking out servants' rooms and stairwells to no effect.

"It's a fine big house," Ruthann told her mistress after one of these pointless expeditions, "but I don't see why you have to know the length and breadth of every room in the place." They had been going through the unfinished east wing, where piles of bricks for the fireplaces and glass for the windows littered the rough floors, splinters caught in Ruthann's skirts and fine sawdust whitened her stockings. She was feeling a little testy about Ellen's insistence on exploring Fernshaws so thoroughly.

Ellen sighed and took Ruthann's hands in her own. "Ruthann, can you keep a secret?"

"If you're planning on running away again," Ruthann said promptly, "I'd just as soon not know it, thank you very much. Master was powerful bad-tempered last time. Blamed me for taking you to the Gypsy camp." She giggled. "I'd a' been turned off for sure, if he wasn't so set on getting you back, and if he'd thought he could find another girl within ten leagues who'd serve alone in Red Harry Graeme's house full of foreign pirates."

"I'm not going to run away," Ellen promised. "And we'll have a proper staff for Fernshaws soon, with plenty of other maids to keep you company."

Ruthann gave a little sigh. It had been rare fun while Ellen was away, being the only girl among all these men, and them under strict orders from Red Harry to treat her with respect. Oh, well, she'd known it couldn't last, and it would be fun to have somebody else to gossip with. To compare notes, for instance, about the mistress's strange behavior. Ever since she came back, she'd been acting plain daft. Snapped at Red Harry whenever he came near her, then burst into tears over the presents he left in her rooms. And nearly every day she wanted to go and search through another part of this great half-built house, with Ruthann trailing behind her over dust and bricks and raw lumber. "Well, if you're not trying to run away, what are you doing?"

"Harry's got a prisoner here," Ellen told her. "I need to find him."

"No, my lady. Not here." Had no one told her mistress that the Scotsman was being kept in the old peel tower? Ruthann shook her head. Why couldn't Ellen have asked earlier and saved them all this traipsing around?

Ten minutes later Ruthann was regretting her revelation. Following Ellen around the unfinished parts of Fernshaws might be a bore, but at least the roof was on in most places and they could keep dry while they poked about. Now Ellen had her on a horse, heading back to the peel tower on a miserable wet summer afternoon with a nasty sharp wind blowing inward from the ocean. The woolen cloaks they'd wrapped over their clothes blocked the wind, true, but they also soaked up the damp drizzle and extruded it again with a powerful odor of wet sheep. If she'd had any sense, Ruthann reflected as she bounced miserably along, she would have saved telling the mistress where Guthrie Bell was until a nice bright sunny day, when it would have been a pleasure to go on a little expedition.

It was almost a relief when they got turned back by the guards who rose out of the hills halfway there.

"Sorry, mistress. You're to go no farther than this. Red Harry's orders."

Ellen swore at the men in English, Scots, and Spanish, but got no results except a few chuckles and a compliment on how fast she'd picked up Harry's favorite vocabulary of Spanish curses.

"I ought to know those words well enough by now," Ellen said on the gloomy homeward journey. "They're about all I ever hear from him. And I'll probably learn a few new ones when he finds out I was trying to see Guthrie."

"Then why were you trying to see him?" A nice boy, the young Scotsman, but Ruthann personally considered he didn't have his head screwed on tight. Anybody who'd even contemplate stealing Red Harry's woman was crazy; anybody who would do it and then linger within Red Harry's reach for the inevitable counterstroke was lucky if nothing worse happened to him than being locked up in an old stone tower.

"I had to make sure he was being treated all right. It's my fault he's here."

Ruthann favored her mistress with a skeptical glance from under the sodden hood of her cloak. She didn't have to say what she was thinking. This was the man who'd been trying to marry Ellen in Scotland before Harry interrupted the wedding and brought them both back here. If Harry heard that Ellen had been sneaking off to visit Guthrie—as, now, he undoubtedly would hear—the news wasn't likely to make him any fonder of the Scotsman.

"Oh, all right. I wanted to see him because Harry forbade me to." Ellen twisted the reins around her fingers in an effort to explain what had seemed so clear in her own mind. The patient mare slowed to a walk, stood still, dropped her head and nibbled on grass while Ellen struggled with her words. "Harry thinks I don't love him. He's jealous of Guthrie. And as long as he keeps Guthrie locked up where I can't visit him, I've no way to prove to him that Guthrie really doesn't mean anything to me. But if I went to see Guthrie and just treated him perfectly casually, normally, as an old friend, then Harry would have to believe me. You see?" she appealed to Ruthann.

"Mmm. Sort of. You think it'll make Harry trust you if

you sneak around behind his back to visit the man he's jealous of."

Ellen let out a sharp, exasperated breath. "It seemed like a good idea at the time. Never mind, Ruthann. Why are we sitting out here in the rain, arguing about something that didn't even happen?"

"Blest if I know," muttered Ruthann behind her mistress's back as they resumed their homeward journey.

Ellen did not feel that the abortive expedition had been a total waste. After a week of chilly silence from Harry, she would have welcomed anything that broke the ice between them. If her visit to Guthrie convinced him that he could trust her, good. If it inspired him to fight with her, good. Maybe a fight would clear the air. Anything would be better than the frigid, punctilious courtesy with which Harry had treated her ever since she explained why she'd left him. Instead of trying to understand what good reasons she'd had at the time, he had chosen to brood over the fact that she could ever, for one solitary moment, have believed him capable of murder. Which seemed to Ellen to evince a remarkable degree of childish sensitivity for a man who'd spent the last eleven years sailing the Spanish Main, looting and killing and justifying plain piracy as patriotism.

Let him shout at her for trying to see Guthrie! Maybe at the same time she could shout a little sense into his deaf ears.

By the time they got back to Fernshaws, Ellen was spoiling for a fight. She was disappointed not to find Harry waiting for her in the courtyard, even more disappointed when a message sent by Eleazar informed her that he was in Carlisle and would not return that night. What was the good of flagrantly disobeying his commands if he wasn't around to know about it?

Even when he returned from Carlisle, Harry did not deign to mention Ellen's attempt to see Guthrie. The only way she knew that he'd heard about it was that her riding privileges were suddenly suspended. The first time she sent for her mare to be saddled, Yohannon appeared instead of the stable lad. He informed her that Harry had given orders not to let her have any of the horses. In fact, she wasn't to be allowed out of the house.

"I must have exercise," Ellen complained.

"The long hall on the first floor is a very pleasant place to walk." Yohannon stared hard at Ellen; she had the feeling he was trying to convey some message that he dared not say aloud.

"Very well. I'll take my exercise there."

"Not now. In two hours."

The words were breathed so softly that Ellen could scarcely believe she'd heard them.

"What?"

"My apologies, mistress, but those are the master's orders. You're not to ride out until further notice." Yohannon's eyes flickered upward, and Ellen, glancing in the indicated direction, thought she saw a black-haired figure at one of the upstairs windows. Could Harry be eavesdropping on their confrontation? Just in case, she ranted at Yohannon a while longer before retiring to her chamber. Anybody who'd listened would think she had gone to her room to sulk. Instead, Ellen paced up and down and counted the minutes until two full hours had passed.

At first she thought the hall was empty. The cloudy day let in only a dim, diffused light that showed a long barren room with a pile of chairs and bolts of cloth at one end. Ellen felt a momentary disappointment. Yohannon had only been teasing her, or she had misinterpreted his words. Then there was a movement at the shadowy far end of the hall, a familiar yellow head appeared in the midst of the furniture and hangings piled there, and Ellen cried sharply, "Guthrie!"

"Ellen. I could hardly believe it was you." Guthrie rose from his kneeling position and came forward to take both her hands in his somewhat dusty ones. He smiled down at her, and she was relieved to see that he looked perfectly all right. "What's going on? Some villainous-looking dark Moor of a fellow told me to wait here, that Red Harry wanted to see me about the ransom terms."

"Harry left for Carlisle an hour ago." Ellen had watched him go from her upstairs window. He'd been making a lot of mysterious trips lately, but this time she hadn't been hurt that he didn't tell her where he was going or trouble to say good-bye.

"Then what's this about? Did you arrange it?"

Ellen shook her head. "I haven't that power. I think Yohannon did it. He must . . . feel sorry for me." A stupid lump in her throat made it hard to finish the sentence. She hadn't realized, until now, how evident the estrangement between her and Harry must have been to his men. Somehow that made it more real; not a silly quarrel that would be cleared up as soon as Harry stopped being childish, but a solid barrier between them, harder to pass than Solway Firth at high tide.

"Sorry for you! Why? Has he hurt you? Oh, God! That monster. I've suffered agonies, Ellen, knowing you were in his clutches again, and it's all my fault. He beats you, doesn't he? Or worse . . ." Guthrie didn't specify what he meant by "worse," but Ellen thought she could figure it out. How shocked he'd be if she told him that was the best part of her marriage—these days, the only good part.

"I don't see how you can blame yourself, Guthrie. And he's not a monster. He's my husband."

Guthrie gave a theatrical groan that set Ellen's teeth on edge. "Worst of all!"

"Yes, I thought that's what you meant."

Guthrie paced up and down and pressed one hand against his forehead. "You cannot imagine the torment it has been to me, lying alone and imagining what he must be putting you through. I've suffered terribly."

"Cheer up," Ellen said heartlessly, "it's not all that bad."

"You're so brave, Ellen. How can you bear being married to that maniacal killer? Being caressed by hands still red with your mother's blood?"

"He's not a murderer."

"Of course, you want to believe that." Guthrie halted his pacing, took Ellen's hands in his and looked down on her with a pitying, understanding smile. "Poor Ellen, you're only a weak woman after all, and you had to give in to him. Has he seduced you with his false glamour, or are you just bravely making the best of it?"

"I'm not bravely doing anything!" Ellen snatched her hands out of Guthrie's warm, slightly damp grasp. "Will you stop being dramatic and listen for one minute, Guthrie Bell? God help us all, I used to think Harry was immature until I tried to talk to you! He's an infuriating, self-centered, jealous man, but he didn't kill my mother. Fish-Mou' did. And I've got the proof of it."

Guthrie took a back step and stared at her.

"What proof?"

Ellen couldn't bear to recount the terrible, frightening scene in which Fish-Mou' had tried to rape her while whispering words of love to her long-dead mother. Even thinking about that day made her sick. But she could at least tell Guthrie about the Graeme silver and gold she'd found in Fish-Mou's box chair.

"Your precious cousin had loot from Fernshaws hidden in his chamber. A picture frame, an inkwell, a dirk, all with the Graeme arms. Obviously he stole Harry's ring in the same raid and then dropped it by my mother's body to throw suspicion on the Graemes."

"And where's this supposed loot now? Can you show it to me?" Guthrie demanded. "Not that I'm saying it would prove anything if you did, mind you."

Ellen remembered the pale crackle of flames rising above Fish-Mou's proud new roof. "Well, er, actually I suspect it got melted down in the fire."

"Poor Ellen," Guthrie murmured, "you're grasping at straws, aren't you? You want to believe this bloody-handed pirate innocent, so you have to pick on somebody else to blame—and who better than a dead man? I shouldn't be surprised if your sufferings have turned your brain. Don't worry, my love. As soon as I'm ransomed I'll come back with an army, if need be, to free you and bring you safely home to Scotland."

"Please don't bother!"

"Are you afraid he'll threaten your life if we attack? I think you'll be all right, my darling. The man seems quite insanely attached to you. In any case, you'd be better off dead than left at his mercy. Your nightmare is almost over, my love. I'll take care of you from now on."

Guthrie swooped down and enfolded Ellen in a hug that crushed her nose against his broad chest.

"Damn you, Guthrie, let me go!"

Her mouth was muffled in the folds of his shirt; the protest came out as "Muhmuhmuh!" which Guthrie could interpret as he liked. She pushed with both hands against his chest, and he relaxed his arms a fraction, but only so he could tilt her head back and cover her mouth with his own. Ellen squirmed unavailingly and only got bent slightly backward for her pains. Obviously Guthrie was too intent on playing out his own drama of passionate love to understand that she didn't want to participate. She quit struggling and waited for him to come up for air, reflecting bitterly that if he didn't let her breathe soon, she was probably going to faint in his arms. Which should leave her just the way he liked his women—limp, complaisant, and with nothing to say.

"If you're quite through with my wife," said a cold, sarcastic, English voice behind her, "I believe we have some unfinished business to discuss."

Guthrie raised his head and let go of Ellen so suddenly that she staggered. Harry caught her arm and helped her regain her balance.

"Thank you," she gasped with her first full breath. "I thought he was never going to let me go."

Harry's blue eyes were hard and dark. "It's a little late to try to convince me that you were unwilling, madam wife."

"You let her alone!"

Guthrie aimed a wild punch at Harry's head. Harry caught his wrist, twisted it slightly, and sent the off-balance Guthrie staggering ludicrously back into the pile of furniture at the far end of the room. Before Guthrie regained his feet, Yohannon and two other men had slipped past Harry and taken Guthrie's arms.

"You may remove that to the peel tower," Harry told them with a nod at Guthrie's flushed face. "I'm done with it."

"What about our 'unfinished business'?" Guthrie shouted. "I'll fight you for her! Give me a sword and we'll settle the matter here and now!"

Harry raised one eyebrow. "As far as I am concerned, the matter is settled. I have her. You don't. And I intend for it to stay that way. Why should I bother to run you through the body to emphasize the point? My unfinished business was with my wife. We have private matters to discuss. Come, madam."

Ellen accompanied Harry out of the room with as much

dignity as was consonant with being towed rapidly along by the upper arm. At the door Harry paused and looked back at Yohannon. "On second thoughts," he said, "keep the boy here. I'll talk with him later, after I've finished my discussion with Ellen. I would advise you," he told Guthrie in dulcet tones, "to be seated. I may be quite a while."

Once they were outside, Harry released Ellen's arm and bowed to her, motioning her to precede him up the stairs. Ellen picked up her skirts and swept upstairs in a freezing silence. Guthrie's shouts of rage followed them halfway up the grand stairway. Then there was abrupt silence, as if someone had clapped a hand over his mouth. The only sounds then were the swish of Ellen's skirts and the pad of Harry's feet in soft leather shoes.

She did not turn to face him until they were in the bedchamber with the door closed.

"I assume you set all this up with some ridiculous idea of trapping me in an affair with Guthrie?"

"Not so ridiculous," Harry corrected her. "It seems to have worked. I overheard some of that affecting scene before interrupting it."

"Then you heard me defending you."

"What a pity," said Harry, "I seem to have missed that part. I heard you and Guthrie making plans to send an army over the border to rescue you from my evil clutches."

"No, you heard Guthrie making plans. If he'd given me a chance to slip a word in edgewise, I'd have told him he was dreaming."

"He was indeed," Harry agreed. "Neither he nor anybody else will have a second chance to steal you away from here."

"That's not what I meant! I meant I don't want to be rescued."

"Funny, I didn't hear you say that. And Guthrie wasn't talking all the time. There was a long period of silence. In fact, that's what inspired me to interrupt you."

"If you must eavesdrop," said Ellen with a curl of her lip, "I wish you'd do it right, that's all. If you'd heard our conversation from the beginning, you'd know I have no desire to betray you. Especially not with Guthrie Bell. You can't hold me responsible for his fantasies."

"No? But you play such a large part in his dreams, surely you must have contributed to them."

"Believe what you will." Ellen turned away and leaned against one of the tall carved bedposts. "I'm tired of trying to convince you, Harry. I am here with you of my own free will, I'm your wife, I am trying to love you, but you're making it very difficult for me."

Harry slipped one arm about her waist from behind. "Try harder," he suggested, his voice a soft insinuating murmur in her ear. "Actions speak louder than words . . ." His other hand slid around to cup her breast.

Ellen let her body relax against his. His lips brushed the nape of her neck, and all the fine fair hairs there tingled under his touch. Her forehead rested against the hard carved wood of the bedpost; she smelled the sweet oil used to polish the wood, felt the silky smoothness of it under her hands.

"That's my sweet Ellen." His lips traveled along the line of her jaw; she turned her head to meet his kiss. Her mouth was bruised from Guthrie's awkward embrace. Harry's lips healed the soreness, warming her center, drawing her soul to meet his. She slipped one arm around his neck, melted into him, lost herself in the sensual sweetness of a moment outside time. She could feel his heart beating against her own breast; the fine-drawn tense muscles in his shoulders quivered under her hands. As his kisses traveled down to the curve of her neck, she half closed her eyes and sighed with pure pleasure. This was real, Harry holding her close, his lithe, wiry body demanding hers. The games he played of jealousy and mistrust were as unreal as bubbles bursting in the froth of a stream; the love that flowed between them was the current, swift and sure.

"Is it a little easier to love me now?"

"What?"

"You said I was making it difficult for you to love me. I'm trying to make it easier." The fastenings of her gown were falling away under his hands, and Ellen's anger at the way he'd manipulated her was falling away as quickly. When this was so wonderful, how could everything else between them go so wrong?

"That wasn't . . . what I meant."

His hand slipped into the half-opened bodice, caressing her breasts until she thought she would faint from pleasure. "Do you object?"

Slowly, languorously, Ellen moved her head back and forth. "Why are we always quarreling?" she murmured.

"I don't know. Maybe we should just stay in bed all the time."

"But it's broad daylight," she protested mildly when Harry lifted her onto the bed with her half-fastened gown falling about her.

"Mmm? When did you become shy?"

"They're waiting for you downstairs." Even in the midst of this sensual daze, Ellen blushed to remember Harry's last insinuating words to Guthrie. "Guthrie will think—"

"And he'll be absolutely right." He knelt over her, kissing her everywhere that his busy fingers uncovered her skin, until she could think of nothing but where his lips and tongue would tease her next. She was almost beside herself with frustrated excitement when his mouth enclosed the crest of her breast, pulling at her in a tender, testing action that made the center of her body melt into a delicious sweet warmth.

"Now, about that unfinished business . . ." Harry's weight was close on top of her. She cried out with surprise and pleasure as their bodies joined, feeling the warmth of him deep inside her. The quickening tempo of their mutual need became a part of her, her rapid heartbeat echoing the pulses of delight that controlled her. She could no more withstand the forceful pull of that rhythm than she could have kept her feet from dancing to a faerie piper's tune. All that had stood between her and Harry, her anger at his tricks and the pain of knowing he didn't trust her, was forgotten in the ecstasy that claimed her now.

"Harry," she breathed on a long, outgoing sigh as the music rose to its climax. She felt perfectly at one with him, feeling his involuntary quivers of passion as her own, holding him close within her and wishing they could stay that way forever. Her heart was pounding and her legs trembled as if they had been dancing from noon to night on a faerie mound. But the gray light of a cloudy afternoon still filled the bedchamber with its diffused radiance.

They lay quietly for some time. Harry's head rested on her breast; Ellen gently smoothed away the springy black curls with their hint of red, watching the slight tremor of his dark lashes against his cheek. He was awake, she knew, but neither of them spoke. Ellen was content for the moment just to lie in the warm circle of his embrace, letting the ugliness of their quarrel vanish in the soft joyful aftermath of their loving.

"Do you know now that I love you?"

"I always know it—in bed." Harry sighed and drew away from her slightly. "It's the rest of the time that doubts plague me."

"Then let's stay in bed forever." Ellen twined her arms about him and pulled him back to her.

Harry inclined his head to trace the ivory line of her arm with tiny nips of his teeth, interspersed with kisses. "I need you, Ellen. You have to stay with me. I'll make sure of it."

"You don't have to."

"That's a matter of opinion." His mouth was hard against the soft inner curve of her arm. "Whether I have to or not, I'll *be* sure of it. You're my wife, Ellen, and next time your father sees you, I want a flock of black-haired Graeme sons 'round your skirts to underscore the point."

Ellen thought her heart would burst from happiness. "I *thought* you were being a little less cautious than usual."

"Not at all. I've changed my objectives, that's all. Keeping you is more important to me than ending the feud."

"We couldn't do both?"

"One thing at a time." Harry's fingers trailed up and down the white curves of Ellen's body, making her shiver with delight. "First I'll make you love me, then I'll work on your relatives."

"I do love you," Ellen whispered. She nipped at his earlobe. "And I'm tired of arguing about it. If you don't believe me, I'll bite your ear off!"

"Ouch!" Harry let go of her to raise one hand to his ear. "I believe you would, you wild woman. Am I bleeding?"

"What sort of a pirate worries about a little blood?"

"Well, don't you see," Harry explained with great seriousness, "if you mangle me too ferociously, I might not be able to put a gold ring in there when next I go to sea."

"Would that hinder your acceptance among the fraternity of swashbucklers?"

"Terribly. Everybody who is anybody pierces bits of their anatomy and dangles gold from it."

"Mmm. Maybe you could pierce something else?" Ellen's lips traced the line of dark hair that arrowed down from Harry's chest toward his flat stomach.

"Oh, no. Not in your present mood. I'm not trusting you with anything that sensitive." Harry's fingers tangled in her hair, trying to stop her downward motion; then, as she reached her goal, he sighed and his hands relaxed. "Oh, well, perhaps I'll have to take a hostage of my own to ensure your good behavior."

It was soft and slow and very sweet, this loving, with time to enjoy all the details of existence. The springy feeling of Harry's dark-haired thighs under her cheek, the scent of lavender and dried herbs from the linen sheets, the high clear trill of birdsong outside—all blended into a shaking ecstasy that left them both breathless for some time.

"You taste like the sea," Harry murmured lazily.

Ellen blushed again. "Don't. It's not—"

"Not proper?" Harry guessed. "To talk about it? Do anything you like in a curtainless bedchamber in the broad light of day, but keep your mouth shut? Oh, no, that wouldn't have worked too well, would it? Perhaps—"

Ellen laid two fingers over Harry's mouth. "Whatever you were going to say," she told him, "don't. I'm feeling marvelously in charity with you right now, don't spoil it with lewd talk."

"Mmm." Harry nibbled at her fingers until Ellen snatched them away. "All right. I'm all for a pleasant home life. In pursuit of which, I have decided to set Guthrie Bell over the border without waiting for ransom."

"Oh, thank goodness!"

"Were you so concerned for the boy?"

"Oh, don't start that again," Ellen pleaded. "If you must know, I was afraid you were going to have him stay here at Fernshaws while you wrote to arrange a ransom."

"Wouldn't that be pleasant for you? The company of your dear old friend?"

"I might have thought so at one time," Ellen admitted, "but now I don't think I could stand it."

"Too difficult playing the two of us off against one another?"

Ellen ground her teeth and wished some part of Harry were between them. "You insist on misinterpreting everything I say. I am not in love with Guthrie Bell. I don't even like him very much anymore. He's just as egotistical as you, and just as bent on seeing his own version of everything."

"Hmm. Where does that leave your feelings toward me?"

"Somewhat less charitable than they were a few moments ago, believe me." If Ellen could have flounced off the bed in her state of nudity, she would have. As it was, she had to content herself with a disdainful stalk across the room to retrieve the garments Harry had flung off the bed as soon as he got them off her. He lay back, unashamedly naked, arms laced behind his head, and watched her with a grin of enjoyment.

"Can't you leave Guthrie Bell alone?" Ellen grumbled as she struggled back into her clothes. "Guthrie Bell this, Guthrie Bell that—anybody would think it was you who were in love with him, not I."

"I thought you said you weren't in love with him."

"You know perfectly well what I mean!" Ellen thrust her head through the petticoats and emerged, tousled and glaring, with the scraps of her bodice in one hand. "I'm not in love with him. I'd be perfectly happy to never see him again."

"That, no doubt," said Harry silkily, "is why you have been bending heaven and earth for a se'enight to get a chance of speaking with him." He pulled on his own garments, which, Ellen noticed, he had not tossed across the room. Only her clothes got the treatment of wild abandon.

"I thought you might give over your silly suspicions if you saw that I could speak with him without jumping into bed with him."

"Ah, yes." Harry's tone was creamy smooth. "That was indeed a very suspicion-quelling scene I happened on in the hall just now, wasn't it?"

"I hadn't expected him to grab me." Ellen pulled her bodice together any which way, all crooked and with half the laces not in their proper holes, and stared Harry in the eye. "Now you get this straight, Harry Graeme. I do not love Guthrie Bell. I do not even particularly care to see Guthrie Bell again. He bores me. Even talking about him bores me. I am flat delighted that you're putting him back over the border, and if you ever bring up his name again, I shall scream!"

"And yet," said Harry, "you were about to marry him."

Ellen stuck both fingers in her ears, shut her eyes, and screamed at the top of her voice until the sound of a quietly closing door told her that Harry was gone.

CHAPTER
❧ 19 ❧

The gray walls of Carnaby Irvine's peel tower presented a forbidding appearance at the best of times. In this stormy June, when the Scots king was taking castles and burning houses in his own west march to put down the rebellion of the Catholic lords, when beacons were loaded with oiled wood to blaze announcement of the expected Spanish invasion, the old tower seemed to be crouching low to the earth, its shuttered windows like closed eyes, the iron gate before the main door grinning like a cornered badger's show of teeth.

Inside, Guthrie Bell and Carnaby Irvine put their heads together over a table and drew maps of the border country with their fingertips dipped in a puddle of spilled wine. Carnaby's men could be trusted; the Bell men who now followed Guthrie had their master, Fish-Mou', to avenge; Verona Irvine, who might possibly have objected to the plans they were making, was safely upstairs nursing a horribly burned man with one eye put out, a man who cursed all the Irvines and Graemes impartially even while Verona nursed him. Even so, Carnaby and Guthrie instinctively lowered their voices while discussing how to get Ellen Irvine free of the bloody pirate who held her in Fernshaws.

"She's well, she's safe?" Carnaby asked for the hundredth time, scanning Guthrie's face for any sign of evasion.

"Well enough. As for *safe* . . ." Guthrie shrugged. "What woman is safe in Red Harry's hands?" His eyes flickered. "Don't ask me for details, Carnaby. We have to get her out of there."

How could he tell Ellen's father of the humiliating scene when, held by Harry's ruffians, he'd watched Harry drag Ellen away by brute force? Sneering at Guthrie, letting him know plainly just how he intended to abuse her. Worse, how could he tell Carnaby about the screams he'd heard from the bedchamber?

"Only one thing could have persuaded me to leave her there," he said at last, "and that was the hope of getting your help to free her."

And that was not quite true either. Even that hope wouldn't have taken Guthrie from Ellen's side until he was physically thrown out of Fernshaws. But he couldn't bring himself to tell Carnaby about Harry's sarcastic taunts when, doubtless after beating Ellen into submission, he'd come back downstairs to inform Guthrie that he was to be put over the border into Scotland at once.

"Oh, go on, get out of here!" Harry had snapped when Guthrie appeared suspicious of this sudden freedom. "I don't want you around here. She doesn't want you around. I'm supplying you with a horse to ride and a guide to see you don't fall off the horse and wet your pants in a burn between here and Scotland, God forbid anyone should say harm came to you at my hands. What more do you want?"

"I want to know that you'll not mistreat Ellen."

"Believe me," said Harry, "the shoe is on the other foot. You'd better get out, boy. You're not man enough to tame her."

"And you are? By beating her? By threatening her? By killing her like you did her mother? I'll see you damned first!"

Guthrie's ill-advised attempt to launch himself at Harry's throat had had the predictable result. Five strenuous minutes later he was sprawled on his seat outside the front door of Fernshaws, with a black eye and a bruised hand to add to his spiritual bruises. Somewhat to his surprise, the promised horse and guide were waiting there.

"I'll come back with an army," he promised himself before riding away with his pride bruised worse than anything else.

Carnaby's tower was closer than Fish-Mou's, and it was there he'd ridden, to find that Johnny Bell's new home had burned to the ground while he was dragged unconscious into captivity at Fernshaws. Johnny himself had survived by a miracle when the bed on which he lay collapsed, wrapping him in heavy brocade hangings that put out the flames around him. No one could explain how he had come to be stabbed through the eye with an iron candle spike, but they assumed it had been a piece of casual brutality on the part of some of Red Harry's men. The surgeon who tended him said that a fraction of an inch more and the spike would have penetrated the brain. In private, having heard Fish-Mou's delirious ravings, the surgeon thought it was a pity the spike hadn't done just that.

Now the Bells and the Irvines were grouped together for one final, deadly raid to put Red Harry Graeme, the murderer and kidnapper and rapist, out of their lives for good and all. Only one thing restrained them.

"We have to get Ellen out of there first."

Carnaby had said that almost as many times as he'd asked Guthrie to confirm that Ellen was safe and well. And every time, Guthrie felt a twinge of guilt at the thought that he'd tamely ridden away from Fernshaws, leaving her there. But what more could he have done?

"Will she leave?"

Guthrie studied the pattern of splinters and wine splashes on the tabletop, tracing idle patterns with one broad thumb. Ellen ought to leave. How could any woman stay with a beast like Red Harry? And yet in their one meeting she'd claimed that she didn't want to be rescued, that she considered Harry Graeme her husband, that he was innocent of her mother's blood.

"She says she loves him." The words felt like having his

own entrails dragged out of him. "It's pride, of course. She refuses to admit she made a mistake when she let him out of Johnny's cells. She'll never ask us to rescue her."

"Is she too proud to meet you again? If you got a message to her?"

Guthrie raised troubled eyes to the gray-haired man who faced him across the table. "I . . . don't know."

"Too proud to meet *me?*"

He shook his head slowly. "I don't know. I don't understand one damned thing about her," he admitted in a rush of injured feelings and bruised love. "But—I think she's infatuated with that pirate. She won't hear a word against him. She refuses to believe the truth."

"Then," said Carnaby slowly, "maybe she'd meet us to save his life. She has some crazy tale to make him out innocent, doesn't she? Let her know I'm willing to meet her and hear the story. If I'm convinced, I'll call off the feud and shake hands with young Graeme. Otherwise, he'll never know a peaceful night in that rebuilt mansion of his."

"You wouldn't really make peace with Red Harry?"

"Perish the thought!" Carnaby shook his head so vigorously that his thinning gray hair flew out in an incongruous halo around his face. "But thinking I might, that'll draw Ellen out. Once I have her safe, she'll see reason soon enough. And then we can strike at Red Harry with all the men in the marches, to put this English murderer out of the way permanently."

The series of lightning-swift raids into England that followed this decision tired Harry Graeme and his men, cost them cattle and houses, but seemed pointless otherwise. Harry spent sleepless nights guarding one of Fernshaw's outlying farms while Carnaby's men slit the throats of cattle at the other end of the fertile valley; labored through another night throwing buckets of water on the blaze that had been Ruthann's father's prosperous farmhouse; and sat up through two more nights holding the hand of a wounded man.

"No priest," Jenkyn o' the Side had croaked through his arrow-pierced throat. "No minister. A man o' the cloth leads a sheltered life, d'you see. He'd not understand—certain things—but Red Harry would." He could die peace-

ful, Jenkyn said, if Red Harry Graeme were there at his side,
to hand him over to the Lord and explain certain irregulari-
ties in a man's action-packed life.

Jenkyn was two long days and nights dying, and in the
gray dawn when he gave his last sigh, Ellen saw tears in
Harry's eyes. When they left the best bedchamber to pace up
and down in the long gallery, the windows along the side of
the gallery showed an ugly plume of smoke going up where
new burnings had taken place.

Harry cursed his own carelessness.

"You can't be everywhere at once," Ellen tried to comfort
him. "And you must rest sometime."

"Later."

With that word he was off, his face gray with fatigue and
sorrow, to ride to the ends of the valley and see what could
be done for the folk burned out of their homes. "Yohannon,
go with him!" Ellen pleaded. "Make him wear his armor.
Make him stop and eat something. Make him . . ."

Yohannon was in the saddle and gone, a guard of archers
riding behind him, before Ellen could think of any more
prescriptions for Red Harry's welfare. She sat down on the
mounting block in the center of the courtyard, wishing she
could just stay there and let out the tears of grief and
frustration welling up inside of her. Gentle, clumsy Jenkyn
gone—the valley slowly being wasted from one end to the
other—and Harry with eyes like something being burnt up
from the inside, as he tried to be everywhere at once and
stretch his guards to cover all the fertile valley that belonged
to Fernshaws.

The lady of Fernshaws couldn't bawl her heart out on the
mounting block like a kitchen maid.

The lady of Fernshaws ought to be thinking of something
she could do to help Harry defend his lands. Because it was
her fault, wasn't it? Oh, Harry hadn't said anything to her,
but they both knew that the raiders who struck out of the
night—and struck again, and again, and again—were
Carnaby Irvine's men. If Ellen had been in one of the
burning hamlets, she would have seen men who'd dandled
her as a baby putting the torches to English roofs, and
laughing as they worked.

She had failed completely to convince Guthrie Bell of

Harry's innocence—failed, Ellen thought miserably, because she'd lost her temper. She hadn't even had the courage to tell Guthrie exactly what Fish-Mou' Bell had tried to do to her. And Guthrie had been unconscious all the time he was locked up in Fish-Mou's cells. All he knew was that Ellen had let Red Harry loose and Harry's men had fired the house and taken him with them as a hostage. *Naturally* he didn't believe her.

Which meant that Carnaby didn't either. He still thought Harry Graeme had killed his wife. He was still bent on vengeance for that. Only he was afraid to attack Fernshaws direct, afraid Ellen would be hurt; so instead he waged this war of attrition that was slowly killing Harry.

Most raids, Ellen thought bitterly, had some reasonable purpose. Lifting cattle or sheep, usually. Which meant that the raiders had to go by known paths, and had to get away with a herd of lowing beasts, and had to make it home before a pursuit could be mounted. Each limitation cut down on the incidence of successful raids, made it possible to defend against attacks, turned it all into a game where the cleverest and quickest fellow won.

But what defense could there possibly be against Carnaby Irvine's project of wanton destruction? Where a proper reiving party consisted of many men, had to go where there was loot to be taken, and was slowed on the return by the need to herd the beasts they'd stolen, Carnaby suffered none of these limitations. One man alone could slip through the night to drop decaying sheep's guts down a well and poison the water; two or three armed men could turn a group of peasants out of their houses and burn the rooftrees; a group of five could slaughter a herd of cattle and disappear again, slipping over the border by separate, secret byways.

If only she could talk to Carnaby herself!

Ellen was still seated on the stone mounting block, elbows on her knees, chin on her fists, when her sleepy musings were interrupted by shouts and the sound of horses galloping just outside.

At last Carnaby had attacked Fernshaws.

"The fire! It was just a ruse to draw Harry off!" In the midst of her fear and excitement, while the few men Harry had left at Fernshaws rushed to defend the house, Ellen felt a moment's relief that the expected attack had come here and not elsewhere—not at Harry, for instance. Then she thought of what it would do to Harry if he came back from yet another disaster scene to find his new mansion a gutted heap of blackened timbers and rubble like the Fernshaws of eleven years ago.

"Ruthann, call the serving girls. Tell them to bring buckets. We can soak the walls from the upstairs windows." Ellen was on her feet again, a leather bucket full of water in her own hands, almost happy at the need for direct action.

By the time they'd established a chain of girls from the kitchen-yard well to the windows, the attack was over, and all Ellen had accomplished was to get water splashed along one outer wall and most of a red Turkey-work hall carpet.

"I never liked that carpet, anyway." Ellen sank into a chair and gazed ruefully at the angry red lines on her palms where the wire handle of the bucket had pressed. "But why would they go to all that trouble just to gallop around the house two or three times and get everyone excited?"

Her question was answered when she went upstairs to the big chamber she and Harry shared, now comfortably furnished with carpets and cushions and soft window draperies that rustled back and forth in the summer breeze. In the middle of the floor was a rock with a piece of paper tied to it.

Ellen stared at the scrap of paper wrapped around a stone, as if it might, in her hand, turn into an adder and bite her. She knew without looking at it that Guthrie had taken this means of getting a message to her. The brief attack had been only a diversion, a way to let him get close enough to the house to throw something in through her open chamber window.

"Merciful Heavens, will he never give up?" she murmured. Thank goodness Harry was away from home—he would have been bound to think the worst! But, of course, he had been drawn away by the burnings at the far end of the valley, so Guthrie could try to communicate with her.

He would be wanting her to come away with him, or at least to meet him secretly somewhere. The sensible thing to do would be to ignore the note. No, she couldn't do that. He'd only try again. Eventually Harry was bound to notice;

one couldn't expect a man to remain oblivious forever to rocks bouncing in at his chamber window, and it was certainly hopeless to wish that Guthrie might think of some subtler means of communication.

Well, then, a sensible woman would hand the note to her husband without reading it—without even unwrapping the black length of waxed string that bound it to the rock—so that he couldn't possibly suspect her of encouraging Guthrie.

She did not dare do that. What might Guthrie have said in the note? Protestations of love, promises to take care of her after she left Harry? He didn't seem to have grasped the situation at all. And Harry would take his most fantastical words as evidence that she still thought of running away with him.

Very well; she would read what Guthrie had written, and then she would either throw the note in the fire or take it to Harry, depending on what he had said. Neither was a very good solution, but anything was better than meeting Guthrie again and giving Harry more reason for his suspicions.

Ellen bent stiffly to pick up the rock. Her fingers were cold and clumsy; the string binding the note was hard to unknot, and as she jerked at it in frustration, it cut into her hands.

When she finally unfolded the paper, she read over the few sentences in Guthrie's bold handwriting, shook her head slowly, read them again, and folded the paper very small—small enough to fit into the tight, broad embroidered cuff of her undersleeve. She would have to talk to Harry, but it might be better if he did not know the suggestion came from Guthrie Bell.

Several hours later Ellen stood outside the long hall on the first floor where she'd met Guthrie. Harry had returned from a long day at the end of the valley, tired and muddy, with no more than a quick kiss of greeting for her before he plunged into discussions with his lieutenants. They had been shut up in the hall for over an hour now; the short summer night was drawing in, Harry would need to sleep and eat before dawn came all too soon, and she still had not had a chance to talk privately with him. If she didn't interrupt this interminable planning session, she was likely to get nothing of Harry but his snores in her ear and his muddy boots on the counterpane when at last he fell exhausted into bed.

Summoning up all her courage, Ellen pushed the door open and walked into the long hall where Harry, Eleazar, and Yohannon sat around a table covered with maps and letters. As she entered, Eleazar made a quick involuntary gesture to pull the maps toward him.

"The guards at Caerlaverock—" Yohannon, his back to the door, started to say something about powder stores; Eleazar's quick movement alerted him and he stopped in mid-sentence.

Harry looked up, dark brows slanting together in the beginnings of one of his quick daunting frowns; then he recognized her, laughed, and clapped Eleazar on the back. "No need to worry, old friend, it's only my lady come to refresh our tired eyes." He got up, smiling, and took Ellen's hands. "What, empty-handed? No posset for tired men?"

Behind him Yohannon casually slid a stack of letters over the open map; Eleazar leaned forward on the table, covering the remaining surface of the map with his broad forearms.

"Indeed, Harry, 'tis time you rested." Ellen took advantage of the opening he gave her. "Can you not leave this tedious business awhile?"

Harry shook his head. "I'm sorry, love. But we'd all be grateful for a cup of wine, hot, with spices and honey, the way you mix it. 'Twas chill riding for a summer day, with the wind blowing sea spray upon us until I think my bones are turned to cold saltwater."

"Sea spray? But—"

The smoke they'd seen that morning was at the eastern end of the valley. What had Harry, Eleazar, and Yohannon been doing at the coast? Ellen's eyes narrowed. The flat reaches of Solway Firth, near the sea, were a fine place for a body of horsemen to cross over into Scotland. The maps Eleazar and Yohannon were trying to conceal from her showed a stretch of coastline, though she couldn't recognize it from the brief glance she'd gotten. And the talk of powder and shot sounded as though Harry were planning a very serious expedition indeed.

"Are you going into Scotland?"

"Now whatever could have given you that idea?" Harry's

own eyes were flat blue, like glazed pottery, giving nothing away, and he kept steering her toward the door. "Go along now and mix us that wine posset, love, and send one of the kitchen maids along with it. I'll see you later—in our chamber—hmmm?" The quick kiss on the tip of her ear, the murmured last words, created a momentary cocoon of privacy around them. Ellen felt like a traitor, with the sharp folded corners of Guthrie's note sticking into her wrist under the cuff of her sleeve and Harry, unsuspecting, murmuring love words to her.

"I *need* to talk to you."

"Yes, love. Later. I've business to attend to now." Harry put her outside the door with gentle, loving force, and had turned back to his lieutenants before it swung shut. Ellen caught three words in Spanish, something about a ship, and then she was alone again, looking at a closed door.

A useless visit? No, not quite. She'd learned enough to be tolerably sure that Harry was planning a massive retaliatory raid against her father. By sea? Was that what the ship was for—so they could land a body of men on the coast and strike inland, rather than coming from the border as anyone would expect? Ellen frowned. That didn't seem like a terribly clever move just now. Everybody knew that the Spanish were assembling a great fleet to invade England; they might already have set sail. King James had feared that Herries and Maxwell, the rebellious Catholic lords, might have invited the Spanish to invade by way of this section of the Scottish coast. Ever since he subdued the rebellion, he'd been manning castles along the coast, setting men to light beacons in the event of an invasion, even refusing to sell his extra gunpowder to the English fleet because he feared he might have use for it himself. Perhaps she should point out to Harry—casually, without letting him know of her suspicions!—that no sane man would try a clandestine landing on the Scottish coast in this particular summer.

She'd bring the wine posset in herself, Ellen decided, and maybe she would be able to piece together a little more of their plans. How much time did she have to talk Harry into Guthrie's suggestion of a meeting? Without, of course, knowing it came from Guthrie! Oh, life was getting too complicated! It all made her head hurt. Maybe she'd have some wine posset herself.

They were through with their planning session when she returned with a tray of steaming cups; standing before the unlit hearth, maps and papers safely put away in one of the locked chests that served as window seats. That was a disappointment, but it was more than made up for by the fact that Eleazar and Yohannon drained their cups and took their leave almost at once, leaving Ellen alone in the twilight room with her husband.

She studied his face in the waning light as he drank the wine posset, taking not more than a few sips before he put the cup down with a slight nod. He was always abstemious before action; Ellen had lived with him long enough to learn that much. And though his face still looked drawn and tired, the lines etched by fatigue were lifted and lightened by a dancing excitement, a contagious quiver of half-suppressed smiles. Oh, yes, the signs were clear enough. He was planning some direct action on his own account, something to wipe out the frustration of the last weeks. God send, it might not be within the next two or three days!

"I know what you're planning," Ellen blurted out without preamble.

Harry raised one dark brow and stretched out his hand for the wine cup. "Do you indeed? Listening at the door, were you?"

"I didn't need to. It's obvious to anyone with the least sense—anyone who knows you at all."

"The devil, you say!" Harry regarded her with more interest. "Do you think the Scots have figured it out too?"

Could he really be so foolish as to think that Carnaby wouldn't be expecting a retaliatory raid? "They'll be waiting for you."

Harry's eyes flashed a warning blue. "You didn't warn them, did you?"

Strange, how it still hurt, that he could accuse her of such a thing. "I wouldn't. But they're not stupid. It's the obvious move." Ellen thought of the one argument that might appeal to him. She moved forward and took the wine cup from his hand, entwined her fingers in his and traced the embroidered slashes in his doublet sleeve with her free hand. "Harry, Harry, I never thought you'd be so dull-witted as to do the obvious."

"I had rather hoped it might be a surprise," Harry admitted.

"Can't you try other means? If only you could talk it over with them, you might be able to come to an agreement."

"Diplomacy has been tried." Harry withdrew his fingers from her own and took up the wine cup again. He did not drink, but stared thoughtfully down into the depths of the cup, swirling the dark red liquid about as if he could read his fortune in the spirals he created. "Tried, and failed. It's too late to go that route."

"Is it?"

He set the cup down on the table so suddenly that wine splashed over the edge and sprinkled the bare table with bright red drops. Ellen caught her breath at the unlucky omen.

"Yes. Much too late. And don't keep trying to talk me out of it, Ellen. It's what I came here for."

"Yes," said Ellen dully, "I know." He'd returned to Fernshaws for revenge. Her discoveries had come too late to stop the feud; her father and Harry now had new wounds to avenge, new battles to fight. "But I'd hoped . . . you might find other things that mattered more to you by now."

"I love you," Harry said. "But that doesn't turn me from my duty."

Duty? To kill, burn, maim, and slaughter? Ellen shook her head in passionate revulsion against the code of the border, the code she'd been raised in. What had seemed only right, when it was a case of her family against others, looked like plain murder when it was husband pitted against father. "And I love you," she cried. "But they're my people too—shall I forget that?"

Harry's face closed down, unreadable and blank as a defended fortress. "And I thought you were concerned for my safety," he said softly.

"I am! I'm concerned for everyone's safety! Don't condemn me because I can't forget who I am and where I come from!"

"Then," said Harry, "don't you condemn me for exactly the same thing?"

It wasn't the same thing at all, Ellen wanted to tell him. This battle wasn't between Irvines and Graemes, Scots and English; it was between life and death. And she and Harry were irrevocably, forever, on opposite sides. He had put on the black uniform of Death, and no word of hers could make him forsake it. She turned away, desolate, and did not see the puzzled look in his blue eyes.

A word of explanation then might have saved them both months of needless suffering. But not knowing how deeply they had misunderstood one another, neither of them proffered that word. Harry let Ellen go from the room without voicing his puzzlement that she should feel so passionately about his plans to help England against the Spanish threat, and she gave up her attempt to talk him out of slaughtering her family.

As she wearily mounted the broad stairs, the sharp edges of Guthrie's folded note pricked her wrist under the embroidered cuff of her sleeve. There was that one hope left. She would meet Guthrie and try for an explanation, even though she had to go alone and secretly.

CHAPTER

❦ 20 ❧

A rising ripple of hills, high curves of sparse pale grass continually swept by the east wind, lay between the hamlet of Ravenstane Rig on the English side of the border and the immense standing stones called the Three Dancing Maidens on the Scots side. It had never been satisfactorily settled which country owned this barren land. Scots and English alike grazed their cattle on it in the infrequent times of peace; Scots and English alike avoided the high empty hills when war or feud might bring a troop of light-armed riders galloping across the ridge in either direction.

Guthrie had asked Ellen to meet him by the Dancing Maidens, on the Scots side. His note assured her that they would be in no danger of being observed. When she reached the meeting place she understood why. If Guthrie had been possessed of a sense of humor she would have suspected him of exercising it at her expense. The five houses comprising Ravenstane Rig were now five blackened and empty shells. The fury of the blaze had scorched the leaves off a sheltering tree behind the biggest house; the continually whistling little winds that blew across this desolate waste had kept a smoldering fire going along the great rooftree.

Ellen tethered her horse to the scorched tree and walked up the hill to the meeting place. The three standing stones were dark, brooding presences against the pale blue sky, hulking outlines that almost seemed to move in menace as she approached them. The wisps of cloud blowing across the sky behind the stones were responsible for that illusion. Ellen was not afraid to approach the stones, not in broad daylight. All the same, she nearly jumped when one of the stones split itself in two and the smaller part walked toward her.

"Startled you, didn't I?" Guthrie grinned down at Ellen and reached to take her hands in his.

"Not a bit of it. After all, I was expecting you." Now that he was before her, she could see why she hadn't noticed him at first. His jerkin and trews of mouse-gray leather blended with the gray stone, while his dark green shirt could have been the moss on the rocks. A soft cap to match the shirt was pulled down low over his blond hair. "You're dressed like a reiver," she blurted out.

Guthrie grinned again. "Am I? Perhaps I'll have to steal something from the English, then." He seemed uncommonly pleased with the effect of his small surprise. Or was something else making him smug?

Ellen didn't know why she was so nervous; she'd made quite sure that she was not followed from Fernshaws. But she couldn't keep from glancing around at the long crests of the hills falling away into Scotland. The rustling noise she heard to her left was only the breeze stirring the tufts of pale grass along a ridge; the shadow she glimpsed to her right belonged to a soaring hawk, no menace to creatures as big as Ellen and Guthrie.

"You can tell my father he's made a small mistake," she said. "Ravenstane Rig doesn't belong to Harry. He'll have all the landowners of the border out against him if he burns so indiscriminately."

"Will he? Perhaps instead they'll turn against the pirate who's settled in their midst and brought this trouble down upon them."

"Harry's no pirate! At least," Ellen corrected herself, "not anymore. He only wants to settle down and live peaceably on his own land."

"And peaceably kill a few Irvines whenever he gets the chance. Ellen, you must come out of there! Don't you see that you are his best weapon against Carnaby? We daren't attack Fernshaws while Harry has you."

"So you burn out defenseless villagers instead?"

Guthrie shrugged. "They're used to it. If it weren't us, it would be somebody else. They'd no business to be settling this close to the Scots side anyway."

Ellen studied his face in silence, searching for some sign of the boy she had grown up with. "You've grown hard, Guthrie."

"Aye. Maybe now I'll have more success with you. You seem to have a preference for murdering brutes!"

Ellen's hand struck him across the face before she thought. "You'll take that word back! Harry's no murderer, and well you know it, if you weren't too pigheaded stupid to believe the evidence! Fish-Mou' Bell was the killer who put the blame on Harry!"

Guthrie grabbed her by the shoulders and pulled her to him. "D'you think you're safe, accusing a dead man? Think again. Johnny survived the firing of his house. He lived to tell us how one of Harry's men stuck an iron spike through his eye for the sport of it—probably on Harry's command. Is that the kind of man you want to live with, Ellen?"

Ellen could feel the high thin edge of hysteria sharp within her, making her laughter forced and brittle. "He's aye a fine liar, Fish-Mou' Bell. 'Twas I struck him down, Guthrie, to keep him from raping me while you lay unconscious. And I thought I had killed him—I wish I had!"

"You don't know what you're saying," Guthrie told her. "You're hysterical. You couldn't hurt a man, Ellen. You're too sweet and gentle."

His arms were tight about her, imprisoning her hands. "You don't know me," said Ellen between her teeth. "You never have. You're in love with a picture you painted yourself, Guthrie, and it's nothing to do with me if the picture happens to have my face on it! I tell you I tried to kill Fish-Mou', and I wish I'd succeeded. You didn't see his mad face when he had me alone in his chamber, you didn't hear him calling me by my mother's name, you didn't feel his fat hands tearing the dress off my body! *Don't tell me what I wouldn't do!*"

"You're making it up." Guthrie sounded uncertain. "You have to be. Johnny wouldn't attack you—he wanted us to marry. He suggested it."

"I'm sure he did!"

"Besides. He *can't.* Red Harry's men took care of that. Hasn't he suffered enough at the hands of the Graemes, Ellen, without you blackening his name besides?"

"Believe what you will." Ellen felt too tired to struggle any longer. "The wound he took was an accident of battle, not some beastly plan of Harry's. And maybe he couldn't have raped me, but he had plenty of alternative ideas. Of course he promoted the marriage, Guthrie. His idea was that you should get sons on me, while he had me to play with the rest of the time."

"Having previously murdered your mother and cast the blame on Harry."

"Yes!"

Guthrie shook his head pityingly. "Ellen, Ellen, will you never give up? You can't prove one wild accusation by piling another in its place. There are no witnesses to any of these things you allege against my uncle."

"Of course there aren't," Ellen flashed. "I never said he was stupid—just mad and vicious!"

"Whereas there's a weight of evidence against Harry. Look at your own story, Ellen! On one side, a respected member of a good Scots family, a man who's been a friend of your own family for years; on the other, a bloody-handed pirate and a girl who's so beglamoured by his dark charm that she runs from safety to his arms. Ellen, Ellen, Ellen, give him up. Come back to your family. Let the men who love you and care for you get rid of Red Harry for you. You're safe now, Ellen, I have you safe, I won't let you go again."

His voice was low, soothing, as if he were trying to weave a spell of words about her while he rocked her against his broad chest. Ellen felt cold and helpless, and she began to regret the care she'd taken to slip away from Fernshaws unobserved. She had failed entirely to convince Guthrie,

and his jest about "stealing something from the English"
began to take on sinister meaning to her. Oh, why had she
been such a fool as to come alone? She hadn't the strength to
get away from him, if he decided to force her to come back
to Scotland with him. She would have to use her wits to get
out of this and safely back to Fernshaws.

Back to Harry.

The image of him, standing with his legs spread and
hands on his hips, smiling at her with those wicked blue eyes
dancing with merriment, was so strong that she could
almost believe he was there beside her.

"I don't know, Guthrie." Ellen let her knees sag slightly so
that more of her weight leaned on Guthrie's arm. "I'm so
tired, so frightened. You'll do what is best, of course. You
always do."

"Yes, I do, don't I? I'm glad you finally recognized that."

How unbearably smug he sounded! Ellen rested her
forehead against his shoulder, looking down at the ground
so that he couldn't see the horrible face she felt compelled to
make. She had to make him feel confident enough of her
that he would let her go; more, she had to get him occupied
so that she could get to her horse. If flattery would save her,
flattery he should have.

"Yes, Guthrie. You must guide me. But—forgive me—I
came away from Fernshaws fasting, and now I feel too weak
to ride on." If he went to his horse to get something for her
out of his saddlebags, she might have a chance to run back to
the English side, to get to her own horse.

Guthrie frowned. "I don't know, Ellen. I've nothing with
me, and we must get well away from here. Can't you make it
a few miles at least? Perhaps later we can stop at some
cotter's for refreshments."

The silly gowk! Ellen raged inwardly. He'd set out for this
meeting without food or drink in his saddlebags, as though
the frontier he and Carnaby had ravaged were a prosperous
high road lined with inns. She'd have to think of something
else.

"Perhaps you're right. I'll just go back to get my horse.
No, you'd better stay here—she is shy of strangers, that
mare, she might nip you if you come too close," Ellen
improvised.

Damn the man! He insisted on walking beside her, one arm about her waist for support. How would she ever get away? Oh, well, they were walking toward her horse and away from his. If she could persuade him to let her mount, to spare her the exertion of walking back up the hill, then she'd be mounted and he'd be afoot and some distance from his own horse. Ellen relaxed. Yes, this was even better than her first plan. She could even put up with Guthrie's kissing her ear and murmuring sweet promises at her.

Only a few steps more and they'd be at the tree where she'd tethered the mare. They were almost there now, just passing the blackened shell of the first burnt-out house. The four stone walls still stood, surrounding a pitiful heap of ashes where the roof timbers and the thatched roof had collapsed in the center. Through the empty doorway Ellen glimpsed a flicker of movement, as though a vagrant breeze stirred up the ashes for a moment. Distracted, she almost forgot to respond appropriately to Guthrie's love words. He paused and looked at her expectantly. Had he asked her a question?

"You know best, Guthrie." That should be a fairly safe answer, whatever he'd said.

Guthrie's tender smile nauseated her. She forced herself to smile up at him in response, saw his eyes flicker toward something behind her, felt a hand on her shoulder tearing her away from him even as his smile changed to a look of slack-jawed amazement.

"I've mentioned before that I don't care for your unfortunate habit of laying hands on *my wife,* Bell."

Harry stepped between her and Guthrie, one hand on the hilt of the short, serviceable knife which he used to more effect than most men could use a sword.

"It's her decision," said Guthrie. "And she chooses to go with me."

"No, I don't!" Ellen said, her protest drowned out by Harry's simultaneous statement.

"I don't care what you two have agreed; *my* decision is that she stays."

Guthrie was smiling again, standing easily in front of Harry as though he enjoyed this encounter. In the midst of her shock Ellen felt a small, niggling worry. Why wasn't

Guthrie more afraid? Harry was armed, he wasn't, and he himself thought Harry a cold-blooded murderer who'd feel no compunction at striking down a wounded man.

"Ah. But nobody asked your opinion, *Red Harry Graeme!*"

The last words were pitched higher, almost shouted; a moment later Ellen saw why. The high ridge behind the Three Dancing Maidens was a-glitter with steel helmets, men rising out of hiding with their weapons ready. She threw herself in front of Harry, felt his arm jerking her backward by the wrist; he yanked the mare's reins loose by breaking the branch they were tied to, leapt into the saddle and hauled her up before him. His heels thudded into the mare's sides; the horse dashed forward, almost directly at Guthrie. Ellen had a confused impression of Guthrie's large hands snatching at the reins, a swerve of the mare in mid-stride and a crashing impact that almost jolted her from her precarious seat. Harry's arm was around her, tight enough to hurt, maybe to break a rib or two, but that didn't matter as long as he helped her stay on the mare. Ellen worked one leg up and over the mare's back, clamped her knees on either side, and only then looked back to see Guthrie rising from the turf while his men and Carnaby Irvine's came down the long sloping hill after them.

"We always . . . seem . . . to wind up riding double!" Harry shouted in her ear. The wind of their passage whipped Ellen's hair loose about her face and turned up her skirts and petticoats into a frothy sea about her knees. "It's a good thing you stole my best horse to run away on."

"I didn't run away!" Her voice was weak against the rising wind that pulled at them as they crested the hill.

"What?"

When she tried to turn around to shout into his face, his arm held her too tightly. "Oh, no, my sweet, you're not leaving me this time."

Fuming, Ellen gave up the attempt. Explanations would just have to wait until they got back to Fernshaws. She had enough trouble winning an argument with Harry under the best of circumstances; give him the added advantage of being able to talk into her ear while the wind blew all her words away, and she'd never get anywhere.

But would they get back? Ellen shut her eyes and prayed. It seemed to her that she could hear the pounding hooves of the pursuit almost upon them already. She opened her eyes and saw men all around them—but English, not Scots.

Of course. Even Guthrie hadn't been fool enough to come alone to a meeting on the border. Why should she think Red Harry would do so? Yohannon was riding on one side, Eleazar on the other, and Harry's men fanned out around and behind them. She was as safe now as if she were already at Fernshaws. Ellen relaxed and almost enjoyed the ride back, now that she knew she was safe against being taken by the Bells and Irvines.

Once there, Ellen found that Fernshaws was no longer the haven she'd prayed for. Peace might be something not to be found again under the same roof with herself and Red Harry Graeme.

From the outside it seemed peaceful enough, the great square block of a house with candles lighting all the windows against the blue-gray of a long summer twilight. On the inside it resembled a battlefield, as Ellen and Harry carried their running battle from room to room. Shouting, pacing, interrupting themselves occasionally to gulp down a glass of wine or pick up some of the cold food Ruthann had left out, they raged through the house without settling a single one of their private differences.

"What do you mean, you weren't running away?" Harry shouted at her almost before they'd entered the house. "Am I not to believe the evidence of my own eyes? Did I not see you with your head on the shoulder of that gormless boy, letting him seduce you back to Scotland before my face?"

"You saw me trying to get away from him!"

"You looked mighty compliant to me."

"I had to trick him. I was trying to make him feel secure."

"Oh, yes. You're very good at that. I had almost begun to trust you again!" Harry took Ellen's arm and thrust her before him into the great hall where candles were lit and food set out. "Come in here. I'm not minded to make a public display of our differences. We can talk in private."

"What's there to talk about? You've made it perfectly clear that you don't trust me, and there's an end on it." Ellen marched over to the table and picked up a gingerbread

knight with marchpane icing. The weakness she'd feigned
for Guthrie was truly upon her now; her head was swimming and her knees shaking, and she wanted to cram sweets
in her mouth. She wanted to lie down too. But she was too
angry to relax.

"I don't. Trust you. But I'd like to." Harry leaned against
the wall, one booted foot propped on a low carved chest,
and watched her with his arms folded.

"Then I suggest you cultivate the faculty. It'll never come
without practice." Ellen bit the head off the gingerbread
knight with a vicious snap of her small white teeth and
followed it up with a bite of his marchpane lance. The
sweetness rushed into her blood, making her head spin but
giving her momentary strength.

"Wouldn't you like to help me? I'm all agog to hear your
explanations of just why you bribed my servants, stole my
best mare, and sneaked over the border to meet Guthrie
Bell—all alone—if you didn't intend to run away with
him."

Ellen licked the last of the marchpane icing off the fancy
cake, slowly and deliberately, while she thought how to
convince Harry. "I wouldn't have gone alone, Harry, if I'd
thought you would come with me."

"Less than totally convincing!" Harry jeered. "What
woman brings her husband to an assignation with her
paramour?"

"All I wanted to do," said Ellen, "was to stop the fighting.
I thought if I could convince Guthrie that you hadn't killed
my mother, maybe he could convince my father, and then
they would stop attacking us, and then—maybe—you
wouldn't have to go into Scotland and attack them."

"How noble-sounding! But it would carry more weight if
you had any reason to think I meant to continue the feud."

Ellen stared.

"But I heard you planning it! Last night only, Harry, I
begged you not to raid into Scotland, and you wouldn't even
listen to me!"

It was Harry's turn to stare. "Last night . . . Oh, *that*. Was
that what you thought I meant to do?"

"You admitted as much to me. It's no good, now, trying to
say you'd no such plan."

Harry began to laugh: great, gasping, crowing laughs that took all the breath from his body and bent him nearly double with each convulsion. "Oh, you precious fool! Almost," he gasped between laughs, "almost I believe you. Even you couldn't make up such a tale. And me worrying my brains out that you'd guessed and had gone to spill my secret to the Scots by way of young Bell. You really didn't know?"

"Know what?" But Harry had gone off again into whoops of laughter, and when he straightened, his eyes were watering from laughing so hard and all Ellen could hear was his voice repeating, "Almost I believe you . . . almost . . . almost . . ."

Ellen felt at once very tired and furiously angry. How dare Harry drag her around, call her a liar, shout at her, accuse her, and now *laugh* at her? Was she to spend her entire life defending her every action against his baseless suspicions? Her shoulders sagged under the weight of it all, the long bloody history of raids and counter-raids that she was trying to stop. How could one girl by herself end a feud when the men on both sides lived for nothing but fighting?

"If you can't believe me, pray for faith," she told him. "I'm not going to defend myself any longer. It's been a long day. I'm for bed."

"Oh, me too, sweet silly heart of mine. Me too." Harry reached for Ellen as she passed him.

"I'll not lie any longer with a man who doesn't trust me!" Ellen snatched her skirts out of Harry's unsteady grasp and slapped him across the face with all her force. Her open hand stung from the blow; Harry straightened up and she saw the red marks of her fingers standing out against his cheek. Suddenly afraid, Ellen picked up her skirts and ran for the staircase. Harry was close on her heels, but he slipped on a rug at the landing and she managed to reach their chamber ahead of him, turn the key in the lock, and shout renewed defiance through the keyhole.

"You'll not come in here until you're ready to believe in me, Red Harry!"

"I'll come to you whenever I please!" Harry's voice shook the panels in the door. "You're a fool, Ellen, and we have to talk, and I'm not explaining myself through a locked door. Now let me in!"

"Why? So you can bully me some more? Go ahead. Say anything you want to say from there. Maybe you can even convince me."

"And what'll you do if I fail? Run back to your father's house?"

"At least he doesn't call me a liar every day and twice on Sundays," Ellen shouted through the door. "It would be a refreshing change, being among folk who know that I mean what I say."

"I'll not let you go!"

"I'll not live as any man's prisoner!"

A thud against the door was the only answer. From the sound of it, Harry was using one of the tables in the hallway as a battering ram.

"Break down that door," Ellen screamed between thuds, "and I'm away to Scotland!"

The heavy thuds stopped abruptly. Ellen backed toward the bed and sat down. Was it possible that she'd made Harry back off with her threat? Was he ready to talk like a reasonable human being, instead of one minute accusing her of adultery and the next minute laughing himself silly and trying to drag her into bed?

"'Reasonable' and 'Red Harry' are words that don't belong in the same sentence," Ellen muttered. More likely he'd gone downstairs for a pike or an antique halberd with which to split the panels of the door. No, she heard his voice outside. He was talking to somebody else; the words were muffled by the door, she couldn't hear what he was saying. She stole to the door, knelt down and peered through the keyhole.

Harry had turned away from the door; his back was toward her. Even though she couldn't see his face, his posture and the tense, quick tattoo of his fingers beating against one thigh betrayed his sense of urgency. He was talking to a man who stood just below him on the stairs, breathing heavily. Yohannon? Eleazar? No, the messenger raised his voice now and she could mark the broad Northumberland accent; he must be one of the North Country men who'd gravitated to Harry's ship during his years at sea.

"Ah tell yees, t'sheep's raady noo, an' she'll no' wait!"

Ellen grimaced. These Englishmen with their broad accents—she couldn't understand half of what they said. Why couldn't they talk in good honest Scots? And what was all this fuss about a sheep? Oh, he must mean a *ship*. So she'd been right in guessing that Red Harry meant to raid from the sea, making a quick strike inland at her father's lands! And so much for his contention, just now, that he never meant to attack Carnaby at all! Ellen's hands clenched into fists as Harry dismissed the man with a pat on the shoulder and turned back to the bedchamber door. She retreated on tiptoe toward the bed, not wishing to betray that she had been listening.

"Ellen?" Harry's voice came low and muffled through the door.

"Ellen, I have to go now. It's urgent."

"I'm sure it is," said Ellen bitterly. "Pray, don't let any desire to salvage what's left of our marriage stand in the way of your masculine need to burn, loot, and destroy! Why should I have expected you to be different from any other man of the borders?"

But he had been different, when she'd first known him. What had happened to the man who would risk having his raid discovered and himself killed rather than frighten a little shepherd boy? Had the bitterness and distrust between them hardened him?

"What's that? I couldn't quite hear you." Harry paused, and Ellen heard his feet shuffling on the floorboards just outside. Indecisive? Red Harry Graeme?

"Well, never mind. I have to—well, it's best you shouldn't know. If there's trouble afterward, you should be able to convince them you're innocent."

That sounded as if he didn't expect to return from the raid. What was this, a suicide expedition? Ellen flew up from the bed, hands clenched at her breast. "Harry, don't go!"

It was too late; by the time her shaking fingers managed to turn the key in the stiff new lock, the door swung open to an empty hall and the sound of horses galloping away.

CHAPTER

❧ 21 ❧

Harry had certain small detours to make along the way, waiting men to alert and plans to set in motion; the July day was fading into cool blue dusk when at last he rode into Carlisle. Eleazar and Yohannon had led the rest of his men straight on to the small harbor at Rokele, where the ship awaited them. They were a rowdy crew, laughing and shouting with the anticipated joy of going back to sea, a good deck underfoot, a good salt wind blowing in their faces, and no more of this landsman's messing about with horses and cattle. The thought that many of them would probably die in the coming battle did not seem to trouble them unduly; and Harry, who was troubled, could not find it in his heart to quench their merriment. Better to let them wend their roistering way down to the sea, celebrating without thought of the morrow.

He was surprised at himself, at the black pall that had hung over his spirits ever since he left Fernshaws. He did not feel like himself at all, Red Harry Graeme, the most daring Englishman ever to raid the Spanish Main. What had happened to the boy who used to go into action juggling a knife in either hand, a jest on his lips, and a bawdy word to encourage the crew?

"The boy's grown up," Harry told himself, "and about time too."

But there was more in it than that, he knew. In the years since he'd left home, he had cared very little for life—his own, or anybody else's. After a gossiping North Country seaman had brought him the news of the burning of Fernshaws, Harry had crossed the line from daring to foolhardiness, from courage to reckless death-seeking. He looked back now on some of the exploits of his seafaring years and shook his head with a wry smile. An unbiased observer would have said that Red Harry Graeme didn't really want to live, perhaps felt he didn't deserve to live. By the strict code of revenge and counter-revenge that governed the borders, he should have been back in England, burning out Irvines and Bells in retaliation for what they'd done to his family. Instead he'd spent years risking his neck on the Spanish Main, as if to prove that whatever kept him from returning to England, it wasn't cowardice.

And when at last he'd returned, wealthy now and able to finish the feud, hadn't he been relieved that England's danger and Frankie's need forced a different role upon him? The old feud had provided convenient cover for his activities this summer upon the border, but he had not been free to pursue it to its logical conclusion—and now, understanding Carnaby's motive for burning out Fernshaws, he was glad that he hadn't.

None of which explained why, now when the time for action was upon him, he was riding into Carlisle town with a leaden heart and a strong desire to turn around and make for Fernshaws again.

For Ellen.

And she thought he was headed over the border to raid her father's lands, to carry on the feud. And she was there in Fernshaws, hating him for it. If only there'd been time to explain!

Harry shifted in the saddle, reined his horse in to avoid trampling a child in the street, and stared moodily at the red glow of sunset reflected in the pools of water between the cobblestones. The fine ship he was taking command of would soon look like that, its deck spattered with red wetness. He'd never minded the prospect of death before. But the prospect of not coming back to Ellen—that he minded horribly.

What odds did it make? Harry told himself to stop worrying about the girl. He had proof enough that she was a false jade, forever sneaking off to her lover Guthrie Bell behind his back, making up sly stories about how all she wanted was to make peace between the families. So what if he hadn't been able to explain his plans to her before he left? It wouldn't matter to her what his reasons for leaving were; now that he wasn't at Fernshaws to keep an eye on her, she would be away to Scotland as she'd threatened.

Harry's lips tightened to a thin line, and an old fishwife scurried out of his way. The silver-shining fish packed into the wicker creel on her back reflected the last dying sunlight; the gleam of their scales made him think of chests of Spanish silver. What good had all the wealth of the Indies done him? It hadn't bought Ellen's love.

No. He wouldn't go into battle believing her false. What had she said to him in that last bitter quarrel? "If you can't believe me, then pray for faith."

Harry raised his eyes to the sunset sky, glowing with red and purple clouds behind the tall peaked gables of the houses on either side of the street. "I will believe in her," he vowed. "I *do* believe." He would come home victorious, and she would be waiting for him at Fernshaws, and he would give up the sea for good and together they would build a new life in the new, grand mansion he'd raised on the Graeme lands.

She would be waiting for him on the lowest steps of the great central staircase, dressed in her simple green gown and with her silvery hair loose about her face, the way he loved her best. Harry fixed that image in his heart as if it were a talisman to keep him safe through the battle. It was so real to him that he no longer saw the crowded street through which his horse picked its way, the open market stalls about the cross or the liveried men who grouped themselves around him as he crossed the marketplace.

A tug on his horse's reins roused Harry from his reverie.

He scowled at the man who'd presumed to stop him, a squat beetle-browed fellow in a blue stuff doublet. "And what may you want, sirrah?"

"Lord Scroope wants a word with you."

"The warden? Oh, aye. I was just coming to call on him."

"We'll escort you," said the beetle-browed man with a grim smile, nodding to someone behind them. Harry twisted around in his saddle and saw with a prickle of apprehension that there were six more men in dark blue doublets riding just behind him. Two on either side spurred their mounts and came up beside him, and the man who'd accosted him went on in front. He was well boxed in—not, Harry thought, that he couldn't have won free if he chose, but he could hardly do so without creating an unseemly brawl in the marketplace. And what was the point? He'd been going to call on Scroope anyway; it was only courtesy to let a man know when you were about to commit serious annoyances upon his neighbors to the north. And Scroope should understand that he had the queen's warrant for what he meant to do.

The warden's chamber was on the second story of his house, a long narrow room with a desk at one end and piles of papers almost blocking the light from the one casement window behind him. Through the small glass panes Harry could just make out the glimmer of daylight and the long slope of a roof just below the window level. In front of the window, his face cast in shadow, sat a man he barely recognized from his boyhood memories.

Henry, the ninth Baron Scroope of Bolton, had held patents as warden of the west march and captain of Carlisle since 1563. Harry remembered him as a vigorous, ruddy-faced man with mud on his boots, who wore his spurs indoors and out and talked largely of hunting hounds and the game to be found on both sides of the border. It was somewhat a shock to find that the large healthy man of his childhood memories had aged into a fat, querulous old man with thinning hair and a sagging chin that drooped over the high starched ruffles of his collar.

It was even more of a shock to find that the warden was in a towering rage with him.

"Queen's patent? Queen's patent?" Scroope repeated in a

voice that trembled with anger. "You're a damned wee liar, Harry Graeme, and if I were the man I used to be, I'd put ye over my knee and skelp ye! Do you not know it's march treason, what you've done?"

"But I've not done anything—yet," Harry protested, somewhat bewildered by this tremulous outburst. He glanced toward the small leaded panes of Scroope's study windows and saw only dark blue sky and dark leaded rooftop. The deepening sky outside perfectly matched the blue doublets of the liveried guards standing before each window and the door. In an agony of impatience Harry drummed the fingers of one hand against his thigh. If he wasn't at Rokele soon, they'd miss the evening tide on this perfect, calm, moonless night. There'd never be a better night for his plans, not to mention that news of the ship in harbor would soon get out and make his work that much more difficult. And Frankie was waiting for him! He groaned inwardly and tried to break into Scroope's aggrieved, whining lecture. He'd as easily have crossed the Solway at high tide.

"March treason," Scroope repeated, thumping his desk with a chased-silver paperweight representing two dogs bringing down a stag. "Treason, d'you hear me, and I could hang you for it if I chose. Do you understand the scope of a warden's powers, young man? I'm the law of England here on the border. I'm empowered to receive fugitives, to take my lieges against thieves and to days of truce, and to try all resets, witchcrafts, slaughters, thefts, and any other capital crimes—of which this is certainly one. Not that I'm about to hang a Graeme of Fernshaws, but damnit, man, you've put me in an awful bad light with her majesty! What she'll say when she hears of it, I dare not think. She'll say I can't control my own march, and she's right, when my gentlemen of the west march defy me and go behind my back like this! She'll say I'm too old to be warden. She'll say—say—" A paroxysm of coughing interrupted the complaint. Scroope bent forward over his desk, spraying the papers in front of him with rheumy spittle.

"And exactly what am I supposed to have done? Sir," Harry added with barely concealed impatience.

"You know damned well what you've done, Graeme.

You've married a Scotswoman. Without the queen's knowledge or consent. *Or* my license."

Harry blinked. Good Lord, was that what all the fuss was about? "Oh. Yes. I did forget to tell you about that. My apologies, sir. But, my lord, that's not important. I have to tell you what I'm here for—"

"You're here to be taught proper respect for your elders!" Lord Scroope interrupted him. "And it's no good you saying you apologize and all that, and will I please grant you a license after the fact. For one thing, too many people know about it. Can't be hushed up. For another, this is absolutely the wrong year to be trying to get a quick pardon for consorting with the damned Scots. Short of powder and shot as we are to fight the damned Spanish with, and the Scots king sitting on a bloody great horde of gunpowder and refusing to sell it to us because he thinks he might need it himself—"

"That's what I'm here about!"

"Eh? Don't interrupt. I know you're here about the marriage, young fellow, that's why I sent my servants to bring you in. And here you'll stay till the matter's cleared up. You'll have to spend some time in prison—well, I'll put you up in my own quarters, and there'll be no guard if you give parole. But it's the least I can do, to keep you close-held until I've word from the queen what to do about you. Otherwise she might be accusing *me* of march treason next!" Lord Scroope chuckled and leaned back in his leather-covered chair, interlacing ringed fingers over a chest sunken with old age.

"I can't do that, sir," said Harry politely. "Tonight I must be at Rokele. Frankie's sent the ship, you see, and we have to get to Caerlaverock tonight, then join him in the south as soon as we can get there, and—oh, hell. I'm making no hand at all of explaining this. Look. This is a highly unofficial mission—the queen doesn't want political trouble with the Scots over it. If I'm caught, she'll be free to disavow me. You, too, sir. That's why you weren't notified. But—You were saying about the powder and shot? And the Spanish invasion? Well, just because the Scots won't sell it to us doesn't mean—"

"Tell me about it over dinner, young fellow," Scroope

interrupted him. "Officially you'll be my prisoner, but unofficially we can all be gentlemen together—assuming you don't do anything foolish." A meaningful glance around the room reminded Harry that at least four men stood between him and the door.

"Sir, I *can't* stay!" he tried again.

"Nonsense. I mean to report to the queen that your cooperative attitude and contrite heart are a strong recommendation for pardon—and by God, as long as I'm watching you, you'll *be* cooperative and contrite! Is . . . that . . . clear?" Lord Scroope's rings flashed as he waved a stubby finger at Harry. "You've made a good beginning by coming here so promptly, even before you were sent for. I only got the complaint this afternoon. Of course, under the circumstances," he added with a chuckle, "you'd know you were being turned in, what? Family quarrel, eh? These mixed marriages never do work. And you shouldn't have wed an Irvine, young fellow. The old feud's too deep in their hearts for a single marriage to make peace."

Scroope squinted down at one of the papers before him, and Harry felt his stomach give a queer lurch. He'd never seen Ellen's handwriting, and he could hardly have recognized it at this distance; but he felt a cold foreknowledge.

"Who reported my, er, march treason?"

Scroope gave a watery chuckle. "Didn't I just tell you? Your own kin, lad. Seemingly the lady's tired of the marriage and took this way out."

The complaint had come in this afternoon. If Ellen had sent a swift-riding messenger straight to Carlisle as soon as Harry left, Scroope would have had the papers on his desk while Harry was still making his detours and stops on the way to Rokele.

Did she hate him that much? Harry fought to retain his vision of the smiling girl on Fernshaws steps, waiting for him to return victorious from the wars. It wouldn't work. She must seriously want the marriage dissolved, or she'd not have done this to him. So much for love and faith. What was left for him now? Nothing but war—and no smiling old senile fool of a warden was going to cheat him out of this war.

He glanced again at the small leaded panes. Outside was a tiled roof sloping down at a steep angle almost to the ground, and at the corner of the roof he could just see the stable where his horse would be waiting.

"Well," he said with a shrug and a smile, "it seems I am your prisoner, my lord."

"Glad to see you're seeing reason at last!"

"If I could just read over the complaint for myself?" Harry edged nearer the desk and put one hand on the shoulder of the blue-coated servitor who stood protectively between him and Scroope. His fingers tensed momentarily on the man's shoulder as he gathered himself for action; Scroope looked up, some awareness of danger dawning on his gray face, but he was too late to shout a warning. Harry used the guard's shoulder as a vaulting pole to help him spring onto the desk. His booted feet muddied Scroope's papers and he kicked the silver paperweight directly at one of the liveried men who'd moved in to take him. It landed with a crunching sound that spoke of a broken nose, and the man staggered back howling, with both hands clapped over his face and blood spurting between the fingers.

Harry scooped up the silver inkwell and threw it at the other men in a wide splattering arc. While they were blinded by the ink, he wrenched open the casement window behind Scroope's head and leapt for freedom in one desperate jump that landed him scrambling and sliding on the tiled roof. A slide, a crabwise reach, a gutter to hold on to, and he was all but free, the stables just below him and Scroope staring out the window behind him, purple-faced with fury.

"I'll give your regards to Frankie!"

"Who the hell is Frankie?" Scroope bawled out the window.

"Sir Francis Drake!" Harry shouted before he let go of the gutter and landed on the ground with a jarring thump.

His horse was right there, and still saddled. The star of War was in the ascendent; the star of Love had fallen through the sky, a blazing meteor soon to become a cold burnt-out relic. With Scroope shouting incoherently above him and the feet of his pursuers clattering on the stairs, Harry mounted and made for the open country behind

Carlisle. He had his freedom and he was going to a good fight, and there wasn't anything else in life that a man should care about; and perhaps, if he kept this busy all the way to the Channel, he wouldn't have time to notice the cold aching void where his heart had once been.

"Sir Francis Drake," Ellen repeated, staring at the smiling dark face before her.

When Eleazar had slunk in the door, head hanging, she'd thought he had come to tell her that Harry was dead. It turned out that his shame was for having deserted Harry at the last moment. "I couldn't leave you, mistress," Eleazar confessed. "You'll be needing a man here to help you defend Fernshaws, I'm thinking, if there's any trouble—and trouble there will likely be, after what Harry's planning to do."

"Burning my father's lands?"

"Nothing that small." But Eleazar's story was so wildly improbable that she was still having trouble taking it in.

"Sir Francis Drake!" she repeated, and began to laugh with a touch of hysteria. "Oh, God. Harry's dear old friend Frankie. I never guessed. Well, one wouldn't. He never talked of the man with any trace of respect. How was I supposed to know that his old roistering seafaring master, the man who drank him under the table in forty ports of the Spanish Main, was one of Queen Elizabeth's most honored servants?"

"There's a fine line, these days, between piracy and serving the queen," said Eleazar. "It's not always easy to tell which side of it a man stands on. But what Harry is about now is definitely the queen's service, on Frankie's—I mean, Sir Francis Drake's—direct orders. It's what he came here for. To spy out the Scots' supplies of powder and shot, and to be prepared to steal it if King James refused to sell it to us. The English fleet is desperately short of ammunition."

"And the Spanish have been hoarding it for years, preparing for this invasion." Ellen nodded. "What if they invade Scotland? *My* country. Did Harry happen to think of that little detail?"

Eleazar shrugged and spread his broad, pink-palmed hands. "Is there a Scots fleet ready to fight the Armada?"

They both knew the answer to that question. King James

had been far too busy putting down internal rebellions to pay any attention to the threatened Spanish invasion.

"But there's an English fleet. And Frankie's in charge of it—and he needs powder—and Harry's gone to steal the stores of ammunition in Caerlaverock Castle, to carry it south. I can't think why he didn't explain to you."

Ellen frowned, remembering some of their puzzling past conversations in which Harry's answers had not seemed to make sense at the time. "I think he did," she said slowly. "That is, he thought I'd already guessed what he was up to and that I was angry because he meant to steal from Scotland."

"Aren't you?"

"I'm not wildly pleased about the notion," said Ellen dryly, "but even I can admit that Sir Francis Drake is like to make better use of the powder than our Scots king. I just hope the Spanish don't decide to land their armies at Caerlaverock, that's all."

"We must all hope that."

"And that Harry comes safe home," Ellen whispered to herself. But would he come home at all, after their last bitter quarrel, and believing her false, as he surely must? What if he decided to stay in the south, or—worse—to sail off somewhere with his old friend Frankie, once the two of them had defeated the entire might of the Spanish nation at sea?

She had no way of knowing. All she could do was wait, and hope that her waiting at Fernshaws would prove to Harry that she was true to him.

The breaking of Caerlaverock Castle set the border abuzz with gossip. Was it true that Red Harry Graeme, the English pirate, had scaled the cliffside walls alone, a dagger between his teeth? That he had tied the keeper of the castle to his own desk, threatening to blow up the seven tons of gunpowder stored in the bowels of the castle unless the keeper gave him the keys and his aid in loading it on the ship? That, having secured the ammunition he came after, he hoisted an English flag paired with a skull and crossbones atop the castle before he sailed off with his crew of bawdy sea rovers, leaving half the women in the Scots west march pregnant?

Ellen, knowing from Eleazar that Harry's plan had been a much simpler and less dramatic matter of bribing a guard and slipping in through a postern door, was able to discount the more lurid parts of the stories that Ruthann brought to her each day as the legend of Red Harry Graeme grew. She had a little more trouble keeping calm about the rollicking ballad that sprang up to commemorate the exploit, especially with its chorus about the twenty pregnant girls Harry and his crew had left behind.

"You know it's all romancing and imagination, mistress," Eleazar said soothingly. "Harry'd not carry on in such a way, neither would he let his men."

"I know that," Ellen snapped. "He wouldn't have had time."

But folk kept singing the ballad, and no word came from the south where Harry, having brought the powder and shot to his old friend Frankie, was presumably awaiting the approach of the greatest fleet ever to menace England's shores. As the stormy summer days went on with no news from the south, Ellen's nerves stretched taut and she felt as though the whole world were holding its breath in the still heat, waiting for the blow that was to fall on England—on the fleet of little ships assembled by Drake—on Harry.

She was positively testy with her father when he, hearing the news of Harry's exploit and his subsequent departure, came over the border to bring her home.

"I'm not going." Ellen faced him down in the long hall at Fernshaws, where the windows winked with beveled diamonds of glass set between strips of lead and threw incongruous rainbows across Carnaby Irvine's face.

"You'll do as I say, or you're no daughter of mine!"

"I'm Harry Graeme's wife first, and your daughter second. And I stay in my husband's house."

Carnaby snorted. "D'you think he'll ever be back here? He's gone back to the sea trade, the only life he knows. And if he does dare show his face in England again, the warden in Carlisle will have him up on charges of march treason for marrying a Scotswoman."

"What?"

Carnaby chuckled with satisfaction. "Don't know why I

didn't think of that earlier. Sent the letter myself—pity, it must have arrived too late for Scroope to arrest Harry before he left the country. Now will you see reason, Ellen? Come along with me. I'll not let you wait out barren years alone in this great empty English house."

"I . . . stay . . . here." Ellen was glad of Eleazar's protecting presence behind her, of the serving men and the remnants of Harry's crew that he'd gathered together and armed to provide some guard for the house. She was even more glad that Carnaby had come with only two men for escort, not expecting a fight.

Carnaby grumbled but had no way of forcing Ellen to come back with him. When he hinted that he could come back with enough men to put Fernshaws to the torch again, Ellen told him plainly that if he did so, she'd die in the flames before she went back with him. At last he went away, grumbling about stubborn disobedient daughters that no man should be cursed with; and Ellen stayed behind, wondering if his predictions were true. Would Harry ever come home again?

"The mistress has a headache," Eleazar told Ruthann, noting Ellen's pallor and the knife edge of a frown between her brows. "Take her upstairs. Make her rest."

"Would you really burn to death rather than leave here?" Ruthann asked when they were settled upstairs. She stroked Ellen's long fine hair as she combed it out.

"I don't suppose so," Ellen said. "No. It's always better to live. As long as you're alive, there's something you can do. But as long as Carnaby thinks I might be hurt, he'll not dare attack Fernshaws. And . . . maybe he'll feel better about the marriage soon."

"Why?"

Ellen gave a small, secret smile and felt the tightening seams of her gown. "I may spend years alone here, but not barren years, I think."

Ruthann squealed with excitement and dropped the comb she held. "How far along are you?"

"I was hoping you could tell me that," Ellen confessed. "I haven't done this before."

"Neither have I. We'll ask my mother. She should know,

having brought seven of us into the world and helped my two aunties deliver theirs—ten children they had among them, and all but two lived. She's a rare good midwife, my mam, and you couldn't ask for better to ease your lying-in." Ruthann stopped, blushed, and twisted a lock of Ellen's pale hair around her own fingers. "That is unless—I mean, you'll doubtless want to have real ladies with you."

"I don't think my Scots friends would venture over the border for the occasion, and my acquaintance on this side of the border is not wide," Ellen said dryly. "I'd be grateful to your mother for her advice now and her help later, Ruthann. Of course, Harry will be home long before the baby is born, and he may have his own ideas."

"Of course," Ruthann agreed, trying not to let the doubt she felt show in her face.

"And stop twisting my hair! You're pulling!"

Ruthann's mother, called to Fernshaws for consultation, poked and prodded and questioned Ellen at length. "You're sure the child couldn't have been conceived before June?"

Ellen felt her face turning bright red. Everybody in the countryside knew that Harry had carried her off in April. They must be wondering what the two of them had been doing for the first two months of the marriage. Well, let them wonder. She wasn't about to explain Harry's strange notions about not getting a child of mixed Irvine-Graeme blood, or to give details of the interesting techniques he'd shown her for taking their pleasure while avoiding such an eventuality.

"Positive," she said, and left it at that.

"Well, if I hadn't known better, I'd have said—but let it pass, let it pass," Mistress Turner grumbled. "Aye, you're carrying, mistress, and a big healthy babe it looks to be. A boy, no doubt, from the size of it, and I shouldn't be surprised if you felt him kicking you in the next month— that would be early, to feel a first baby, but there's clearly a lot of life in this one."

Ellen had already been aware of small fluttering movements within her, but she held her tongue. If Mistress Turner said next month was the earliest she could expect to

feel the child, then perhaps she'd been imagining those first
faint signals.

"End of February," Mistress Turner concluded after some
muttering and counting on her fingers. "Maybe sooner, for
that's a big one you're carrying. Wouldn't he be a bonny
Saint Valentine's day gift for his daddy, now?"

Ellen wondered if Harry would be home by Valentine's
day.

July stretched on into a stormy August, with gusts of wind
and rain that flattened half the crops. The news from
Carlisle was that the unseasonable wet weather had cast a
chill into old Lord Scroope's bones; he'd taken to his bed
and was likely not to rise from it again. The news from the
south was that the storms they felt here had swept on down
to the Channel, where the Spanish fleet had disappeared
after a series of battles off the south coast of England. They
might be coming north, to try a landing in Scotland. No one
knew anything about the fate of a pinnace called the *Rover's
Delight*, last seen heading south from Scotland with a load
of powder and shot for Drake's fleet.

Through August and September all of England and Scotland awaited news of the vanished Spanish fleet, and Ellen
waited for news of Harry. Was he dead, wounded, or merely
off to rejoin his fellow sea rovers?

"I'll go south myself to get news of him," she grumbled to
Ruthann.

"You're in no condition for the journey."

"I know. Thank God for these hoops! At least I can look
decent, though I'm uncomfortable enough underneath.
Who'd believe this child was only four months along? He's
going to be a giant." Ellen gave her hoops an irritable twitch,
trying to move the bulk of her skirt around to disguise her
swelling waistline, and plodded heavily up the stairs to her
chamber.

She'd meant to lie down for a while, but the sight that
greeted her from the windows of the long gallery drove all
thoughts of fatigue and complaining from her mind. She
glanced casually at the window, then gasped and pressed her
face to the glass, trying to see more clearly. Between the

seacoast and the blue hills of Scotland a golden spire of flame leapt into the air; it grew and opened like a flower atop the cliffs at Rokele, far above the castle.

The great beacon at Rokele had been fired. Was this the first warning of the Spanish invasion? Ellen held to the casement frame and stared into the night, eyes straining to see the coastline that she knew was invisible. Her imagination peopled the sea with Spanish sailors, the hills with an army landing secretly in the night. Then another flare sprang up, and another, and another: from the Wardshill to the Lochmabonstane, from the fells of Hardenknowes to the high bare fields below the Dancing Maidens, the border was alight with beacons. Ellen gave a little gasping sob of relief and her fingers let go of the thick iron bars.

It wasn't the Spanish; only the Scots. Her own people. Ellen had no fears for herself, but she didn't want to see Harry's house and goods whisked away. Men used to violence, and in a hurry, might not pause to consider whether the Irvine name was sufficient to protect the magnificence of Fernshaws. At the very least they would do well not to tempt such men with unguarded cattle or a house standing open as if to receive them. "Ruthann! Eleazar!" she called down the stairs. "The Scots are over the border! Get the men armed and start drawing water. And lock all the shutters downstairs."

In the scurry of preparations against the Scots raiders, Ruthann and Eleazar both tried to persuade Ellen to remove to some safer, more defensible place than this new manor house of Fernshaws, but she adamantly refused. Her presence might yet be some kind of protection for Harry's fine new house. If she left his men to defend it against the Scots without her, the reivers would have no reason to stay their hands, and some of Harry's followers might be killed unnecessarily. If she left the house empty and undefended, they would return to find only a blackened shell like the remains of the first Fernshaws.

"Harry will come home," she insisted, "and he will not find his house burned down."

"D'you think he'll care for the house, mistress? It's you he'll want safe!"

"Och, get away with you, Eleazar. I'll be safe enough; no

Scot who wants to live in peace on his own side of the border is going to attack Carnaby Irvine's daughter."

She felt much less sure of that when she saw the scarred man who was leading the first wave of reivers, a gross man with a patch over one eye and his face horribly disfigured by burns.

CHAPTER
❦ 22 ❦

In the southern counties of England, October was autumn: a season of brightly-colored leaves, high-piled hay ricks, and barns just filled with the last of the harvest's bounty. On the Scottish border October was the beginning of winter: cold gray skies and a cutting wind, men and beasts huddled together in low-ceilinged stone buildings.

In just three days of hard riding, Harry and his quietly grumbling men had crossed the imperceptible boundary between the comfortable autumn of the south and the hard, bleak, early winter of the north. The hills they rode over now were as barren and inhospitable as a storm-tossed sea, showing no friendly gleam of light from inn or house to comfort the traveler. Men in these parts shuttered their houses tightly at dusk or before, set guards who were likely to question the stranger at the gate with six inches of steel blade, and drove their cattle into tight stone-walled enclosures. Here and there, as they crossed a high ridge or followed a sheep trail over the sparse pale grass of the hills, the blackened burnt-out shell of an empty dwelling stood in remembrance of someone who'd omitted these sensible precautions.

"Home," said Nine Nebs Geordie cheerfully when they passed the landmark of the Stone Riggs, smoke-blackened stones laid out in a row like a giant's furrow. "Not far now." He drew a deep breath of satisfaction through the slivered nostrils that had earned him his byname, savoring the cold emptiness of the air with its faint hint of peat smoke and burning timbers.

"Home," agreed Yohannon, shivering under his furred cloak. What had possessed Red Harry to set such a mad pace north, after two months of recuperating from his wounds in the pleasant atmosphere of the English court, was as much a mystery to him as to the rest of the troop. But since they had worn their nether parts down by three days in the saddle, and since they were this close to Fernshaws, he could only agree that they might as well press on through the gathering dusk until they reached the great house. "Fires," he murmured, more cheerfully. "Warmth. Hot food, by God!"

Harry, riding at the head of his men, constantly scanning the horizon with quick glances, could have explained his haste to Yohannon and the rest if he'd been in the habit of explaining himself and had the time to spare. It was true enough that in the weeks following the short, sharp sea battles with the Spanish there'd seemed no particular reason to return to Fernshaws. Several of the men were wounded, and he himself had taken a nasty cut on the thigh while boarding the Spanish flagship; they needed time to rest and recuperate, and the ladies of Portsmouth were eager to felicitate the returning sailors, just as the more richly dressed ladies of the queen's court wanted to receive Harry and Frankie and the other captains.

For a while he'd even toyed with the idea of setting out to sea again. Before Harry's wound had healed, word had begun drifting in of a ship wrecked off the northern coast, another adrift and seemingly helpless, many more coming aground on the Irish rocks where the peasants slit the Spanish nobles' throats for their fine armor. By September it was believed, as was later found to be true, that the fleet had broken up in the great storm that ended the fighting; a few remnants might have limped home, but it would be many and many a year before Philip of Spain could muster another such attempted invasion against the shores of England.

Once they knew for sure what had happened to the Spanish fleet, Frankie said, it might be time to follow up their victories at sea with a few more attacks on land. How would Harry like to help him singe the king of Spain's beard again?

For a man with a warden's prison waiting for him at home, and with nothing in particular to go home for anyway, Harry supposed it seemed as good a pastime as any other. He no longer felt any great desire to go back to sea. But then, since Ellen had so decisively ended their marriage, he felt no great desire for anything. Perhaps he and Frankie would sail again—someday.

Harry's lackadaisical, heartsick daze came to an abrupt end on the day when he was summoned without warning to an audience in the queen's privy chamber.

He had, of course, been received by the queen after the battle, together with a host of other captains. They'd been thanked collectively for their part in defending the country. Scrolls had been passed out—not grants of land, as some of the gentlemen had audibly hoped, but gorgeously illuminated letters of thanks for their service. For his special services in procuring powder and shot for her majesty's fleet, Harry had been knighted, as had several other men who'd distinguished themselves in the fighting. The queen's careful watch over her budget was well-known; gold paint and taps of a blunted sword were a sight cheaper to dispense than grants of income-producing land. Harry, forewarned by Frankie, had expected nothing more. This second summons left him more apprehensive than hopeful.

"What's it about?" he demanded of Frankie on his way to answer the summons.

Drake shrugged. "You're a personable young man. Her majesty likes to be surrounded by such. Perhaps she means to offer you a place at court. Wear your best doublet, with the seed pearls."

"I'm flattered," said Harry dryly. Frankie's hypothesis did nothing to allay the prickles of apprehension that ran up and down his spine; still, he managed to stop on his way and put on his best doublet of black velvet.

The paneled chamber was small and lit only by one narrow window overlooking a private garden. She received him seated, with three gentlemen of her court standing behind her. Walsingham looked disapproving, but then he usually did. The other two were unknown to Harry.

"So. Our North Country pirate. What keeps you at court so long, Sir Harry? We should have thought you'd be eager to return to the dubious charms of the frontier."

He'd been right, Harry thought, to feel apprehensive. He dropped to one knee and looked up with an appealing, slightly crooked smile. "If I have displeased my queen in any way, my one desire is to make amends." From here he could see that the harsh redness of her hair was not natural, nor was the famed whiteness of her cheeks. But the eyes were real, and their eerie, compelling brightness made all else unimportant.

And she'd said something else, and he—God help him!—had been looking instead of listening. "Your majesty?"

"Your thoughts wandered, Harry Graeme. Tell me what was so interesting that it made you lose track of what we were saying to you."

"I was thinking," said Harry, "that the men who made songs in praise of the queen's incomparable beauty were no flatterers, though once I believed them so."

A brief smile lit a face that was tired under its white paint and powder, and Harry knew that his backhanded compliment had pleased her more than some flowery speech. "I see it's true, that the men of the North Country have rough tongues but honest ones. One of my courtiers would have said he believed every word of all the songs. Do you not weary for your own country, Sir Harry Graeme?"

"Who could wish to be anywhere but at the court of Gloriana?"

"It has been known to happen," said the queen. "I am surprised you don't wish to return to your Scots wife."

So that was it. The complaint had followed him south. Harry supposed he should not be surprised; you couldn't kick a warden's windows out and knock down a half dozen of his servitors without spawning some annoyed letters. At least he wouldn't be in trouble now, not for a marriage ended so decisively. The thought was small comfort.

"Your Majesty, I confess to having imprudently married a Scotswoman without your license or Lord Scroope's. I had been away from England for some years and was not aware that I was breaking the law, and I beg your pardon for it. The marriage is now at an end and should cause no further complications for your realm."

"You tired of the lady so quickly?"

"She never cared for me," said Harry bleakly. "The marriage was connected with some family feuds which I was attempting to settle in my own way. My attempt failed, and I understand that the lady is now back in Scotland. Since the marriage was illegal, there should be no bar to her concluding a union with her Scottish suitor."

"I . . . see." There was some secret amusement in the faerie eyes, so wide and bright. Well, Harry had been warned that the queen liked young men about her, but not their wives. Doubtless she was pleased to hear that he no longer considered himself a married man. "Sir Harry, I am surprised that a man of your stamp gives up so easily."

"Easily! You don't know—" Harry swallowed his protests. One did not contradict a monarch.

"I think," said Elizabeth, as if pondering a weighty decision, "yes, I do think, Sir Harry, that you should go north and make another attempt to settle these family feuds of which you spoke."

The long, tapered fingers brushed the scroll in her lap as she spoke, and light danced from her many rings and from the jewels with which the seams of her gown were sewn.

"I fear the warden of the west march would not be well pleased to see me in his territory again." The scroll was his pardon, then, or she'd not be sending him back. She was only pretending to make her decision now. It had been made already, and there'd been some argument about it, or why was Walsingham frowning so thunderously?

"I beg to differ with you." When monarchs are painfully courteous, watch out for traps at your feet. Harry watched the wide pale eyes, unblinking. She seemed all made of light, and the reflections of her jewels were the least dazzling part of her. "I think you will have no difficulty with the warden."

"You've sent to Lord Scroope?"

"Lord Scroope is dead. And the new warden is not yet in Carlisle."

"Dead!" A small breath, one he hadn't known he'd been holding, rushed out of Harry. Not surprising. No. Scroope had been an old man. But the force of his authority had kept something like peace on the English side of the border for many years. Now . . . He remembered the orgy of English raiding that had accompanied the treason of the Scots warden. The same thing would be happening now, in reverse. "Then who's keeping the peace? Someone should—" He stammered to a halt, tongue-tied under those bright, watchful eyes. The queen would not be pleased if he presumed to advise her on the governance of her realm.

"I see you now agree with me," said the queen. "It took time for the word of Lord Scroope's death to reach us in the south; it will take time for the newly appointed warden to travel north. I think he should leave at once. How long will you require to take your leave of our court ladies, Sir Harry?"

"I? I—But—"

"Try not to stammer. And close your jaw. It's unbecoming in a warden of the marches to stand like a gap-mouthed boy. Who best to guard these reivers of the land," inquired the queen rhetorically, "than a reiver of the sea? I have discussed the matter with my gentlemen here, and after some time they saw matters as I did. A warden of the marches must come of a good family, and it helps if he has been raised in the marches and knows their ways; on the other hand, an extensive network of local relations can cause problems of favoritism. And he must always be able to balance the conflicting claims of justice and discretion, willing to take some risks and perhaps to bend the letter of the law a little in order to enforce the spirit of our peace. You," said Elizabeth of England, "through no fault of your own, appear to fit the requirements as to family and upbringing exactly. As for the rest, Lord Scroope was sometimes hindered in his duties by a too strict interpretation of the written law. Somehow I feel that will not be one of your problems."

Harry grinned. "No, Your Majesty. May I go now, Your Majesty?"

"So eager to leave us," she sighed.

"Well. I've to call my men together; they're lodged all over the city. Mounts to arrange too. And—" Harry felt his tongue tripping over the words. There was work to be done, a land to guard, a home to rebuild. Nothing that could make up for the loss of Ellen, but a task that he at least desired to set his hand to. "And armor to get in order, if we're to set off—you did say at once? Because the Scots will be over the border, if Scroope's dead. I should be there. In your service," he added, remembering tact at last.

Fourteen hours later he was riding out of the bright southern autumn, with men behind him who were just now sobering up from a two-month celebration of their victory over the Spanish. Three days after that, cold and sober and wary again, they were in among the walled farmhouses and solitary peel towers of his home country, with their blank shuttered eyes, and the smoke of Scots reivers rising just over the horizon. Harry saw with grim satisfaction that his predictions had been exactly right. In the warden's absence it was open season on the marches.

They paused once to hang two men, not Scots but English scum, from the rooftree of the house they'd been firing. Their deaths would be cold comfort to the woman whose man they'd killed, but Harry took her up on his own saddlebow and carried her five miles to a stout-walled farm where she could mourn in peace.

He was almost glad now that Ellen had left him. It wouldn't have done for her to be at Fernshaws with this wave of wildness pouring over the border. He wondered, tiredly, if she was wedded to Guthrie Bell yet, and if Guthrie were one of those coming over the border to take advantage of the warden's presumed absence. He might yet have the opportunity to make Ellen a widow, and all in the course of duty; but what good would that do him? She'd still hate him. One couldn't go on kidnapping a woman time and again. By the third time it took on the overtones of farce.

"Quite a change," said Yohannon cheerfully, riding up beside him as they left the farmhouse. "From hell raising to peacekeeping. I've known a time when you would have comforted the grieving widow in your own inimitable way."

Harry snapped at him, then repented and set himself to

produce a string of bawdy jokes that had the men grinning in their hard saddles through these last miles of the journey, reassured that their captain was himself again.

"What was I tellin' ye? Warden or no warden, but they'll never make a douce respectable gentleman out of Red Harry Graeme!" Nine Nebs Geordie called to his friends after one particularly obscene series of puns between Yohannon and Harry.

Harry raised one hand to still the answering laughter and cheers. He pointed mutely to the line of hills ahead, black against the darkening sky. First one man then another shut up and peered forward at the reflected glimmer of flames against the low clouds. Somewhere behind those low hills a house was being fired.

When they'd all seen it, Harry reined in and turned to Yohannon. "What do you think? I know they're tired, but we'd best see to that little disturbance before we stop at Fernshaws."

The men galloped over the low hills and came to a halt atop a rise. The fitful wind parted the low clouds that both reflected and dissipated the light of the fire, and Harry realized they were on the fringes of Fernshaws itself. He led the horsemen up the crest of the last long, low rise and saw men in armor rolling tarry barrels under the carved stone pilasters of the front door, other men plunging torches into the mass. Along the south side of Fernshaws a similar fire was already sending out its gouts of oily smoke and wicked, sharp-tongued flames. A dark-haired woman who might have been Ruthann Turner was hanging half out of one of the upstairs casements, shrieking defiance at the men below. From the two windows at either end of the gallery, their casements opened just a slit, came a steady fire of crossbow bolts that annoyed without stopping the men at their task.

"That'll be Eleazar," said Yohannon. "But who's the other crossbowman?" He found he was speaking to the air. Harry was already charging down the long slope, putting the spurs to his horse while, with the expertise of long practice, he pulled his loaded harquebus forward from the shoulder sling and fired on the men with torches from behind. Yohannon spared one sigh for the impatience of youth, stood in his stirrups and let out a high-pitched warbling yell that brought the rest of the troop thundering down behind Harry.

The first moments of the attack were blind confusion and noise, and the advantage of mounted men over those on foot. After the first charge there were trampled men moaning on the ground and others slashed apart by the vicious cuts that can be delivered by a man coming down on a horse with the full weight of his body behind the arm. Harry saw with surprise that most of the men he rode down were wearing Bell badges, not Irvine; he didn't have time to think about the matter in detail. Whoever they were, they regrouped with startling speed and effectiveness; his harquebus was empty now and he'd retreated to the short curved sword he always used aboard ship. For some intense minutes of cutting and thrusting and stabbing, pivoting his horse to avoid a stomach-slashing blow from a man on the ground, sending Scots flying sideways and before him, he didn't have time to think about anything but surviving from one minute to the next and killing as many raiders as possible.

The Scots were well-organized and well-disciplined, but they hadn't been prepared to be pinned between Harry's men in the foreground and the fire of crossbows from two separate wings of Fernshaws behind them. Those who could still stand broke and ran before long, and half of Harry's men followed them, whooping with the excitement of the chase.

The men who remained trampled the fire and watched one man of the attacking force wheel his horse and return to the fight: a stocky, thick-lipped, scarred man with the Bell scarf of red and green looped crosswise over one shoulder and around his waist. The bright hues were darkened now by the brownish-red of drying blood.

"A neighborly call, Fish-Mou'?" Harry circled the older man and jabbed lightly at his horse with the short sword. "It seems my people haven't made you welcome. Why don't you get out of the range of their crossbows before somebody picks you off?"

The withering cross fire from above had dwindled to a few slow shots. "I think they're running out of bolts," said

Johnny Fish-Mou' Bell. "And it's too dark for good aim now." There was no sign of strain on his scarred face, no hint in his one good eye that he knew his own luck had run out as well. "I would have smoked the bitch out if you hadn't shown up in the worst time. As it is, you can have her, and good luck!"

Harry glanced up at the house, momentarily distracted. Ruthann was still visible at the open window. "You went to all this trouble for *Ruthann Turner?*"

Fish-Mou' laughed. It was a horrible sound, like scales clashing against one another; his fire-scarred vocal chords refused to obey his commands. "Not the maid—the mistress. I owe your lady something for this." He touched the sunken wreck where his eye had been. "I'll collect another time."

"Ellen?" Harry looked up toward the windows, unbelieving. Did he catch a flash of long pale hair in the western casement, a white hand holding a heavy crossbow? "Ellen!"

In that moment of inattention Fish-Mou' Bell set spurs to his horse, wheeled and threw himself down along the horse's neck in a dash for the safety of the hills. His horse was fresh, while those of Harry and his men were lathered from the last desperate gallop to Fernshaws and the short fight that followed; he might have made it but for two things.

One was the line of tarred barrels that his men had been ready to fire when Harry interrupted them. A dropped torch had ignited them where they lay, a blazing obstacle that forced him to check his horse in mid stride and attempt a clumsy, unplanned jump.

The other was the last crossbow bolt from Fernshaws, sent whizzing through the cold dark air to strike Fish-Mou' where he crouched low over his horse's neck. With deadly aim it buried itself in the roll of fat exposed between the brim of his salade and the upper edge of his steel-plated jack.

"Ellen?"

With one swift glance to make sure his men had matters under control, Harry was inside and plunging up the wide central staircase to the upper gallery, where a white-faced girl, her hair loose and her hands blistered from wielding the heavy bow, fell laughing and sobbing into his arms. From the other end of the gallery a black shadow advanced, bowed formally, and lit a branch of candles. In the wavering light the shadow became Eleazar, his night-black face and hands blending into a suit of black velvet. "Your wife didn't kill Fish-Mou'," he informed Harry. "I did."

"He took my last bolt away!" Ellen interpolated indignantly, between squeezing Harry's neck too tightly and laughing with relief.

"I didn't think you should have that killing on your conscience. Besides, I'm a better shot."

"I already killed him once. It wouldn't have burdened my conscience any more to do it again. Besides—"

Harry clasped Ellen to him, remembering how she'd been troubled with nightmares after her first bloody encounter with Fish-Mou'. "Besides, love," he said gently, "Eleazar *is* a better shot." His voice hardened. "And now will you kindly explain to me just what you are doing here? I never built this house to stand up against a raid of this size! Why in the name of all that's holy didn't you take refuge in the old peel tower where you'd have been safe! By God, next time I should leave orders for Eleazar to pick you up and throw you into the tower, willy-nilly! I should—I should—" His hands slid down to her waist in unconscious illustration of his meaning, but he could no longer clasp her as tightly as he'd been used to. His fingers didn't meet at her spine anymore, and his thumbs slid over the soft rounding of her stomach under the stiff fashionable dress she was wearing.

Harry gulped down the last of his tirade and stammered in surprise. What could he say? She was carrying his child. And she hadn't left him.

"So you didn't run back to Scotland after all?"

Ellen shook her head, smiling. "I never meant to, Harry. Only you left before I could tell you so. I was angry—but not that angry."

"Angry enough to inform on me to Lord Scroope, though."

Two faint parallel marks appeared between Ellen's high, fair brows. "What are you talking about? I didn't even understand that you meant to steal the powder from Caerlaverock until after you'd gone. And I told nobody. And if I had, it would have been the Scots warden, not the English one!"

"Somebody sent a complaint against me to Lord Scroope," said Harry slowly, watching the smoke-smudged face of his beloved. "On the grounds that I'd married a Scotswoman without his permission or the queen's. He tried to have me locked up. Would have interfered sadly with bringing the powder south to Frankie."

"And of course you leapt to the conclusion it was my doing!"

"You seemed a wee bit annoyed with me when we left. Besides, he told me so . . ." Harry stopped and rubbed his chin. "No. No, he didn't. I got that impression, that's all. He said it was the doing of my 'kin'."

"My father," said Ellen with weary resignation. "He's never been reconciled to our marriage."

"Well, he'd best reconcile himself now, for you seem to be carrying the evidence of it under your girdle! When's it due?"

"February, I think."

Harry couldn't keep the silly, pleased grin from splitting his face. "We'd better get Carnaby over on this side of the border for a nice public wedding as soon as possible. Seeing he keeps trying to deny the legality of the last one, I don't want him getting any ideas that this boy of mine is more Irvine than Graeme."

"It could be a girl," Ellen reminded him.

Harry smirked. "Not my child. Graeme men have powerful seed. We get boys. Four brothers I had, and not a girl in the house to lighten the atmosphere."

"And do you think it's tactful to have a large public wedding at this point? Given that Lord Scroope tried to arrest you for marrying me, maybe we shouldn't repeat the crime in public. The new warden should be appointed any day now, and I don't want him to start his regime by locking up my husband."

Harry's smirk broadened. "He won't. I can guarantee that."

"How?"

"Come to bed, and maybe I'll tell you. Eleazar, help Yohannon collect what's left of Fish-Mou's men, and stitch up any of them who are bleeding too fast to give us a good ransom. It looks as if I've got some repair work to do on Fernshaws, and the Bells might as well pay for the first installment."

Once they were private in the chamber, Harry and Ellen vied with one another to spill out explanations and accountings for the long months of separation. Harry's fists clenched and his jaw hardened when Ellen told him how Fish-Mou' had threatened to burn Fernshaws unless she came out to him, and how she'd seen their scanty supplies of ammunition all but gone—the powder spent, the few men who'd stayed at Fernshaws wounded, and no defense left but herself and Eleazar with the two crossbows.

"You'd not have gone to him?"

Ellen's eyes darkened, remembering. "No. He would have burned Fernshaws anyway."

"You should have gone to the peel tower."

"And leave your home undefended? Harry, if it had been anybody but Fish-Mou' raiding, they'd maybe have left the place alone out of respect for an Irvine. That was why I stayed. I couldn't bear to think that when you came back—if you came back—you'd find your home burnt to the ground for a second time. Not when it was the Irvines' fault the first time."

"Hush, now!" Harry gathered her in his arms before the tears of weakness could start spilling over. She'd put aside her smoke-stained gown for a loose nightgown of gathered white silk that slid, soft and enticing, over the new bigness of her belly and parted over the fullness of her breasts. "We'll hear no more talk of faults and blame. There's been hot tempers and hasty actions on both sides, and misunderstandings enough to fuel a month of sermons. I'm here to start a new era."

Ellen looked up at him through long silvery lashes that veiled the doubt in her eyes. "No more feuding?"

"No more," Harry agreed. "'Twould be improper in the

new warden of the west marches to engage in family feuds in his spare time, don't you think?"

Ellen had to hear the whole story of how the queen had granted Harry the wardenship in reward for his services in saving England from the Spanish Armada practically single-handed, and she refused to believe it until he shouted for Nine Nebs Geordie to bring the scroll of his appointment up from the saddlebags below.

"Och, that's no' the part I don't believe," sniffed Ellen when she read the actual words. "It was the part about her rewarding you for your great services to England. More likely she was at her wits' end how to keep the biggest roisterer in the marches peaceful, so she's set the fox to guard the chicken run, poor queen!"

"Poor Harry," the ex-pirate said with a rueful smile, "shackled to his own sense of responsibility. She's a clever woman. If I didn't take the wardenship, the next man to the post might feel it his duty to clap me in jail for offending against the peace of the realm. I could hardly refuse."

Beneath the words, Ellen sensed an undercurrent of pride and deep satisfaction, and she allowed herself to draw a long breath of relief. He was home for good now, her sea roisterer, her wild young pirate. He had broad acres to guard, a fine new house only slightly singed around the edges, a position in the society of the border, and . . .

She shifted position, trying to take her increased weight off his knees, and Harry's arms tightened around her. "Trying to get away?"

"I thought—I'm too heavy for you now." Ellen pulled at the edges of her silk robe, trying to cover herself better. "So big and ungainly, and months to go yet!"

"Big, yes. Beautifully round and full of our child. Not ungainly." Harry's palm smoothed over the curve of her belly, and she shivered with involuntary, perverse desire. "Beautiful," he repeated, lowering his lips to brush across her swelling breasts. "Perfect. I don't want you to change."

In spite of herself, Ellen giggled. "Too bad. I understand that's a natural part of the process."

"Enough!" His arms tightened around her and his lips

went over her mouth, stopping her laughter. His kisses were brighter than the candles on the mantel, sweeter than the wine that stood poured out and untasted in cups of chased silver. The round laughing cheeks of the cupids on the brim of the wine decanter glimmered in the candlelight, until Harry's face came between her and the light and she clung to him for life and breath. As if to prove how little her new bulk mattered, he stood easily with her still in his arms and lifted her onto the bed in a single movement.

There he stood looking down at her for a long moment, his face dark and unreadable, with the candle flames dancing a red-tinged halo around his dark head. Ellen reached out one hand to draw him down beside her, but he seemed unable to move.

"It's a miracle to me, to see you here. I'm only now beginning to believe it. I was so sure that you had gone back to Scotland," he said slowly. "To that boy . . . what was his name?"

"I never loved him."

"You stayed at Fernshaws. You didn't have to—but you stayed. You didn't know I was coming back—but you stayed."

"You might at some point begin to deduce that I love you."

Harry laughed and came into her open and waiting arms, his hair still damp from hasty washing, the candles burning brightly behind him. "I might. Or I might ask you to prove it again . . ." Then his mouth was on hers, greedy with the months of deprivation, and Ellen surrendered to his unspoken need with her own hunger. They'd been apart too long—and in another month she would be too big for such goings-on—if indeed she wasn't so already! The desperate eagerness of their long-delayed joining was slowed by the necessity to be inventive. In haste and laughter and desire they enjoyed one another, freed of all the unspoken lies and misunderstandings, the old ghosts banished at last. It was a night of pure joy, so intense that it could not be contained in memory. Later Ellen would remember only candles burning against the uncurtained windows, reflecting their pale glow

300

back into the room; a sense of lightness and freedom released from her heavy body wherever Harry's fingers glided over her skin; his hands tangled in the silvery net of her hair, drawing her close to him, and at the end, the sweet, long-delayed fulfillment that reverberated through her like music.

CHAPTER

❧ 23 ❧

On the north shore of Solway Firth, in a field about three hundred yards above high-water mark, stood a stone seven feet high and eighteen feet around. Its weathered granite surface had seen assemblies of blue-painted men with quivers of arrows, mounted on shaggy northern ponies for a raid into the rich south lands, and it had seen the retaliatory marches of Roman legionaries with their polished helmets and shields, their leather sandals swinging forth in the prescribed regular step that carried them through the miles of heather and waste. Later it had witnessed the arrival of men in horned helmets, who came to raid and rape and stayed to farm the tempting rich land around the firth; and later still, the Norman conquerors who laid waste to the north of England had paused at this great gray stone that marked one of the traditional boundary points between Scotland and England. Now, in the civilized years of Elizabeth of England and James VI of Scotland, the Lochmabonstane was a recognized gathering-point for gentlemen in trunk hose and plate armor, their tents pitched on either side of the stone while the wardens of the marches heard complaints and set fines for the damages done by either side during the last three months.

On English days of march truce, the meetings were held at Rokele Castle, where the English warden and his retinue could be lodged in comfort for the days of bargaining, quarrels, single combats, and impromptu football matches that sometimes did more damage than out-and-out battles. In this cold October month it happened to be the Scots' turn to hold the truce days, and they traditionally chose the Lochmabonstane in its empty, windswept field, where both sides could be equally miserable.

Harry apologized to Ellen for the discomfort of the long journey and the drafty tent; she pushed her windswept pale hair out of her eyes and laughed in his face. "Don't be thinking you brought me for your own political ends, Red Harry Graeme! I'd have been bound to come anyway, for I was wild to get out of the house and see a bit of amusement, and by next march days I'll be too big to travel."

"You're too big *now*," said Harry, passing one hand lovingly over the curve that neither hoops nor farthingales could disguise any longer. They'd argued long and loudly over whether she was to come with him on this, his first day of official action as English warden of the west march. Ellen had begun by ordering Ruthann to pack for her, acting as though there was no question of her biding at Fernshaws. Stopped by Harry, she'd pointed out a great many reasonable arguments, beginning with the importance of letting both sides see the strength of their marriage and ending with the hope that together they might effect a reconciliation with her father before a new series of even more destructive raids broke out.

To all these arguments Harry had opposed the simple, reasonable statement that he wasn't risking his heir by letting Ellen ride a horse when she was already bigger than the poor mare.

He couldn't quite remember how she had persuaded him that by letting her ride to the Lochmabonstane in a cart he had made a brilliant compromise and won the essentials of his case. Did it matter? Here she was, cheeks bright with the chilly snap of the wind, hair blown about her face like a pale bright halo, and eager as a child to plunge into the merriment around the wardens' tents. On the flat shore somebody was getting up a horse race; Nine Nebs Geordie and a few of Harry's other retainers had already sneaked off to start an impromptu football game in which the object was to drown as many as possible of the other side in the sucking sands of Solway Firth; closer to the tents, the sellers of hot frumenty and gilt ginger nuts were doing an excellent trade.

"You'll go nowhere without me," Harry told her. "And our first task, before I get tied up in wardens' business, is to find Carnaby."

"Red Harry Graeme, ye wee cheatin' gomeril, come out and fight me like a man!" roared a bull-throated voice behind them.

"I think we've accomplished the first task." Ellen turned and made a perfunctory curtsy to her father, who was standing with balled fists on his hips, his hair tousled in the autumn wind, while behind him a dozen armed retainers copied his dour glower. "And it's nice to see you too, Da," she said with a smile that did not reach her eyes. "I do hope you weren't planning violence on a day of march truce. The penalties for that are rather severe."

"By God, I ought to drub yon man of yours up the Lochmabonstane and down the other side!" Carnaby's hand shot out to grab Harry by the collar; the younger man evaded the motion with a single quick sidestep.

"And for which of my many misdeeds are you castigating me now, sir?"

"Da," Ellen put in, thrusting her ungainly bulk between the two parties, "Da, listen to me! Harry didn't do it—what you're thinking of."

"Are you trying to tell me he didn't kill Fish-Mou' Bell before I had a chance to get me hands on the slimy rotter?"

Ellen's jaw dropped and her pretense at ladylike poise vanished. She opened and closed her mouth several times before speech returned to her. "As a matter of fact, he didn't. But I thought—I thought—"

"You probably thought a lot of nonsense, like most females." Carnaby's scowl softened and he raised one hand to tentatively touch his daughter's swelling body. "You should ha' talked to me direct, lass, instead of to that great gowk Guthrie Bell. But then, women never do have a lot of judgment, and least of all when they're breeding. I recall your mother—" He shook his head and blinked violently. "Well, that's neither here nor there. Point is, Ellen lass, Guthrie didna' want to believe what you were telling him. He wanted to believe Red Harry guilty of everything from murder to rape to picking pockets in Carlisle high street, so that he could be justified in taking you for himself. Took him these months to think it over, decide there might be something in your story, decide he might ought to warn me against Fish-Mou'. By which time it was too late. Fish-Mou' was healed of his wounds, old Scroope was dead, and he'd gone over the border after you. I rode after him, of course, but on the way we met what was left of his men limping back with some story about Red Harry Graeme rising from the sea to ride them down on a fire-breathing black stallion."

"They exaggerate," said Harry. "It was a gelding."

Carnaby gave an unwilling chuckle. "Never mind. You've got one hell of a nerve, Graeme. My quarrel with Fish-Mou' goes back a good many years more than yours. I had first rights to kill him—and I wouldn't ha' done it so quick and easy."

"My quarrel also is of long duration," Harry proposed with unnatural meekness. "I owe him the deaths of my family and the destruction of Fernshaws, sir."

Carnaby nodded slowly. "Well, better you should blame him than me. All right. But there's another thing they told me, and on seeing this silly lass of mine, I see it's true. Big as a barn she is already, and by February she'll be too big to get up the double stair at Fernshaws. Now what are you going to do about that, boy? You can't keep carrying her off. 'Tain't decent. And I want her properly, legally wed before the bairn comes— no hole-in-corner wedding with Wee Erchie too drunk to see the book before him, this time! And *you* can't wed her, or the English warden will throw you in jail again."

"Oh, I very much doubt that," said Harry with a faint smile. "Shall we go in and ask him about it now?" He raised the tent flap that was painted with the arms of England and motioned his father-in-law to step inside.

"Harry, Ruthann and I will just go and get some ginger nuts while you're explaining to Da," Ellen said, making her escape while her husband was caught between the tent flap and Carnaby Irvine. As she lumbered down the hill toward the horse racing, a bull-throated roar echoed from the tent behind her.

"They've got a bear in there! It's a bear baiting!" squealed a boy of ten or eleven who'd been kicking his heels at his father's side, running up the hill to see the fun.

"Not so fast, Geordie Johnston," Ellen told him, "it's only my father finding out that he's related by marriage to the English warden."

Some time later, when she hoped that Carnaby would have had time to calm down, Ellen ambled back to the tent. Her stomach was uncomfortably full of ginger nuts and hot pies, her purse comfortably heavy with the proceeds of several good wagers at the racing, and her arms laden with pinwheels, carved hobbyhorses, and painted wooden dolls for the baby.

Outside the tent a long line of cold, bored men waited for the warden to hear their complaints against the Scots raiders. Ellen gave them a sympathetic glance, raised the tent flap and slipped inside, leaving Ruthann to entertain the waiting men.

Carnaby had recovered from the news with remarkable speed, it seemed. He was already busily laying down his conditions for the wedding to Harry. "No hole-in-corner affair this time, you understand? I want folk to see my lass is legally wed and with the full support of her family."

"Agreed." From Harry's restrained tone Ellen could gather that they'd been over this point several times before.

"And if you insist on having it at Fernshaws, we'll have to wait till the next days of march truce so the Armstrongs and Nixons and all can come over the border in safety from you wild Englishmen."

"Agreed."

Ellen frowned. "That's too late, Da. I don't want to waddle down the aisle looking like a pregnant duck." She dropped her packages and sat down heavily, one hand on the small of her back.

Carnaby regarded his daughter with a fond smile. "You're waddling now, Ellen Irvine," he told her. "How about Christmas, then? Usually get a few peaceful days between Christmas and Epiphany."

"How about now?" Ellen suggested. "Wee Erchie's barely started drinking. He's still sober enough to read the words over us."

"I'm not having you married from a tent in the fields," Carnaby said, brushing this suggestion aside. "D'you want folk saying we had to hurry?"

Ellen smoothed the farthingale over her swelling middle and grinned. "I think they'll notice anyway, Da."

"We'll compromise, then. Christmas it is. Go buy some ginger nuts while your man and I work out the details." Carnaby turned back to Harry. "I'd always planned to dower her with the lands her mother brought, but you being an Englishman, that won't work. Would you take a few head of black cattle in exchange?"

By Christmastide Ellen was hardly able to lumber up and down the broad stairs at Fernshaws, and her temper was rapidly fraying under the stress of listening to Aunt Verona and Ruthann Turner and Mistress Turner plan for the wedding party.

"Couldn't we just elope?" she asked Harry when they enjoyed a rare private moment in the hall downstairs.

"We've tried that, remember? Your father wants it done publicly this time." Harry strained over yards of gathered green silk to kiss Ellen's flushed cheeks. "Besides, even Red Harry Graeme couldn't throw you over a saddle and gallop away with you now. It'd have to be a farmer's cart, and I refuse to do anything so graceless."

"I just wish it were *over.*"

"It will be," said Harry, teeth clenched. "This time you are going to be well and thoroughly and publicly married, and I will personally kill any member of your family who throws a spoke in the works."

"I'll help."

Just then Aunt Verona bustled in, full of the news that Ellen's new petticoat with the pearl and gold embroidery in the shape of oyster shells had arrived to be fitted, and the man was here about the turkeys, and could Harry please pay him and think of some place to keep two-dozen turkeys until tomorrow, when they were to be slaughtered.

The petticoat had to be let out.

"Aunt Verona and Mistress Turner were up two nights, letting in more material at the seams and stitching pearls over the alterations. How does it look?" Alone in their chamber while guests gathered downstairs, Ellen turned slowly and majestically for Harry to admire the wedding dress. Oyster-colored satin gathered over her full breasts, then swept in tiers toward the floor, each layer weighted with a scalloped edge of gold embroidery around clustered pearls. Her hair was caught back in a gold net knotted with more pearls, then released to flow down her back like a waterfall of pale, gilded moonlight. Halfway through the slow pirouette she paused, caught her breath for a moment, then continued with one hand outstretched for balance.

"Beautiful." Harry's voice was rough. "A little tight, maybe. That doesn't matter. I like your shape."

"I'm shaped like a *whale!*" Ellen said crossly. "Don't remind me!" She bit her lip and held on to the back of a chair for a moment, then let out her breath in a sigh. "Is it time to go down yet?"

"Almost. What's the hurry?"

"The laces are too tight."

"Ellen, you're not *wearing* stays. You refused. Remember?" Harry looked worriedly at his enormous, seven-months-pregnant bride. "That's why the dress had to be let out so far."

"Oh. Yes. Well. Something's pinching."

"Should you sit down? Won't that crease the dress?"

"I don't—oh!—don't care." Ellen lowered herself carefully onto the chair she'd been holding on to. "I need to sit down. No, I need to . . ." Her voice trailed off and her eyes crossed with an expression of intense concentration.

"You need," said Harry, "to come down to the hall with me. The guests are here, and the preacher, and I promise you that I will personally kill any man who interrupts this wedding now that we've got it all arranged." He offered Ellen his arm to help her rise; her fingers bit into his sleeve, almost hurting him.

"I think . . . you might . . . change your mind about that," Ellen gasped, hauling herself upright on Harry's arm. "Call Verona."

"What?"

"That Graeme son . . . you've been talking about . . . is about to interrupt the wedding." Ellen gave up the struggle and sank back down on the chair, her skirts billowing about her like shining silvery waves laced with gold foam. "Call Aunt Verona! *Now!*" Her voice rose to a near shriek on the last word.

Mistress Turner was first into the chamber, bustling in with a word about nervous young girls who thought every ache and twinge meant they were giving birth. With one look at Ellen's face she changed her tune. "All right. This is real. How long have you been having pains? Since before dawn? Why didn't you tell me? Thought you could get through the wedding first? Silly girl, you're not going anywhere. What are you standing there like a great gormless lump for, Harry boy? Get out, this is women's business. Light the fire. Get out of my way. Bring some water. Strip the bed. Where's that useless girl of mine when I need her?"

Ruthann arrived hard after her mother, then Verona Irvine, then Effie Armstrong with her own ideas after having borne seven great Armstrong boys. Shoved out of the chamber by the flood of chattering women, Harry listened white-faced and tense to the small sounds that filtered through the door until his father-in-law found him and dragged him downstairs by main force.

Some hours later, when Harry had personally depleted a large part of the supplies of bride ale, a beaming delegation of ladies invited him upstairs again to meet his wife and newborn child.

"It doesn't look like a seven-month baby to me," Ellen whispered when Harry knelt by the bed and buried his face in her long silky hair. She showed him the red-faced, squalling bundle. "Look, fingernails and eyebrows and everything! Do you think some of your theories about how to make love without getting children might be slightly in error?"

Harry patted the squirming little thing absently on the head. "Could be." A blindly waving little fist opened, caught his finger and drew it toward an insistently sucking mouth. Harry laughed and gently extricated himself. "Hungry already, little man? Wait a while. We've something to do here."

"What's that?" Ellen asked in some apprehension as Harry stood up and looked toward the door.

"The minister's still here, and most of the guests. I thought I'd save time by having a wedding and a christening together."

"Such efficiency! Did you plan it this way?" Ellen began to laugh. "I wouldn't put it past you." Her head fell back on the pillow and she crooked her arm to take the baby again.

"I'm a very crafty man," Harry agreed. "Remember that I managed to get myself a wife and end a feud while stealing powder for Frankie's ships. Combining a wedding and a christening is small-time in comparison, don't you think? It's about time you learned, Ellen, that I am very efficient and all my plans work out exactly right—even," he said, beaming at the lace-wrapped bundle in Ellen's arms, "even those I wasn't expecting to happen quite so soon. Now, before I call the minister, what shall we name this little man?"

Ellen's white cheeks dimpled. "Maybe not *all* your plans work out exactly as you intend," she teased.

"Of course they do. What do you want to call him?"

The saucy grin grew wider. "Eleanor."